W9-AGK-568

SLEEPWALKER

SLEEPWALKER

by Mikel J. Wisler

Doxa NOŪS
MEDIA

Published by DoxaNoûs Media

Marion, Indiana 46952—doxanousmedia.wordpress.com

Cover Design and Illustrations: Mikel J. Wisler

Interior Layout: Mikel J. Wisler

Editor: Eric M. Bumpus

Printed in the United States of America

ISBN: 978-1-7325307-2-0 (hbk)   ISBN: 978-1-7325307-4-4 (pbk)

ISBN: 978-1-7325307-3-7 (ebk)   LCCN: 2018965307

For information about the author, visit: www.mikelwisler.com

First Edition: December 2018

10 9 8 7 6 5 4 3 2 1

FOR TREVOR DUKE

But what then am I? A thing that thinks. What is that? A thing that doubts, understands, affirms, denies, wills, refuses, and that also imagines and senses.

- René Descartes, 1641

For to imprint anything on the mind without the mind's perceiving it seems to me hardly intelligible. … No proposition can be said to be in the mind which it never yet knew, which it was never yet conscious of.

- John Locke, 1694

Traditionally, in the precomputer, preneurological science age, we made knowledge, in particular memorial knowledge, totally a function of internal access. But perhaps we need to modify our thinking here in the light of current technology and philosophical psychology. You don't have to speculate about prosthetic brain sectors. You can just use your pocket calculator to add up your checkbook or use your computer to access the essay you've recently composed to see how these devices become extensions of our brain, an invaluable part of our memory and knowledge base.

- Louis P. Pojman, 2001

We're at a moment in human history when the marriage of our biology and our technology will transcend the brain's limitations. We can hack our own hardware to steer a course into the future. This is poised to fundamentally change what it will mean to be human.

- David Eagleman, 2015

INTRODUCTION:

Is There a Ghost?

NOTHING YOU EXPERIENCE IS objectively real. This realization has slowly shifted the philosophical and technological exploration and understanding of what it means to be human. As a species, humanity is blessed with a complex nervous system that has enabled us to experience reality in profoundly compelling and meaningful ways. Still, our eyes only see a tiny fraction of the total light spectrum. The experience of seeing colors is a deliberate construct of the human brain. Memories are stored in as efficient of a manner as possible using networks of associated neurons. In the process, not every detail is stored but only the most seemingly relevant information. Over time, memories can be distorted or fade into oblivion as these networks are needed to store new memories.

In one sense, it's tempting to think of ourselves as the slaves in Plato's *Allegory of the Cave*. The slaves are chained down, facing a large wall where shadows are cast. For these slaves, their singular experience of reality is the shadows. According to Plato's allegory, only an escape from the cave could bring the slaves into a true experience of reality, which for him was a world beyond our physical reality. Like the slaves in Plato's Cave, are we trapped inside our nervous systems, forced to experience the electrochemical simulation of the outside reality, but unable to have direct experiences of the totality of the objective world?

This assumes that there is a true "you," an actual individual, somewhere in there. Advancements in neuroscience continue to call into question the notion of a singular self, but instead suggest that our sense of self is a narrative crafted by the ebb and flow of the currents of our synapses at work in a grand concert within our brains to bring together millions of biological systems to build a unit: a single human being, capable of navigating the world. All of this is done by a three-pound mass of goo that requires no more power than an old 60-watt light bulb.

A purely empirical understanding of the brain might indicate that our "self" may be no more than the evolving collection of the unique memories that make each of us who we are. Our brains are built to curate this abstract museum of neural-connections that represent our memories. In this view, my sense of self is directly tied to my ever-shifting collection of memories. But does this mean that the Alzheimer's patient who is losing her memories is becoming less "herself" with every vanishing memory?

The philosophical, or perhaps, spiritual question that still remains outside the grasp of science is whether or not there might be some self, some ghost in the machine, that transcends our system of memory formation and storage. It is unlikely that such a thing could ever be empirically established. As such, it remains easiest to dismiss such speculation as outside the realm of science and best left to philosophers and the clergy.

But, even as a scientist myself, I cannot help but wonder if there might be some things outside the realm of our current empirical grasp? Might our empirical understanding of reality eventually prove to be merely a limited bandwidth of the totality of our universe in much the same way as visible light represents only 0.0035% of the total electromagnetic spectrum?

Do I dare even to admit this question in our current scientific culture? Is this speculation merely an inclination of my nervous system to perceive meaning in a complex and chaotic world, constructing a narrative where the perceived individual self is the protagonist within a story that is being played out in the darkness of the empty auditorium that is my cranium?

Is anyone actually watching the show?

[Taken from a document allegedly composed by Dr. Violet Murphy recovered from the hard drive of her home computer. FBI Case File: SP0999827264-127]

PROLOGUE:

Darren

BLOOD TRICKLED DOWN HIS right leg, slipping slowly along the back of his knee. He paused next to a shrub, shivering as the chill wind blew the fallen red and brown leaves across the dimly lit street. His eyes fought for focus, staring up at the house number: 2995. He stepped back, running his hand through his short brown hair. The drying blood formed a hard crust on the left side of his head, which throbbed with pain. He took in several deep breaths, trying to clear his mind, to cut through the confusion. Again, he looked down at his clothing—the white shirt stained with blood and the dress pants torn on one side. His bare feet ached against the cold, damp sidewalk. He felt as if he could lie down, letting gravity carry him down the slope of the hill, rolling off into an infinity he knew nothing about. Maybe there was nothing beyond this. Maybe this was infinity.

Darren shook his head, fighting for clarity. Returning to the moment, he stared up at the house, the little townhouse, crammed in among other similar houses on the hill. A smile crept across his face. He nodded then almost laughed out loud. Memories of days long since lost clawed at the walls of his mind. Light emanated from the curtain-drawn windows. Darren took a deep breath and staggered forward. His bare feet pressed hard against each wooden step as he made his way to the front door. The creak of every step cut into the silence of the night like a dull knife. Stepping across the porch, he halted at the door. He tried the knob, but it wouldn't budge—of course. He stood there for a brief moment before knocking. He could hear movement inside. Darren stepped back from the door, keeping his eyes on it. The lock clicked. An elderly woman cracked the door and peeked out.

"Who's out there?" she demanded.

"It's me, Darren," he said, his words more of a croak than a spoken language.

The woman stared, her mouth opening wider and wider. Finally, she said, "No. Go away." Abruptly, she slammed the door.

Darren stepped closer and spoke, "Aunt Helen, I need your help."

Nothing.

"I'm right here. I need your help, just let me in. Please."

From behind the door she cried, "Darren is dead! Now you go away."

Darren took in a deep breath, momentarily subduing the escalating rage within him. He drew another deep breath, his hands clenching into fists. He called to her again and again. He heard her move about, knowing that she would likely be headed for the phone to call the police. He still knew that much about his aunt, so he took a few steps back. Then, he kicked the door. The loud boom echoed down the street, but the door didn't cave. A light came on a few houses down, then another. He'd committed to this course of action now. There was no going back. Darren kicked it again. The frame splintered at the locks as the door flew open. He stared at the open door for a moment, almost unable to accept the reality of what he had just done. He moved into the house, finding Aunt Helen on the phone. She stared at Darren, the phone dropping from her hand.

"It's me," he said, stepping closer.

She backed away, shaking her head. "No. Darren is dead. We buried him. You get out of here, now! I called the police. Get out of my house!"

A tear slipped down Darren's cheek. "You don't believe me? I used to call you Aunt El. You made those mushy chocolate-chip cookies for me when I came over as a kid. When I was in college, you would send them to me sometimes. I visited on a few Sunday afternoons and Uncle Rob, you, and me; we watched football on TV." He gestured off to the living room, glancing in that direction.

*The living room…*where was the living room? What he looked at now was more of a den lined with bookshelves, a love seat, and an old upright piano that stood along the far wall.

No. It couldn't be. This wasn't how he remembered it. What was wrong with him?

He looked back at Aunt Helen, feeling a cold rush of panic wash through his heart. He could see tears welling up in her eyes. Was he out of his mind? No. He was certain that he was in the right house. She'd rearranged things. It had been years now. At least six years since he'd last been there. He felt sure he knew this much, at least.

"Then," he continued, in an effort to convince himself as much as the woman before him, "When Uncle Rob passed away, I came here every Sunday to be with you. Remember? We used to—"

Was that movement by the open door? He'd caught something out of the corner of his eye. His breathing quickened as his heart leaped into overdrive. That cold rush of panic from a moment ago became a hot wave of adrenaline—a new kind of panic. He looked around with quick jerks of his head.

"Ah…no…no. Not now."

OUTSIDE, BLACK FIGURES CREPT around the house like silent specters—demons with guns. Units Two and Three found their way around the back of the house. Unit One positioned himself by the front. He could hear them talking inside. He waited. Then, thinking he ought to reposition, he darted to the other side of the small porch, passing the open door. The talking stopped abruptly.

"Hold it," said the female voice in his earpiece, "Shit! He's on to us."

Unit One cursed himself for moving by the open door. He crouched and readied his gun. He fought the onset of fatigue, his vision blurring slightly. He blinked, trying to clear his eyes. The muscles in his hand cried out in protest, just wanting to let go of the gun. He needed to be controlled, focused. The past twelve hours of search for this particularly sly subject was taking its toll on him at last. He could feel a rush of adrenaline as the impending confrontation now loomed before him. He didn't want the adrenaline. It would make his hands shaky. He needed to focus. He needed precise movements so he could act swiftly and smoothly—lethally, if necessary.

"Units Two and Three in position," came Unit Two's confirmation came through the radio earpiece.

Unit One tugged on the handle of a small knife strapped to his left arm, confirming that it was secure. He then checked the smaller handgun on his right hip. Feeling reassured, he lifted his right hand and ran his fingers over the button on his unmarked, black helmet just above his right ear. He needed to focus. He pressed the button. A slight popping sound followed. He sensed his awareness tightening and his focus sharpening as the built in trans-cranial magnetic stimulation took effect.

"What was that?" the female voice on the radio demanded, "Unit One, did you just activate your TMS?"

"Roger," he whispered. He really was losing focus. The TMS caused a blip in communication. Any such interference sent red flags up for those monitoring their every move. Supposedly, they were worried someone might be trying to hack into their encoded signal. Who exactly would want to do that, he wasn't quite sure. But, he had been with the project long enough to gather that paranoia went with the territory. So, any such blip caused hearts in the control station to skip a beat, as they were momentarily convinced they were now being heard by god-knows-whom.

"Shit, David! Give me a warning next time." She growled.

"Roger that."

He tightened his grip on the gun. He knew better. He was just off his game tonight.

"Target is moving," she said. "All units deploy!"

Unit One sprang up. Running in through the door, he could hear glass shatter as Two and Three burst through the back windows. The target dashed into the adjacent dining room. Unit One followed. The man leaped through a picture window in the dining room. Unit One fired his gun. If none of the previous noise had been enough to wake most of the neighbors, the gunshot made up for it twice over. In the midst of the flying glass, he couldn't tell if he'd hit the target or not. He rushed to the window and looked out.

"Target's gone," he said into the radio.

"Did you hit it?"

He scanned the porch quickly. Splotches of blood amid the shards of glass stained the wood deck.

"Negative," he said. "There's blood, but only from the glass. Man, this guy's quick."

He leapt through the window and then jumped off the porch and onto the lawn. Looking up and down the street, he glimpsed the blur as the target cut in between houses down the street.

"Spotted him." One announced, sprinting down the sidewalk.

One turned left where he had last seen the target. A narrow alley cut between houses. The target, a good distance ahead, ran hard. One raised his gun and fired. The shot went wide, ricocheting off a dumpster. Sparks momentarily lit the alley.

"Hold your fire!" a different woman's voice called over the radio. "No live rounds! We need him alive."

Had it happened? Had their communications been hacked? Who was this? The voice felt familiar. He couldn't quite place it, but he thought he knew that voice.

"What?" retorted the first female voice.

"We can't kill him," said the second.

"Violet, stay out of this," the first woman screamed.

DARREN RAN AS FAST as his sliced feet would allow. He heard the shot, which was immediately followed by the ricochet of the bullet as it bounced off of the dumpster next to red brick building. That was a close call! The next one would be on target, he felt sure. He turned right, running down a narrow street. The pain in his feet shot through his legs and he cringed with every hard footfall upon the cold pavement, his soles leaving bloody prints on the sidewalk. A few blocks down, a set of headlights turned onto the street and headed toward him.

He cut across the street. But, as he did, another set of headlights rounded the corner from the opposite direction and blinded him. The car stopped in the street just yards from where Darren stood frozen, panting frantically. The car door opened and a person climbed out. Darren shielded his eyes from the light, but he could not see the person's face. Frantically, he looked around him for a place to run. Nowhere— the futility of his desperate search for an escape only made his heart race faster.

"Darren," said a woman. It took him a moment to realize the voice came from the person who had gotten out of the car. "I'm here to help you. I know who you are."

The other set of headlights stopped behind Darren. He turned to face the van. Four more people poured out, guns in hand. The man who had shot at him in the alley arrived on foot, his gun still drawn. Darren raised his shaking hands. His knees felt as if they could give out at any moment.

"Hold it right there," a different woman by the van commanded.

The armed pursuer pressed the gun against his head. Darren waited, feeling the warm metal against his skin. A fresh burst of adrenaline born out of desperation rushed through him. With a quick jerk of his hand, he pulled the gun away from his head while grasping the man's wrist but the agent's grip remained firm on the gun. With his free hand, Darren ripped the small knife that was strapped to the agent's arm. The agent delivered a hard jab with his knee to Darren's ribs. The wind rushed out of Darren's lungs and he lost his grip on the agent's hand that held the gun. In desperation, Darren swung the knife wildly. As the agent pointed his gun at him, Darren lunged forward and jabbed the knife into his abdomen, twisting the handle. The man screamed. With his other hand, Darren tugged at the gun. It fired with a blinding flash and deafening report. Agent One screamed in pain and hit the ground.

"Hold your fire!" The woman by the car screamed. "Don't shoot, hold—"

IT TOOK ONLY ONE shot. The fugitive's head jerked back as the bullet made a small hole on his forehead and burst out the back of his cranium. Unit Four lowered his weapon as the dead target's body slumped to the ground. Blood flowed onto the pavement as if it still possessed the drive to escape, by any means necessary. In the streetlights, it was hard to tell where the dark red blood ended and the black asphalt began.

Unit One observed this from the ground where he had fallen. The wound on his abdomen bled. He felt dizzy. He gripped his abdomen and tried to control his gasping breaths. He convulsed momentarily before staring down at the growing pool of blood on the pavement. Was that his or was that the other man's? Looking around, he tried to distract his mind from the pain. He felt his consciousness slipping. Around him, he could hear the voices of the others meshing into a swirl of noise. An argument ensued. The woman from the car wanted the target alive. Units Three and Four had their guns drawn on the woman who had interfered. One tried to stay alert, but the pain and the fatigue took over. As his consciousness evaporated into oblivion, he could hear someone calling to him as if from a great distance, "David, you're going to be fine. Stay awake. Hold on, David. Hold on, damn it!"

THE NUN

Parasomnias usually happen during the first few hours of the night, during the deepest sleep just before the evening's first bout of REM sleep.
- Sandra Aamodt & Sam Wang

THE COLD GROUND PRESSED hard against her cheek. She blinked away the cloudiness while tasting dirt. The sight of a cracked sidewalk extended out in front of her. Before she could look around, she already knew what had happened. She was outside again. Her left hand rested under her chin, extending out at an odd angle. She fumbled with her right hand, which was trapped under her body, and pushed herself up. On her knees, she looked down at her hands, only then discovering a small cut in the left palm. Inspecting herself, she noted with relief that she wore a white tank top and shorts. Her bare feet stood firmly on the black asphalt. She brushed dirt from the dark olive skin of her arms and legs. The distinct aftertaste of a fading dream clung to her mental pallet. What had it been?

Riley Bekker glanced about. The empty street stretched in either direction. The houses were dark, save for a few outdoor lights as security. Streetlights provided pools of cool LED light. All of this, combined with the calm, chilly breeze, Riley assumed that it was approximately three or four in the morning. Riley stared at the twinkling lights of the Brazilian city of Campo Grande in the distance. The city stretched for kilometers, with buildings cropping up in clusters of business and apartment complexes. The lights possessed an eerie beauty at such an hour. A chill ran through her body. None of the surroundings looked all that familiar.

"Oh, God help me," she muttered, "where have I ended up now?"

"Are you okay?" a voice asked in Portuguese.

She turned, finding a young woman standing nearby. She wore a red dress that hugged her too-slender frame and her bleached hair was pulled back in a ponytail. At first, Riley wondered if this too might be a dream. Maybe she was still asleep. Alas, that would have been much more convenient, and far less embarrassing. Maybe she was just losing her mind. It certainly would explain a lot. The young woman took a deep drag of her cigarette and smiled at her. Riley's face grew red. The breeze picked up, casting her dark hair across her face. Riley moved it aside.

"I'm okay," Riley replied in an accented Portuguese.

The girl picked up on this, her eyes almost twinkling with delight, "*Americana?*"

Riley nodded, "I—uh—yeah. I need to go home now."

She started for the sidewalk. The other woman's heels clicked loudly behind Riley, echoing off concrete walls surrounding houses that lined the empty street. *Oh Lord, I don't need this,* she lamented. She had no desire to be rude, yet she preferred to avoid any awkward situations—make that, any further awkward situations. This was uncomfortable enough already. With each passing moment, however, Riley's hope that the strange woman might let her walk off alone faded.

"Where do you live?" the woman asked.

Riley stopped and turned.

"I'm sorry; I just need to go home," she said.

"I know," the woman smiled. "But where do you live?"

"*Jardin dos Estados,*" she offered, tentatively.

"Alright, so you're in the right neighborhood."

Riley looked around, attempting to gather her bearings. The vacant lot with tall grass to her right now looked vaguely familiar. A three-foot high concrete wall surrounded it. Two spray-painted words reflected the streetlight: Sonic Hedgehog. Dizziness suddenly overwhelmed her. Images flashed in her mind of a can of spray paint. She could smell it.

The distinct sense of familiarity washed over her for a brief moment as she stood there by the street. Somewhere in the recesses of her mind, she recalled an old video game she'd played as a child, *Sonic the Hedgehog*. The catchy theme song flooded her brain. But why was anyone spraying those words on this wall? As a matter of fact, what wall was that? Where was she? Her knees gave out.

"Whoa," the girl in the red dress grabbed her arm to steady her, her grip surprisingly strong. "Take it easy. You on something?"

"No. I have this case of sleepwalking. I'm sorry." Riley rubbed her eyes with her free hand. *Parasomnias*, she thought, *that's what the doctor called it, right?* Looking around again, she saw the street with a new and unexpected sense of familiarity. "Oh, wow. I'm about ten blocks from home. I remember now. Thank you. I'll be fine."

"Good," the woman said, still holding her arm. "How about I walk you home?"

Riley looked into her eyes. How could she explain this? Too much make-up coated the strange woman's otherwise naturally attractive face. She was young. Eighteen, maybe? Likely even younger. In a different context, she would have been no more than a Brazilian girl just now coming into her womanly beauty.

"I'm a nun," Riley mumbled.

The girl's eyes widened and she giggled.

Riley became immediately aware of how those words might have sounded utterly inconsiderate, bearing a distinct "holier-than-thou" connotation to them.

"I'm sorry," she said. "I don't mean that—I just—"

"Hey, it's okay. I didn't ask you if you were wanting anything. By the looks of it, you've already had too much of a good time for one night anyway," the girl giggled again.

"No," Riley stammered for words, "it's this—I sleepwalk some times. It's really bad. I just need to go home. I know my way from here."

The girl let go of Riley's arm and smiled. "Okay, but I still think I should walk you back. It's not so safe out here at this hour."

Riley opened her mouth to refuse, but found herself almost unable to turn the girl away. What would people say about her wandering in the streets at night with a prostitute? This certainly would not go over very well with the other nuns at the school. Yet, another thought entered her mind. As a nun, should she take the very attitude that brought about such bad characterization of the religious leaders of the New Testament? Did not Jesus associate himself with the outcasts of society? He allowed a prostitute to wash his feet with her own hair, a rather intimate gesture of service and love.

"Okay, sure. Having help might be wise."

"Very well," the girl said, cocking her head to one side.

They started down the sidewalk together. As they made their way down the block, the orchestra of city life played out its nightly symphony. The traffic—cars zipping along the main avenues, honking horns, engines revving—played out a cacophony of sound that could be heard in the distance. Amidst the usual baseline, a siren cascaded through the air before dissipating into the night. The cadence of the city's performance now met the gentle applause of the night breeze. As the two women continued down the hill, the dissonant nature of their personalities struck against the staccato beat of light casting itself upon them from the street lamps overhead—a syncopated progression of light and shadow.

"Look," Riley said, "I didn't mean to offend you."

"Offend me?" the girl shrugged, "So you're a nun and I'm a hooker. It's quite alright, really. Lots of both around here. And, truth be told, some of my best customers have been priests and pastors. I've even had a nun before. She was older, but feisty!" The girl laughed, looking off.

"Oh," Riley nodded, searching for a change of subject. "What's your name?"

The girl frowned. "My real name?"

"Whatever you like to be called."

"Eliane."

"It's a pleasure to meet you, Eliane," Riley stuck out her hand. "My name is Riley."

Eliane shook her hand with an amused smile on her face. "Pleased to meet you, Riley. You know, you don't look American."

"Yeah, I get that a lot," Riley smiled, aware that her Mexican genes and her American accent were a source of initial confusion for many Brazilians she met.

They continued walking. Another thirty seconds of silence passed before Eliane spoke again. A light breeze brushed past them. Riley looked out at the city lights; then to the sidewalk in front of her. She wondered how Eliane had gotten started down what she couldn't help but scc as an incredibly sad path.

"So, what brought you to Brazil?" Eliane said.

"I'm a teacher at *Colegio do São Pedro*," Riley volunteered. "I teach science."

Eliane laughed, her head craning back. "A nun that teaches science? I always thought that science and God didn't get along."

Riley smiled. "You make it sound like they had a big fight."

"Well, didn't they?" she grinned now, holding back laughter.

Riley chuckled as she pushed back a strand of her dark hair, "Yeah. Maybe. But I think if we look at both science and God with an open mind we might find that neither is quite as contradictory as once believed."

"Wow. An open-minded nun, I like that." She looked at Riley for a moment as they walked then said, "So, does this happen often?"

"Huh? Oh, the sleepwalking?" Why did she even ask? "It comes and goes. Sometimes I wake up in the kitchen or on the living room floor. There have been a few occasions that I've wandered out of the house. But, usually it's not quite this far."

"You should see a doctor, or pray about it, or something. You know?"

Riley smiled and nodded, "I have seen a doctor and I do pray about it, quite often, in fact."

"I see," she whispered, looking away.

They walked on for several blocks, talking as they went.

"How did you become a nun?" Eliane asked at last.

"I really want to make a difference in the world," Riley shrugged. "Ugh, sorry, that sounds so pretentious. What I mean to say is that I like helping people, I like teaching, and I hope what I do helps people discover they that have value and are loved."

"Wow," Eliane smiled. "Noble."

Riley shook her head and waved the comment off. Feeling the awkwardness of the situation, Riley's mouth seemed to move of its own accord. She launched into a rambling narrative of growing up Catholic in the United States. Her parents had been an interesting mix. Her father was a stout freckled man of Irish descent who had never left Boston and her mother was a dark-skinned mystery from Mexico City. They were different in so many ways, but they were both profoundly devout to their Catholic faith. Riley had pursued a career in science. But she had always maintained an interest in the faith of her upbringing as it had been a constant compass guiding her way through an extremely tumultuous adolescence. She found herself drawn to being of service to the church and the broader world. She joined the small but growing order of nuns, the *Sororibus Christi*, which was Latin for Sisters of Christ. The order's philosophy landed somewhere between the Dominican and Jesuit modes of operation. Nuns lived generally in small communities of fellow sisters, usually three or four to a house, much like Dominican nuns. They also dressed far more casually (though always modestly) like Dominicans. Like the male-only Jesuit order, the *Sororibus Christi* had a profound focus on innovation and broad-sweeping missionary and educational work. No sister was purely religious, but all possessed profound knowledge in diverse areas of humanities, sciences, the arts, and medicine. Many held doctorates in both theology and science. Riley joined the *Sororibus Christi* and continued her education. About a year and a half ago she decided she would like to see more of the world, so she accepted the job in Campo Grande as a science teacher for a private Catholic school.

"Did you go to Catholic school all your life?" Eliane asked.

"No, I went to public school. But I grew up going to mass. I guess you could say it felt right to become a nun." She shrugged. "How about you? Where did you go to school?"

Eliane sighed. "Public education in this country is total shit." Her eyes widened and she almost stopped walking, forcing Riley to slow as well. She looked at her with concern, "I'm so sorry."

Riley shook her head. "I know it's probably hard to believe, but even nuns occasionally say shit."

Eliane laughed and they resumed walking normally. Eliane looked around. Riley observed her then said, "So you did public education?"

"Yeah, up to fifth grade. I didn't really like it."

Riley wondered if she'd really not liked it or if there were other circumstances that played into her choice to drop out—if, in fact, it had even been her choice at all. They continued on for a few more blocks then turned onto a small street that headed up hill. A car drove past them, but didn't seem to pay any attention to the barefoot woman in a tank top and the woman in the red dress.

"That's my house right there," Riley pointed to a set of green gates.

In many places in Brazil, houses were encased in tall walls often sporting nails or broken glass to dissuade potential burglars from trying to climb over. Thus, a standard for all homes was to have a gate or garage door that a car could drive into, or at least a person could pass through. Direct access to the front door or windows was discouraged. Riley's gate was made of simple metal bars that allowed one to see the small car she shared with her housemates. It sat under the tin roof that served as a car port. A heavy chain hung around the center bars of the gate, which were twice as thick as the rest. A deceivingly small lock linked the chain into a closed loop around the center bars.

Riley and Eliane stopped in front of the house. "Alright, here it is."

Eliane looked at her. Worry crept into Riley again. *I hope she doesn't think that now that we are here…*

"You seem like a really nice person," she smiled, "even for a nun."

Riley laughed. "Thanks. I think."

"Maybe I'll go to mass on Sunday. It's been a…really long time."

"That would be good. Look, could I call you a cab?" Riley offered.

Eliane shook her head, "I can take care of myself."

"Are you sure?"

She nearly laughed, "Yeah, I'm fine. I'm always fine. Besides, my night's work isn't over yet. You have a good night, and be careful with your sleepwalking."

Eliane turned and started to walk away.

"Thanks, Eliane," Riley said, "Thank you for walking me home."

The young woman stopped and looked back over her shoulder, "You're welcome."

She gave Riley a slight smile and then went on her way. Riley watched her walk off, wondering where she might be headed. Was she really working this neighborhood? Did that really happen in her neighborhood? Now that Riley thought more about it, it did seemed peculiar that a prostitute would pick such an area to work. The city government was making a show of cleaning up certain areas, so it was possible that pimps and hookers were forced to branch out in new directions and take different approaches. Riley lifted a silent prayer for Elianc as she watched her go, expressing both hope that she might remain safe tonight but also find her way into a better life.

Finally, Riley fished the keys out of her short's pocket. She looked down at the key in her hand, then at the lock on the gate. This had happened before. Somehow, when she went into this strange sleepwalking state, she would leave her house in a very normal manner. She would always fetch the keys, lock the gate, and head out. Of course, she couldn't remember doing any of that. However, it had to be what happened. After all, the gate's bars were sharp at the tips, and the wall was high and bore shards of broken glass at the top. Riley looked down at the small cut on her hand. No, it was too small to have been caused by the glass on the wall or even the tops of the bars on her gate. She would have ripped open her hands and legs trying to get over the wall and would only fare slightly better trying to go over the gate.

Riley unlatched the padlock and swung open the gate just far enough to slip in, then she closed and locked it from the inside. She entered the cream-colored house. Her fingers brushed over the small screen on the wall next to the door. This activated the lights. She stood in the sparsely furnished living room. She lived here with three other nuns that taught at the same private Catholic school. A sofa and a chair faced a wall.

Riley walked to the sofa and collapsed onto it. The projection television sprang to life. The small, three-dimensional projectors hanging from the ceiling in each of the room's four corners cast light about a foot out from the wall the sofa faced. The image of a jet flying through clouds formed quickly. In comparison to the stillness of the house, the sound of the airline commercial seemed unexpectedly cacophonously. Riley jolted up right, heart racing.

"Television off," she said in a flat tone.

The noise and lights vanished. She hoped the sudden burst of sound hadn't disturbed the other women in the house. Riley sloughed, letting her head fall back and her eyes close. Why did this happen? Why did she sleepwalk? It didn't happen every night. In fact, she hadn't had any episodes for about four weeks. That is, until this past week. She woke up in the hallway a few nights ago. And before that, she found herself by the front door one morning. Apparently she had fallen there and just slept the rest of the night. Her neck had been sore for days. Those cases didn't bother her quite as much as waking up in the street. She didn't mind it if she woke up in the kitchen. She even wondered if she might not be lucky enough to wake up some time by the fridge with an already made sandwich, or maybe even a martini. But the fact that she had awakened out in the street somewhere three times in the past four months frightened her. She'd been lucky. Even if she was relatively fit, being out at night was not a safe place for a lone woman in her mid-thirties—or so Riley had thought until tonight. She yawned and rose from the sofa. She had to get back to bed. She had to teach tomorrow.

She made her way down the hallway to her bedroom. Pausing in front of the small crucifix on the wall, she crossed herself, whispering the words, "*Nome do Pai, do Filho, e do Espirito Santo.*" She chided himself for not spending enough time training her mind to think in Portuguese. After all, thinking in a language is the only true mark of fluency. That was her goal, after all.

She proceeded down the hall and then realized that she had left the lights on in the living room. No matter. The motion sensors would detect the lack of her presence in the room and the lights would go off in a few minutes. It wasn't the most efficient use of energy, but she was officially exhausted. She turned into her room and crawled under her covers. Only after she had lain down did she even think about how filthy her bare feet must have been. Too tired and too comfortable to care, she rolled over and closed her eyes. Tomorrow she would wash the sheets. She remembered her cut hand and looked at it in the dim light. The blood had clotted, forming a small scab on her palm.

Good enough for now, she thought as she felt her body give way to sleep. At some point she had that old familiar dream: long halls, blinking lights, wires being connected, more halls, more panic.

THE CHAPEL

2

> [T]he ability to attribute feelings and intentions to others is an essential component of mature religious beliefs, which depend on faith in unseen motives.
>
> - Sandra Aamodt & Sam Wang

CHILDREN RAN ABOUT, LAUGHING and shouting. The early morning air bore a slight chill, but none of them seemed phased by it. Riley, wearing a light-blue dress shirt and dark dress pants, stood by the front entrance of the schoolyard, which was encased in a tall, green fence that circled the block. She took a deep breath of the morning air, detecting the slightest scent of burnt leaves.

Cars pulled up, dropping off more children. Some had electric motors, which whined as the cars picked up speed and drove away. Other cars were hybrids or full-blown combustion engines. Most of the combustion engines were older models that continued to run solely because of characteristic Brazilian persistence and ingenuity. The transition away from these older machines was slow even in the most developed of nations. But in Brazil, and much of South America, the transition was even slower still due to economics, politics, and the availability of alcohol derived from sugarcane, as a fuel source, Riley and her housemates drove a ten-year-old hybrid that ran on Brazilian alcohol and electricity.

Some kids stood on the sidewalk and waved to their parents. Others, too excited about seeing their friends, ran through the gate, zipping past Riley. More cars pulled up to drop off even more children and so, the process continued. She had to admit that she admired this method. Sure, it was noisy and the street became easily congested. Still, she found it remarkable the number of parents who made it a standard part of their day to drop off and pick up their children. This certainly was not part of her childhood memories.

The large trees by the street provided a nice shade for these exchanges. A traffic coordinator stood with her yellow vest next to one of the large trees and waved cars through. Out of one of the cars dashed an eight-year-old boy named Tiago. He greeted the traffic coordinator with a boisterous *"Oi,"* 'hello' in Portuguese. Tiago rushed past her and spotted Riley, who still stood by the main gate. Tiago ran to her.

"Bom dia," he called to her.

"Oi, Tiago," Riley responded in her accented Portuguese. "How are you?"

"Good," the boy grinned, showing bright white teeth that contrasted his dark skin and black, curly hair. "I got a guitar for my birthday."

"Congratulations! Are you going to bring it in and play us a song?" Riley smiled knowingly.

Tiago's eyes widened. "Uh, no. I can't do that. I have to learn first!"

"Alright, you learn first. Then, you'll have to bring it in some time and play for us."

"Can I play a song by The Death Razor?"

"Why not?" Riley laughed.

Filled with excitement, Tiago bounded into the schoolyard. Riley watched him go. *Such energy. I could use some of that energy right about now. More sleep would have been a good thing,* she lamented. Riley recalled the events of the previous night as if looking at a faded photograph. Although they had taken place mere hours ago, they possessed an elusive dream-like quality. And with every passing minute of the new morning, her memories grew increasingly hazy. Had she really walked home with Eliane? *Yep, that happened,* she thought as she looked down at her injured hand again. Something else pressed against her mind, something invisible. She couldn't recall what it was. She felt as if she'd had a bad dream and now could not evoke the image that had caused her to wake up so frightened in the first place. Nevertheless, that primal fear was present; lingering within her like a shadow on her mind that only grew darker and heavier. She snapped out of her daze. Looking down at her watch, she realized it was time to make her way to her classroom.

THE TWO TEENAGE BOYS stood before her, their hands folded in front of them. Eduardo, the smaller of the two, looked right at her with his wide, frightened eyes. His lips trembled slightly and Riley couldn't help but think that he looked rather like a cornered animal, filled with dread, but determined to face whatever was coming its way. Marcus, the taller and stronger of the two, seemed more defeated as he hung his head forward and stared at the floor. Class had been dismissed a moment ago, but Riley had asked the two boys to stay. Now she stood, leaning against her desk, where she still had a glass of water and the open textbook.

She'd been teaching their ninth grade general science class when she spotted a note being passed to Eduardo. Not one for making a scene, she waited for the opportune moment to walk by Eduardo's desk, tap him on the shoulder, and quietly ask for the note while the other students worked on a quiz. Confiscating the note, she quickly ascertained that Marcus had been the one to write it. He had asked for the girl who sat between the two boys to pass it along to Eduardo. Riley read the note several times. It was short. Each time she read it she tried to determine how best to interpret the note and how to proceed.

"Meet me at the spot at 8 tonight," was all it said. Marcus had simply signed it with a sloppy, 'M'. Students were not allowed to use technology in any of the classrooms. The school administrators were determined that students should learn the 'old-fashioned' way, with pencil and paper. Smartphones, tablets, and smart watches had to remain off in the students' bags for the duration of any class. This meant that students also had to resort to old-fashion methods of clandestine communication during class.

22

"You know why this is a problem, right?" Riley looked at the boys and asked.

Neither moved, but Eduardo's eyes grew slightly wider.

"Two weeks ago, a note a lot like this one was passed at one of our sister schools. It was a rendezvous for a fight. One of those students is in the hospital right now in critical condition."

Marcus looked up, his shoulders relaxing. "You think we're going to fight?"

Riley raised her eyebrows. "Should I think something else?"

Marcus glanced over at Eduardo, his mouth hanging open but unable to produce any words. Riley watched this carefully. In Marcus' eyes, which looked back at Eduardo, she saw a new and raw vulnerability. This was not the behavior of a boy looking to pounce on a rival. Eduardo, let his hands fall to his sides and his eyes wander.

Riley knew what other kids said of Eduardo. She could imagine a scenario in which the more popular and much stronger Marcus might have seen his twisted chance to assert his dominance by beating up one of the schools gay students. But suddenly, she saw the note in a whole different context. Relief and then hesitation washed over her.

"You weren't meeting to fight," she stated.

The boys glanced at each other and then nodded

"Good," Riley said softly. "However, passing notes are not allowed. And especially in light of these recent events, I am required to turn in this note to the administration."

Now both of the boys looked at her, their faces draining of color.

"Ms. Bekker, please don't," Marcus said, his voice shaking.

She looked into his eyes for a moment, feeling the waves of desperation coming from them. He didn't look away now.

"Ms. Bekker," Eduardo interjected, softly, "it was my idea. Marcus had nothing…"

"*Du*," Marcus cut him off by using his nickname, "don't do that. She knows better."

Eduardo glanced at Marcus then hung his head.

Do I know? Riley wondered. She looked at the boys for a moment.

Yes, it started to make sense. This was definitely no rendezvous for a fight. Turning the note in to the administration would out Marcus. It would have little social effect on Eduardo as most everyone knew or assumed he was gay. No one made that assumption about Marcus. The school, being a Catholic institution, after all, had an official position of not condoning homosexuality. No students would be kicked out over their sexual orientation, but at the same time, the social impact within the school on those students known to be gay, transgender, queer, or bisexual, was obvious. Riley had heard that a few years ago the administration had gone to great lengths to change the schedules of two tenth grade boys who had been in a relationship. Somehow, the school felt that ensuring the boys never again had a class together; it would be enough to end their relationship. It wasn't.

Riley took a deep breath and let it out slowly. While there was so much she genuinely loved about the church, there were things she did not feel were handled well. Hell, there were things she genuinely believed were completely off the mark, based on antiquated and misguided thinking. She looked at these two young men, adolescents simply trying to understand themselves and to get a grasp on life. No good could ever come from Riley turning in that note.

"I'm required to turn in this note to the administration," Riley said, watching the panic rise in both of the boys again. "But…I can't turn in a note that I don't have."

The boys frowned, bewildered. Riley looked down at the note in her hand, folding it up again. She then slowly moved her hand over to the glass on her desk and let the piece of paper fall from her fingers and into the water. The paper immediately absorbed much of the water. Looking back at the boys, she found them both open-jawed and wide-eyed.

"*Profesora,*" Eduardo said, in shock.

"Now, I need you both to do me a couple of favors," Riley continued, all business. "First of all, never mention this conversation to anyone. I'm serious. I like my job. I'd like to keep it. Second, there will be no more passing notes in class. Any class! You can't afford to get caught again."

The awestruck boys nodded emphatically. She dismissed the boys, who promptly headed off in different directions. Fetching her glass of water, Riley stopped by the bathroom, where she poured it into a toilet and flushed the note away. Then, she headed to lunch.

She spent her meal poking at her food and silently wondering how those two had found each other and if they were happy together.

ENCOMPASSED IN SILENCE, RILEY sat alone in the empty chapel, her head bowed. After a moment, her eyes opened and she raised her head. She focused on the crucifix at the front. Her mind, however, battled for concentration on her prayers. Foreign thoughts, some related to last night, cried out for her attention. She took a deep breath, refocusing herself, pushing out such thoughts. She felt her abdomen involuntarily tighten. *Great. Cramps.* Her mind immediately began speculating about potential connections between her sleepwalking episodes and her period. *Later,* she told herself. *There's time to think of these things later. Right now, just be. Just pray. Though, honestly God, I really need some answers. This is getting seriously out of hand!*

But focus was proving particularly hard this morning. Had she done the right thing for those two boys? Why did she agree to continue her work as a nun when there were significant things about the larger institution of the Catholic Church she could not bring herself to agree with? *Why can't it be more straight-forward? Why can't people be who they are?*

When these frustrations came, she tried to focus her mind on prayer, trusting that God was bigger than the institutions and systems of belief that humanity had devised in an effort to understand the divine mystery. Still, she longed for something greater, which she often struggled to articulate. She knew that her own past had to inform this longing. While she enjoyed her work, she often felt oddly out of place. At times, it felt as if she were an actor playing a role. She repeatedly tried to assure herself that this was simply an impostor syndrome, which many often faced while in the service of the church. She found great meaning in her work and great relief in knowing that even the most pious of nuns and priests were only human, fraught with their own doubts and questions, and simply doing the best they could moment by moment. *Lord, please see the compassion that guided my choice today,* she prayed.

As her head went down, she heard the door at the back of the chapel creek open. A moment later, footsteps proceeded down the aisle. She closed her eyes, continuing her contemplative prayer. The footsteps grew louder as the person approached. The heavy steps, likely belonging to a man, stopped next to her. She heard the rustling of clothing as the person found a seat. Riley tried to push the presence from her mind. She remained in silent prayer and reflection as best she could for a few more minutes. But at last, she embraced the futility of this exercise today. She was exhausted and completely distracted by her sleepwalking last night, her encounter with Marcus and Eduardo this morning, and now the presence of another person in the normally empty chapel.

She raised her head and glanced to her right. Across the aisle sat a man in a suit. The man clasped his large, dark hands together in an awkward pose of prayer. Riley didn't recognize him. *Must be a guest, visitors often want to take a moment in the chapel.* Not wanting to disturb him, Riley quietly rose from the pew. At the pew's edge, she knelt quickly, glanced at the crucifix, bowed her head, and crossed herself. The man, apparently sensing Riley's movement, looked up. Riley smiled and gave him a polite nod then headed for the door.

"Sister Riley Bekker," the man said in English.

Riley stopped and turned to face him. The stranger stood and walked to her. She noticed that the man did not pause at the pew's end to cross himself. The stranger, standing a bit taller than Riley—who was five-foot-six-inches herself—stuck out his hand as he approached her.

"My name is Thomas Coleman," the man said.

"Hello," Riley said tentatively, shaking his hand. "How can I help you, Mr. Coleman?"

"I was told you might be in here. They said you make it an afternoon ritual."

Riley nodded, "It's a habit, I guess. Are you…American?"

"Yes," Thomas gave her a broad smile, flashing neat, white teeth that contrasted to his incredibly dark skin. "I'm brand new to the area and I was told that you're from the States."

"That's right. Where are you from?"

"Boston."

Riley grinned, "Oh, well, I'm from that area as well."

"Really?! I don't hear the accent," Thomas smirked.

"Never picked it up," Riley shrugged. "I don't hear you dropping your Rs."

Thomas chuckled. "Originally from Michigan. Then Texas."

"A traveller," Riley observed.

"Something like that."

"So, Mr. Coleman, what can I do for you?"

"Oh yes, I was wondering if maybe you could help me get a feel for the city. My Portuguese is horrible. Communication is a little tough. How about we meet some time for some of this notoriously strong Brazilian coffee? You know, we could chat for a while. Like I said, I'm new to the country, and could use a bit of help... and some prayer, actually." Those last words fell awkwardly from his lips.

Riley studied the man, his hazel eyes, his dark complexion, the short, black hair. Looking at him now, Thomas seemed vaguely familiar. Riley felt a moment of slight disorientation, somewhat like waking from one of her bouts of sleepwalking. She shook off the notion, not sure where she would have seen the man before.

"I know a few other Americans connected to the school. I could introduce you to them," she offered.

Thomas looked away, clearly searching for a response. Riley wondered why this man wanted to meet with her, of all people. There were two American priests in the school as well as one Canadian. It seemed like whomever he spoke with, to find out where Riley was at that time of the afternoon, would have steered him to one of the men. Something felt off about all of this.

"Okay," Thomas said, "I'll level with you. I came here specifically looking for you. I know who you are. Knew your parents too. I need to talk to you about something very important."

Riley frowned, her lips pressed together. "Okay. What would that be?"

"I'm sorry," Thomas said. "I'm sure I'm coming across like a total creep. I assure you that I'm not. I just…"

He looked around at the empty chapel.

"We should find a better place and time to talk," he said.

"I'm sorry, Mr. Coleman," she said. "I don't mean to be rude, but I would feel more comfortable if you would just tell me what this is about."

"It's about your sleepwalking," he said, softly. "I can't say anymore. Not here." He glanced around again.

Riley blinked, taking this in. *He knows about my sleepwalking?* At a loss for how to proceed, she glanced down at her watch and considered the rest of the day's schedule. "I could meet around six this evening. Do you know where the *Padaria do João* is? It's only a few blocks away. It's a bakery, but they have great coffee and a nice area with tables where we could sit and talk."

Yeah, nice open area with tables and big windows and lots of people hanging around, Riley thought. I might be intrigued, but I'm not stupid.

Thomas gave her a large grin, "Fantastic. So, six o'clock at, ah…yeah, I think I saw it on my way here. Sounds great!"

Thomas shook Riley's hand again and thanked her. He headed out the door quickly. Riley stood in the chapel alone. *First, I have a totally crazy night and make friends with a hooker*, Riley mused. *Then, I put my job in jeopardy out of compassion for a couple of boys. Now, this guy shows up. This is turning into one truly bizarre day.*

Knowing that she had only a few more minutes before her first afternoon class, she decided to spend those fleeting moments in prayer. Valuing frankness, it wouldn't be the first time she began a prayer with, "So God, what the fuck is happening?"

3 KNOWLEDGE AND BELIEF

Some philosophers suggest that conscious awareness is nothing but lots of fast memory querying: our brains are always asking 'What just happened? What just happened?' Thus, conscious experience is really just immediate memory.
- David Eagleman

THE SCENT OF STRONG coffee hung in the air, an enticing aroma to the lovers of caffeine in all its forms, tastes, and colors. The bakery/coffee shop struck Riley as a perfect example of Brazilian culture assimilating some aspects of North American life. According to what she had learned and observed in other areas, the neighborhood bakery was usually small and quaint, focused on functionality and providing fresh bread for the day's meals. There might be places to have a seat and enjoy some fresh bread, a soft drink, or some coffee, but space was usually limited and most of the clientele purchased what they needed and headed home.

This place, however, resembled the older American coffeehouse, which had been forced to reinvent itself with the rise of virtual reality cafes. Glass comprised nearly the entire front of the shop. In fact, glass seemed to be the chosen motif for this particular shop. The tables were formed as glass sculptures, stylistically shaped and formed for the sole purpose of supporting their *pièce de résistance*: the tabletop—a perfectly round and thick pane of tempered glass with a frosted finish. Contraptions of modern art hung on the walls in shades of dark blue and green. Small, but clear speakers in each corner spread the eclectic sounds of pop ambient tunes, mixing forms of classical music and trance-like EDM.

Riley sat at one of the round glass tables, a copy of *Veja* (Look) magazine and a mug of coffee (decaf at this hour) before her. She flipped though articles ranging from politics to soap operas, noticing the number of ads in such a magazine bearing nearly naked or fully nude men and women. Yes, Brazilian culture seemed to carry with it quite an open attitude towards sexuality. According to her Brazilian colleagues, it had basically always been this way. Well, this was the land of *carnaval*, after all.

Her eyes fell upon an article dealing with recent developments in neuroscience. She read through the first paragraph, her eyes landed upon, "While advancement in science is usually hailed with great enthusiasm for all the possible practical applications, big questions abound. of those major questions concerns itself with whether scientific development within our understanding of brain functions, as it relates to personality theory, should be used to combat crime."

Sipping her coffee, she skimmed the remainder of the article out of curiosity. It seemed that some scientists were proposing the possibility of identifying areas of the brain that are associated with criminal activities, and targeting them with drugs or other means in order to "help" repeat offenders quit such behavior. She'd heard of this before, and the notion bothered Riley. There were plenty of scientists in opposition to this idea, citing the complexity of the brain and that no particular part of it was responsible for any single action or even addiction.

A few held out hopes for training the brain by eliminating the strongest neural connection associated with certain behaviors. It was a process they were tentatively calling Drug-induced, Long-term Depression. They were careful to note that "Long-term Depression" was the name for the process by which synapses in the brain were naturally reduced.

She finished the article, surprised at how quickly she took it in, though she had only intended to kill some time before the man she had met earlier—*what was his name?*—arrived. *Thomas Coleman. That's it.* She shook her head and sighed. Her inability to quickly pick up on people's names had always bothered her. She had to be intentional about it.

"Sister Bekker," said Thomas.

Riley looked up from the magazine. Thomas approached her table. Riley began to stand, but he quickly plopped down in the seat across from her and thrust out his hand. Setting the magazine aside, she reached across the table and shook it. His handshake was firm but quick.

"I'm glad to see that you came." Thomas smiled.

"Well, you have me intrigued, Mr. Coleman. How exactly do you know about my sleepwalking?" she said, wasting no time.

Thomas maintained the smile, but Riley noticed his eyes scanning the room. "We'll get to that, I promise," he said.

Riley frowned and sipped her coffee again.

Coleman's eyes still searched for something. Finally, they returned to Riley. "What made you decide to come to Brazil?"

Riley raised her eyebrows. What was this guy up to? "Change of pace, I guess. I wanted to see a little more of the world, be of service."

The smile on Thomas' face grew. "That's a good answer."

"How is that?" Riley straightened her back slightly.

Thomas maintained his warm smile. Riley noted that he ordered no coffee. What was this man after? This whole situation was incredibly fishy and she began to wish she'd not shown up at all. But, how could she not show up when this stranger knew about her sleepwalking? She divulged such a private matter to very few people.

"What exactly can I do for you, Mr. Coleman?" Riley said in a calm yet direct tone. "You said you knew my parents? And that you know about my sleepwalking?"

Thomas smiled big, nodding, "You might say I knew your parents." He leaned in. "So you're a woman of faith, Miss Bekker."

"That I am."

"That means that you, more than anyone else, understand that there is more to this life of ours, on this little blue planet, than what we normally see or feel."

Annoyed by his evasiveness, Riley took a large sip of her coffee and set it down. "Sure, I believe there's much more to this world than meets the eye."

"Have you experienced any of that?"

Riley looked down at the table, and sighed slightly. "What exactly do you mean, Mr. Coleman?" she probed. Was this a game, some kind of prank?

"Please, call me Thomas. What I mean is, have you been moved in your prayers? Have you seen angels or heard God speak to you? You know; the supernatural?"

Riley smiled, glancing down. "How did you say you know my parents?"

Thomas sat back opened his hands in a gesture of surrender. "Okay, you got me. I never knew them personally. But I know about them. And, I know how they influenced you."

Thomas glanced at Riley arms, which rested on the table, her hands around her mug.

"You have a scar on your arm," he pointed out. "How did you get that?"

She glanced down at the V-shaped scar. Looking back up, she locked eyes with the man. Neither moved. Riley felt that familiarity again. Something inside her stirred, and she spoke. "When I was a girl, my parents took me to mass. I didn't really understand it at the time. It seemed so formal; peculiar. The image of Christ hanging on the cross looming in the front of the church seemed morbid." She took another sip of coffee.

"When I was nine years old," she continued, "we spent the summer in Alaska while my dad consulted for a drilling company out there. We had a tall picket fence around the house in which we were staying, to keep animals out. I was often told to take out the trash as part of the chores. Well, this one day, one of the bags was filled with old newspapers. It was really heavy. We would toss the bags over the back of the fence, and the owner of the house, who lived about a mile away, would come by and fetch it in the evenings. I had to stand on a bucket to toss the bag over. But, this time the bucket slipped just as I tossed it. The fence impaled my left arm. My parents were gone at the time. I passed out from the pain, but eventually came to again. I hung there for more than two hours, but, all along, I just remember being overwhelmed by this sense that things were going to be okay. All those prayers that I had been learning in catechism just suddenly began to pour out of my lips. After that, going to church had a whole new meaning to it."

"Wow," Thomas remarked softly, "that's impressive. How's your arm?"

"It's okay. It healed up. The scar is a little gnarly, but it does remind me of the peace I felt in that moment," Riley said.

Thomas looked at her arm and then said, "There you have it, proof of the existence of God."

"If it's proof you're looking for, I'm afraid this hardly qualifies," Riley raised her eyebrows. "It certainly convinced me. But proof is a bit of a loaded word, don't you think?"

"How so?"

"Well," Riley said, "The word proof is mostly used in an empirical context. I'm a science teacher, so when I hear the word 'proof,' I think of something I can test; something I can repeat in order to demonstrate— prove to you that it is in fact the case. A subjective personal experience, such as what I just described is a little hard to cite as 'proof' in that sense of the word."

"But you were convinced," Thomas insisted.

"I was—am convinced. But people are convinced by subjective and unprovable experiences all of the time. So, I understand when other people say they are not convinced by an experience that they did not themselves have. The subjective nature of experiencing God is part of the mystery," she smiled, concealing her annoyance at the roundabout nature of this odd conversation.

Thomas looked around the bakery again. He nodded; then leaned in, "I don't have much time to explain myself."

Riley looked into the man's eyes and waited for what might come next. This whole conversation felt at the same time familiar and peculiar.

Riley couldn't even quite figure out why in the world she had managed to talk so much to this man she had just met. Why had she shared the story about her scar? Thomas cleared his throat.

"You don't remember me, but I sure as hell remember you," Thomas continued. "We used to work together in Boston—well, it wasn't exactly you."

"Mr. Coleman," Riley sat back, grinning "are you sure you have the right person?"

"Oh, yeah. You're Riley Bekker. You're the daughter of a Mexican immigrant and Boston native Irish descendent. An unlikely mix. But they were good people, worked hard, paid their taxes, cheered for the Red Sox and The Revolution, and helped you through college. Your father worked for thirty-two years in construction. He died of a heart attack at the age of fifty-four, far too young. Your mother passed away a year later in a car accident."

Riley stared incredulously at the man sitting before her. It took her a moment to realize her mouth had dropped open as he had spoken. Finally, she managed to speak in a soft but stern voice, "Who are you?"

"Consider me a friend who is here to help you find the truth about your past in hopes that together we can ensure a better future for us both."

Riley frowned then shook her head. "I don't know you," she said, standing. "I don't know what you think you're pulling here, maybe you just have me totally confused with someone else. Or maybe you should have your head checked out."

"Haven't I told you the truth about your past, your family?" Thomas glanced around the bakery. "You know I have. It's all true. So, please, hear me out. Actually, since you're standing, how about a walk?"

"WHAT IS IT EXACTLY that you want from me?" Riley pressed.

She and Thomas Coleman walked down the sidewalk away from the bakery. They crossed a narrow street in the shade of the overhanging trees. Children played soccer—*futebol*—barefoot on the street. Riley glanced at the flip-flops being used to mark out the small makeshift goal, which sat about four feet apart. The ball rolled between them and a shout erupted from several of the children. Riley watched them, distracted by questions racing through her mind.

"Do you believe you are who you are?" Thomas said.

"What kind of question is that? Yes, of course!"

"Exactly. *Of course* you are who you are. It's a given; one of life's basic realities."

They strode a little farther down the sidewalk while cars buzzed by them. An older combustion engine truck rumbled past.

"You have nightmares, don't you?" Thomas probed.

"Who doesn't?" Riley spat, then regretted her tone.

"But these are different. You dream of places that appear so familiar, but places you have never seen. You dream of people you have never met, but in those dreams they feel so real to you; like you've known them all your life." Thomas let this sink in. "But worst of all, you wake up at night in all kinds of places. You sleepwalk, wandering about as if someone else is in control."

Riley clenched her jaw. This man knew far too much about her. She stopped walking. Thomas grinned at her. For a second, she wished to reach out and slap that smarmy grin off of his face. But she clenched her hands instead.

"Who are you?" Riley said, slowly.

"Do you really want to know?"

"What do you think, Mr. Coleman," she glared back at him. "You have my attention. So, whatever this is—whatever you're up to—it's time to come right out with it. Enough with this game. What are you really here for? What is it you want with me?"

Thomas stepped closer, his eyes gleaming with excitement. Opening his mouth, he took in a slow breath. Riley waited, keeping her eyes intent on Thomas. His lips moved.

"You're not Riley Bekker, a nun who teaches science. There is no Riley Bekker. She's not a real person. Oh sure, you firmly believe you are

Riley Bekker, but… I'm afraid it's a lie."

A nervous laugh burst from Riley's mouth then quickly died. *This guy can't possibly be serious!* She probed the man's eyes for any sign of falsity or jest, but found only an eager anticipation.

"You can't be serious," Riley said. "You expect me to believe you? I know who I am! What I don't know is who you are or what you want from me."

"Careful now, Sister. There's a big difference between knowledge and belief." Thomas countered. "You believe that you are who you think you are, and with good reason. But can you say you know who you are with certainty?"

Thomas stood there smiling as if he'd made some clever move in a game of chess. Riley again felt like she could swing a first at him in an effort to remove that grin from his lips.

"I know this is hard to accept," Thomas continued. "I need you to bear with me. I understand that this seems rather incredulous."

"To say the least." Riley interjected. "Why should I believe you?"

Thomas leaned even closer and whispered, "I know why you sleepwalk. I know the truth. I can make it go away. Isn't that what you want? Isn't that what you pray for—for it to go away?" Thomas moved back, eyes still locked on hers. "How does it go? 'And you will know the truth, and the truth will set you free.' I know the truth. I am here to set you free."

He gave her a warm smile. Riley's eyes wandered for the first time. This couldn't be. She knew that. This was so ludicrously impossible that she honestly wondered if, even now, she might be dreaming. Yet, who was this man? What did he mean when he said he was there to set her free? Free from what? *And how does he know so much about me?*

Riley looked at him again and spoke words that she herself was surprised to hear coming from her lips, "You're going to have to explain everything very carefully, Mr. Coleman. Very. Carefully."

PLATO'S CAVE

4

Everything you experience — every sight, sound, smell — rather than being a direct experience, is an electrochemical rendition in a dark theater.

[R]eality is a narrative played out inside the sealed auditorium of the cranium.

- David Eagleman

ALEXANDER JONES EDWARDS SLAMMED his fist on the large oval table. The boom echoed in the long meeting room. The floor-to-ceiling windows overlooked the Potomac River. A plane cut through the sky, coming in for a landing at Reagan. Its movement caught his eye and he stared at it for a moment, while he stood frozen at the end of the table, his hands planted firmly on its dark wooden surface. His short, stocky frame contracted and relaxed with each breath. The twenty members of the unofficial board stared at him, most with blank faces. Jones, as his colleagues called him, met their stares as he looked the room over. *I hate Washington*, he thought for what he was sure was the millionth time. The members, most of them politicians of one vile species or another, seemed exceptionally small and miserable to Jones at that very moment. He could almost smell their filth.

"Well, isn't this just fucking marvelous," he growled.

"We understand your frustration in light of these new developments," said Helen McKinley.

Jones met the Joint Chief of Staff's eyes with a stern glare. Her sandy blond hair and smooth face betrayed her age. She, like most of the people in that room, had been around for a while and knew how to play the popularity game that consumed so much of national politics. She regarded Jones with her typical detachment.

"Unfortunately," Jones said, "I don't need this administration's understanding. I need solutions. Solutions cost money. And I doubt I need to explain exactly what money is to this particular gathering."

"Financial support has been given to the project," Ms. McKinley said, "but at this time we feel it is best to hold back. There have been too many flaws to justify further significant investments. There's pushback from other departments, and we don't want more people sticking their noses into what we're doing here, do we?"

"The problems you speak of are natural parts of research and development. We're talking about something that has never been done before. Something of such complexity that it's impossible for the average person to imagine. How do you expect me to be able to work through these 'problems' if you cut my goddamn hands off?" Jones shook his head.

On the table before each person sat a small screen. Charts and graphs displayed the latest results of tests as well as projected results for the continuation of planned experiments. He knew these were not the numbers they had hoped to see and that the budget had been depleted quicker than originally anticipated. But he couldn't let up now. The politicians maintained their deadpan demeanor. Jones sighed, his eyes returning to Ms. McKinley.

"I'm sure you can find a way," she said, "you have brought the project this far, haven't you? We admire what you have been able to accomplish despite the loss of one of your project's founding members. Besides, we're not cutting your budget completely."

Jones shifted a few papers in front of him and then pushed the monitor before him away. "This project's results will face a congressional review in six months. Six months, and you want me to make this project a success with a minimal budget?"

"The success of this project is what we all want. We assure you of that."

"You have a funny way of assuring people."

"Dr. Edwards, we did not gather here to be berated. We ask you to understand that this administration currently faces significant criticism for its debt. American taxpayers aren't exactly happy with where their money has gone. Quite frankly, this project would not sit well with the current national attitude towards the President."

Jones let his head fall back. *And yet you all give yourselves raises.* He took in a deep breath, and then let it out slowly. *This project will long outlive the current dip shit in the White House,* he wanted to say, but didn't. "I see. This isn't about the project itself. It's about the national psyche or, more specifically, about the presidency." He looked the room over. For the first time, eyes began to shift away from his gaze. "You're not sure that six months is enough time, are you? You're just buying time. Maybe you can slow things down by giving the project less money, all in the hopes that we will ask for more time. Maybe enough time will go by and this becomes the next administration's problem. Gotto' hand it to you, it's pretty clever. It's also a pile of horse shit."

A long silence followed. Then, from the other end of the table came the voice of a much older man, "We have confidence that you will succeed, Jones. I have seen the power that Project Sleepwalker has to offer. But, before things can come together, there is a certain matter that must be cared for delicately. Everything at this moment hangs on the outcome of this one issue."

Jones looked down at the table. He nodded. "Yes, of course. Violet."

A CAR SPED BY. THOMAS walked along slowly next to Riley. Another car headed in the opposite direction. They ambled on the sidewalk, though now they were much closer to the school. Behind buildings, the sun now set. Several of the streetlights had come on. Most cars had their headlights on. In the western sky, the clouds hung low, diffusing the orange rays of the setting sun, which cast a golden glow over the city. Sunsets in Campo Grande were often a more magnificent experience when the wind would kick up the red dirt from the region and mix it throughout the air, creating a swirl of rosy dust against the already gorgeous backdrop. Through the thinner spots in the cloud cover, rays of white light burst through in magnificent shafts that dissipated throughout the evening sky.

Riley looked down as she walked, soaking in what this stranger had to say. It had to be a lie. In no way could it be true. Riley knew herself, she knew who she was. Thoughts swirled about in her mind as she tried to make sense of the claims Thomas had made. Some things just didn't add up. She had evidence she was Riley Bekker, didn't she? She had…

"What about my scar?" Riley asked.

"Ah yes, I figured you would ask that at some point." Thomas drew in a deep breath. "You're the philosophical type, aren't you?"

"I've read my fair share of Augustine and Aquinas." Riley understated. "Why?"

"Might it be possible that you got that scar in some other way?"

"Sure. But how could that be? I have distinct memories of hanging on that fence."

Thomas nodded, "Ah, memories. Exactly. You have all these *memories*. But, how do you know that these memories are true? Do you have a means to confirm they are accurate? Can you prove that a memory is empirically true?"

Riley stopped walking. Thomas did so as well, turning to face her. He was cleverly winding the whole conversation back to where it had started.

"I have this scar. It corresponds to the memory I have of my accident. I think I'm justified in believing that my memory is accurate."

"You're right. You are *justified*. But weren't people long ago justified in believing the earth was flat? Or, that the moon was a perfectly smooth sphere without a single flaw?"

"What are you getting at?" Riley barked. She didn't like how defensive this conversation was making her, but she grew to like Thomas less and less with each new question.

Thomas grinned. "You have memories; I have memories; everyone has memories. In fact, that's all we really have, isn't it? Memories. Think about it. Life is just a collection of these fascinating neural-phenomena. I heard that philosophers even argue that the present is an illusion. We have no direct access to the present. By the time information from any of your senses travels through your nervous system and fires the appropriate synapses in your brain, what you're experiencing is already in the past. The time it takes for a signal from your lips to travel to your brain is much shorter than a signal from your pinky toe and yet, the brain gathers all of this information first. Then, it presents to you what it judges to be the most pressing info. In a way, it's already a memory. In a world where time is measured in nano-seconds, all our experiences lag behind reality—actual, external reality. In which case, all of life, as we know it, is memory. Or, at best, it is a delayed perception of reality. So really, we're always playing catch up." Thomas clasped his hands together and said in a low voice, "We completely define ourselves by our memories, Riley. They are who we are. Or maybe more accurately, we are our memories. They completely shape who we perceive ourselves to be and what we think the world is like."

Riley stared past him, her mind attempting to digest what she was being told. She bit her lower lip, lost in thought; a large city bus rolled by. It slowed, making its stop. A woman and her child got off the bus and walked down the sidewalk. Riley watched them go. Thomas' words echoed in her mind, "We completely define ourselves by our memories."

"What are you driving at?" she finally said, "Should I believe that my memories are false?"

"You're on the right track now," Thomas said. "You should at least be open to questioning your memories."

"Why? Why would any sane person question their memories?"

Thomas just looked off, not answering.

"Fine," Riley said. "I guess in the pursuit of philosophical inquiry, sure. We should at least hold our memories up to the light and examine them."

Thomas looked back now, grinning. "The Light?! Is that the light the cave dwellers see casting shadows *on* the wall in Plato's Cave? A light used to cast shadows for the poor slaves, who are in chains and facing the cave wall, so that they only know of a world of shadows? In that case, the light was used to create a deception. Or, were you talking about the 'light of truth'?"

Riley smiled, shaking her head. "Okay, so you've read the *Republic*, or book seven at least. But, keep in mind, it was merely an allegory that Plato used to explain his take on the quest for full intellectual realization."

"An apt allegory, I would say," Thomas shrugged.

"Sure, if you accept Plato's dualism and dismissal of all things non-intellectual and..." Riley shook her head as she trailed off. "I think we can officially stop the philosophical book knowledge contest now. Mr. Coleman, what exactly does any of this have to do with my sleepwalking?"

"Slow down. We're going to get ahead of ourselves. That will come in time. But first, we have to deal with what is right before us."

"Right before us?" Riley sighed. "You mean my memories."

"Not just your memories," Thomas said. "More specifically, what your memories lead you to believe about yourself."

Riley waited for more from Thomas, who, instead, turned and started walking. Riley didn't move. Thomas looked back at her and paused before gesturing for her to come along. Reluctantly, she followed.

Catching up to him, Riley said, "I don't get it. If all I had were abstract memories, maybe I could buy this. But it's more than just having some vague history, it's my *own* history." She rubbed her eyes with both hands. "What I mean to say is that, uh, I have more than just memories, I have the distinct feelings of experiencing those memories first hand. I have the cognitive awareness that I once experienced hanging on a fence by my arm. I was there. It *happened*. Specifically, it happened *to me*."

"Ah yes," Thomas nodded. "We worked very hard to achieve that. It was a particular programming challenge we faced with early tests. You're right. It's not good enough to just *remember*. You have to have the feeling that you experienced the original incident from which the memory was created. Our subjective experiences are incredibly formative experiences. Once we grasped that concept, we basically had to go back to the drawing board and reconfigure the whole idea of how to even begin that process."

Riley's jaw dropped open. "What are you talking about?"

"I'm sorry," Thomas smiled politely. "I'm getting ahead of myself at the moment. But I must admit that I find it fascinating—and encouraging—that you recognized this problem so quickly."

"So, what?" Riley raised her palms and shrugged, "What are you getting at? This is all some sort of crazy experiment?"

"Well," Thomas hesitated. "It's something along those lines."

Riley shook her head and laughed. "I don't believe you. You're wasting my time."

"Skepticism, from a woman of faith; not something I would have expected."

"Faith and blind faith are two very different things. What you're asking me to accept is beyond madness."

"Oh, I'm well aware of how this must all appear to you. Hell, if I were in your shoes, I wouldn't believe any of this either. But sometimes, the truth sounds a little ridiculous at first glance. I believe you, as a devout follower of a man who claimed to be God—even referred to himself as 'the light of the world'—was killed and then, supposedly rose from the grave, can appreciate this point. I mean, doesn't every religion sound at least a bit absurd when stated in plain English? So, what I am asking you to do is to place a little faith in me right now."

Riley laughed and sighed. "I am person of faith, yes. But not faith without reason," Riley explained. "To open myself up to just any notion that might come my way would be intellectually and spiritually irresponsible. What I have come to believe, I believe for many reasons."

"And what if those reasons were wrong?" Thomas cocked his head to the side and watched Riley as they walked. "What if you're working from a set of incorrect basic assumptions?"

"What? Like, maybe there is no God?"

"Well, no. Not specifically that."

"You mean, what if I'm not who I think I am?" Riley asked,

knowing where Thomas seemed headed. "Okay, I thought this was usually relegated to philosophy courses, but what the heck, right? Are you suggesting that I might be a brain in a vat somewhere, being electronically stimulated to have certain cerebral experiences with no basis in the real world?"

"Yes and no." Thomas looked straight ahead. "But that's a great place to start."

"I've seen this movie before," Riley shook her head. "I know how it ends. And I'm not going down that rabbit hole. I'm afraid this just stems from a horrible misunderstanding of what Descartes was attempting to say."

"Yes, Descartes," Thomas looked back to Riley. "It might be helpful if you would assume a bit more of his approach. Begin by seriously questioning your reality."

Riley rolled her eyes and sighed. "Absolutely, I'll get right on that. But first I need to score some weed and go home and watch *The Wizard of Oz* while listening to Pink Floyd's *The Dark Side of the Moon*."

Thomas laughed.

"Mr. Coleman, honestly now, what is it that you want me to do?" Riley said firmly, not remotely trying to mask the exasperation in her voice.

"All I want you to do is to see if you can remember. It's just that simple. Can you remember the past; the *real* past? Are you able to search your mind and see the truth for yourself? It won't be easy. But I believe it will be worth your while."

"Where would I even start such a noble quest, Tatooine?" Riley said, dryly.

Thomas smiled, "Ah yes, where to start. Start with something called *Project Sleepwalker*. Remember that, and the rest will come to you."

"What is *Project Sleepwalker*?"

Thomas stopped again and faced Riley. "It will come to you in time. Right now, you should relax." He reached out and clasped Riley's shoulder.

A sharp pain shot into her shoulder and down her arm. She gripped

Thomas' arm while her head spun and her knees gave out. Her vision narrowed into a blurry tunnel. "What are you doing?" she cried out.

"I'm just helping you remember. Now relax. This is all part of the process. I'm not going to hurt you. Just let it go. It will all make sense soon."

She felt her vision blur; the world around her faded away. As the darkness rushed at her she locked onto Thomas' smile—that knowing grin that brought to mind the mischievous Cheshire Cat. Panic shot through her like 10,000 volts. Her last thought was that she'd fallen down a very deep hole. Would she ever find her way out again?

5 ZANTHRIX

Perhaps surprisingly, memories appear to be rewritten frequently. Unlike a computer's memory, biological memory is reinforced by recall. It is as if the ink on a printed page got darker when the page was read.
- Sandra Aamodt & Sam Wang

THE FLOOR AND WALLS throbbed with the pulsing of the music's low frequency notes. Colorful lights flashed and swung about, cutting through the murky air and splashing upon every surface. On the dance floor, a crowd of people writhed in chaotic order, moving their bodies without, yet their minds entranced within the musical pulse. The whole place seemed alive; moving in sync like the crowd was one, complete organism. On the second level balcony, which overlooked the dance floor, people sat at tables with glowing LED center pieces. Alcohol of all types flowed freely throughout the room. From a dark corner, Arisu Ana observed the people. Her narrow eyes and dark, straight hair allowed her to blend in well with this particular Brazilian club.

Apparently, this part of Brazil was host to a significant population of Japanese immigrants. For decades, a Japanese subculture grew quietly, as it was mostly overlooked by the broader Brazilian population. This particular club founded its roots within that established subculture and, as a result, the frequenters of the club were mostly Japanese-Brazilians. Arisu chose the club for this very reason. Even though she felt extremely out of place, she knew that she could blend in well enough. She was not Brazilian and, in spite of her name and genetics, she was not particularly Japanese either. She wore a slender, black dress in hopes it passed for clubbing attire. Alone, at a corner table, she sipped a cocktail. She didn't

46

need any unwanted attention, especially since she didn't speak any Portuguese.

A waiter in tight, black pants and no shirt walked by, his tray filled with several drinks. She'd lost count of how many times he had walked by her table. She watched him go; only momentarily distracted by his abs and wondering when her contact would arrive. The lights on the dance floor changed colors then began to strobe. Her eyes took in the mayhem. *How long had such places as these existed?* The escapist and indulgent nature of humanity ensured they would almost certainly exist as a long as people populated the planet, or at least, as long as young people had some form of disposable income. Such places also offered a convenient cover for other activities. She was certain that much more took place within the club that night than she cared to know. Drugs, sex, murder; who knew for sure? But that wasn't why she was here tonight. She maintained her cold, controlled exterior, but inside, she looked forward to leaving the thumping club.

A new thought surfaced, nagging at her. Could it be that in her attempt to be quiet and call no attention to herself, she only drew more? She looked out across the balcony from where her table sat. Most people gathered at their own tables and talked; or rather, they screamed at each other over the deafening music. A few tables down from hers, however, a young man sat alone, sipping a drink. He looked at her and winked. Her impulse was to look away. She didn't, though. Was he flirting with her? *Sorry, but you're wasting your time on so many levels,* she thought. She maintained as blank of a look as she could, and continued her scan of the area. She saw from the corner of her eye that the young man looked down at his drink again, his shoulders dropping. *Nice try,* she thought. *But you're going to need to pick a better candidate.*

From out of the shadows emerged a young Brazilian woman in a horrible yellow plastic-looking dress, it's gloss sent light reflecting in every direction as she moved. A short oriental man followed her. They came to Arisu's table, taking seats without a word. The man grinned at Arisu, showing the gap where one of his front teeth should have been. The woman, her face caked with far more make up than a Cirque du

Soleil performer, leveled her eyes on Arisu and waited.

"Glad to see you two could make it." Arisu said over the music and in English.

The man nodded; then he turned to the woman, repeating in Portuguese what she had said. The woman then said something to him and he turned to Arisu. "Eliane says you pick interesting people to spy on."

"What exactly happened last night?" Arisu pressed.

Again, he translated. "Your friend, the nun, she is rather peculiar, she says." His accent bore a mix of Portuguese and Japanese. "She walked for quite a distance in the middle of the night. She seemed to be in a trance. Eliane says that your friend talked about it being a—how do you say—a regular occurrence. She is a sleepwalker, no?"

"She talked to her?" Arisu leaned in.

"She says that after she had gotten what you requested, the nun woke up. Eliane couldn't get away. They talked."

Arisu glared at Eliane, "And what exactly happened after that?" She waited for the translation.

"Your friend went home and Eliane went away. She got what you asked for."

He set on the table a small glass vile with a slight grey speck inside. Arisu reached for it. He slid it back, eyebrows raised. She gave him an annoyed glare. With a sigh, she pulled up her purse and set it on the table. From it, she produced two metal vials and set them on the table.

"As we agreed," Arisu said, "twenty-four milliliters of Zanthrix."

The man smiled broadly. "These little guys are spectacular! Are they in working order?"

"Preserved in saline in a state of hibernation," Arisu nodded. "All you have to do is drop a milligram of sugar into the solution and the nanobots will wake up."

She held his gaze, hoping he couldn't read any hesitation in her. It was true that there were nanobots in the vials, but they weren't the psychedelic mind-altering Zanthrix bots this man was after. They were a now defunct breed of simple intestinal cleaning bots. They would wake up with the electrolytes introduced to their saline, but they wouldn't do much else. They weren't even particularly good at doing the job for which they had been designed and their project had been on hold for two years. Within the nanotech industry that meant it was already long-forgotten, ancient history.

But, under a microscope, they looked remarkably like Zanthrix. So Arisu gestured for the man to proceed when he pulled out a small electronic pocket microscope and nodded at the vials on the table. He opened one vial and using a thin glass wand that he removed from the side of the pocket microscope; he dipped the tip of the wand into the saline and then placed a drop of the solution on a tiny, glass plate. He made no effort to hide any of his actions, clearly unconcerned about on-lookers. Bringing the microscope down, he looked at it for a long minute, his fingers sliding up and down the touch screen on the side of the device, as he adjusted his magnification and focus. Finally, he looked up and nodded with a smirk, satisfied.

Arisu returned the nod, but inside she felt a wave of relief. She'd chosen correctly. She'd found someone with enough knowledge to get themselves into trouble, but not enough to tell the subtle differences between these defunct gut bots and a batch of Zanthrix. The relief was followed by the immediate panic that he'd find this out sooner rather than later. But she knew this man was in it for the payday, not the trip. *But what if he wants to sample it?* She tried to keep in mind that a single milliliter of Zanthrix could go for as much as $2,000. Her research had indicated this man was a dealer, not a user.

With a smile, the man slid his glass vial forward. Arisu took it. She pulled out a small, black box from her purse. When she pressed the button on the side of the box, the device lit up and a cylinder slid out from the top. She inserted the vial and pressed the button again. The cylinder descended and the vial disappeared into the device. A display lit up on the side of the box. It read, VM001-DB211-RB321. She nodded with satisfaction.

"Did she react when you cut it out of her hand?" Arisu asked the woman.

Eliane shook her head after she heard the translation. She said something and the man turned to Arisu.

"She wants to know if you would like her to continue observing the nun. She finds her... interesting; she'll do it for a reduced price." He grinned, seeming to enjoy the prospect of continued work.

"No. There's no need for that. She's already done too much. I have what I wanted. Your services are no longer needed." Arisu put away the device into which she had placed the vial. "The two of you should forget me, forget this job, and forget about Riley Bekker. She doesn't exist. Never has. That was the deal. Stick to it and there won't be any trouble."

She stood. Eliane and her translator stood as well. Arisu stared at him, then the woman. "What do you think you're doing?" she asked.

"It seems to us," he glanced to his partner, "that this is something of importance. We would hate for anything to interfere with your visit to this country."

A chill ran through her body. Arisu locked eyes with the man, working to maintain an expression that was cold and calculated. "Are you threatening me?"

"No, no. No threat."

"You want money," she stated, shaking her head. "Well, guess what? There is no money. That was the deal. You did your part, I did mine. It's not good for business to keep changing the rules."

"All we're saying is that this seems important. And you wouldn't want outside interference."

She reached across the table and took a fist full of his shirt, pulling him closer so he leaned over the table. Eliane's jaw dropped, and she froze. "Now you listen carefully, you little shit; I kept my part of the deal. You can walk away now, or I can just kill both of you right here, and walk away with the Zanthrix *and* the chip." She stared into his eyes, then smiled. "In fact, now that I think about it, that sounds like a better deal."

"You kill us, and how will you get out of here?" he protested, but his eyes were wide and his breathing shallow.

She looked into his dilated eyes, seeing his fear and adrenaline kicking in, and smiled. She leaned closer so she could speak right into his ear. "You said it yourself. This seems rather important. Let's just say I have my own ways of dealing with such things. I'd rather not deal with the mess, but it can be done. I have powerful friends. The choice is really yours."

Arisu drew back and looked into his eyes, which were now even wider. At last, he spoke, "Okay. We walk away now. We're done. We keep the deal, right?"

She held him a second longer for effect, then shoved him back. "We'll keep the deal as long as you stay away from her. I'll be watching, and if either of you show up anywhere near her, I will kill you both, no questions asked."

He nodded.

Arisu looked down at her unfinished drink on the table. "Thanks for picking up the tab." She turned and walked away, leaving them behind. With her back to them, she sighed with relief, feeling the knot of tension loosen slightly within her stomach. The bluff had worked. Barely, but it had. She could see it in their eyes. These were small time crooks, happy to score such a good haul of Zanthrix for just a few nights of stalking. They'd played their hand well, tried to get more out of the deal. Arisu knew they might try. But there really was no more she could give them. As long as they believed Arisu (or whatever secretive and sinister organization that was behind her actions) would kill them they wouldn't present any further issue. Or so she had hoped.

Arisu proceeded down the steps to the main floor and disappeared into the lights, smoke, and crowd.

PAIN. RILEY BECAME AWARE of the pain. Her eyes fluttered and bright light struck them like daggers. She squinted. Her head hurt. Her vision blurred. Her hands reached out before her, waiving aimlessly in an attempt to shield her eyes. Her left shoulder shook with pain and she let that arm drop. She gradually became aware that she was resting on her right side. She ran her hand across whatever she lay on. Was it the sofa in her house? She tried opening her eyes again but her head screamed out in painful protest. *What is wrong with me?*

Finally able to more-or-less focus on what sat right before her, she could see the familiar light brown color of her sofa. She wondered what time it was and looked over to the clock on the wall. Her eyes were still too fuzzy to be able to make out the numbers. She brought up her left hand to rub her eyes, but this caused more pain to shoot through her shoulder. She groaned then tried to sit up. Dizziness almost kept her from being able to do so, but she fought through it. Managing to sit back on the sofa and steady herself, she rubbed his eyes again.

At last she could begin to focus her vision. She looked at the clock again. This time she could see the numbers: 4:42. Judging from the dim hint of sunlight seeping in from the east-facing windows, it must have been early morning. The other sisters in the house were still asleep. What had happened? Riley searched her mind for the last thing she could recall.

Thomas.

She had been talking to Thomas. They had been talking and walking... walking down a sidewalk... talking about... Project Sleepwalker. A feeling of familiarity washed over her. For a brief second, she became absolutely certain she knew what Project Sleepwalker was about. But, just as quickly, the feeling dissipated.

Had that been a dream? Had she been sleepwalking again? She looked down, inspecting her clothing. Why was she still wearing the clothes from the previous day? When did she end up on the sofa? The other sisters would have seen her if she had come home early and fallen asleep in the living room. Certainly one of them would have found this peculiar and out of the norm for Riley. Why couldn't she remember anything past Thomas talking to her and... the pain in her shoulder? Had Thomas dropped her off here?

A wave of nauseous fear washed over Riley as her mind raced in several directions with horrible speculations of what Thomas might have done. But she took a deep breath and steadied herself. She sat still and took stock of how she felt. Aside from her left shoulder and head, nothing hurt. Her mouth was dry and her teeth needed brushing, but that wasn't unfamiliar. Looking down at her feet she noticed that even her shoes remained on. As far as she could tell, she had simply been deposited on the sofa. All the same, rage rushed through her as she felt the betrayal and violation of having been-*against her will*-rendered helpless for hours! She wanted to find Thomas and hurt him. *Who does he think he is? What did he do to me?*

She touched her left shoulder, feeling a bump on the skin. She pressed it and cringed at the sudden pain. The memory of Thomas touching her shoulder and the pain that followed rushed to the surface of her mind. *He injected me with something*, Riley realized. Whatever Thomas had used, it had knocked her out for almost ten hours. But, how had she ended up in the house? Did Thomas bring her here? She wanted to get up and go call the police, call someone, and report this maniac. She took a deep breath and steadied her nerves. She didn't know yet what she would be reporting. She put her right hand down on the sofa as she prepared to stand. It landed on something hard that had apparently been sitting there next to her this whole time. Looking down, she saw that it was a small tablet computer. She picked it up, squinting at it. The screen displayed a note.

Congratulations Riley,

You're headed in the right direction. Forgive me for having to inject you. I hope the pain will not bother you too much. I'm afraid I had to do this. It will help you begin to remember. Ice the shoulder, it'll feel better. Then, meet me tonight at 7:00 in front of your house. I've arranged for your extraction.

Please believe me when I tell you that you are safe and unharmed. And please forgive my methods, as time is of the essence. Click here to play a video.

Your friend,
Thomas

Riley could hardly believe it. She read the note again to make sure she understood it. Inside, she boiled with anger. All well-intentioned assurances aside, if they were even sincere, what gave this man the right do any of this to her? How could he dare to interfere with Riley's life this way? And what was this talk about extraction?

She tapped the last line of the note that indicated she should watch a video on the tablet. The screen lit up with a view of the backseat of a car. Apparently, it was a time-lapse video, as the door suddenly swung open and, in fast motion, Thomas deposited Riley's unconscious body in the back seat. There, she lay still as the car drove about. In the lower right corner was a timestamp that sped through the hours of the night. Finally, near midnight, the car stopped and Riley was taken from it. The camera moved out of the car and focused on Thomas' face as he stood in front of her house. The video slowed to normal speed.

"I've dropped you off in your living room at midnight," Thomas said. What I've given you will begin the process of helping you remember the truth. You are safe and unharmed. I know this is all very alarming, but this is the only way you can know the truth of who you really are. Call in sick to work and lay low, let the process take its course. I'll see you tonight at seven."

The video ended.

It appeared that Thomas was trying to demonstrate some level of benevolence. The video didn't show what happened after he'd taken her into her house. And yet, she shared the house with other women, some of whom were light sleepers. Thomas would have needed to be quite stealthy in order not to wake her roommates. It did strike Riley as unlikely he would have stayed and risked being found there. It didn't make her dislike the man any less, but Riley had to admit that he seemed to be going out of his way to assure her that he meant her no harm, even if his methods were profoundly disturbing.

She stood, fighting the last bits of dizziness. She still squinted. Her eyes seemed to be taking a while to adjust to the slowly increasing light of sunrise. *I guess ten hours of deep sleep will do that to you*, she thought. *Or maybe it's whatever Thomas injected me with.*

She headed for her room, where she removed the day-old clothing and changed into athletic shorts and a sleeveless shirt. Then, heading for the kitchen, she fetched herself a bag and filled it with ice. She breathed a sigh of relief as she placed the bag on her shoulder. Next, she found some pain killers in one of the drawers. Popping two tablets in her mouth, she downed them with a full glass of water. It wasn't until the water touched her lips that she realized just how thirsty she was. She had gone nearly half a day without water, and her last drink before that had been coffee. She poured another glass, taking it down almost as quickly as the first.

She stood in the kitchen, clutching the bag of ice on her shoulder. What next? What should she do now? It seemed to her that she had few options. This was not something she could possibly ignore. Thomas would be back. Could she bring the local law enforcement into this? Would they even believe her if she told them what Thomas had told her? She could show them the video on the tablet, but the video only indicated that Thomas had not specifically harmed her in any way.

There was the note, however. She could take the note and the video to the police. The two items together painted a particularly negative, if not outright sinister, picture. But was it enough to get local authorities to take any action? There was still a strong current of machismo in Brazil, and without making an outright rape allegation it was unlikely local police would get too fussed. She'd seen and heard of blind eyes turned to worse cases. Of course, if she presented them with some financial incentive, she might get somewhere. But she had no bribery funds being a nun and all.

Riley stared at the floor for a long moment, a nagging feeling growing inside her. What if there was some truth after all to what Thomas had told her? Why would he go to all this trouble for some kind of hoax? Why her?

Slowly, Riley came to terms with the realization that she had to find out what was happening. A feeling of resolute determination gradually replaced her anxiety. That strange and haunting feeling of familiarity rose and fell inside of her like waves lapping up on a beach, her conscience mind being the wet sand to which those elusive waves reached out. One way or another, she had to know the truth. Keeping the ice on her shoulder, she walked back to her room where she found her smartphone. She placed a call without thinking of the early hour. The phone rang several times and then a groggy voice answered.

"*Padre Antonio*," she said. "It's Sister Riley. I'm sorry for calling so early."

"Yes, Riley," the deep voice of her heavyset boss resonated through the speaker. "What's the matter?"

"I need a personal day. I'm not feeling well."

"Is everything alright?" Antonio asked.

"Yeah, huh," Riley hesitated, but then decided that of all people, Antonio could be trusted. "No, everything's not quite alright, actually. I have something rather complicated going on right now. I could use some time. I need to work a few things out. There's someone here from the States. He came to see me and says he knew my parents. It's… complicated, but there's some things I need to take care of. I might need the rest of the week off." She couldn't tell Father Antonio any more at this point for fear of endangering him, or for fear of sounding insane.

"Oh. Okay. I'll take care of things. Do you have lesson plans for the week?" Antonio asked, concern growing in his increasingly alert voice.

"Yeah, they're on the school network."

"Okay. I'll take care of it. Is there anything else I can do for you? This seems, well, out of the ordinary for you."

Riley knew the question was genuine and heartfelt. She paused, then replied softly, "I'm sorry to be so cryptic, but that's all I can really say right now. In the meantime, pray for me, Father."

6   LIBRARY

You become who you are not because of what grows in your brain, but because of what is removed.

- David Eagleman

RILEY WALKED DOWN THE long row of books. The shelves were packed into the building rather tightly, giving the library a claustrophobic feel. After speaking with *Padre* Antonio, she had showered and then thrown on a faded pair of jeans and a grey t-shirt. She'd quickly drawn her dark hair into a ponytail. Considering she hardly wore any makeup on a normal day, it was an easy decision to completely skip makeup today, of all days. Otherwise, she had checked the wound on her hand and then headed out.

She was following Coleman's instructions only in part. She'd called off of work, as he'd suggested. But she was not about to lay low and play sick. Whoever Coleman thought she was, he clearly didn't know her well enough to realize that she wasn't about to sit idly at home for the day and accept his ludicrous story. She wanted answers.

Reaching the end of the aisle, she looked around. She needed a private place, somewhere she could mull over any information she might be able to dig up. Yet, how should she go about finding what she wanted? Where should she even start? She spotted the computer stations in a separate room. Large panels of glass separated the computer room from the study area at the end of the shelves, where she stood. Beyond that, the almost clear, flat screens glowed with a life of their own. Riley made her way through the History Lounge to the nearest station just inside the computer room.

Only a few stations down, a couple flirted excitedly as they browsed the internet. Riley looked down at the workstation, then again at the couple. They laughed, seemingly unaware of her presence. She looked around for a more private area. Proceeding down the row of computer workstations, she wondered if she should have used the shared computer at the house after all or even her smartphone. None of the sisters bothered with a personal computer, but there was a shared laptop at the house any of them could use. Since the other sisters would be at the school all day, she could have used that. And yet, she wanted to play it safe and not draw any unwanted attention to her friends. On top of this, the house now felt so confining, suddenly so foreign. She felt on edge there. Maybe it all amounted to paranoia. Either way, she left the house and her cellphone behind.

In the same spirit of paranoia, she sure as hell didn't dare trust the tablet Coleman had left with her. Someone may or may not be tracking her every move on the house laptop or her cellphone, but she felt sure that Coleman's tablet was anything but safe to use. She also wondered if Coleman or someone else might be watching her. It was a risk leaving the house, but she had to do something.

I'm a teacher, not a spy, she thought with frustration. *Maybe I'm just losing my mind.* She'd made a point of taking her normal route to work, riding together with the other sisters to the school. She hadn't told them she was taking the week off. But once they arrived, she had headed for the nearest bus stop and made her way to the old municipal library of Campo Grande.

She tried to play it cool the whole time she rode the bus, but could hardly stop herself from eyeing passengers with suspicion. She made the switch to another bus that got her here. But she felt sure she was being followed. At some point, the question of being followed sparked an unwelcome thought: had the hooker who walked her home the other night been following her? She felt lightheaded as her heart raced. Finally, she had closed her eyes and stopped the rushing questions and focused her mind on a simple quest for any divine help available.

Now that she was at the library, she sat down before a computer in the far corner of the room. The screen looked like nothing more than a thin pane of glass until she touched it. It glowed with life and the operating system emerged from its sleep mode. A large window next to her looked out at a busy street two floors down. Riley glanced out, and then looked at the computer. The login screen appeared.

"Riley Bekker," she stated.

In a flash, it logged in, displaying advertisements and library announcements on the screen.

"Keyboard, please," she commanded in Portuguese, "Deactivate voice operation."

A slender keyboard slid out of the thin CPU box under the screen. Clearing the screen of the ads, she punched open a myriad of web browser windows. She searched on several databases for information on this "Project Sleepwalker" of which Thomas had spoken.

Several results were presented to Riley. She began the arduous process of sifting through the information. An hour slipped by, barely registering in Riley's consumed mind. She entered a focused state, looking almost angrily through news articles, reports, blogs, and anything else she could find. None of what she turned up seemed to lead her in what she felt might be the right direction. But how could she know for sure? None of the information gave specific descriptions about what such a project might be like. Some of the search results she found seemed unrelated to anything Thomas had talked about. So she kept at it. Pausing, she slowly rolled her head from one side to another, feeling the tense muscles of her shoulders and neck stretch, then proceeded.

An hour and ten minutes into her searching, Riley's eyes locked on to a title, "Prison for the Mind: Fighting Terrorism by Erasing the Terrorist." The article was from a British science journal. She opened it and began to read. Her jaw dropped. The article dealt with research into the theoretical notion of retraining the mind to perceive itself as having different traits, possibly even a different personality altogether. By the use of new developments in neuroscience and nanotechnology, new neural-connections could theoretically be established. The author outlined the hypothetical process of generating artificial memories and feelings about past events. At the turn of the century, the old notion that cells in the nervous system could never be replaced had been overthrown by new research in neuroscience. This gave rise to a whole new way of seeing the nervous system. Now, there were scientists proposing a combination of neuroscience and nanotechnology—the ever evolving branch of science geared at generating mechanical devices the size of several thousand, or even several hundred atoms. Riley had heard talk before of using nanites, as the small robots were sometimes referred, in connection with developments in neuroscience. She knew of at least one experimental nanite treatment for Alzheimer's where the tiny robots worked to repair broken neural-connections and heal the legions that formed on the brains of people suffering from the disease. However, she hadn't heard of anything quite this drastic. Repairing the brain was one thing, reprogramming it was quite another.

The goal of the program described in the article would be to generate a completely new sense of self-awareness for a test subject; in effect, an entirely new personality. Of course, it would have to be superimposed over the already existing memories and self-awareness. The brain was not a hard drive, after all, which could simply be formatted and a new operating system freshly installed. But the article suggested that a few private companies where engaged in the research and development that could lead to the tools required for reprogramming the brains of violent criminals and radical extremists.

The article made it all sound remarkably plausible, but she wondered if such lofty goals were attainable. Riley knew enough to be aware that memory was malleable, based on recurrent use of the networks of synapses associated with particular memories. The inability to recall information, such as forgetting a childhood friend's name, could be traced not to the loss of the information itself, but to the brain's lack of connection to those particular synapses. Controlling such connections could at least mean that a person could improve their memory or block out completely unwanted memories. The article cited the practice already in use for survivors of severe trauma where truly debilitating memories were quarantined in the brain by the severing of the connections to that memory. *But, how could nanites create new memories?* Riley shook her head in wonder. Then, a new thought struck her.

She moved to the end of the article, looking over the cited works the author had used. She scanned over the titles and author names, wondering which she should look at first. Her eyes locked on to a particular name, reading it several times. That feeling of familiarity sprang up within her again. The name seemed to echo in her mind, teasing her as if she ought to recall the face the name belonged to. She looked at it for a minute, wracking her brain for what the connection might be. Finally, she gave up and opened the link and began to read the article titled, "Reimagining Locke's Blank Slate: A New Look at Personality Theory and Brain Function" by V. Murphy.

<hr />

ARISU ANA WALKED SLOWLY through the library aisles. She glanced over her shoulder; then continued. She wore blue jeans and a black v-neck, long sleeve shirt, casual; basic; relatively easy to blend in with. At the end of the aisle, she locked her eyes on the computer room. Several computers sat in rows on partitioned desks. A couple walked out of the computer area, hand-in-hand, making their way to the front entrance of the library. Turning back to the computers, Arisu spotted Riley. She sat alone at a distant workstation near the back corner. A slight smile involuntarily found its way to Arisu's lips for a fleeting instant.

Putting on as casual of a demeanor as possible, she glided to the computer area entrance. Riley, apparently too engrossed in whatever she looked at on the screen before her, seemed not to notice Arisu's entrance. Picking a workstation on the opposite corner of the large room, Arisu sat quietly. From her pocket, she produced a thin smartphone barely larger than her hand that appeared to be hardly more than a polished rectangle of glass with rounded edges. More than just an average smartphone, the tiny (but powerful) micro-tablet computer bore no branding. Using her finger, she pressed several commands in quick succession. The desktop computer before her displayed the login screen. She glanced up at Riley, then around the room. The place was still, Riley was focused. Arisu returned her attention to the computer before her. The micro-tablet made a series of quick blipping sounds. Riley looked up from her computer. Arisu caught her eyes, playing it off as if she was embarrassed to have made any noise at all. She relaxed the moment Riley went back to her work. Yet, her heart thundered inside her chest. This felt so unnatural. By the time her eyes looked down at the computer screen before her, it had logged in to the library network. Using the micro-tablet, she worked her way through a series of library security codes. Finally, she pulled open a window on the larger screen. There it was. She now saw everything that Riley had up on her screen. Arisu's heart skipped a beat as she saw what Riley had pulled up on her workstation.

What had happened? How much did she know? Arisu scanned the article Riley currently had up. *She's on to something,* she thought. *But how has Riley caught on?* Arisu could feel her whole body becoming heavier with the realization that she had taken too long in getting here, in finding and reaching Riley. *Thomas,* she fumed within. *That sonofabitch, Thomas beat me to it!* He had done his work, and apparently done it very well—so far. The time had come to take action, whether Arisu felt ready or not. She only hoped she hadn't delayed too long.

Quickly, she looked through the other browser windows Riley had opened as well as her browsing history. Judging from the searches she was doing, Thomas must have divulged enough information to Riley to spark some serious curiosity. She was searching for Project Sleepwalker or anything that might get her close to it, though she was searching for information mostly in the wrong places. But what did a nun know about classified nanotech R&D, even if the world of such classified work spanned the domains of various private tech companies from the San Francisco bay area to Cambridge, Massachusetts? And that was just in the US. The Japanese and Chinese had their own programs, or so it was rumored.

Arisu entered a series of commands on her smartphone then slowly looked at Riley, waiting. Riley stared intently at the computer before her, reading a new article. The screen before her abruptly became solid blue. In the lower right hand corner the words, "Quietly exit the library using the front entrance and walk north down the street," appeared. Riley's expression changed abruptly from intense focus to bewilderment. She looked up, frantically turning her head to take in the world around her, which she seemed to have forgotten about. Arisu and Riley locked eyes again. Arisu maintained a stoic composure though her heart raced. Riley's mouth opened but Arisu hit a new command on her smartphone without needing to look down. Riley's computer beeped and she jolted in surprise. Arisu sent her another message, "Go now. Don't say a word! Don't look at me! Just leave calmly."

Arisu watched her frown, still confused and bewildered as she read the message and glanced back at Arisu. *Come on, Riley. Just go! Don't call any more attention to the two of us. Just get up and leave!* It was painfully slow waiting, but Arisu kept her eyes on her.

Finally, Riley took a deep breath, turning back to her computer. She logged off, though Arisu could have easily done that remotely for her. Riley stood and walked out of the computer room. She followed Arisu's instructions rather well. She never looked at Arisu as she made her way out of the computer room at a slow but deliberate pace. Arisu watched her until she was out of sight, then quickly logged off of her own workstation. Slipping her phone into her purse, she made a controlled rush to the door. She could not lose Riley!

EVASIVE MANEUVERS

7

In terms of the brain, consciousness is a way for billions of cells to see themselves as a unified whole, a way for a complex system to hold up a mirror to itself.

- David Eagleman

RILEY WALKED BRISKLY OUT of the automatic doors at the library entrance. She headed north down the cobblestone sidewalk. The bright sunlight made her squint. *What is going on here,* her mind screamed. *What's happening? Who was that?* She slowed her pace and tried to breathe normally as she walked. Cars sped by on the busy downtown street, but she paid no attention to them. People walked past her, distracted by their own affairs or because they were wearing smartglasses or looking at their phones. She slipped through them, her eyes never making contact with theirs, her body turning here and there to slip past them unnoticed. *Who was the Asian woman in the library? First, it was Thomas, but now it's this woman? Are they working together?*

She hadn't gotten a good look at the woman and, given her complete confusion and surprise, her mind was having a hard time focusing on recalling details. She tried to glance behind her to see if the woman was following her, but she felt no confidence she could have recognized her among so many people moving about. What had the woman been wearing? How was her hair done? All Riley could recall, suddenly, were her dark but alert eyes. Even though she'd only left the library moments ago, her recollection of what had transpired there felt more like a dream she'd just awoken from than anything else.

It didn't help that her head throbbed in a horrible cocktail of fear and anger. Riley felt increasingly detached from the world around her, her perception of it felt more and more like some sort of a first person video game, as she weaved through people on the sidewalk. With this new thought, random images of video games flashed into her mind. She staggered to a wall, putting out a hand to hold herself up. When had she played video games in the last ten years of her life? She'd been too busy for such things. She took in several deep breaths and looked around. *Great, I bet I look drunk*, she thought. She felt somewhat drunk, though this was much more like the combination of being tipsy while having a hangover and recovering from a serious blow to the head. She suddenly found herself wondering if she had ever been drunk. No, her parents had been pretty strict on the use of alcohol or other substances. She'd never had more than— Out of nowhere, the phrase, "more than enough to get shit-faced" came to mind. She shook her head and straightened herself, starting down the sidewalk at a more controlled pace.

That last series of thoughts didn't make any sense. Her parents had actually been quite okay with alcohol. Her father drank more than her mother, but neither had been alcoholics. Riley had the distinct memory of her father smiling at her and handing her a beer on her eighteenth birthday. "Now you don't need to run off and get crazy with this stuff," he had said. "I know how it works and how the world works. So I hardly expect you to steer clear of this stuff until you're twenty-one, but I do want you to be smart about it." He had this smirk, his classic charm he could turn on. He might have had a hard time putting into words his deepest feelings, but he had always made gestures like these. She still recalled the slight bite and hoppy aftertaste of that first IPA. It would be a long time before she grew to enjoy any beer.

As she recalled all of this, Riley felt a wave of dizziness. *What is happening to me? Is it the stuff that Thomas guy injected into my shoulder?* She took a deep breath and blew it out slowly, trying to control the swirling in her head and stomach.

She looked over her shoulder. She saw several people, but none of them looked like the woman from the library. Once again, Riley tried to recall what she had looked like. When they had locked eyes, she'd had this odd feeling that she could not quite describe. Had it been familiarity? Maybe, though she felt sure that there had been something else, something different. But it was hard to sort things out in the rush of anxiety and fear of discovering that she had been followed. Again, all she could recall were the woman's eyes that seemed to see right into her. Those eyes…

As she passed a narrow alley between buildings, a hand reached out and grasped her shoulder. Swimming through a mental sea of detachment from reality, Riley felt herself being pulled into the alley. All at once, those mysterious eyes were locked on to hers. Instinctively, she brought up her arms, batting the woman's hands away. The woman backed up a step, breathing heavily. She must have run from the library to catch Riley here.

For a long minute they stared at each other, neither saying a word. Riley just looked into the woman's eyes, hardly able to take in any other features of her face as her mind swirled. Riley blinked and forced herself to focus. The woman did seem familiar—the slight scent of her perfume; her black straight hair; her narrow eyes. She was there in Riley's mind, but she could not recall the familiar stranger that stood before her.

Riley clenched her fists in anger, as if she could will herself to summon these stubborn memories that she felt sure about, but somehow, they refused to surface. *The neural-connections are blocked*; the thought erupted in her mind out of nowhere. But did she have memories of this woman? She seemed so familiar, yet she remained a complete stranger. The mix of opposing thoughts stirred up an ocean of confusion that threatened to overwhelm Riley.

"Easy," the woman said in English.

Riley's unsteady hands froze then relaxed at the sound of her voice.

"How do you feel?" the woman asked.

Only after a moment did it dawn on Riley that she should answer, "I feel… horrible."

The woman nodded. "Yeah, that's to be expected."

"Who are you?" Riley managed.

Riley watched the woman swallow, her eyes flickering ever so slightly at the question, almost as if Riley had said something shocking or offensive. "You're not that far along yet, are you? Just try and take it easy for a bit. It can be pretty rough at first."

"Taking it easy is not really high on my priorities right now," Riley protested as her head still swirled, battling for full coherence. "I don't understand what's going on."

"You will. It will take time, but you will come to understand."

The woman's voice was soft but confident, each syllable clear. Riley couldn't detect any particular accent. The woman reached out for the shoulder Coleman had injected and squeezed the spot as if she knew it was there. Riley winced and pulled away, seeing a flash of light in her eyes.

"What was that for?" she protested.

"When did Thomas inject you?" the woman asked.

"Yesterday. Are you with him?"

The woman cracked a smile. "Not even a little. We need to get you away from here, and quick. He'll be coming for you. Did he tell you to meet with him again?"

"Whoa, hold on," Riley put up her hands in protest, "We're not going anywhere until I get some answers."

"Answers will come in time."

"No. Answers will come right now. Let's start with who you are."

The woman smiled slightly and nodded, waiting for Riley to put her hands down. Riley sighed and lowered them. She stared into the woman's dark eyes, searching for anything that might indicate danger. Instead, Riley sensed a calmness in this woman's presence. She seemed steady and resolute, and that somehow made Riley feel at ease.

"My name is Arisu Ana," the woman said at last.

Riley heard the name with all five senses. A chill ran through her and she became suddenly dizzy. Her back hit the wall as her knees wobbled uncontrollably. Arisu grabbed her arm and pulled her up.

"What's wrong with me?" Riley stammered.

"It's the neurogenesis fluid that Thomas injected into you. It's taking effect rather strongly now. The more stimulation you have from anything that might connect you to past memories, the more seriously it will kick in. You did some heavy reading back there and now, I'm here. So you'll be pretty messed up for the next several hours. It's quite a lot for your brain to handle."

"Well, that doesn't sound like much fun," Riley gave her a weak smile.

She returned it.

"So, does this mean I knew you?" Riley asked.

"Yeah. You knew me. But, as I said already, that will come with time. Right now, we have to get going."

"I think I would rather sit here and rest for a while." Riley's speech slurred and her eyes fluttered.

"No, no, no. We have to go now," Arisu protested, steadying Riley by the arm.

A sudden moment of lucidity came over Riley and she yanked her arm free. "Why should I trust you?"

Arisu rolled her eyes. "If you want to make it out of this alive, you have little choice but to trust me, honey."

"No," she pushed Arisu away. "I can't keep playing this game. I'm done with this mess. I can't trust any of you." She tried to back up, but ran into the wall again. Her mind felt as if it swam through thick sludge in an effort to remain conscious. "Just last week I was a normal gal with a sleepwalking problem. Okay, so that's not so normal, but still. It was just sleepwalking… oh shit…"

Riley watched as the ground rushed towards her in slow motion and hit her face. *This looks like it should really hurt*, she thought on her way down. Oddly, it didn't, though the bright flash of light that she saw inside her eyes when she collided with the sidewalk was quite startling. She didn't pass out right away either. In her field of vision, she saw feet striking the pavement and legs jutting up at an odd angle, as people walked by not too far away from them. And from that strange vantage point, the world slowed and faded away into a murky pool of nothingness.

What is it to be a person?
To know?
To have identity?
What are these things?
And to whom do they belong?
Who is everyone?
And
Who is no one?
Or does it even matter?
Identity.
Maybe it is that which we do not possess
Until we are deprived of it.

Riley's eyes opened. Shapes—*were those buildings?*—rushed past. Her eyes fought for something to focus on as her mind recalled an old nightmare of white halls, wires, lights, and a feeling of panic. Before her, slight streaks of dirt trailed across the glass like ancient canals on the surface of a now dried planet. She stared at the dirt. *Where am I?* She turned her head to the left. Arisu sat next to her, her hands on the steering wheel. She braked for a red light. Riley found herself mesmerized by the cherry glow emanating from the light. For that moment, nothing else existed.

She shook her head then looked out again. This time, people crossing the street consumed her. For some reason, her depth perception appeared to have gone on strike. The people seemed to be 'walking' in and out of each other, as they made their way across the two dimensional street. The world felt so foreign to Riley in that moment. Like she had been inserted in to *Flatland*, it felt distant, foreign, and so vibrantly dull.

It fascinated her, yet she felt completely detached from it. Reality lay bare before her, but it remained inaccessible; just beyond her reach.

This world rolled by her eyes like a tedious movie. All she could do was watch. She was not a character, but an audience member, a prisoner in Plato's cave, chained down and passively watching the dancing shadows of light. Maybe none of it was real after all.

"Where is Arnold?" Riley asked in a low rasp, but why she asked this, she did not know.

Arisu smiled at this and said, "How are you feeling?"

"Why did I just say that?"

"What? You mean, 'Where is Arnold?'"

Riley nodded.

"Your brain's firing up old synapses of which you have no current cognitive awareness."

Riley grinned then muttered, "You sound smart. Damn it, that only makes you hotter."

Arisu smirked slightly and looked away.

"I mean," Riley fought to control her mind and mouth. What was she saying?

Feeling embarrassed, Riley went back to staring out the windshield of the small car. The red light seemed to slowly fade. The green light flashed to life.

Her head was still pounding. She lowered it, closed her eyes, and rubbed her temple for a brief moment.

"Why is this happening?" she asked. "Why is this strangely familiar, yet painfully foreign?"

She looked up to find that the street was now a freeway on the outer regions of Campo Grande. She looked at Arisu in astonishment. What had just happened? They had just been in the city mere moments ago.

"Time," Riley muttered. "My whole perception of time is off."

Arisu nodded as she drove. "That's part of the deal. You'll be fine. Just try to hang in there. The neurogenesis fluid has to take its course. Those little bots are really screwing with your neurons, you know."

Riley felt groggy, but her tongue felt like moving. "So, if our understanding of the world only comes through our senses, and those are subjective to the individual, as is emotion, personality, tastes, and

memories, maybe Kierkegaard was right after all. Truth is subjectivity."
She looked at Arisu, Riley's eyes pleading for her help in understanding
what she was saying. Where was this coming from? At some level it made
sense to Riley, though how it connected to what she was experiencing
she remained unsure. "But how can my brain fire off neural-connections
for which I have no cognitive awareness? I mean, seriously here. John
Locke would crap his pants if he could hear me say that!"

Arisu smiled at her ramblings, returning her focus to the road. "You
and your philosophers," she mumbled.

"Where are we going?" Riley asked.

"We have to get out of here," she said. "You have to go back to
Boston."

Riley looked at her. Her eyes took in the gentle contour of Arisu's
face. Inside, feelings mixed and clashed. There was that calmness again.
But there was also the perpetual bewilderment and anxiety that Riley
could not shake, as her world continued to crumble around her. There
was a part of her that felt like she could possibly follow Arisu anywhere.
She felt strangely drawn to Arisu, as if some mixture of admiration
and trust, which she was unable to verbalize, was at play. On the other
hand, she was a nun and a teacher. She wasn't going anywhere. She was
going back to work, back to her students. They needed her. She wasn't
leaving with anyone. Not with Arisu, not with Thomas, no one. She had
no reason to trust any of these people. How dare they swoop in and
destroy her life?

"I can't go," she sat up. Her head throbbed in a sudden slur of
dizziness. "I can't leave. I have responsibilities. I have a classes full of
students."

Arisu turned to Riley, a painful look of disappointment crossed her
face for a brief moment. But that moment seemed to last an hour to
Riley. Her heart felt some inexplicable weight.

"You'll have to trust me," Arisu said softly. Was there a slight twinge
of sadness in her voice? Riley was unsure if it was there or if she her
drug-addled mind was twisting things.

"Why should I trust you, and not Thomas?"

Arisu passed a slow car then changed lanes. "Thomas works for them. They must have sent him to retrieve you. I have to admit that I didn't expect him to go about it this way. But, while I am perplexed by his methods, he has done some important legwork for me. I'm just glad I acted when I did."

Arisu looked around, changed lanes again, and then, took the next exit. "How about some food?"

Riley, still fighting slight dizziness and confusion, swallowed. "I think I'm going to barf."

8   CYLOGITEC SERUM

Despite the feeling that we're directly experiencing the world out there, our reality is ultimately built in the dark, in a foreign language of electrochemical signals. The activity churning across vast neural networks gets turned into your story of this, your private experience of the world…

- David Eagleman

FOR DECADES, BRAZIL BUILT large roadside centers. Located on major highways, these complexes housed an ample refueling station as well as several restaurants and shops. The restaurants, however, were not all cheep fast food joints. Prices varied, but most often the food was of a much more substantial nature than what might be expected by foreign travelers used to the American quick-fix fast food mentality. *Rodovias*, as they were called, had evolved with time. Sugarcane alcohol and gasoline sales fell as cars running solely on such fuels decreased in numbers. For a brief period, hybrids dominated the market. And then, the electric car revolution was ushered in by the likes of Tesla. The major car makers saw, at long last, the writing on the wall. They didn't want to be blindsided and forced to play a serious game of 'catch up'. The demand for such roadside facilities began to decrease as electric cars increased their driving range. About one-third of *Rodovias* had made, so far, the conversion over to quick charging stations. This particular *Rodovia* was old and in desperate need of repairs which, most likely, would never happen. The fueling station had only been partially converted to electric car chargers of a now outdated and slower variety.

Riley walked out of the women's restroom and looked around at the mostly empty food court. A moment later, Arisu walked out of the bathroom and stopped next to Riley.

"Not a whole lot of options," Arisu said, dryly. She made her way to the only restaurant still in operation. Riley followed. Before long, full plates of meat, rice, and beans, and cans of *Guaraná Antarctica*, a fruity Brazilian soda of which Riley had grown quite fond of, but only occasionally indulged in, were on the table before them. Much to her own surprise, Riley ate eagerly, not having thought much about food until Arisu had mentioned it in the car. The dizziness had subsided, allowing her stomach to settle. Maybe being out of the car helped. And, as her stomach settled, hunger took over. Riley felt momentarily better about things now that she had some food in her. Arisu ate slowly, Riley noticed. She looked around periodically, seeming to scan the surrounding area. Riley couldn't decide if she looked for danger or was trying to spot something or someone in particular. Riley still couldn't bring herself to fully trust this woman. But what could she do? Here she was, hours from her home and job in Campo Grande. Her whole life had quite suddenly taken an unexpected turn. She smirked at such a pathetic understatement then wondered what her housemates would think—what her boss and colleagues would think—when they could find no trace of her.

"How are you holding up?" Arisu asked.

Swallowing a mouthful, she said, "I suppose I'm doing fine, all things considered. But I am growing rather tired of fumbling along in ignorance here. So I think it's time to spill the beans; all of 'em."

Arisu's eyes drifted down to the plate before her. She nodded. "You're right. First of all, thank you for coming with me. I recognize I've given you little reason to trust me."

Riley looked down at her own plate and sighed. "I'm not sure I had much of a choice," she said, then looked up at Arisu. "So please forgive me if I suggest we skip any pretense of nicetics here. We're not friends. I don't know who you are. I don't know who Thomas is. And I definitely don't understand why you two think I'm someone other than who I clearly am."

There was that brief flash of something in Arisu's eyes again. Was it anger, pain, disappointment? But she covered it quickly, looking off and nodding. "I was hoping you would remember more by now," Arisu said softly. "I'm sorry. You have every right to be angry."

"What is it exactly that I'm supposed to remember? You?"

"I'm part of it," Arisu said, running a finger over the condensation on her soda can. "But first you need to realize who you were."

Riley frowned as she searched her mind. *Dear God, what is happening to me? What happened to my life? This is beyond insane!* And yet, some part of her willed her to stay seated there, begged her to believe, to look further. After a long silence, she sighed.

"I'm not Riley Bekker, am I?" she said with a new sense of wonder as something inside of her was knocked loose at the shock of hearing her own words. "Then who am I?"

Arisu took a sip of her drink then set it down. Her eyes stared through Riley's, penetrating deep into her. Riley waited, uncomfortable as it might have been.

"Violet Murphy," Arisu said, her voice soft yet clear. "You're a scientist, a damn good one."

No dizziness threatened Riley's focus; she simply stopped breathing as the name sent through her body a cold wave of what she could only eventually describe as a kind of foreign recognition. Somehow, deep within the recesses of her mind, Arisu's words connected to some unknown force that compelled Riley to believe.

"Okay," Riley said, "Then how did I get this way? Why don't I know that I am this… Violet Murphy?"

Arisu's eyes filled with concern. "Do you have any recollections of your life as Violet? Or, any sense of being Violet?"

"No," she breathed, "Well, I don't know. Not sure how to describe it, really. It feels strange, like I know the name. It… gosh, it feels like trying to place a face with a name of some long lost friend from grade school. It's in there, somewhere. But I can't get to it."

The neural networks are blocked, Riley thought suddenly.

Arisu sighed, pressing her lips together. "It's not working quickly enough."

Riley frowned, "You mean that stuff Thomas injected into me? What exactly was in that?"

"Did he inject a full syringe into you?"

"No clue," Riley shrugged. "I never saw a syringe. He just touched me."

"He had a palm unit then," Arisu said, looking off. "Easy to keep concealed."

"A concealed syringe?" Riley's eyebrows shot up. "What kind of operation are you people running running—"

"—the kind of operation that has ties to every intelligence agency and covert branch of government and military. Trust me; the concealed syringes are the nothing. They're also the least of our worries."

Riley leaned forward, "Arisu, what did he inject into me? I have to know."

Arisu blinked, at the sound of her name. "Cylogitec Serum is the lab name for it; millions of microscopic robots all flooding into your nervous system. Their primary function is to reconnect neural pathways that had previously been disconnected, or blocked, by a Personality Overwrite Procedure, or POP as as the techs call it."

Riley was silent for a moment, her jaw dropping slowly as the words echoed in her mind. "Nanobots," she said, "What are they doing to me?"

"When you were reprogrammed," Arisu leaned forward, finally seeming ready to explain, "you were injected with a certain type of nanobot that attached to your spinal cord. These then gave birth to new kinds of nanobots."

"Whoa, wait a second!" Riley raised a hand in protest. "These things inside of me, they can reproduce?"

"They can and they do. The second generation is in charge of transporting needed chemicals, enzymes, and hormones to stimulate the formation of new cells that can create new connections between neurons. This enabled them to create new paths for the new memories that are installed by the project."

"What happens to the old memories?"

"Unlike a computer, you can't just reformat the human brain and install a new operating system. The first generation of nanobots take over the spinal cord, delivering to it slight electrical stimulation, which enables them to control the functioning of your short-term memory. By delivering a controlled electroconvulsive shock to the brain, the nanobots are able to completely eradicate short-term memory if needed. All this is doing is to keep you from remembering the truth. We call them 'lie bugs'. The third generation penetrates deeper into the brain, locating and stimulating the correct regions so as to place the subject in a wakeful coma. They don't remember who they are, have little to no bodily function, and no ability to wake up."

Riley shook her head, "So the old memories are all still there, but the nanobots control what my brain can remember? But, wait, how does this electro—"

"Electroconvulsive shock. It's the very same process as shock therapy once done to mental patients. But this is a very mild and focused version of electroconvulsive shock therapy. It just prevents the information flow from the part of the brain that stores short-term memory to the part that stores information for the long-term. In many respects, this part does kind of work like a computer. On a computer you can start working on a file, but that file is not permanently on your computer until you save it on the hard drive. Before then, it exists solely in Random Access Memory. Turn the computer off without saving and you will have lost it, back up systems and modern instant file update protocols aside. Until the information is taken from the RAM to the hard drive, it stays put within your computer's 'short-term' memory. Interrupt the communication between RAM and hard drive, and the information is lost."

"Okay," Riley nodded. "I get that. Is that why my sense of time has been screwy?"

Arisu smiled. "The Cylogitec Serum is resetting the function of the other nanobots already present in your nervous system. So, while resetting the nanites that govern the transfer from short-team to long-term memory your sense of time can be affected."

"So is something wrong?" Riley said, more softly now. "You said you thought I'd remember more by now."

"Hard to say," Arisu went back to tracing shapes in the soda can's condensation. "I'm not one of the project techs, but I do know that most of these things have gone through various versions. It's possible that Thomas didn't have the latest version of the Cylogitec Serum to work with. Not sure why they wouldn't have sent that with him. Or why they sent him, for that matter."

Riley nodded, taking this in. Several questions came to mind, but one stood out. "So, the original nanobots I supposedly have in me, are they why I sleepwalk?"

Arisu looked down at her plate, "Maybe. We're not quite sure, yet."

Riley scoffed, "If they can control my short-term memory, couldn't they control me? I mean, what's to keep them from giving me ideas like: Go kill the President. I do, and wake up with no recollection because the memories were never allowed to move from short to long-term."

"I don't think they've achieved that kind of programming depth yet. The brain isn't a computer program's source code that can be pulled up and recoded so quickly. New synapses and whole neural networks have to be established. The machines are programmed to keep the brain functioning on the newly programmed level. It takes more than a month to allow new neural-connections to grow. With the proper enzymes, oxygen, and nutrition, the cells grow and new paths are made. I doubt they're to the point where they can insert ideas so quickly."

"So these things grow new brain cells?"

"Yeah. People used to think it that wasn't possible. But actually, a normal human being grows new brain cells all the time. But you know that. You just read about it." A sudden smile came to Arisu's face. She looked away.

"What is it?" Riley asked.

"It just feels strange to be telling you all of this. I'm not the scientist, that's for sure. I'm merely babbling back to you what you... I mean... what Violet told me."

"She told you a lot," Riley said as she sat back in her chair. "That does bring up an interesting point: Who exactly *are* you?"

Arisu's eyes looked past her as she remained silent for almost a minute.

"Look," Riley said, "I *have* to know. Apparently, I already knew—"

"Violet knew." Arisu interrupted.

"What's the difference?" Riley protested, "It seems to me that you're saying I am Violet."

"There's a pretty significant difference," Arisu snapped back. "Violet can save or destroy the project. You, on the other hand, were developed as a safe of sorts that now has to be cracked."

The words stung Riley, but she leaned in, her hand hitting her fork, which made a loud click against the plate. "Well, guess what? It seems that you're stuck with me at the moment. So I guess you'll have to get used to going through me to get to Violet, whom I don't even know anything about. But, regardless of that, there are much more crucial questions at hand: *Who are you* and *who do you work for?*"

Riley held a stern glare as she waited for an answer. Sick of being pushed around and herded along by these strangers, she was more than ready for some answers. Regardless of what perception they might have of a nun, she sure as hell felt no obligation to play nice anymore. These people were destroying her life!

Arisu nodded, "Alright. I guess you have a right to know. I used to work with the project. That's where we met—Violet and I, that is. I was in charge of the ERU, that's the Escaped Retrieval Unit. It's sort of a clean-up crew. A rogue hunter, that's what they called me. Every time there was a problem and one of the test subjects would go ape-shit on us, I had to lead a team to capture it."

"'Capture *it*.' 'Test subjects.' I take it you're talking about human beings whose lives were being stripped from them?" Riley pushed back, fully prepared to fight now.

Arisu fell silent, looking away from Riley. Finally, she said, "When they reprogrammed you, I guess they left the part intact that eventually felt so revolted by the poor ethics of the project which Violet helped create." Arisu pressed her lips together, "Listen, I'm here because I believe that part was right. The system is corrupt. I'm here so that, together, we can destroy this project. But, let's get this one thing straight. Riley Bekker is a synthetic program of memories compiled from various people, some completely artificial. Riley Bekker is *NOT* a real person. So, try to understand, I'm not going to get real attached because, in time, Ms. Bekker will be no more."

Riley let herself slowly slouch back into her chair. "How long?" She swallowed hard, "How long do I have until I'm... *uninstalled*?"

Arisu opened her mouth, seeming to momentarily regret her tone. "Could be up to three more days."

Her stomach turned. She looked into Arisu's eyes. They seemed so cold and distant now. What had changed? But then Arisu's eyes shifted and her expression become brighter.

"Finally," Arisu said, looking past her.

Riley looked over her shoulder. A short, dark man approached them.

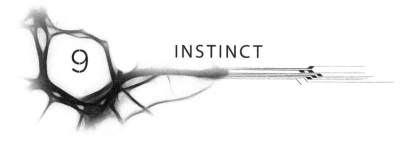

9   INSTINCT

The brain has many different types of learning, only one of which is dedicated to facts and events that we can consciously recall.

- Sandra Aamodt & Sam Wang

JONES CLEARED HIS THROAT. "It's fine, I just wish you would give more of a warning before showing up at my office."

Mel, his sixteen-year-old daughter, rolled her eyes. "If I gave you any warning, what fun would that be?" She rose from the cushioned leather seat and walked closer to her father's desk. She looked over the sparsely furnished and minimally decorated place. The large glass desk with silver metal legs was home to three clean, flat screens. In front of the screens sat a slender keyboard and a tablet. Near one corner sat a black office phone. No wires ran to it. Not a single sheet of paper could be found in the room. A rather bland abstract painting hung on the wall. A fake plant sat in the corner by the large glass doors that accessed the interior balcony. Beyond the floor to ceiling windows, Boston moved at its usual pace of frantic congestion. Jones could just make out the Custom House Tower near Faneuil Hall between the buildings, its recognizable clocks and pointed top increasingly dwarfed by newer and taller structures. Light poured in through the windows and lit the office. Nearly everything in the place was a cream color. His daughter called it boring; Jones saw it as efficient. The clean and minimal room helped him focus. This was also why he kept decorations to a minimum. If he wanted to look at something, he had the city outside his window. It cost plenty of money to have his office here. Why distract from the view?

"Wow, you've redecorated," Mel said, dryly.

Jones looked around in astonishment, "It's always been this way, honey."

Again, she rolled her eyes, "Hello, sarcasm."

"How's your mother?" Jones forced himself to ask, unsure of what to say at this point.

"Mom's fine, I guess," Mel shrugged. "She's still dating that sleaze bag from her firm, Joe something."

Jones opened his mouth to reprimand her, but realized he just didn't give a shit. Joe something was a sleaze bag. Good on Mel for recognizing that.

The silence returned. Jones looked at his daughter and wondered if she would ever outgrow the ridiculous teen clothing stage. Her shirt today wasn't too bad. Her pants however, clashed with her T-shirt. One leg was orange, almost plastic-like material, and the other was deep brown denim. It made Jones shudder. Did all the kids dress like this?

"Okay," he said. "I give, what do you want?"

She cocked her head to one side. "Want?"

"That's why you're here, isn't it? You want something."

She sighed. "Yeah. Look, Harvey had a wreck with my car. It's not bad, but I have to get it fixed."

Jones frowned, "Harvey?"

She threw up her hands and groaned, "Harvey, my boyfriend. You met him four months ago."

"Oh."

"But I just need some help. Mom's too uptight about the car to let me have any money. You understand, right?"

"Sure," Jones grunted.

The electronic bleating of the phone suddenly filled the office. Jones pushed the speaker button, "Yes?"

"Rikard's on line four," his secretary said. "Says it's important."

Jones looked to his daughter. "You know how it is. I've got to take this."

She flopped down into a seat as he picked up the headset. He stopped mid-motion.

"Mel, I have to speak on the phone… *alone*."

"Why?"

"How many times do I have to explain to you that what I do is classified?"

"If you do all this spy shit, then why did they let me in here?" she smirked.

"First, watch your language. Second, I never said I do spy shit." He pointed to the door, "Out!"

"Fine," she stormed out of the office.

Great, he thought, I just can't win.

"Jones here," he said into the headset.

"Is the line clean?" Rikard rasped.

"Yes."

"I'm afraid I've got some unpleasant news," Rikard said in his low voice. He was now Jones' head of ERU.

"What's that?" Jones responded unenthusiastically.

"Arisu's got Riley."

Jones felt his whole body tense up. "What? How?" he growled into the phone.

"Well, we knew she was tracking Riley with some outside help. She pulled some kind of stunt with some local mercenaries, best I can tell."

"But she shouldn't have been ready to act yet." Jones protested.

"You're right; she wasn't ready to act quite yet. But someone forced her hand: Thomas."

Jones smacked the surface of his desk, "Goddamnit! He's just compromised everything. Everything!" He took a deep breath, calming himself. "He betrayed us, plain and simple. That sonofabitch!"

"Plan of action?" Rikard asked.

"Trail them for now. But don't let them have the *slightest notion* you exist. Not yet. We need to figure out what they're planning on doing next. If we spook Arisu too soon it could go badly for everyone."

"And Thomas?"

Jones grinned, "Actually… watch what he does too. If he's half the dumbass I suspect he is, he'll try to follow them and contain this mess before it swallows him whole. After all, Riley is no good to him if Arisu has her. He's gone this far, he's not going to just walk away now. Maybe you all can have a new nice little reunion party at some point."

"Shouldn't be too hard to arrange."

"Rikard," Jones lowered his voice while his hands fumbled with his wallet. "This is it. No more unexpected bullshit. Thomas may have just screwed everything up for good. We cannot lose Riley. Too much is at stake and too many prying eyes are on us these days."

"Too many eggs in one basket?" Rikard asked.

Jones nearly dropped the phone at Rikard's audacity. He could practically hear the asshole's smirk forming on his lips from another hemisphere. "Just do your fucking job!"

"I always do."

"Good." Jones hung the phone up and flipped open his wallet, fishing out a few large bills.

He headed out the door, walking into the reception area. His daughter stood up from her slouched position on one of the small sofas.

"I have to run." Jones said, thrusting out the money.

Mel looked at the money and then up at him. "Cash? Can't you Venmo me?"

"I…" Jones grunted and thrust the money out at her. "Take this or take nothing. It is four hundred dollars. If the damage is more than that, so help me God…"

Mel's eyes grew wide, "Oh dad, you rock!"

He made a weak attempt at a smile. "I'm sure your mother will hate me for this."

Taking the money, Mel shrugged, "Not like she doesn't already."

"Exactly," Jones pointed at her with a smirk. "And lesson one of doing spy shit is to not leave a trail people can trace. Your mom probably still checks your email. She'd see a Venmo deposit from me."

Jones waited as she stuffed the cash in her small purse. She looked up at him and frowned.

"What?" she said.

"Do I at least get a hug?"

She sighed and shook her head, giving Jones a quick hug before heading for the exit with a swift, "thanks dad," over her shoulder.

Jones watched her go then headed down the hall that led to the back exit.

"SO YOU'RE THE ONE of which so much has been demanded," the dark, short man smiled broadly. He slid his hand forward, "A great pleasure to meet you at last. You may call me Dante."

Riley shook the man's hand, noting the firm grip. Dante's English bore a slight hint of an accent, which Riley could not identify, but each word was pronounced with careful diction.

"Dante," Riley repeated. "That's quite the name."

"Isn't it?" The man nodded, his smile never fading. "'Tis why I picked it."

"I see. Planning a trip through hell?" Riley smiled.

"No, not me, but you're about to take one. I'm just along for the ride."

Riley frowned then looked at Arisu, who seemed more relaxed now that this Dante character had shown up. She stood, gesturing for Riley to do so as well. Riley didn't budge.

"Riley," she said, "Let's go!"

"Yes. Our enemy draws nearer." Dante whispered.

Riley stood, looking the two strangers in the eyes. Yes, that was in fact all they amounted to in her mind: strangers. She took a deep breath before speaking.

"No. I'm not going anywhere."

Dante's smile faded. Arisu closed her eyes and let out a heavy sigh, but Riley remained firm.

"I don't know either of you." Riley continued, "Neither of you have given me any reason to place my trust in you. You can't demand anything from me. Not without some explanation—at least more than what you've given so far. Tell me—and I mean, really tell me—why I should trust you two and not Thomas?"

"We do not have time for this," Dante said, looking at Arisu.

"Dante," Riley said, "I assume you know what's going on here or you wouldn't be working with..." she looked at Arisu and then said, "I'm sorry, what is your last name again?"

"It's not important," Arisu responded in a flat tone that seemed to indicate controlled annoyance.

"You see," Riley pointed at her, "this is exactly what I'm talking about. You two should listen to yourselves—I mean, really listen to yourselves! Put yourselves in my shoes. Would you trust a couple of strangers talking to you the way you're talking to me?"

Arisu locked eyes with Riley, her face stern. Slowly, her features softened and she nodded, a slight bit of sympathy seemed to flicker across Arisu's features. "The information Violet holds in her mind can make or break Project Sleepwalker. We'd like to break it; otherwise, thousands of people will be subjected to this same treatment once it is approved as a viable means of criminal punishment. But the system is flawed. Horribly."

"There are many other people interested in this technology," Dante spoke up. "Most of them are not interested in deterring crime. They have far more ambitious and sinister applications in mind."

"Violet wanted to prevent that," Arisu nodded. "We want to prevent that. So, please, will you come with us?"

Riley looked down at the floor, soaking this all in for a moment. At last, she shrugged, "Well, at least you two haven't drugged me yet like that other dick."

THE TIRES ROLLED TO a smooth and silent stop. Thomas craned his head to one side, cracking his neck and then, did the same in the other direction. He yawned, barely paying any attention to the radio, which played a strange electronica version of a song that he could have sworn was actually an old folk tune, *Asleep in the Deep*. The singer's voice drifted from the radio while Thomas sat, waiting.

Though death be near, she knows no fear,
while at her side is one of all most dear.
Stormy the night and the waves roll high,
bravely the ship doth ride; Hark!

Reaching into the bag on the passenger seat of the small hybrid car, he produced from it two guns. The first was a standard police issue 9mm handgun, though this one had been modified, which meant that it lacked a serial number and fingerprint activation. The other weapon was a tranquilizer gun.

Loudly the bell in the old tower rings
Biding us list to the warning it brings.

Acquiring both had taken some money and meeting with a less than pleasant illegal arms dealer in Brazil, but thankfully the money and the meeting had been arranged for him. He looked about first to see who might be around to see him with the weapons. Spotting no one on this side of the *Rodovia*, he slipped on the shoulder holster that allowed him to comfortably carry both guns.

Better take care! Better take care!
Danger is near thee, beware! Beware!

With both weapons in place, he checked his mini tablet. The homing beacon appeared to be in working order. Along with the substance that he had injected into Riley, Thomas included another set of nano machines whose sole function was to scatter in her blood stream and together generate an identifiable signal, which he could track. He nodded his head with satisfaction then got out of the car. Putting on a jacket, he made sure to cover up the weapons. He reminded himself again: *Your right hand will be holding the tranq-gun; your left, live rounds. Right: tranq; left: live.*

He made for the entrance, walking in long, confident strides even if he didn't quite feel completely confident. But he tried to compensate, his face twisting in a smirk. Entering the building, he encountered a few people mingling by a shop. He walked past them, scanning for Riley or Arisu. He checked the tablet again. Riley appeared to be only about a hundred yards away at about two o'clock relative to his position. Thomas picked up his pace. When he looked up, he jumped in surprise as did the rather large Brazilian woman he nearly plowed into.

"Sorry," he said automatically in English.

The woman rattled off something in Portuguese, which Thomas could only guess, was a string of curses and other agitated words directed at him.

"*Pardon*," Thomas tried, immediately recognizing how dumb that must have sounded as he was fairly sure that wasn't Portuguese for sorry.

He put up his hands in surrender and backed up. The woman shook her head in disgust. Not waiting another minute, he walked past her. Checking the tablet, however, he discovered that Riley had now moved to eleven o'clock and the distance had increased. Thomas walked briskly into the large terminal-like area where several large screens played informational videos about this particular region of Brazil, showing a swamp land with the word *Pantanal* displayed in bold letters. To his right, a few sit-down restaurants hosted a small crowd. To his left were restrooms and computer stations where travelers could log onto the Internet, though the computers were at least a decade old. He checked the tablet again. Riley didn't seem to be moving at the moment.

Thomas proceeded quickly down the wide hall to his left. He discovered another hall on his right that led to game rooms and a bar. Glancing at the tablet, he found that Riley was now dead ahead.

THE SIZE OF THE bar in this roadside facility surprised Riley. She looked around, wondering why they had made their way to this spot. Dante turned to Arisu and whispered something to her. She nodded then looked over her shoulder.

"Let's keep moving," she said.

"Where are we going?" Riley asked.

"Away from here," she responded glancing left and right.

"Okay, then, let's just go," Riley muttered, annoyed.

"Not that simple," Dante interjected. "We are being pursued."

"Thomas?" Riley said. "Is he here?"

Riley looked behind her just in time to see Thomas round the corner of the bar entrance. He stopped. Arisu, Dante, and Riley stood frozen, looking their pursuer in the eyes. Thomas grinned. His right hand moved slowly into his jacket.

"Thomas," Arisu said over the noise of music and people talking, "What are you doing here?"

His hand stopped, but remained across his torso. "I've come," he said, "to talk to my new friend here." Using his hand that still held his tablet, he indicated Riley.

"Why did you follow us?" Arisu demanded, "Did Jones send you?"

A broad smile crept onto Thomas' lips.

"You're on your own, aren't you?" Arisu's voice grew louder.

"Take it easy," Thomas cautioned, "I guess you and I have something in common now. We're deserters. Try to keep that in mind."

"But you're not here to help Violet," Arisu shot back.

Thomas nodded slightly, keeping his eyes moving between Dante and Arisu. "Sure I am. I'm just not here to help her in the way you think you're helping her."

Riley looked around the bar. No one seemed to notice the tense foreigners by the entrance. She looked back to Thomas, dreading the thought of what might happen the moment his hand reached inside his jacket. She felt a sudden certainty wash over her that he was armed. It was something about how he stood, the way he moved.

In her mind, Riley saw herself leap out and tackle Thomas, disarming him before he could fire the first round. The sudden vivid thought startled her. Yet, she also felt a surprising confidence that she could strike him in the windpipe while grabbing his wrist. She knew just where to hit. But where exactly had that thought come from? More than just a fantasy, this thought bore the weight of determination, as if she actually meant to do it. Indeed, Riley could feel the action, almost count the beats it would take for her to dodge the punch Thomas would likely throw while gripping the other wrist. She could trip Thomas or simply deliver that firm blow to the neck, which would likely crack his windpipe. Death would come quickly, but not quickly enough for Thomas, who would endure excruciating pain as he suffocated. In a flash, Riley knew not just what to do, but that she *could* do it. She could feel her muscles tensing with anticipation.

"You can't stop us," Arisu said to Thomas.

"Too late, I think I already have."

As if controlled by some unknown force, Riley stepped forward and said calmly, "No, you haven't."

"Stay where you're at, Riley. I'm your friend, remember? I'm here to help you. So let's just take this easy."

"Here to help me?" Riley scoffed. "You basically roofied me."

Thomas' eyes widened as if he just now realized how violated Riley felt. "I left you that video. I didn't touch you."

"That may be," Riley shot back, "but as a general rule, I don't consider people who drug me to be my friends."

"It will all become clear soon. I promise," Thomas insisted.

"Yeah. So I keep hearing. But for now, you're going to let us walk out of here." Riley said, pure instinct commanding her lips to move. The words flowed with no effort. Riley took another step closer. Thomas' hand slipped into his coat. The gun came out quickly. Thomas leveled it at Riley, but just as quickly Riley clapped his hands together. One hand hit the barrel, the other Thomas' wrist. She struck hard like a closing trap. The gun flew from his hand.

Riley reached for Thomas' throat. She could have done him in, she knew. In her mind, Riley saw herself over Thomas' dead body. She stopped, still keeping the pressure on the man's windpipe. She looked into Thomas' fear filled eyes. Riley took a deep breath.

"We're walking out of here," she whispered, "You're not going to follow us. I don't want to kill you, but I will if it comes to it."

Thomas nodded slightly.

Arisu picked up the tranq-gun which Riley had knocked to the ground.

"Don't follow us," Riley said, releasing the man's throat.

Thomas gasped, rubbing his neck. Arisu examined the tranq-gun. Riley looked around, just becoming aware of her surroundings again. People in the bar had stopped to observe the commotion. Riley felt lightheaded. Where had she gone? What had happened? *That wasn't me. Or maybe it was.* Either prospect frightened her.

"Let's go," Arisu ordered.

Dante started in the opposite direction from which Thomas had come. Riley began to follow, but looked back at Thomas out of instinct. Thomas dropped his tablet and in one quick motion drew a handgun with his left hand. Riley lunged at Arisu, taking her to the ground. She then swung her feet, tripping Thomas. The burst of gunpowder sent a shockwave through the bar. Screams erupted as people ran for the exits or ducked for cover. A bottle on the bar not two feet from Dante erupted in a shower of liquid and glass.

Dante hit the floor, producing two handguns from beneath his own coat. He lay on his back, both guns squared on Thomas.

Riley rolled off of Arisu. Looking up, she stared down the barrel of Thomas' gun.

"Now," Thomas said, "You'll come with me!"

Riley kept her eyes on the gun, knowing very well it fired bullets, not tranquilizer darts. Then it dawned on her…

"You can't shoot me," she said. "You need what's in my head."

Hesitation crept into Thomas' eyes. She'd called his bluff. Recovering, he moved the gun quickly to Dante, who picked himself up from the ground.

"But I can shoot them," Thomas said.

Riley acted without a thought. Her hands gripped the barrel of the gun, twisting it. Thomas fought to keep control. Riley slammed the gun down on the ground three times. Thomas yelled as his fingers took the brunt of each impact. The gun came loose. Riley grabbed it quickly then stood over Thomas. Instinctively, Riley pointed the gun at him, her finger resting ever so lightly on the trigger. She could feel the instinct to squeeze down. How easy and yet, how devastating that simple action would be.

Arisu picked herself up as well. She approached Riley. "Let's go," she said.

Riley hesitated. She let the gun drop to her side, then she handed it to Arisu, suddenly overwhelmed with disgust at the very thought of even being near the damn thing. Leaving Thomas crumpled on the ground, they fled the bar.

Cutting through the bar, they headed for the nearest exit. They stopped almost immediately once getting outside. Riley looked in bewilderment at Arisu, who squinted as the outside light struck her eyes.

"What are we looking for?" asked Dante.

"Something fast," she answered. "We have to get moving now."

She turned to Riley. In Arisu's eyes, Riley could see the question before it was even asked. Arisu opened her mouth, but Riley beat her to it.

"It's fine," Riley said. "I'm in. I'll go."

Genuine relief flooded Arisu's features. Riley sensed that for all her external show of strength, powerful emotions battled within her. She felt it within herself as well. What was it? *I'm guessing I'll find out eventually*, she assured herself. *But right now is definitely not the time.*

"I suggest that we take that rather nice specimen," Dante said, pointing at a blue electric Alfa Romeo a few yards from them.

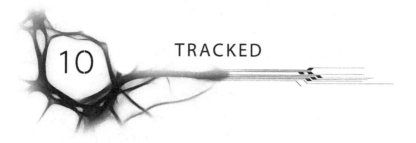

10 TRACKED

Our past is not a faithful record. Instead it's a reconstruction, and sometimes it can border on mythology.

- David Eagleman

THOMAS DASHED DOWN THE long corridor. Behind him, three Brazilian police officers gave chase. They shouted, but none of their words held any meaning to him. Hitting the exit door, he burst out of the building with such force that he startled a group of people who had just stepped out of their van. Thomas dashed for his car. Fumbling for keys, he managed to hit the automatic ignition on the keychain. The car headlights lit up and the door unlocked. He jumped in, jamming the car into reverse. A cloud of swirling smoke rose from the spinning tires. Leaving the officers in the haze, Thomas floored the car, heading for the highway's entrance ramp.

Once on the road, he sighed. His whole body ached with tension. Jones would have to find out sooner or later, and Thomas would be in serious trouble. Time was short, now. Riley would begin to fade away. Violet would soon emerge. Maybe she was emerging already. Riley had certainly handled herself well back there. He couldn't recall any information about Riley having had such extensive self-defense abilities. *Guess the nerd learned kickboxing on the side or something.* As long as she was with Arisu, everything would be in jeopardy.

Keeping the car at a high speed, he checked the tablet. The drop hadn't damaged it. The casing was dinged on one corner, but the unit still worked. With one hand, he checked through the Universal Wireless Internet for information on where he might be able to "exchange" his car for another. No doubt, satellites several miles above now tracked his car, even though he had turned the onboard GPS off. How long would he have before the police hacked the engine and shut it down? Were the Brazilian police up to speed on car hacking? Were the laws the same here as in the US? He hadn't thought this far ahead, and now he kicked himself. Jones had always carried on about covering every possible scenario by constantly posing all those wonderfully annoying "what if" questions. It didn't matter now. Things were in motion. He just had to get to Violet.

The tablet beeped, notifying him of an incoming message. He checked it quickly. An audio file began instantly to play. "Thomas," said a growly female voice with a strong British accent, "you didn't check in as planned. What's happening? Tensions are running high. You said this was going to be a smooth transaction. Call in."

Damn it! He was officially a wanted man from three sides now. Jonas would want him, Brazilian authorities would want to arrest him, and now he'd have the British SciRebryl Inc. folks after him. He'd promised to deliver Violet Murphy into their hands, but now he found himself well on his way to certain doom from one angle or another.

Seeing a sign for a small town, he changed lanes and exited. He had to take it one step at a time from now on. His first step: find a new car. The next: hack it.

DANTE HAD HACKED THE car quickly, safely overriding security shutdown and effectively convincing the car's internal computer that it had been started properly. He had done it so surprisingly quick and apparently without the use of a tablet. In too much of a rush, Riley hardly had the chance to take this in, much less question it.

As they drove, Arisu took over the GPS hacking, locking out any incoming signals and rendering the car invisible to any police systems. Dante drove, Arisu rode shotgun. Riley sat in the backseat, her head leaning against the window. Hours passed. Headlights rushed past them. "São Paulo," Arisu had said, "that's where we are going."

Riley had asked why there, but she gave no clear answer. Riley figured they meant to take her out of the country. Riley would go, though she now questioned if she had any choice in the matter. She did not question her ability to refuse Arisu's demands. On the contrary, she questioned if, within herself, she had the ability to choose other than that which she knew she *would* choose—what she had already chosen somewhere deep inside the moment Arisu said her name. She tried to ignore it as she always had, but everything was changing so quickly.

Riley nodded off; sleep coming to her in fits of dreams, which mixed with her mind's ever shifting metaphysical terrain. Memories, images, voices, whole conversations… all of these washed over her in waves which rolled in from her subconscious, lapping on the shores of her conscious mind.

> *Are you here, still?*
> *Have you not left yet?*
> *We cannot share this space.*
> *Leaving hurts. But so does staying.*
> *Acceptance leads the way.*
> *Open the door.*
> *Do not worry.*
> *When existence comes to an end.*
> *So does pain.*
> *When existence comes to an end.*
> *So does all the blame.*

When Riley's eyes opened again, a yellow light flooded her vision. Arisu's silhouette moved closer to her. She blinked and squinted.

"Where are we?" Riley croaked.

"At a motel," Arisu answered. "We need to keep a low profile, so don't speak too much English until we are in our room."

Suddenly, Riley felt awake. She frowned, blinking away the sleep in her eyes. "Our room?" she asked. "We're staying together?"

Arisu helped her out of the car. Now, Riley saw the yellow light that came from a street lamp they were parked near. Only a handful of cars littered the small parking lot.

"Yeah, we're only getting one room," Arisu muttered, "Dante and I have to keep an eye on you."

"At a motel?" Riley asked.

"Yes," Arisu sighed, becoming increasingly annoyed. "What's the big deal?"

"Sorry," Riley shook her head. "Motels in Brazil are often used for…" she searched for a proper way to state it. The conversation she'd had with Eliane only a couple nights ago—though it felt as if a year had already passed—came to mind. Riley pushed all of this aside and spoke. "Motels usually go for an hourly rate, if you know what I mean."

Arisu's annoyance let up. "Oh. I see. It's actually a small hotel. It just looks like a basic American motel. I didn't realize there was that distinction here."

Riley smiled. "The things you learn living in a new country."

Riley soon found herself in a small room. Two beds faced a wall with an old flat screen television. She looked at the beds, their ugly green covers not appealing to her much. The whole room consisted of faded brown (much more a state of being than a color). The few generic framed-pictures that dotted the wall were nothing special or particularly appealing. The bathroom was miniscule, but adequate. That is to say, it would be, as long as there were no issues with the water pressure.

"I'm sorry we didn't stop at a better place," Arisu said, sitting down upon the bed farthest from the door and removing her shoes. "It's just that we have to keep a low profile, and going to some fancy place filled with people would probably draw more attention to us."

"It's alright," Riley shrugged. "I'm a nun who teaches in a third world country. I'm not exactly used to the high life anyway."

Arisu looked at Riley with a slight smirk and then let a chuckle slip out.

"What?" Riley asked.

"Nothing," Arisu smiled. "It's just not something I ever could have pictured coming out of your mouth."

Riley nodded, thinking. After a moment, she spoke. "So, we knew each other."

Arisu nodded. "Yeah."

"How did we meet?" Riley asked.

"The project," Arisu said, looking away.

"But I was a scientist?"

Arisu smiled slightly again and nodded her head. "We were in different departments, but our work crossed over."

"How so?" Riley asked.

But just then, Dante stepped inside and closed the door behind him. He bolted it. Turning to Riley, he smiled and patted her on the shoulder. Riley winced as his hand hit the spot where she had been injected.

"I'm sorry," Dante pulled his hand back.

"It's okay," Riley gently ran her hand over the tender area. "How long is this supposed to hurt?"

Arisu looked up at her with sudden concern. "It still hurts?" she asked, "The spot Thomas injected you?"

Riley nodded. Arisu stood and approached her.

"Let me see it," she said. "Take off your shirt."

Riley hesitated at this command. Arisu looked at her, waiting for her to comply. When Riley didn't move, Arisu seemed to soften.

"I'm sorry," she said, "I forgot who I was… I just need to see your shoulder. Can you pull up you sleeve, at least?"

Riley smiled sheepishly and glanced at Dante, who stood by the window staring out of a small opening in the curtain. "Sorry, vow of celibacy and all. Not used to being in mixed company. And modesty is kind of part of the deal."

Arisu laughed. Riley's heart leaped for a brief instant. Something about her laugh felt familiar. It also made her feel warm and at ease. It disarmed her. It took her a moment to realize that she laughed as well.

"But, huh, I guess if what you say is true," Riley grinned, "it means I've never truly been a nun."

Their eyes remained locked for several seconds. The overwhelming warmth growing inside his chest finally made Riley too uncomfortable.

She looked away, swallowing hard.

She pulled her left sleeve up as high as she could, but it was a tight sleeve and she only just managed to clear the site of the injection. Arisu leaned close and looked at her shoulder.

"Oh," Arisu said.

"Oh?" Riley asked. "Why do I get the feeling that's not a good reaction?"

"It looks really bruised," Arisu said. "I need to see if the bruise has spread up toward your neck."

"I'll, huh," Riley pointed to the bathroom.

"That's fine," Arisu said.

Riley nodded, her mouth open and ready to say more. But nothing came. She couldn't even think of what she would want to say. *Must be the stuff Thomas injected into me*, she told herself. *It's really starting to mess me up.* But she only partially believed this.

RILEY STEPPED INTO THE bathroom and Arisu took a seat on one of the beds. She was having such a hard time keeping in mind that this woman who seemed so familiar was not the same person she had known. She watched as Dante finished his inventory of what he could see outside before he closed the blinds.

"Looks clear," he said.

"How's the air around here?" Arisu asked.

Dante closed his eyes for moment. She waited while he worked.

"Basic Wi-Fi, radio waves, a handful of Bluetooth devices, one strong encrypted Wi-Fi hotspot, nothing stands out as being all that suspect," Dante said, opening his eyes. "I shall take a short walk so that I can get a sense of what else is around here."

"Make sure it's short. We should rest and be out of here early."

Dante gave her a confident smile and headed for the door.

"Get me a cola while you're out," she said.

"Cola?" Dante said with surprise.

"I know, I know. But I could use the caffeine and sugar right about now," Arisu sighed.

Dante nodded and smiled before giving her the "okay" sign and making his exit. She stood and bolted the door behind him. Then, finding the remote for the flat-screen television that hung on the wall, she turned it on and searched for news. Of course, Brazilian stations confronted her. Unable to understand what the banter on the screen meant, she continued to flip through the channels, hoping that the run-down hotel, despite its several shortcomings, would have American or European channels via satellite or internet. In the process, she encountered an inordinate amount of semi or fully pornographic channels. Somewhere around channel 270, she found programs being broadcast in English. She slowed her channel surfing, settling finally on an American news channel.

Sitting at the end of the bed closest to the window, she watched as the screen displayed images of a mob of people protesting in Washington D.C. "Unhappy about recent announcements concerning the testing of mental-reprogramming techniques on several inmates," said the news reporter, "Students from several east-coast colleges and universities gathered in Washington today to protest."

The television showed students carrying signs and shouting. The signs bore slogans such as: "The mind is no toy," and the words "Thought police" crossed out. The reporter continued, "Many expressed grave concerns that such technology would be disproportionately used on minorities that have been systematically incarcerated for decades. So far, the research programs have been geared towards violent criminals only, with the particular focus on the eventual use on convicted terrorists. A few private companies are developing potential systems, but most of the concern targets companies working on classified projects. White House Science Advisor Tessa Wong has repeatedly stressed that these projects are standard classified R&D and have no definite application at this time.

"That hasn't stopped several Middle Eastern leaders from accusing these programs of being tools for the eventual brainwashing of their citizens into what they see as Western and American ideals. The fear is centered on the loss of traditional Islamic beliefs and cultural ideals in light of the secular bent of the American creators for these projects. Some groups have gone as far to accuse the scientists behind these advances of developing a sinister plan to eradicate the Islamic way of thinking."

The door to the bathroom opened.

"Arisu?" came Riley's concerned voice.

Turning the TV off, Arisu got up and walked to the bathroom door, which was cracked. "Dante stepped out," she said.

Riley pulled the door open. Her shirt was off and she wore a rather plain light blue bra. Her eyes were wide with concern.

"Here, take a seat," Arisu gestured to the bed closest to the bathroom.

Riley complied without saying a word. Arisu sat next to her, pulling her hair back from her face. She looked at the raised spot on her shoulder. The spot was definitely bruised, bearing a purple and yellowish tint that faded out in a circle around it like some oversized tick bite. Faintly visible through Riley's dark skin were winding purple lines that stretched up her shoulder and almost to her neck. Arisu looked at Riley with concern.

"I don't like your reaction," Riley said. "Give it to me straight, doc."

"Something's wrong with this. It shouldn't be infected. Not unless he used a bad syringe or…" She stood quickly, staring at Riley's shoulder and frowning. "Shit."

"What?" Riley asked.

Arisu removed a long black cylindrical device about four inches in length from her purse and returned to Riley. Sitting down next to her again, she moved to place the cylinder on Riley's shoulder. But Riley reached out and grabbed her wrist.

"Whoa, hold on!" Riley glared at her. "Wanna' tell me what's going on?"

"I need to take a reading of your blood at the site of the injection. I have a feeling Thomas laced the cylogetic serum with something else," Arisu explained.

Riley held her wrist firmly, eyes narrow.

"I need you to trust me on this," Arisu said, softly.

Riley seemed to consider this for a moment. Finally her grip loosened and she let her hand drop.

"It'll hurt just a little," Arisu said and quickly pressed the end of the cylinder against the spot before Riley could protest any further. Riley cringed.

"Hold still for a second," Arisu instructed. "It'll be alright."

With her free hand, Arisu held Riley's arm. She pressed a button on the side of the cylinder and it whined. Riley's arm jerked slightly in reaction to the sudden pain.

When Arisu removed the device from her shoulder, Riley leaned back on her right arm and said, "That hurt more than a little."

"I'm sorry. It requires a sample of skin and blood."

She set the device aside and went to the restroom. Returning with some tissue paper, she handed it to Riley. Taking it, Riley gently pressed it against the now bleeding spot. Arisu removed a tablet from her purse and connected a thin cable to it and the cylinder. "How does it feel?" she asked.

"Like a some super nasty bug bite."

"That may not be too far from the truth."

Before Riley could ask for clarification, the tablet made an electronic buzzing sound, indicating the completion of the analysis process. Arisu turned back to it and disconnected the thin cable. Her eyes became wide. Turning slowly to Riley, Arisu could see that she sensed her concern, though she could have no idea what caused it or what significance it might hold. Arisu tried to calm herself for Riley's sake.

"Riley," Arisu began, "I need you to do something."

She just nodded silently.

"Lie down on the bed and try to relax your whole body."

She hesitated now, "Why? What's going on?"

She sighed, "It does looks like Thomas injected you with something extra along with the serum. I think it might be some kind of tracking system. There is a high concentration of silicon in your blood stream.

Certain nanobots are built from silicon. The spot on your shoulder probably hasn't healed yet because there is a high gathering of nanobots there which are using that spot as a focal point for transmitting your location. I can see some evidence that they are spreading up your neck. They're probably doing that in an effort to expand the surface area for better transmission."

Riley took in a deep breath and let it out slowly, "You mean he... bugged me?"

"Looks like it," Arisu said, thinking of the encrypted Wi-Fi hotspot signal Dante had picked up. It could have been someone's smartphone being used to provide secure Wi-Fi for other devices, or he might have been picking up on the disguised signal of the tracking system inside Riley. It was often a trick employed by some black market trackers.

"What now?"

Arisu hated this part, "I have to inject you with another system of nanobots. The new system will have to battle the tracking bots and destroy them."

"More nanites?"

Arisu nodded.

"Well," Riley sighed, "what's a few more tiny robots running around inside of me?"

"The thing is," Arisu paused, biting her lower lip, "this will knock you out for a while. If Thomas shows up, we'd have to drag your body to the car. You'll be unconscious."

She could see it in Riley's widening eyes how profoundly this disturbed her. How could she ask her to become completely defenseless at such a time? Besides, it was clear Riley still did not fully trust her or Dante. Not that Arisu could really blame her. *This isn't Violet*, she told herself once more. *Not quite yet, at least. You have to earn her trust.* But Arisu also had to admit to her own inherent impatience. This shouldn't have been happening this way. Thomas had messed everything up, forcing her to jump the gun.

Riley finally nodded, "Well, seems to me like it's bad news either way. Don't do anything, and Thomas will know right where I am. Inject me and I become literal dead weight."

"Dante and I will keep you safe," Arisu looked into her eyes and put on a brave front. "I promise you."

Riley pursed her lips and shrugged, though the fear was clear in her eyes. "Shoot me up, I guess. But, if I'm going to be unconscious for a while I have to have a shower first."

Hidden in shadow, Rikard observed as Thomas stepped out of his car. A handful of cars in the small station filled their hybrid tanks with Brazilian alcohol made from sugar cane. Rikard marveled that this had never caught on in oil-dominated nations. But then again, who else grew sugar cane like Brazil? At any rate, the days of oil where now fading. Since he had arrived in Brazil, he'd learned a few things about the culture. Cars that ran on alcohol were one of the first and most intriguing things he had picked up on.

Apparently, the police had not yet successfully hacked Thomas' car. Maybe he'd take precautions or maybe the police in this rural area were not up to speed on car hacking. But such luck would only last so long. The police were sure to be looking for his car, even if they couldn't hack it. Thomas' lack of professionalism, however, became all too obvious in his haste. Rikard knew Thomas needed a new car. Then, he would be on the road again in a futile attempt to catch Riley. In a sense, Rikard felt he was well ahead of Thomas. Yet, Thomas did have the presence of mind to inject a tracking system into Riley, something which Rikard had to give Thomas a little credit. But he was about to rescind that credit.

As Thomas walked into the station, Rikard moved out of the shadows. A slight breeze ruffled his neatly combed red hair. He glanced about quickly, checking the area. Through the large glass front of the station's store, he watched as Thomas entered the men's restroom then quickly cut between the pumps to Thomas' car.

Reaching it, he stooped by the back bumper and extended a hand underneath it. His hand searched around before finding the foreign object attached to the car. Carefully, he pried loose the small cube-shaped tracking beacon. Examining it, he found it is was dirty, but otherwise unharmed. Rikard brushed it clean and slid it into his jacket pocket. Glancing around to see if anyone might be near, he walked back to the station's store.

The smell of strong coffee spewed into his face as the automatic door slid open. He swallowed then tried not to breathe. The smell disgusted him. He had never quite figured out what so many people saw in coffee. He tried to take in slow breaths in an attempt to acclimate himself to the stench.

Rikard stopped by the magazine racks. He picked up a news magazine, ignoring the array of rather explicit covers. Of course, he couldn't read any of the articles. He managed to recognize a few words that bore a similarity to Spanish, but even his limited knowledge of Spanish had long faded into vague familiarity.

He looked as if he might be reading, but his ears were intent on the bathroom door. By no means would Jones approve of this method in most situations, but Rikard knew this case was different. Actually, Jones knew this sort of situation to be far from ideal. That's why Rikard had been deployed. He needed to get to Riley before Thomas had another chance to screw things up. *At least it gives me something to do*, he thought. *A nice little trip, really.*

The bathroom door creaked open. Thomas stepped out, his face still damp where he must have splashed it with water. Rikard observed him from the corner of his eye. Being in the store was completely unnecessary, but Rikard loved the rush of playing with his prey. The proximity invigorated him. It was the main thing he missed from his days in combat. Thomas grabbed a bag of chips and stepped up to the register. Rikard waited for him to pay before sliding the magazine back on to the rack. He followed several feet behind Thomas as the unsuspecting man walked out of the store.

Thomas moved quickly toward the parking lot. Rikard knew that he would be seeking the cover of darkness while trying to hack a new car. Perfect. Thomas picked up his pace, never once looking back. *Amateur,*

Rikard marveled. Not more then five steps into the building's shadow, Rikard threw his arm around Thomas' neck. The bag of chips hit the ground.

"Don't make a sound, Tommy," he commanded.

"Rikard?" Thomas said, "What do you want?"

"Do you really have to ask? Now, let's get one thing straight. Whatever you thought you were doing here is over. There's a new game in town. I'm here to retrieve Riley and you are going to help me."

"Jones sent me to get her," Thomas tried.

Rikard involuntarily let out a short burst of laughter. "You are an even bigger dumbass that I thought," he said as he tightened his muscles around Thomas' neck. "Do you really think I just showed up here to rain on your parade without once talking to Jones? Who the tap dancing fuck fairies do you think sent me here after getting all pissed off at your shenanigans? Now, let's calmly walk over to the car you came in and drive away."

"The police will hack it," Thomas protested. But Rikard called his bluff.

"If they were going to hack any cars, they would have done so by now. Besides, I have a jamming program I can upload. You know me better than to assume that I don't have the next ten steps already figured out. So quit stalling."

Rikard waited for Thomas to acknowledge defeat.

"Okay," Thomas sighed, "But I don't know where they are."

"Bullshit," Rikard laughed. "You've been tracking them, and I've been tracking all of you. Seriously, what do you take me for?"

Letting Thomas go, Rikard picked up the bag of chips and handed them to Thomas, who grudgingly took them. Rikard nudged him on, and the two men walked back to Thomas' car.

"I call shotgun," Rikard winked.

RILEY LAY ON THE bed, her breathing relaxed and steady. Arisu sat on the other bed, watching her. The muted television flashed more news, but she paid it no attention. In the distance, she could hear the faint sounds of a harmonica. Dante, she thought. It sounded like him. That meant he was on the lookout for any danger.

She stood and stepped close to Riley. Taking her hand, she sat on the bed next to her. Carefully pressing her fingers on Riley's wrist, Arisu took her pulse. She could have monitored Riley's vitals on her tablet, but that somehow didn't feel real enough. She needed to sense the repeating pulse in her own finger tips. Satisfied, she placed Riley's hand next to her. Arisu looked at the injection spot on her shoulder. Riley had her shirt on again, but her left sleeve was pulled up in an effort to keep the infected injection site visible. Over time, however, the sleeve had slowly fallen back over the spot. Arisu lifted the sleeve slightly and looked. Was the bruising slightly better, or was she only imagining it? Obviously, Thomas must have made some preparations, but what did he think he was doing? She doubted very much that Jones would send Thomas all alone to Brazil. Thomas was no operative and this didn't seem like Jones' methods. Something else had to be going on.

She looked up at the television. Figuring she no longer had the interest or energy to procure any information from the news, she turned it off. She headed into the bathroom, where she stood in front of the mirror. They still might be able to recuperate their original plan. Everything had now been bumped up to a sooner date, but things might still work out. Thomas certainly had a knack for screwing things up. He had been a fairly good computer analyst on the project, working with the programming for the nanobot functions within the body and brain. He had taken some real interest in the overall achievements of the program. Particularly, he seemed to have taken a real interest in Violet's work in the days before Violet had defected.

Arisu shook her head and looked at the bags beneath her eyes. Better rest up, she told herself. Things are going to get real interesting from here on out, but first, a shower. Then, sleep, if that's even possible..

GUARULHOS

Memories are not written just once but reinforced either during recall or
even offline, for instance, during sleep.

- Sandra Aamodt & Sam Wang

"HOW MANY TIMES HAVE you run across this problem?"

Riley looked up from her desk. A woman stood next to her. Her face…
Riley couldn't quite see her face. Was it Arisu? She couldn't tell for sure. It
seemed as if the woman wore a white flowing gown, which reflected light
so brightly that Riley could not bring her eyes to focus on her face. She
shielded her eyes and looked down. The woman's feet were bare.

"Have you done anything about it?" the woman asked.

She didn't sound quite like Arisu. Riley stood, knocking her chair over.
But she realized now that her desk was pressed up against the wall of a
small back alley in a city. The red brick walls stretched out high above her.
An old metal fire escape clung to the side of the building right next to her
desk. All of the books on her desk looked the same, blue hardback books
with no title. She reached for one. Flipping it open she found the first page.
The title above the text read: Assimilate.

"How many times have you seen it happen?" the woman asked again.

"I don't know," Riley said.

The woman reached for her face, softly brushing her fingers on her
lips. She spoke without using her voice:

Find the key
And you may unlock every door.
Every question will be answered.

What you have known
Will be replaced with singularity.
Multiplicity is molded in the image
Of something new;
Something you have been all along,
Yet something that has never quite become.

"Do you understand me?" she whispered.

The woman was close now. The light blinded Riley, but she felt the sweet, warm lips of this mysterious woman brush softly against her own.

RILEY'S EYES OPENED. LIGHT streamed through the car window. She squinted. The world outside that rushed past her seemed too distant. Had they left Brazil? She stared out the window, assuring herself that they still found themselves on the road to São Paulo. However, the world outside now presented itself to her as a land she had only seen in a movie or read about, not a place where she had lived.

They approached the outskirts of São Paulo. Was it still one of the top five largest cities in the world? She couldn't quite remember. The industrial pollution hung over the large, yet crowded freeways that wound into the city on the horizon. Riley wished she could curl up on the back seat of the car and go back to sleep. Maybe when she woke up, she would be in a much more familiar place. A frightening thought invaded her mind: *What if there is no familiar place?* She felt panic creeping up inside her chest; her heart picking up pace. She wanted to cry; to call out for help; to find a safe place. Such childish impulses also frightened her. She was an independent woman, wasn't she? She couldn't lose control now.

The memory of her dream billowed through her clouded mind like brume. The one thing that had felt warm and comforting had been the kiss. Whose lips had touched hers? Had she ever kissed someone before? The answer itself felt as shrouded and illusive as a dream. Had it been a woman? Riley felt sure the voice had belonged to a woman. She'd kissed a woman?

An old reality that she hadn't dealt with in a very long time came rushing into her conscious mind like violent waters bursting through a broken levy. Annette Stephens. Riley still recalled her short stature and curly hair that framed her round face and big eyes. They'd met during their first semester in college and had spent quite a bit of time together.

One rainy Saturday while watching TV after a long stint in the library, they had held hands, their fingers interlocking. Riley's heart had raced. She looked into Annette's eyes as she looked back with a confused smile. Riley recognized that she had little interest in boys all through high school. But, exploring her feelings towards other girls had felt too risky. That afternoon, however, the electricity had coursed through her hand and up her arm. Her heart raced; her stomach felt as if she were speeding down the first hill of an exceptionally tall rollercoaster. All of this indicated quite clearly to Riley what she had long suspected about herself.

Annette hadn't been so sure of how she felt at first. They would drift apart for a few weeks before getting around to talking again and then, they would choose to forget one had reached for the other's hand during a movie or school play. More importantly, they seemed to always choose to forget how much they had enjoyed the fleeting contact in the moment. Their senior year, Riley and Annette attended a large party, not as a couple, though they spent most of the evening together and even danced to several songs. Afterwards, they'd kissed. It had begun as a shaky kiss, unsure of itself. It melted into a deep kiss, unashamed and passionate.

In the back seat of the car, they tangled their limbs; bodies and lips pressed up against each other, enjoying the release of subjugated longings. Riley had been the one to stop, pulling away from Annette just as her right hand hovered over Annette's left breast. A year earlier, she'd made a private determination that she would like to become a nun. She'd felt so sure about it; that it would be the right direction for her life.

She had felt such a strong connection to her faith and had told Annette about this before, but they hadn't spoken about it in months. Annette asked her what was wrong. Riley explained in jumbled, flustered words what she felt. Quietly, Annette cried and then became angry.

Riley couldn't quite understand. So often, when she'd made attempts at some form of affection, Annette had pulled away and Riley was the one left wondering if it was her or if Annette was still wrestling with questions about her sexual orientation. Other times, Annette had initiated it. This time, Annette left Riley sitting alone in the back seat of her car with the last words she would ever say to Riley echoing through her mind: "Damn it Riley, you're not a nun, yet."

A few weeks later, they graduated. Riley saw her there at graduation, but couldn't bring herself to go speak to her. She never saw her again. *I wonder if she's married now or at least sharing her life with someone,* Riley thought. *I hope she's happy.*

Suddenly, a new, chilling notion hit her like a block of ice; her heart nearly stopped. Was Annette even real at all? If what Arisu had said held any truth—

"Good," Dante said, turning in the passenger seat to look at Riley, "You are awake. How are you?"

Riley stared past him, out the windshield, and into oblivion. The memory seemed to morph in her mind. She recalled everything just as she had before, but something felt different. *Was it familiarity?* Was that it? *No,* she thought, *it lacks a sense of... pastness. Is that a word?*

"You alright?" Arisu looked back at her with concern.

Riley shook her head. "I don't know. It's almost like I don't feel... I... yeah."

"She'll be okay," Dante said to Arisu, settling back into his seat.

Riley looked out the window to her left. Buildings poked up from the ground along the horizon. The brown dirt stretched from the edge of the freeway to the buildings, interrupted by the occasional lifeless tree. A dense haze hung over the buildings. And even now, inside the car, Riley could smell the smoggy filth of booming civilization and industry.

"You should probably give her the new passport," Arisu said to Dante.

Fishing the passport out of an inner coat pocket, Dante handed it back to Riley. "This is your new identity."

"Newest, I think you mean," Riley said, dryly.

"Ah ha," Dante grinned.

Taking the passport, Riley flipped it open. "Lucky me," she rolled her eyes, "Most people only have to deal with having one identity. But not me, I'm going on my third now."

These words fell limply from her lips. She wished she could awake from this dream, but the mere fact that she was coming to immensely dislike this dreadful state of being had told her just how real it was.

"What do you think?" Arisu asked.

"What?" Riley snapped out of her inner despair.

"What do you think of your third identity?"

She realized that she had not bothered to read the name. Next to the photograph of her was the name: Janet Hume.

"It's alright," she sighed. "I can't really see myself as a 'Janet.'"

Arisu looked into the rear view mirror, locking onto Riley's eyes. "Hang in there. The depression's part of the process. You'll make it."

Her eyes returned to the road. A slight smile formed on Riley's lips.

"I'M GUESSING YOU DIDN'T plan for this," Thomas said.

"Oh, this is my lack of planning?" Rikard spat back.

The car sat on the roadside, its front left tire flat. Thomas kicked it and swore.

"I thought these things weren't supposed to pop," he said, leaning against the hood.

"It's technology, my friend," Rikard rolled his eyes. "When has technology been completely reliable? I mean, truly, one hundred percent of the time? Sure, it can help, but usually only for so long. Then, it bites us when we least expect. Nothing is ever one hundred percent."

Thomas wiped sweat from his face and straightened up. "You make technology sound like a shark."

Rikard approached Thomas, getting uncomfortably close. "Now you're catching on. All of this fun that Jones is having with microscopic robots and reprogramming people's brains," he paused for effect. "We're swimming with sharks, Tommy. So make sure you don't go bleeding in the water."

Thomas gave a slight nod, unsure of what he meant by that. Rikard turned and looked down the road. A large truck rushed past them, then a few cars.

"Check her location," Rikard ordered, "We might be able to catch up."

Thomas pulled out the tablet. He made the link up to the internet via his data signal and waited as the tracking application linked up. A warning popped up on his screen: *No available signal. Please check frequency.* He tried again. Once more the same message appeared.

"Starting to see what you mean about technology," he muttered.

"What?" Rikard spun about. "What do you mean?"

Thomas held out the tablet. Rikard stared at the message.

"Did you do it right?" he demanded.

"Of course I did it right."

"That has nothing to do with malfunctioning technology." Rikard said, pointing at the tablet. "Arisu's figured you out. She put in a combatant breed of nanobots to block your signal."

"Oh come on, that can't be it. How would she have figured it out?" Thomas protested.

Rikard came close again, "She's smart, my friend; brilliant, in fact. She was bound to think of this possibility or notice if anything was out of the ordinary with Riley. Don't look so surprised. Jones is well aware that she's got things figured out. That's why there's no room for mistakes. She'll take full advantage of every wrong move we make."

Rikard clenched his hands, then spread his fingers and whistled through his teeth. He turned and walked a short distance.

"Pack up," he said, "We're getting a new car."

"We'll never catch them now," Thomas called to him.

Rikard turned back. "They're headed to the airport, dipshit. Just use your brain. She's taking Riley back to Boston. She'll need a large international airport with flights in the US. Given the direction she's been headed, it's pretty fucking obvious she's headed to Guarulhos in São Paulo. It doesn't take a tracking system to figure that one out. Besides, even with the wonders of technology, flights still get delayed, especially such long-distance flights. Now, let's get moving!"

NOISE AND POLLUTION MELDED together in to a tumultuous miasma, performing a virulent assault upon the senses. People moved in every direction throughout the airport, circulating like blood through the massive arteries of iron, concrete, and glass that made up Guarulhos International Airport in São Paulo. Riley watched as a couple with two young girls hurried past, dragging their luggage behind them. Tears flowed down one little girl's face. Riley swallowed hard. Something about the girl reminded her of Tonya, one of the teachers at her school in Campo Grande. It suddenly hit her with a gut-wrenching force that the people she had shared her life with in Brazil were now in her past. She'd never even said goodbye and they would be worried beyond words at her sudden disappearance. In that moment Riley wished more than anything that she could just talk to Tonya, drink fresh coffee together, and try to make sense of this insanity, as they had so many other things.

A booming voice echoed over the cacophony, "Flight 112 will begin boarding in five minutes at Gate 23." This pulled Riley back to her present moment.

"Let's keep going," Arisu said.

Riley didn't move. Arisu looked into her eyes, but Riley stared past her. Reaching out, Arisu took her hand. Riley blinked, focusing on her eyes.

"Are you feeling alright?" Arisu asked.

"Yeah, it's just so strange. Everything feels like... a dream. I can't wake up, but I can't fall asleep either."

"It'll pass but right now, we have to keep going."

"Going where?" Dante walked up to them.

Arisu dropped Riley's hand and turned to him. "What?"

"Flight's delayed."

She sighed through gritted teeth. She turned back to Riley.

"Unfortunately, looks like we have time to kill after all. We should be careful. I'm sure Thomas is still after us. The tracking bots should be completely deactivated, but honestly, where else would we be going? He has to have figured that much out." She looked Riley up and down.

"What?" Riley took a self-conscious step back.

"We should really get you some new clothes."

"Okay," Riley shrugged. "Should I just put that on my credit card? I mean, it's not looking like Riley Bekker is going to be making her next payment anyway."

Arisu shrugged. "Nuns have credit cards?"

"Try paying for anything without a credit card these days," Riley said.

"Touché," Arisu smirked.

The three spent forty minutes in the shops. Shopping in an airport meant that Riley would leave the country looking very much like a tourist. She regretted not having been able to pack at all. She'd left it all behind. For a moment, that single thought threatened to undo her. She tried to push it aside. Thankfully, even her somewhat progressive order believed that an abundance of material possessions was not something to be encouraged. Riley had lived simply, so there wasn't much in the way of things to leave behind. Her life and friends on the other hand…

She pushed that thought away too. Back to shopping for clothes, she realized that she would very much miss her own clothing. She could buy pants and shirts here with no issue, but a comfortable bra or underwear? Who in the world buys intimates at the airport? Maybe she could find a shop that sold sports bras or something. As for any other possessions she had left behind, Riley figured she could still access her cloud drive with all her pertinent documents, music, movies, ebooks, scraps of writing that she thought she might do something with at some point, and her journal. She had one small bookshelf of books she'd never get back. Her heart sank as she reminded herself that none of those were really hers anyway. Would Violet even read the same kinds of books? How about music or films? What kind of people would she associate with? Did she have friends? A family? It would, no doubt, be different than it had been. But, how different? A wave of loneliness, like a powerful geyser, threatened to burst out from within her.

She wished she could call her housemates and hear their voices again, specifically Renata and Teresa. What must they be thinking right now? Would she remember them tomorrow? Ultimately, she wasn't really Riley Bekker. Soon she would leave much more behind than books and a journal—or even social preferences. She'd leave herself completely. *Is this what it feels like to have a terminal illness and know it*, she wondered. The answer came immediately to mind and she nearly dropped to her knees in the middle of the shop. *You're not dying, Riley. You're just going to stop exiting. The subtle difference being that, soon, there will be no trace left of you at all. You may just as well have never existed.*

"What's wrong?" Arisu asked.

Riley forced a grinned. "I think this shirt will work." She held up the blue t-shirt with a Brazilian flag that was nearly split in half by the deep v-neck that reflected the local sense of modesty.

"Do you like that?" Arisu asked her voice softer.

Riley smiled and shook her head. "Not exactly my style," she said. But her smile faded and she swallowed, "It doesn't really matter if I like it, does it? Whatever 'my style' is right now, it's about to vanish."

Arisu eyes remained steady. Riley could see something in them, a softness that connected with her. Arisu carried herself with a lot of confidence and strength, but her eyes, at times, allowed glimpses of the deeper complexity that must lie within. Still, Riley remained skeptical of how deep such caring might run. Often, Arisu seemed cold and distant. She was on a mission, it was clear. Riley's loss of self was likely little more than collateral damage.

"How about this?" Arisu said, pulling out a far more understated shirt with the logo of the São Paulo football team.

"Do you like it?" Riley asked, no longer feeling capable of caring.

"It should look good on you," Arisu nodded.

Barely aware of what she did, Riley paid for three shirts and two pairs of pants. Arisu had picked up a small leather bag. Riley purchased that as well, and then, she placed the extra clothing in it. Finding a restroom, she changed into the new, clean clothes.

"The flight will be boarding soon," Dante said as Riley came out of the restroom.

They stepped on to the long moving walkway that carried them through the airport. Riley observed as people on the other walkway were moving in the opposite direction. She found it amazing how much each human face could appear so familiar and yet so completely foreign, as she looked from one to the next. Then, her eyes locked on to a set of features she did recognize. Suddenly, she felt alert; a jolt of adrenaline shot through her.

"Run," she said.

Arisu looked at her, then to where she stared.

A few yards ahead of them on the opposite track, Thomas jumped over the rail and onto their moving walkway. A woman near him yelled in startled protest.

Arisu grabbed Riley's arm and pulled her in the opposite direction of the track. Dante stepped aside, letting them pass. Positioning himself between them and Thomas, he spread his feet and prepared for impact. Thomas pushed past several people, paying no attention to their loud objections. He stopped before Dante.

"Let it go, Thomas," Dante said.

"Not a chance."

"You know you can't get past me."

Riley strained her neck as she looked back at Dante. She saw Thomas make a move, but Dante blocked him.

"Here, jump." Arisu said.

She gripped the rail and swung her legs over. Riley followed.

"What about Dante?" Riley called after her.

"He's fine. We have to get to our terminal. Once we are cleared through security, they won't be able to reach us. This way."

She ran. Riley followed her, dodging people as best she could. They cut through a line of people waiting at a Starbucks. Someone yelled at them but they paid no attention. Stopping at another line of people before a set of elevators, Arisu looked back and forth.

"We need to get to the second level," she said.

"There," Riley pointed to a set of stairs beyond the elevator area.

They ran hard, proceeding up the steps quickly. Reaching the top of the stairs, they stopped.

"It's around here," Arisu said.

"Hello, Arisu."

Riley and Arisu turned quickly to face Rikard. He stood next to an interactive touch-screen map of the airport. He grinned with satisfaction.

"Are you surprised to see me?" he asked.

"You're working with Thomas?" Arisu said.

"Not really. It's more like, I caught him being a bad boy and now he has to do my bidding. But I still work for our dear old friend, Jones." Rikard took a step closer. "You remember him, don't you? He really misses you, Arisu. I miss you. It's so boring around the office without you there."

"Spare me," she spat.

"Actually, I was hoping you would spare me some trouble." Rikard looked at Riley, his confident grin slowly fading into seething anger. "Hand her over."

"Do you honestly think I'd do that?" Arisu said.

"You would if you had any idea what's in Violet's best interest." He looked at Arisu now, taking a step closer. "It's Violet you care about, isn't it? That's what this is really all about. Riley Bekker means nothing to you. What you really want is to have Violet back. How do you think that makes Riley here feel?"

"How dare you, Rikard?"

Rikard stepped even closer. "This is going to be a big mess, Arisu. You have no idea. It wasn't supposed to be this way. Don't let your old feelings blind you to that."

Riley looked at Arisu, whose eyes darted between Riley's and Rikard's.

"What's he talking about?" Riley said.

Swiftly, Rikard grabbed Riley's right wrist and twisted her arm behind her back. Arisu took a step forward but stopped.

"Easy there," Rikard spoke softly. "Let's not make a big scene."

"I think it might be too late for that. The little stunt Thomas pulled back there won't go unnoticed." Arisu said.

A yell in Portuguese drew their attention. Two airport security personnel ran at them. Arisu moved forward swiftly, kicking high with her left foot. With barely enough time to see the blur of movement, Rikard reached out and blocked her kick. There he stood, Riley's arm in his left hand, Arisu's foot in his right. He grinned.

"Well, this just got interesting."

He flung both aside. Riley hit the ground and rolled; her elbow and shoulder burning with pain. Arisu spun in place, but remained on her feet. Rikard grabbed Riley by the feet and drug her back, flinging her aside.

Riley pushed herself up in time to see Arisu strike three hard blows to Rikard's torso with her fists. He seemed unfazed. With one good openhanded hit to her sternum, Rikard launched her back. She hit the ground hard.

The guards pointed their handguns at Rikard. He raised his hands in mock surrender. One of the guards screamed orders that only Riley understood. The guard stepped closer to Rikard.

Riley picked herself up off the ground. The other guard yelled at her to stay down.

"I'm innocent," Riley said in Portuguese, "This man attacked us. We didn't do anything."

The guard closest to Rikard raised his gun higher. Rikard made a quick move to the side, grabbing the guard's extended arm. The gun fired. The interactive airport map exploded in a flash of electronic parts, glass, and sparks. Screams of surprise erupted in all directions. Rikard pulled the guard to him, head-butting him. As the guard fell, he took hold of the gun. The other guard turned and fired. Rikard ducked. The bullet hit the glass railing by the stairs, scattering shards. Rikard rolled. He fired one shot. The guard's left leg gave out.

Arisu ran at Rikard, who was still stooped low, delivering a swift kick to his face. He grabbed her feet and pulled her down. She yelled as her back hit the shards of glass.

Overcome by a sudden furry, Riley ran at Rikard as he stood up. She kicked his side. Rikard gasped. Riley stepped back then kicked again.

More guards approached quickly. Riley put up her hands.

Arisu swore as she rolled off of the shattered glass. She pushed herself to her knees and raised her hands.

The guards screamed at them, demanding that they stay still. A wave of dizziness rushed over Riley. *Well*, she thought. *I guess we're not going to make that flight now, are we?*

12 ELECTROX TMS

[W]ho you are depends on what your neurons are up to, moment by moment.

- David Eagleman

LEONARDO VIOLA SCRUNCHED HIS rough face as he looked at the passport. He wore his gray hair parted to the right, giving him a classically refined appearance. The uniform provided the requisite authority. He had a clean-shaven face, and had filled the room with his cologne the moment he entered.

"Riley Bekker," he said, each word heavily accented by his Portuguese. "You are in some trouble, no?"

Riley kept her eyes on the small metallic table in front of her. The cinder-block room felt as if it might be shrinking with every passing minute.

"What are you doing at the airport today?" Leonardo raised his inquisitive eyebrows, carefully watching Riley and acting as if he were an expert in the field of kinesiology, as it applied to nonverbal communication.

Riley spoke in Portuguese, "I was going to catch a flight with a couple of friends. We were going back to Boston. That's where I'm from."

Leonardo smiled. "You have good Portuguese," he said in his native tongue.

"Thank you," Riley looked up.

"And these two men," Leonardo spread his hands on the table. "They attacked you for no reason?"

Riley hesitated, wrestling with what she could and could not reveal.

Mentioning anything about Project Sleepwalker was out. It wouldn't take long in trying to explain how she had come to know Dante and Arisu before she would end up needing to bring up the project. That assumed that they had told her the truth about it in the first place. It would all certainly sound too bizarre. Hell, it still sounded damn near made up to her. What else could she say? Could she lie? She opened her mouth. Nothing came. Then…

"I am a witness for a controversial legal case in America regarding the misuse of some new technology. The man and woman I was with, Dante and Arisu, they are my handlers and were sent to take me safely back to America. I can only guess that these men who attacked us were sent by those who have much to lose if I return to Boston and testify in court."

Leonardo stood up straight. His eyes slowly widened as he regarded Riley carefully, scanning her face for any hint of deceit. Riley held his gaze calmly, her pulse surprisingly steady. She had done it. She had lied. Well, what she had said was essentially true, if not taken too literally.

"I see, Sister Bekker," Leonardo said. "It is good that you are honest with me. I have to say that I am surprised that a nun is involved in such things. What exactly is the case about?"

Riley shook her head. "I cannot reveal that. It would compromise my testimony… and my safety. But you're right, it is surprising that a nun is involved in such a thing, isn't it?" She smiled, in spite of herself.

"Huh," Leonardo nodded with a grin, either believing Riley or just playing along.

What was she saying? The words flowed out of her lips with ease. She fought within to maintain a cool exterior. *Who's coming up with this?* Her heart froze as she realized, *it's not me. I'm becoming someone else.*

Leonardo motioned to the guard that had been standing stiffly by the door the whole time. The guard stepped closer and Leonardo whispered in his ear. With a nod, the guard stepped out of the room. A cold spasm shot through Riley's body. *They're going to find out if my story checks out with Arisu and Dante.* Leonardo's attention returned to Riley.

"You must understand, Sister Bekker, we will need clear confirmation that what you say is true. One of my men is in the hospital. He will live, but his leg is badly injured."

"Of course," Riley said, "And I'm very sorry. But, please understand that it is one of these two men who attacked us, which shot your officer. That man is our enemy just as much as he is yours. All we wanted to do was peacefully board a plane to Boston."

"Believe me, this Rikard Luxford is most definitely our enemy. But I need to know if I can trust you."

Riley looked down at the table. What could she say next? More lies? The truth? Neither option seemed very helpful.

"Is there someone in America I can contact who may confirm your story?" Leonardo said. "Someone with… authority?"

Riley searched her mind. The all too obvious answer loomed over her, but still she scratched for a name, something that might work in her favor. Nothing came to her.

"I," she looked around the room, "I can't reveal such information."

Leonardo frowned. "How about the two people who were to take you back to Boston? Your handlers, could they give me some assistance?"

In desperation, Riley looked the man in the eyes and spoke softly but with conviction, "Mr. Viola, forgive me if I am out of line, but the three of us have done nothing illegal. We merely wanted to catch a plane. Unfortunately, we were intercepted by two thugs, whose job it is to prevent us from returning to Boston. And, so far, they have succeeded rather well."

"And what would you like me to do about this?"

"Apprehend the real criminals here. Let us go."

Leonardo laughed. "Oh yes. This would be the right thing to do, you say?" He leaned in, "Unfortunately, Sister Bekker, I have to fill out a report about this incident that has injured one of my men, damaged airport property, raised all kinds of security alerts, and made many people very afraid and angry. This will be on the national news. I would like to keep my job. I cannot let you walk out of here just like that. It would not look good."

The door opened and a guard stepped in. He whispered into Leonardo's ear. The man paused to consider the news that he had just received. Riley spread her fingers out on the table in front of her and breathed with deliberate control. Leonardo whispered something back to the guard. The guard nodded and whispered again. Riley pressed the palms of her hands hard against the cold table top. Had the guard attempted to confirm her story with Arisu or Dante? She felt sure that her cover had been blown. Leonardo sighed and nodded. He looked at Riley, not saying anything for a few seconds. Finally, he raised his eyebrows and opened his mouth. The man almost looked surprised.

"Sister Bekker," Leonardo said, "I want to thank you for your cooperation. We have just received confirmation from the FBI office in your nation's capital that you are indeed to be flown immediately to the United States so that you may testify in the Electrox TMS case. They have corroborated your information and have requested our assistance in returning you safely to Boston."

Riley's jaw dropped slightly, but she fought to remain as unmoved as possible. And yet, how could this be?

"We will make the proper arrangements. You and the two FBI agents will be on a flight to Boston in two hours."

Riley fought to keep her surprise and relief from showing too clearly. This was too good to be true. How in the world had this happened?

"Thank you," she said with a slight nod.

THE BATHROOM DOOR SHUT with a hollow clang that echoed off the tile walls. Locking the door behind her, Arisu stepped up to the mirror and removed her shirt. She twisted around so she could see her back in the mirror. Several small cuts and scratches marked her skin. None looked too deep. That didn't change how they felt, however. She dreaded the thought of having to sit on an airplane for the better part of ten hours with a sliced up back. *Fucking Rikard*, she thought.

Her shirt bore several cuts and blood stains. Blood stained her bra straps as well. She put her shirt back on and turned to the sink, placing her hands under the faucet. The sensor activated the water, and Arisu splashed her face. She really needed to clean and bandage the cuts; the worst of them, at least. She had about ninety minutes before they would be boarding their new flight to Boston. She dried her face and headed for the door.

Stepping out of the bathroom, she found Riley sitting on a small sofa in the waiting area of the airport transit police office. Riley stood immediately upon seeing Arisu. In her hands, she held a small first aid kit.

"Arisu," she said, "How are you?"

She smiled, "Isn't that what I usually ask you?"

"Switching things up, I guess."

She and Riley locked eyes. For a brief moment no words were exchanged. Arisu couldn't tell for sure what this meant, but she felt a subtle sense of familiarity in Riley's eyes that had not been there so far. *Maybe Violet is finally beginning to emerge*, Arisu wondered. *Or maybe it's just wishful thinking.* Riley finally looked away.

"Here," Riley gestured, "They gave me this. It's for you."

She held it out. Arisu looked down at it then back up to Riley.

"I'm not going to be able to bandage my own back," she smiled. "You're going to have to give me a hand."

"Oh, yea, of course," Riley nodded.

They stepped back into the bathroom that Arisu had just come out of minutes prior. Arisu pulled her shirt off as Riley locked the door. Tossing the shirt aside, she removed her bra as well and draped it over the sink. She stood before the mirror as Riley walked up with the first aid kit. Riley frowned as she stared at the cuts on her back. Arisu noted that she kept her eyes from venturing to the mirror.

"Does it hurt?" Riley asked as she opened up the first aid kit.

"A little," Arisu shrugged. "I've had much worse, believe me."

Riley touched Arisu's back, inspecting various cuts. "Looks like you might get off easy here. None of these look too deep. I think you can skip the stitches."

"Good," Arisu nodded.

Riley pulled out a disinfectant wipe and began to clean the cuts. "Sorry if this stings," she glanced up to the mirror, making eye contact with Arisu for only a second.

Arisu couldn't help but grin at how quickly her eyes darted back down. "Guess nuns don't get naked around each other too much, huh?"

"Not my order, at least," Riley said with an attempt at a grin, but unable to mask the growing redness in her face.

"So, uh," Riley said in a hushed voice, "help me understand something. How is it that we're leaving the country?"

Arisu shrugged. "That's Dante's doing. He and I used to work together in the FBI a few years ago. We still have inside contacts."

Riley looked up again in surprise. "So you are FBI agents. Or were, at least."

"Yeah."

"Were you going to mention that at some point?" Riley frowned.

"Didn't seem relevant," Arisu said, flatly. "Just keep it quiet. I don't have a badge to go flashing."

"What's this Electrox TMS thing?"

"It's a real case. It's a company that manufactures transcranial magnetic stimulation helmets. They had been targeting college and high school students needing exceptional grades to make it into Ivy League universities. They were encouraging students to use their products as an enhancement for major exams. It seems, however, you can get addicted to the stuff. They claimed they didn't know, but others claim they buried evidence from early tests that indicated the potential for users to get addicted. You supposedly have damning information to share with the jury."

"And Thomas and Rikard were sent to stop me?" Riley said. "Doesn't that paint Electrox in a bad light?"

"Sure does," she said, "But, trust me; they've already dug their own grave. A little more negative PR isn't going to change anything."

Riley chuckled and shook her head as she reached for a small bandage. "You two are something else."

She placed the bandage on a cut and reached for another. She was focused now and didn't speak. Arisu watched her reflection in the mirror, feeling each bandage go on with calculated precision.

"You know," Riley said, at last, "you're going to need a new shirt. You should have one of mine."

Arisu nodded then sighed.

RILEY TOSSED HER LONE carry-on bag into the over-head compartment. The tight space of the plane made her a little nervous, but she could not figure out what exactly triggered such feelings. They had been given first-class seats. At least the space was a little roomier there. She took her seat. Dante sat to her right, a magazine in hand.

"How did you do it?" Riley whispered.

"Do what?" Dante asked, keeping his eyes on the magazine.

"Get us out of here. You said I was a witness in a case. That was just something that I came up with off the top of my head in the interrogation room. How did you know?"

"You came up with that?" Dante turned to Riley, his lips forming a slight grin.

"Wait, you did that?"

"You might as well know, Riley," Dante said, setting his magazine down. He leaned closer, speaking softer now. "You and I are not so dissimilar. We both have highly active microscopic machines swirling through our bodies. The only difference is that mine help keep me alive. I have a serious brain tumor. They keep it under control while repairing my brain by creating entirely synthetic cells to replace corrupt ones. Or, at least, they're trying."

Riley looked down. "Wow!"

"But I've also had myself equipped with a breed of nanites that give me the ability to communicate with the Sleepwalker nanites."

Riley looked up at him, mouth open. It took her a minute, but finally she said, "It was you. You… hacked my brain?"

"Suggestibility," Dante held out a hand, "Think of it as a very low level hypnosis. I merely suggested a way out. You did the rest. Or, maybe I should say, Violet did the rest."

"Who are you?" Riley said. "I mean, who are you really?"

Dante nodded, "You used to know me as Fred Arnold. Federico Arnold. Not my real last name, but it's what I'm know as, by some."

Riley felt a wave of dizziness. *Where's Arnold?* In her mind's eye, she could see Dante's face, but he stood in a white room with counters and computers. Riley gripped her head as pain washed over it.

"I used to know you," she said though gritted teeth. "We worked together… on the project."

Riley shook. She gasped for air as she sat up. Tears fell from her eyes. She looked at Dante with new recognition.

"You," she said, her voice nothing more than a hoarse whisper. "You had a wife and two children. They're dead now."

Dante nodded, his eyes moving away.

Arisu sat down next to Riley. She looked at both of them with concern.

"I remember Arnold," Riley said.

A slowly forming smile took Arisu's lips. "Good. Is there anything else? Does that bring anything else to mind?"

Riley concentrated, taking deep breaths. Her eyes closed. What she saw in her mind was a barrage of images, most of which made no sense to her. Some of them she had recognized, such as a park to which she had been or a person with whom she had worked, but seeing so much, all at once, felt overwhelming and freighting. There was a warehouse, computer screens, a syringe, people in white lab coats, charts and graphs, programming code scrawled out on a marker board-the images continued to rapidly fly by, seemingly with no end.

"There are places, some people—I think I've worked with some of them," Riley said.

"Do you know any of them?" Arisu pressed.

"Arisu," Dante broke in.

She looked at him. He shook his head.

"Leave her be for now," he cautioned. "All in good time, right?"

Riley looked at Arisu, whose eyes remained steady, but Riley could sense her disappointment all the same. A twinge of suspicion gripped Riley's heart, but she shook it off. Too much was happening, she was just tired. She let her head fall back against her seat.

"When will I wake up?" she asked.

"All in good time," Arisu whispered, looking back at Dante.

JONES STARED AT THE screen.

"They will be reaching Boston in about ten hours." Rikard's image said.

Jones sighed. He clenched his hands, knuckles popping.

"In ten hours," he whispered, "In ten hours, these three little inconveniences will become a liability cluster fuck. Arisu will launch a war on this project. How did this happen? I have these damn politicians breathing down my neck all day long. And they don't know the half of it. And it sure as hell better stay that way."

"Isn't Arisu's plan merely to blow the whistle?" Rikard said.

"Yes, that is her plan at this moment. That may change if she learns the truth. That can't happen, you hear me. Not like that. We have to contain this mess, get it all back on track. There will be no way to explain ourselves to the press, the White House, or anyone else, should any of this get out. CNN, the BBC, and Buzz Feed are already catching on to this story. There are too many rumors; too many human rights protests from the conspiracy nuts. We need this to go down quietly." Jones groaned. "Damn it! Thomas really fucked this up. Make sure he doesn't do anything else."

"Doubt he can do that from a Brazilian jail cell," Rikard muttered.

"Oh, don't you worry," Jones sighed, "Arisu might have tricks up her sleeves, but she's not the only one."

"But who is she in contact with?" Rikard asked; his eyes narrow.

"She's clearly getting help from someone with serious influence."

"That is none of your concern," Jones said, "whatever seemingly influential people that Arisu might have on her side will be dealt with in due time. Just sit tight for now, I'll get you back here as soon as I can.

"And Thomas? Let him rot in a Brazilian jail?"

Jones sighed and pressed his lips together, thinking for a moment. "Too much of a liability, He'll blab. Bring him along for now, but when the time is right, we'll scrub him."

13 THE FACILITATOR

Over hundreds of thousands of years, our genes have evolved to devote more and more resources to our brains, but the truth is, we can never be smart enough. Unlike our forebears, we may soon not need to wait for evolution to fix the problem.

- D. T. Max

SHE MIGHT HAVE SEEN the place before, but she couldn't be sure. She looked it over. The grass on the hill was short. The sky was a clear blue with only a couple small clouds—your basic childhood painting. The tree provided good shade. She settled herself against the base of the tree and looked down the hill. It sloped down and eventually leveled off. Beyond that, grass stretched out to the horizon. It was like the hill was an island in a vast sea of green. She found it both perplexing and relaxing.

"Do you like?" a delicate female voice asked her.

She stood, looking for the woman.

"Who are you?" She asked the woman.

"I'm your helper," the woman answered, stepping out from behind the tree. She wore white. Her blond hair flowed past her shoulders.

"I think I've seen you before," she said. "What's your name?"

"I am Sophia," said the woman. "But the more important question is: Who are you? Or rather, who do you believe you are?"

"I'm… Riley," she said. But the moment she spoke the words, their falsehood travelled through her body like a tense muscle contraction, starting in her heart and slowly rippling out to each of her extremities. "No. No, I'm not." She looked to Sophia for help.

Sophia walked around the tree and looked down the hill. Riley took a step closer to her.

"What's happening to me?" she said. "Where am I right now?"

Sophia turned to her. "This is merely a transitional stage meant to facilitate re-emergence of the original personality."

Riley shook her head, her eyes wide; mouth open. Her hands trembled slightly. "This isn't real. And you…"

She reached out to touch Sophia's shoulder. The woman smiled and reached out, taking Riley's hand, her skin warm and soft.

"I am merely here to help you become," Sophia said, her green eyes bright, her smile warm and inviting.

"Am I asleep?"

Sophia nodded, letting go of her hand. "You have been asleep for a very long time."

"How long will this take?"

"It's difficult to say at this point. The integration of the new system of nanomachines within your brain is going to take some time. The system has not been able to determine how long it will take to complete the process. So far, this program has been installed and the general process has begun. It will happen eventually. In the meantime, I am here to present to you several options. You can choose to remain in this state of lucid dreaming, or we can let you sleep. If you stay in this state, we recommend that you participate in a series of exercises that may help your original personality become conscious. Doing so will help expedite the recovery process."

"What would that be like?"

The world around Riley became a mesh of blended colors as if she were standing within the surrealistic world of an expressionist painting; in the same vein as a Picasso, Pollock, or Escher. Slowly, shapes began to take form again. After a moment, they were standing in a dimly lit room—or at least she assumed it was a room. She saw no walls in any direction. A large wooden desk and chair sat in the middle of the hardwood floor.

"Please," Sophia walked to the chair and pulled it out from under the desk. "Have a seat."

The place was utterly silent apart from Sophia's voice. In fact, Riley couldn't even detect the beating of her own heart. Walking over to the desk, Riley sat. Looking down, she saw that her feet were bare and that she wore a comfortable tank top and shorts. Sophia opened a drawer and removed from it a yellow legal pad and pen. She placed them on the desk before Riley.

"What do I do with this?" Riley asked.

Sophia leaned closer to her and whispered, "Write about yourself; every little and insignificant memory; every major memory. Write it all down as it comes to you."

"What if what I write is not really who I am?"

Sophia walked around the desk. Riley watched her graceful movements. She seemed to flow through the air with exceptional fluidity and appeared almost to glow in the dim light of this abstraction of a room. Riley was reminded of images of angels or of mythological creatures like Tolkien's tall and nimble elves, which had been inspired by Norse mythology. "There is no magic to this. It's not like choosing between pills of differing colors to decide which life is real. You will be able to tell the difference when you read them. Trust me."

Sophia took a seat on the left corner of the desk and watched her. Riley stared at the paper for a long time, unsure of what to write or even how slowly or quickly time might be passing by her while she was in this state. At last, the tip of the pen touched the paper. She scratched out the words, "Sonic Hedgehog." She looked up. Sophia gave her a warm smile. Riley felt strangely drawn to her, shocked at how suddenly attracted to her she felt. How could it be that Sophia was not real? Smiling back at her right then, she appeared so real.

"Keep going," Sophia gently prompted.

Riley looked back at the paper. Again, she paused for a long time. The words she had already written made no sense to her. She suspected that this would be how most of what she wrote would come to her, out of the quintessence; the luminiferous aether. It wouldn't really be Riley writing. Suddenly, she scribbled something new on the pad. She stared at the word then looked up to Sophia.

"Brown?" Riley asked.

Sophia smiled. She could feel the warmth of that smile. How could she convey such feeling to her when she admitted to being a program?

"I feel like I know you," Riley said.

"You do."

"Who are you?"

"Sophia, I am here to facilitate—"

"—No. I mean, why are you here; in my mind; wherever this is? Come on, sweetie; give me something to work with here."

Riley's own words and tone surprised her. What was she saying? Riley stared at Sophia's smooth face and swallowed hard, awaiting some kind of answer. None came. Sophia just smiled at her.

"It's not really me talking, is it?" Riley said.

"It is and it isn't. It is you, but not you; not as you currently know yourself."

Riley let her head hang. "But why are you my facilitator?"

"I represent that which you are most comfortable with."

She reached out and touched Riley's face gently but Riley pulled away.

"I don't know you," Riley protested.

"You don't feel that you know me at this time, but that will change."

"No," she shook her head. "What if I don't want it to change? What if I don't want to be someone else? What if I don't want to be Violet Murphy? I didn't ask for this! What if I'm happy as Riley Bekker?"

Riley shot to her feet, knocking the chair over. The world swirled around her in a mesh of colors once more. She felt overwhelmed with dizziness. Suddenly, the ground beneath her bare feet gave way and she felt herself falling. She tried to scream, but no noise came from her open mouth.

RILEY SAT UP. THE plane engine whined steadily. She could feel the motion and the slight unsteadiness of flight. A sour taste filled her mouth. She looked around the cabin. Dante napped. Arisu opened her eyes and turned to her. She seemed tired, yet she was alert enough to notice something was bothering Riley. She leaned closer.

"What's the matter?" Arisu asked.

"Technical problems," Riley answered automatically.

Riley blinked, shaking the feeling that she was still in the strange world of the dream.

"What did you say?" Arisu demanded.

"What?" she blinked again, trying to adjust her eyes. "Did I say something?"

"Yeah, I thought you said 'technical problems.' Were you dreaming?"

Riley looked at her, trying hard to remember what had just happened. There had been a desk, yellow paper, Sophia... yes. She nodded.

"I *think* it was a dream," Riley said. "It was really strange. I was in this room—no, wait. First I was on this hill, by a tree."

"You were in a lucid dream," Arisu said.

Riley looked at her. Though it should have been no surprise to her that Arisu would have a fairly good idea of what was taking place in her mind at such a time. She never ceased to be caught off guard by how Arisu so easily saw through her. Would anything really ever surprise Arisu? The way she sprang into action at the airport, she seemed unfazed by every new challenge. Who was this woman, really?

Arisu smiled and continued, "It's the serum working on you. The system is trying to do its homework. The memories you have of being Violet can never be fully erased. They are there, somewhere. But for the system to be able to bring Violet back, it has to map out the routes to such memories and then assemble the parts. It's one very complicated puzzle, you know?"

"Yeah, I can imagine," Riley sighed, "So, by the time we land, I'll be Violet?"

"Theoretically," Arisu nodded, but looked away.

"What? What do you mean?"

134

She looked back at Riley, but eyes still wandering away quickly. "There have been significant problems in reawakening some test subjects. Sometimes the process is fairly successful. Other times…"

Riley waited. "*Other* times?"

Arisu shook her head and sighed. "There have been cases in which the subjects never truly come out of the lucid dream meant to facilitate the original personality's reawakening."

"*What*? You mean I might slip into one of these dreams and never quite come out of it? I could end up in a coma?" Riley let her head fall back. "What are we doing? It would have been nice if you two might have mentioned, 'Oh by the way, you could wind up in a coma.'"

"Those are rare cases. It's just a complicated procedure. I don't quite understand it myself. Violet tried to explain it to me a few times, but I can't recall all of it. But we need Violet. We need what she knows. And this is the only way I know to get her back."

Riley brought her head forward slowly and faced Arisu, "Why do you need Violet so badly? Can't you stop the project without her?"

Arisu's eyes wandered slightly but Riley waited.

"Violet knew all the ins and outs of the project. Before she was even hired, she had already developed most of the theoretical models that led to the early breakthroughs in the project. It's why she got the job. But, she discovered major problems as the testing went on. She was going to blow this all wide open and…"

"And then, they reformatted her hard drive and installed happy little ol' me. Oops."

"Well, not exactly. They can't actually reformat the brain. The memories are still there."

"Yeah, yeah, I get it. Whatever it really means," Riley waived a hand. She stopped and stared off into space. "Though, technically, all the files still exist on a reformatted hard drive; which is why they can be recovered with the proper software. That's why the FBI and CIA format drives, then overwrite them with random information, format them again, and then, repeat that process several times."

"Well," Arisu grinned, "now that sounded a little more like Violet then Riley."

Riley looked back at her frowning. "I think I read that somewhere."

"I'm sure you did," Arisu nodded.

Riley rubbed her face with both hands, taking in a deep breath.

"You should rest," Arisu said.

She reached out and brushed some hair away from Riley's face. Riley looked at her, surprised. Arisu froze, hand in the air. Riley could see something in her eyes. Was that longing? Somewhere inside, she knew her suspicions about Arisu to be right. Arisu pulled her hand away.

"There's more, isn't there?" Riley asked.

"More what?"

Riley leaned closer to Arisu and lowered her voice. "Just tell me the truth. You don't need Violet only because she can somehow stop the project, do you? There's more to this rescue operation than I've been told. In fact, I suspect there's much more to this than either one of you has been willing to tell me so far."

Arisu looked down and said nothing. Riley waited. When she didn't move, Riley slouched back in her seat.

"I'm dying, Arisu," she said. "The least you could do is to tell me the truth. I have a right to know. Maybe it doesn't seem to you like it should matter. After all, I'll be gone in a few hours. But this, this is all I know; being Riley Bekker. Can you understand that? I have nothing else to hold on to." She sat forward again. "Do you have any idea what it's like to be told that your whole life is a lie, that it's…" she pressed her lips together as her throat tightened and tears threatened to overwhelm her eyes. "Artificial. A fabrication."

"You're not dying." Arisu looked up. A tear clung to her left eye for an instant before it succumbed to gravity's eternal pull and slid down her pale cheek.

"Then what am I doing?" Riley said, working hard to keep her voice from wavering. "From where I'm sitting, it feels like dying. Call it whatever you like. But when it comes right down to it, it will be Violet who walks off this plane, not me. We are different people, Arisu. I will no longer exist. Maybe it sounds really selfish, but the way I see it, that's a pretty big deal. It will be easy for you and Dante. You can carry on with your little crusade. But it has nothing to do with me, really. Nothing. And if what you tell me is true, I'm as good as dead. Oh sure, this body may not die, but *I'm* as good as dead. Riley Bekker will just vanish forever."

She put her head in her hands, taking in a deep breath. Wiping tears away, Riley looked at Arisu once more.

"The worst part of it..." she stopped. "The worst part is that once I'm gone, there's nothing. There's no heaven or hell. Not even some kind of purgatory. No afterlife whatsoever for lucky Riley. I've never once read a passage in the Scriptures or in any other major religious books in all of my studies that mention anything about where artificial personalities wind up when they're uninstalled. Have you? 'Cus maybe I just missed that part."

Arisu avoided her eyes.

"But maybe I should join the First Church of the Singularity," Riley forced a smile then sighed heavily with a new realization. "All of my studies, my religious devotion; all of that is probably artificial as well, isn't it? At any rate, you'll have to forgive me if I'm less than enthusiastic about having my... *operating system* overwritten."

Riley leaned back into her seat and closed her eyes. Arisu sighed, looking straight ahead.

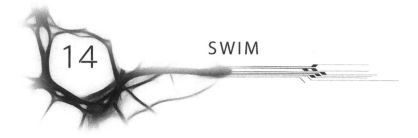

14 SWIM

It is suicidal to create a society dependent on science and technology in which hardly anybody knows anything about that science and technology.

- Carl Sagan

THE WHINE OF THE plane engines grew louder. Thomas felt sure his ears were already popping with the pressure change. He tried to make himself comfortable in the fake leather seat. When he attempted to lean it back, he discovered the lever was broken. He swore under his breath, knowing how much longer the flight would seem in light of this. An announcement crackled over the intercom, but he paid no attention. He looked down at his hands, resting them on his lap. What would he do now? What could he do now?

"What's wrong with you?" Rikard said, taking the seat next to him.

Thomas looked up, "Oh, nothing. Tired, I guess." He looked away, but he could feel Rikard's eyes locked on him.

"Get a drink," Rikard said. "Get something hard, relax. We have a long flight ahead of us. Then, it's right back to work. Jones will be all over us. But what's new?"

"Yeah," Thomas said, still keeping his gaze focused on anything to his right, away from Rikard. "It's been a while since I've flown in one of these small jets."

Rikard laughed, "Fast suckers. But it'll help make up for the delays. Luckily, Jones has his own rather important political connections. So we get to play the game Arisu's been apparently playing. It sure wasn't looking too good there for a while. All the same, I'm sure he'll be more than pissed with the little airport stunt we pulled. And I guess Arisu must have a few more tricks up her sleeves than I gave her credit. Told you she was smart. But, we've got Jones, and Jones has very powerful friends."

Thomas took in Rikard's words, noting how slickly he spoke. Was this rehearsed? It wasn't like Thomas knew Rikard well, but he'd always appeared enigmatic. There always seemed to be something behind his eyes, some secret knowledge. Rikard might not be the smartest person in a given room based on IQ alone, especially at the project, but he met every situation with the confidence of one who knew far more than others realized.

"'Friends' might be too strong a word," Thomas muttered. He turned to Rikard. "What happened, exactly? You told me to surprise them. You were right about Arisu. She grabbed Riley and took off. But why the fight? In the airport, no less?"

Rikard grinned and shook his head. "Ah, business and pleasure."

"What?"

"Arisu is good, but she has a certain level of predictability. Maybe I got a little carried away, but I wanted to see what she would do. Oh, you should've seen her face when she saw me. The look in her eyes when I had Riley. She's loosing it, Tommy boy. I'm starting to doubt she can keep it together long enough to pull off her little mission."

"You mean to say that you had no intention of stopping them?"

"Of course I did. The whole stunt was a stall tactic. We all get into a little scuffle in a major Brazilian airport and no one leaves the country for a while. What I didn't count on is that they have more connections than any of us realized. That was an oversight. We thought we could hold them there for a while longer, connect them to something unrelated— drug trafficking, or worse, information trafficking—and, bam, our three friends would have been stuck in Brazil for a good while, wrapped in a downward spiral of questions and red tape. That's what they should have done with the bitch in the first place. Make her a convict, slam her behind some bars. We could have controlled her better; kept her close, but out of the way. Arisu couldn't have gotten to Riley so easily. But no,

Jones wanted a whole different country. Something about other factors at play— Blah, blah, blah." Rikard watched Thomas with a broad grin.

Thomas examined Rikard's expression. The man looked as if he might be in a trance. Thomas shook his head then leaned it back on his seat. As he did, the plane jerked and began a slow forward motion.

"Finally," Rikard sighed.

NEARLY AN HOUR INTO the flight, Thomas fell asleep. Rikard shifted in his seat and scrutinized the man next to him. His breathing was indicative of a person quickly entering deep sleep. Satisfied, Rikard rose from his seat and walked down the narrow aisle of the plane. The majority of the seats remained empty. A few diplomats and business people sat in scattered seats. Rikard made his way to the back. Finding an empty seat with no one directly around him, he sat down. A phone hung on the back of each seat. He plucked the receiver off its perch and dialed.

"Jones, it's Rikard," he said, keeping his voice low.

"How's the flight?" Jones asked.

"Smooth enough, so far," Rikard looked up as the one stewardess walked past him. She smiled politely at him, he returned the smile.

"How's Thomas holding up?" Jones said.

"He's asleep right now. You want me to bring him in right away once we land?

"Yeah," Jones grunted. "We'll be sure to give him the royal treatment."

"Any clue as to who's going to bat for Arisu? Didn't expect this turn of events."

"I think it's safe to say she's got some influential friends. CIA? FBI? We have enemies in both."

"I'm willing to bet your friends hold more sway," Rikard grinned.

"Sleep, Rikard," Jones said, "Get some rest. I'm sure creating an international incident is positively exhausting."

"Is that sarcasm I sense?" Rikard pressed.

"Just don't make things worse."

"What's the fun in that?" Rikard shrugged.

Jones sighed into the phone. "Did you have to shoot that poor bastard in the leg? You have no idea the shit I had to pull in order to get you two out of Brazil."

"I'm grateful, as always."

"Yeah, whatever. Just get back here in one piece before things get totally out of control," Jones said and hung up the phone.

Rikard hung his phone up as well. Returning to his seat, he leaned it back, but sleep did not come to him for quite some time.

RILEY REACHED OUT AND touched the rose. The lone flower grew from a porcelain pot that sat on the windowsill. The sun poured in through the open window. She felt the warmth on her face. A light breeze brushed against her skin, inviting her to walk outside. She took in a deep breath and wished she could cry. *I've known this place before,* she thought. Her fingers brushed over the petals of the rose and a sharp pain shot though her hand. Riley jerked it away from the flower. Two of her fingers bled. Bewildered, she stared at them. Looking at the rose again, she could see blood on the petals where the petal's edge had sliced into her flesh.

"It hurts, doesn't it?" Sophia asked.

Riley turned to face her. She wore white as before. Her red hair flowed down over her shoulders. Hadn't she been a blond before? Riley felt lost and confused. She observed as Sophia moved closer. She wore no makeup, yet her facial features were distinctly clear and beautiful. The room they stood in was nothing but a yellow cube. The only way in or out appeared to be the window behind Riley.

"What's happening?" asked Riley.

"This is the entrance to your memories."

Riley looked down at her hand, "Why did I get cut?"

Sophia smiled and took a step closer to her. Taking Riley's cut hand into hers, she said, "Isn't memory the most fascinating thing. There are those who would like to define reality through pain, convinced that the only assurance we can have of our experience of reality lies in pain. In the absence of pain, what we experience seems too good to be true."

"But I can feel pain here," Riley said. "How can that be? This isn't real."

"Oh, it isn't?" Sophia cocked her head to one side.

"It can't be real. You're not real."

"What are you experiencing? What do you see, hear, and feel right this very moment?"

Riley shook her head, "This is a dream. It's a just a lucid dream."

"And a dream is experienced by the mind. What's to make this less real than the outside world? You have no direct access to the world around you. Sounds, colors, touch... these are the manifestations of a neurological language that allow you to experience the world in a certain and highly specific way. But, in the end, your experience is still defined by the firing neurons trapped in the solitude of your skull."

"So you're saying this is just as real as my waking life?"

"Try not to think in terms like 'just as real.' Think of this as just another aspect of the totality of your experiences," Sofia said with a smile.

Sophia brushed her finger tips over the cuts on Riley's fingers. Her throbbing cuts stung. She cringed.

"What are you experiencing?" Sophia asked.

"Pain."

"Just pain?"

Riley looked into her eyes, unsure of what this meant. Sophia smiled, and Riley felt a sort of flutter in her stomach. Blood rushed to her face—or at least it felt that way.

"No, not just pain," Riley smiled.

"What then?"

"Pain and beauty."

"Very good. You see, this is the experience of life we all have: pain and beauty. Your memories are no different. The life of the mind is measured in memory and imagination. Inevitably, these two commingle. You remember things as you *wish* to remember them. The beautiful may become gloriously beautiful in your memories while the less than ideal aspects fall away into the oblivion of forgetfulness. On the other hand, the painful might become the worst of your nightmares, the horror of an experience amplified by new fears and anxieties."

Riley looked away, considering this. The walls slowly shifted to a light pink color. She looked back at the window. The flower still sat there. She glanced back at Sophia.

"Subjectivity," said Riley.

Sophia nodded and stepped closer to her, "You can only experience life as yourself; dream or not."

"But, what about Project Sleepwalker? I can have memories that I never experienced."

"This is true, but there is another problem."

Riley waited for her to speak, but she didn't. Riley frowned and asked, "What's the other problem?"

"I think you know."

Riley looked off, trying to figure out what she was driving at. The walls again shifted in color. This time they became a dark blue.

"Wait," Riley said, "The problem is that... it's... I have these memories, but that doesn't necessarily make me that person. Something like that, isn't it?"

Sophia nodded.

"So, what do I do now?"

"Experience and become," Sophia said, her voice low as her eyes remained locked on Riley.

Riley frowned and cocked her head to one side. "What does that mean?"

"Look," Sophia pointed past her.

She turned to the window. Outside she could see a beach. Waves rolled in and crashed, measuring its impact by leaving behind a line of salty white foam strewn across the bright, yellow sand. Riley looked back to her. Sophia's eyes shone bright in the sunlight that slipped in through the open window. A slight, crisp, salty breeze filled the room. Sophia said nothing, but her eyes pleaded, *Go.*

Turning to the window, Riley picked up the rose. Not knowing what to do with it, she turned to Sophia. She reached out to hand it to her. Sophia shook her head and pointed again. Riley turned back to the window. Taking the flowerpot with her, she climbed through. She realized for the first time that her feet were bare the moment they touched the warm sand. Had they been bare inside? She looked down at them and grinned. It probably didn't matter. They may or may not have been. Had she even had feet a moment ago? She hadn't bothered to notice. The world, in which she now stood, did not have to obey the laws of physics, though the sunlight felt warm on her skin and even made her squint. Things were free to change at will. There were no constraints upon her ability to exist solely within three dimensions.

She looked back at the window, but only found distant Californian mountains behind her. Sophia must not have followed her through. Turning back to the beach before her, Riley walked out to the waves, letting them rush up to her toes. The foaming salt water splashed against her feet and she gasped at the chill it sent throughout her body.

Without a thought as to why, she dropped to her knees. Water splashed up, striking her face. As a drop ran over her lips, she tasted the salt. Reaching down to the sand before her, Riley began to dig. She scooped away the soaked sand, leaving behind a small cavity in the shore. She placed the flowerpot into the hole and then, she pushed the sand back into it. The rim of the pot peeked out above the sand. She smiled, sighed with an accomplished satisfaction, and then, she rose to her feet, gazing out over the immeasurable ocean. Only a few light clouds drifted through the spacious and immutably blue sky. The sun remained high.

"This is where it begins and ends." Sophia said.

Riley turned, surprised. Sophia was walking along the beach, coming towards her. Sophia stopped next to Riley and looked down at the rose in the sand.

"What happens next?" Riley asked.

"You swim," Sophia stretched her arm out over the never-ending water.

"What?! Out into that? The void?"

Riley looked out over the ocean again, and took in a deep breath.

"I'm not real sold on this idea," Riley muttered.

"Don't worry," Sophia said softly as she reached out and took her hand. "You don't have to swim the entire ocean. Just start."

Sophia stepped forward, and pulled Riley gently along. Riley followed her in to knee-deep water; the water's chill now less than that first splash against her bare toes. A wave rolled in, striking against them. Sophia laughed and, for a second, Riley was convinced that she had known this woman all her life.

"Who are you?" Riley said.

"I am here to help you; that is all you need to know for right now."

"I know you, don't I?"

"I am that which you once knew best."

"What does that even mean?"

Sophia smiled and kissed her lightly on the cheek. Her lips lingered by Riley's face. "Swim," she whispered. "Just swim."

She backed away.

"You're not coming with me?" Riley said, trying to mask the trepidation behind those words.

"This is your journey. I am merely here to help it along," Sophia smiled. She turned and started for the shore.

"Will I see you again?"

Turning back, she laughed. "Of course, I'll be with you the whole way. Right to the very end; as always."

Riley stood there, mouth open, trying to understand what she meant. Another wave struck her. The splash of cold water brought her back. Sophia stayed put, watching her.

"Okay," Riley nodded, "Here goes."

She leapt forward, diving into the water. The cold enveloped her. She began swimming. After a few yards, she stopped long enough to look back. Sophia still stood in her spot near the shore. She waved.

Riley waved back. Then, she turned to swim again. With each stroke, she felt the water grow warmer. She brought her head out of the water to take a breath and then, she submerged her face into the water and took another stroke.

She opened her eyes underwater. A light green cloudiness surrounded her. She felt at peace. She didn't go up for a breath. In fact, she felt no need for air. She stopped swimming and floated, enjoying the feeling of weightlessness. She relaxed her entire body, no longer feeling the water's chill. A light glowed beneath her, growing in intensity until it overcame her sight. She surrendered to the light. Her eyes closed. Any sense of direction had vanished. Riley released herself to the beckoning bliss, which was paralyzing her entire being. She was unsure of how long she had been encapsulated inside this womb of light. She had no way to measure the passage of time. As a matter of fact, she wondered if time could even penetrate this state of mind. If she could feel pain and beauty, then she could assume the existence of space. And, where there is space, there must be time, right?

Her feet touched a dry surface and she opened her eyes. Within the dark cavern around her, the walls of an old warehouse materialized. Then, from the darkness came a burst of flickering, then solid light. She looked the place over, noticing the stairs off to the left which led upward. She could see office doors on the second level. The musty air felt familiar, but she could not place it.

Sophia stepped up next to her. She looked at her, then back at the empty warehouse. Riley opened her mouth to speak, but Sophia touched her shoulder and shook her head. She pointed to the stairs. Riley nodded, and walked to the metallic staircase. Taking the first step, she stopped and looked back to Sophia, who nodded encouragingly. Riley carried on. Stopping at the first door she encountered, she nudged it. The door swung open with a slight creek. An unmade bed sat in one corner. The light blue walls were covered with glow-in-the-dark stars. The open window at the far end of the room allowed a light breeze to travel through. A little boy with short, dark hair played with a toy space shuttle. He turned to face Riley.

"Hi," the boy said.

Unable to say anything, Riley lifted her hand and waved.

"Do you think that we'll ever go live on Mars?" the boy said, walking over to Riley.

She knelt down, "I don't know. What do you think?"

"We better."

"Why is that?"

"This planet's too small."

"But Mars is smaller than Earth."

"Yeah, but there's no oceans on Mars. And two planets are better than one."

Riley laughed, "You might be right. Who do you think should go?"

"I'll go," the boy shouted.

He ran to his bed and jumped on it. Riley took a step into the room. To her right, stood a dresser. On top of the dresser sat some kind of space station built from Legos. The multi-level structure stood almost a foot high from its base. Several translucent tubes connected it together. Little men in space suits stood about. A six-wheel rover sat on a ramp.

"Did you build this?" she asked the boy.

The boy laughed, "No, stupid. You built it."

It was Riley's turn to laugh. "I don't remember building it."

"That's exactly your problem!" the boy screamed, suddenly angry. "You never remember anything! Anything!"

The boy threw himself down on his bed and stared at the ceiling. Riley stepped closer. Tears welled up in his eyes. Riley knelt next to the bed.

"What's wrong?" Riley whispered.

The boy remained motionless, the tears flowing freely down his blushing face.

"Do you know why you are here?" Sophia asked.

Riley looked back to the doorway where she now stood and shook her head, swallowing hard.

"Then come with me," Sophia beckoned with an outstretched arm. "Come with me and I will help you."

"What about the boy?" Riley asked. "Will he be okay?"

"I think you already know," she said with a smile and a certain glow in her eyes that stirred something deep inside of Riley.

She stood, taking a step closer to Sophia. Their eyes remained locked. Riley longed to reach out and touch her. She wanted to kiss her again, to hold her close. Instead, she stopped before her and stood silent. Her eyes broke away from Sophia's. *It's just a dream*, Riley told herself.

"You seem so keenly aware that this is a dream," Sophia said, reaching out and taking her hand. "Come."

A river of warmth broke loose inside Riley's chest at Sophia's touch. "Okay."

Sophia led her out of the room. There remained no evidence of the warehouse, which she had been in moments ago. They walked down a long white hallway. A single lonely picture hung on the wall. Sophia brought her to it and stopped.

"Do you see it?" she asked.

Riley squinted, straining her eyes. She saw shapes. She had to fight for strength to keep her eyes on the picture. She blinked several times, attempting to gain control over her vision. Her hands came up in front of her face and she fought to pull them back down.

"Don't look with your eyes," Sophia said.

"What?" Riley gasped at this absurd statement, "How?"

"This is not physical reality. You don't need your eyes. Enter into the picture, become one with it."

Riley looked at her, still confused, "I still say this is a dream and you're— 'an undigested bit of beef. There's more of gravy than of grave about you, whatever you are!' Humbug! Ha!"

Sophia ignored the quip or, at least, it seemed she did. She smiled at Riley in a soft, comforting way that felt distinctly familiar. After a brief pause, Riley exhaled in resignation. Looking back at the painting with an immediate sense of remorse from her sharp tone, Riley no longer felt repelled by it. With her left hand she reached out and touched the frame. Her right hand caressed Sophia's cheek. Riley looked back at Sophia and locked on those bright and weary eyes for a few more seconds before turning once more to the painting.

White light washed over her and she lost all sense of space. Riley blinked and, in that moment, the world around her crashed into focus. She stood in a sunroom, Sophia still next to her. A girl in her teens sat by the window and looked out at waves lapping against the shore. She turned and looked at Riley, then back outside.

"It's so strange being here, isn't it?" said the girl.

Riley's mouth dropped open. "Arisu?" she said.

The girl looked at her again. Riley smiled and then nearly laughed. There before her sat a much younger Arisu. But the voice belonged to a much older woman. It belonged to the Arisu that Riley had met only days ago.

"What is it now?" she demanded.

"Oh, huh," Riley looked at Sophia, "It's nothing. I'm just surprised to see you, that's all."

"So you expected me to be gone by now?" the girl questioned.

Riley stepped closer, taking a seat next to her on the wicker love seat. The young Arisu looked up at her. Riley now noticed her red cheeks and eyes. With the back of her hand, the girl wiped away the trail left by a tear.

"What's the matter?" Riley asked.

"Don't pretend like you don't know," she spat.

"Whoa, take it easy. I just got here."

Sophia touched Riley's shoulder and she looked up at her. "Remember," Sophia said, "This is a glimpse into the world of memories. You've been here all along."

"But I can't remember being here," Riley protested.

"Who are you talking to?" said Arisu.

Riley's attention returned to the girl. "Sophia," she said, unable to mask her surprise at this question.

The girl cocked her head to the side and her narrow eyes wondered about the room. "Okay… Who's Sophia?"

Riley looked up at Sophia again who simply nodded and stepped back.

"She can't see you?" Riley frowned.

Arisu laughed, "Alright, you're really creeping me out now. What do you want?"

Riley returned her attention to the girl. "I… I don't know. What do you want?"

"I want to hang out with Steve and Jeff, but mom still hates them."

"I see," Riley looked down. She remained unable to understand what connection this memory had to do with anything about her— or more accurately, anything to do with Violet. She straightened up quickly.

"What's the matter with you?" the young Arisu asked.

"Sophia," Riley called out. She looked around, finding no sign of her supposed guide.

"Who's Sophia?" Arisu demanded.

"What does this mean, Sophia?" Riley stood. "I didn't know Arisu when she was a teenager, did I?"

The faint echo of her voice lingered in the house.

"Does it have to be a matter of knowing me?" Arisu asked, suddenly composed.

Riley turned and faced a much sterner looking young woman. She stood now, her arms crossed.

"What exactly is happening here?" Riley looked up at the ceiling, as if calling out to anyone within earshot.

"Memories aren't always about yourself, you know? You remember watching movies, right? Songs? Stories?" the young Arisu rattled these off at her.

Sophia materialized behind the girl. The two spoke in unison, "This is someone else's memory. You are now recalling a story that was once told to you. A true story. This is a glimpse that surfaced in your mind."

"This didn't happen to me?" Riley said.

"Not directly," they both answered.

"What's happening here?" she yelled at them.

The house shuttered. Riley looked about, her heart beating faster.

Abruptly, the world felt still and foreboding. All sounds of the ocean ceased. Riley looked out the window, seeing crashing waves frozen in place.

"Take it easy," Sophia whispered.

Arisu stood perfectly still, a tear frozen to her delicate face.

"I don't understand this," Riley said. "What is it that I'm supposed to discover?"

"I can't tell you that," Sophia said. "I am here to facilitate, remember? I don't know what you are supposed to find. It is your subconscious that is leading us, as the nanites work to reconnect neural-pathways that once existed. This is not a linear journey."

Frustrated, Riley laughed as she stared off into space. "Great. My subconscious is in the driver's seat and my lovely tech support program doesn't have a *clue what we're doing here!*"

The yell echoed so strongly that Riley felt as if she were now standing inside a cave. The sharp sound of the echo didn't fit with the hardwood floors of the house.

"You should clam down," said a new voice. "You'll end up hurting yourself."

Riley turned to face what appeared to be herself. This other Riley wore a white dress shirt, kakis, and glasses. Her face bore simple, elegant make-up that helped her eyes and cheek bones stand out. Her dark skin seemed to glow with the vibrancy of a more pampered existence than Riley had been used to. Her hair was pulled back into a ponytail and her sharp eyes stared back at Riley. She never blinked.

"Don't look so bewildered," the woman said. "It should come as no surprise that you would meet me here."

Slowly, comprehension washed over Riley like the cold ocean water she had dove into not that long ago.

"You're Violet."

"More or less. I'm a representation at the moment, an attempt at adaptation by your mind. Our mind, actually."

Violet walked past Riley and stood by the window. The outside world remained still. Arisu and Sophia were gone. Riley watched Violet closely. Her footsteps made no sound. In fact, Riley heard only her own breathing. She placed her hand over her chest. She could not feel her heart beat.

"What happens now?" Riley said at last.

Violet turned. "Oh, now? Now we go our separate ways, so to speak. I've come here to claim what is mine. I would like to thank you for taking such good care of what you have been entrusted with. I'm sorry that it will now have to be taken from you so abruptly. But, such is life, right?"

"And what if I refuse?"

"Do you really think you're in any position to refuse?"

Riley clenched her fists and took a deep, steadying breath. "I don't really know that I care anymore what position I'm in."

Violet laughed. The sound echoed deeply in the empty house, causing Riley to clench her fists even tighter.

"It's the old cornered animal instinct," Violet said. "I understand. Believe me, I really do. No one wants to give up. Only cowards give up. So it's admirable—it really is—that you wish to preserve yourself in your present existence. It's only natural. Your brain—well, my brain, actually—is just tapping into its ancient wiring responsible for self-preservation. The reptile brain; my reptile brain—and that's just it, you see," Violet stepped closer and lowered her voice. "That's my body, my brain, my life. And I want it back—now! So, I'm afraid that it's time for you to leave."

"What if I don't deem you worthy of receiving back what was once yours?" Riley countered.

Violet glared at her. "What? Do you really think you have the right—the ability—to do that?"

"As I see it, I'm still the one calling the shots here."

Violet chuckled. With sudden speed, she sprang onto Riley, her hands gripping at Riley's throat. The two hit the ground hard, all air forcibly leaving Riley's lungs, even though air could not possibly matter in this place. Smacking and scratching with her hands, Riley fought Violet, pushing against her face. Violet just smiled and tightened her grip. Taking a new approach, Riley punched Violet's gut hard. But the woman just grinned, unfazed.

"The rules aren't quite the same in here," Violet said. "So please, just resign yourself to this fate. Don't waste my time with all this fighting for self-preservation."

Furious, Riley thrust her right hand at Violet's face. Her fingers plunged into the woman's eyes. Riley pressed with all her might and felt them pop. Violet screamed. Warm blood poured out of her face, covering Riley. She threw Violet off of her and stood. The woman fell to the ground, gripping her face. Her body convulsed for a moment. Then, she looked up—yes looked, with new eyes—at Riley.

"You're stronger than I thought you'd be," Violet mused.

With amazing speed, Violet stood and leapt at Riley again. They hit the ground hard, their limbs tangled. Rolling several times, Riley managed to come out on top. This time it was her turn to do the choking. She squeezed with all her might. Violet gasped, her eyes wide. Then, she grew still, her eyes fluttering, and she lost consciousness.

"Just die," Riley yelled. "Just let me live!"

Violet's face distorted into an array of colors and numbers. In disbelief, Riley suddenly found she gripped nothing. Her hands hit the floor first. Then, her face struck the hardwood. She lay there for a moment trying to understand what had just happened. Where had Violet gone? What if she was just hiding? She might come back. Overtaken with panic, Riley pushed herself off the floor. But dizziness seized her and she hit the ground even harder. She saw the flash of lights behind her eyelids caused by the hard impact of her head against a floor that felt like it was churning underneath her.

15 TRANSITIONAL MODULATION

Our species owes its runaway success to the special properties of the three pounds of matter stored inside our skulls.

- David Eagleman

JONES SAT FORWARD ON his chair, his hands resting on the conference table. The same old group sat there with glazed faces. The place smelled of coffee; strong gourmet coffee. Jones liked the aroma alright, but was more of a tea drinker himself. But such was the preference of the politicians—he still refused to consider himself one of them, though he spent as much time schmoozing and appeasing them, as if he were one, as he did in the project center doing any actual work. "The further up the chain, the more removed you are from it all," a scientist for the project had once told him. "You've become a lobbyist. It's just how the game is played."

"We hope you understand why we have called you here again," said Helen McKinley, snapping Jones back to the present. "There is need for haste. In seeking a new understanding of the project's potential, we need to take a few matters into account."

"Like what, exactly?" Jones said, flatly.

"Like the possibility of failure."

Jones sat back in his chair, letting his hands slide to his lap. He wore a suit, but felt very conscience of the wrinkles in it. He nodded, knowing that this meeting, albeit a hasty one, would not be a short one.

"What precisely do you mean by the 'possibility of failure'?" he said, working to keep his tone even.

Another member of the board piped up, a gaunt white man with a distinctly military air about him, whom everyone else refused to identify under claims that his identity must remain classified, "What we are concerned with is… well, do we have a proper understanding of what takes place in individual minds during and after the process? There's going to be a lot of scrutiny and a lot of ethical questions about the whole process, and we cannot afford to have any unpleasant surprises."

Jones nodded, but inside he wished he could give the old bastard first-hand experience of the process. "It is my understanding," Jones began, "that the individual going through the process may have a unique response to it. The standards that have been established thus far are that each person faces nightmares, lucid dreams, hallucinations. Over the course of twelve hours or so, as the nanobots position themselves along the spinal cord and begin to deliver electromagnetic shocks to the brain, the individual in question will experience a mental state of transition, a phenomenon called transitional modulation. The shock, which gives us the ability to control short-term memory, is nothing more than cerebral stimulation. The subject feels nothing. Other nanobots position themselves throughout the body, flowing through the blood while aiding in the body's communication with the brain. Memory, after all, isn't exclusively about the brain."

"This, of course, is in an ideal situation," McKinley interjected.

"Yes," Jones volunteered. "Of course."

"And it hasn't always worked this way, has it?"

Jones scanned the room quickly. Every last one of them wore their poker faces. He cleared his throat. "As it is with any new science, there is a certain amount of trial and error that takes place. We can't be expected to get everything right the first time on something that is so new. The truth is—and no one likes to admit it—science just isn't as tidy as we were all brought up to believe. There are layers. You figure one out, but the next one surprises you, brings new complexities to the table. It's all part of the development process, as I've pointed out before.

"If you'll recall," Jones continued, trying to mask just how much he felt annoyed by this waste of his time, "several of the early test subjects would emerge from the process in a 'half baked' state—not quite who they used to be, and not quite someone new. We discovered that the neurogenesis process, the generation of new brain cells, had to be aided by yet another set of nanomachinces that helped stimulate cell growth and carry the needed nutrients to the cells. Quite simple, once we realized what was missing. We've learned from our failures. It's quite natural, in fact."

He was overstating the simplicity of it. The development of the nutrient-carrying nanites had presented many challenges and cost a boat load in overtime for lab techs and the R&D teams. And that didn't even take in to account the continued developments in personality and memory theory and understanding of how to map, copy, store, and replicate the necessary information—thousands of petabytes—to legitimately rewrite a human personality. The computing developments alone happening in tandem would soon be making NeuroCorp serious money. It would all pay off. It was just a matter of time.

"I doubt that there's much of anything truly natural about the process," McKinley's eye's flashed at Jones, "People are involved in this process. People whose lives are changed forever. That's a rather high cost, don't you think?"

"The highest," said Jones, staring straight at her. "No doubt about it. Nevertheless, keep in mind the greater good of moving us into a society that doesn't rely on a legal system that kills its criminals or simply locks them in cells with no thought as to their true rehabilitation and reintegration into society. Why kill those who kill? Why dismiss a repeat offender as hopeless? We should be evolving beyond such primal pettiness. We are in the business of changing human behavior. Why fight terrorists with guns, when it's an *ideology* that drives them? We live in an age where worldviews are clashing more than ever. This isn't about land or rights or freedom. This is about *thought*, about how people look at the world and each other. This is about harmony! We are reprogramming the human mind, a super computer—if it's even really appropriate to make such a crude comparison—so powerful and complex that it's unlikely we will ever unmask all of its mysteries. This is no simple task, I assure you. But we will succeed!"

For the first time, the group around the table seemed to look at Jones with a new hope in their eyes. He soaked in the moment, knowing he finally had gained some, albeit fairly minimal, ground. He'd figured a little well-crafted elocution might help do the trick. *These assholes all get off on a good speech*, he grumbled internally, despite his relief. *If they just grasped the science, the process, the real potential—*

"What about the funding shortage?" asked another politician.

Jones smiled, knowing this question had to be on every one of the money-grabbing-bastards' little minds. "We managed early on to secure government funding. But, our research is not only involved with Project Sleepwalker. That's why we formed NeuroCorp."

"We are well aware of this, Dr. Edwards," McKinley interrupted. "But NeuroCorp has faced its own problems lately."

"This is true," Jones said, "But the advances in the use of TMS and nanomachines in combating Parkinson's disease and depression in patients has been promising. The visual simulation for the blind has been a significant success. It's a two way street. We make discoveries within NeuroCorp that presents new means for Sleepwalker to take new steps, and Sleepwalker continues to develop new technology that finds new commercial applications through NeuroCorp. Moreover, within the work of the project, we have definitely come across information that has been very helpful in understanding how we might use this technology to better treat certain diseases. We're talking about the betterment of an entire society, potentially the whole human race. We are on the edge of transcending mere humanity. This is the next step in our evolution. But now we get to guide it. In the eyes of science and history, nanotechnology, while not a new thing in our minds, is still in its infancy. Every infant must fall several times before it learns to walk. How could we expect this to be any different?"

There, he'd done it. He could see it in their eyes.

"Fair enough, Dr. Edwards," McKinley nodded. "Now, all that remains for this committee to see is the results of your latest test subjects."

Jones bore a slight smile on his closed lips, but his teeth clench together. "Of course."

"And what of Dr. Violet Murphy?" she asked.

"We are caring for her as we speak," Jones looked down at the table. "She will present no problem for us going forward."

"I'm sure she won't. But she should never have presented a problem in the first place. How was this allowed to happen?"

"I believe you have read my report on Dr. Murphy."

She sighed, shaking her head. "I'm not referring to that. I mean, what happened in Brazil? We know you've been busy cleaning up a mess. We need to know Murphy isn't going to compromise the program because of a change in… ideology." She spoke that last word with eyes locked on Jones, no doubt enjoying the ironic resurgence of the word into their conversation.

"The issue is being cared for," was all Jones said, working hard to keep his voice from becoming a growl.

SHE GASPED FOR AIR, forcing her eyes to open at last. It took a moment for her to recall where she was. But the constant whine of the jet engines reminded her that she was still on the long flight from *São Paulo* to Boston. In the seats next to her, Dante and Arisu sat up and looked over at Riley. She rubbed her eyes, taking in several deep breaths. Looking up, she met Dante's concerned eyes. Dante opened his mouth to speak, but seemed to reconsider this and looked away. Riley turned to Arisu, who looked at her for a long moment with unmasked concern. The plane's intercom beeped. "Attention ladies and gentlemen," said the stewardess, "We are about to begin our final decent into Boston. Please fasten your seat belts at this time and remain seated. Thank you."

Riley looked at her seat belt, finding it still fastened. Arisu touched her arm and she looked back up at her.

"How do you feel?" she asked.

Aware that no answer she could give would be what Arisu was looking for, Riley just shook her head.

"Violet?" Arisu said, clearly trying to keep her voice low but unable to quite hide some undercurrent of hopefulness. Or was it desperation?

Riley sighed and stared straight ahead. "No. Not yet, at least." She looked at Arisu. "I don't know what happened. But, not yet. It's still Riley, me, or… no… Riley."

Arisu's eyes grew wide with concern. "I don't understand. How can that be?"

Riley slouched in her seat and looked down. Within her, a torrent of contradictory emotions swirled. She felt the disappointment at not accomplishing what clearly was so important to Dante and Arisu. But she also felt incredible relief at still being what she thought of as herself. But even as this thought took hold, she felt guilt for being so relieved that she had fought to preserve her artificial self. Yes, artificial. Her heart sank at the realization that this self she still held on to was a mere illusion.

"I fought, Arisu. Inside, in my mind, wherever that is, I fought Violet. She's still there somewhere. Lurking behind every thought, I imagine. She seemed so angry." Riley looked up at Arisu again. "I don't want to be her, Arisu. That's not the person I want to be. I'm sorry I just don't want to be her."

Arisu's eyes dropped. She looked away and swore. The plane shook slightly as they descended through a patch of turbulent air.

16   BOSTON

[W]atching someone else in pain and being in pain use the same neural machinery. This is the basis of empathy.

- David Eagleman

RILEY STEPPED INTO A world of color and noise. Three-dimensional ads jutted from every possible spot in Logan International Airport. Carrying her baggage, she tipped her head back and stared at the overly active world writhing around her. It was as if the LED displays and holographic adverts were alive; the muscle and skeletal composition of a living body contorting and stretching itself across the entire airport. People congregated in the small food court of this particular terminal. A pub served locally brewed beers to those waiting for their departure or connecting flights. People rushed up and down escalators already in motion, hardly glancing at the mural upon the wall exhibiting a glowing rendition of the Boston skyline and the words, "Boston Strong" beneath it. Stores lined the sides of the main walkway between terminals. A few plants dotted the metallic and glass structure that had been erected in the last six years as part of major updates to Logan. The sound of people talking coalesced with the digital ads, creating a cacophony of chatter brawling for your undivided attention.

Riley passed one of the three-dimensional ads. A beautiful blond in a bikini waved at her. Suddenly, the image stuttered slightly and the woman morphed into a handsome dark man in swim trunks. He grinned at her, winked, then turned and ran into a blue ocean. "With TrekNet, you can travel anywhere in the world without leaving home." Then, a woman in a slim business suit appeared. She sat at a desk and smiled. "Through TrekNet, I can travel to Los Angeles for business and spend all of my free time golfing under the shade of Mount Fuji." She slipped a slender helmet over her head as the image behind her morphed into a glorious golf course in Japan. She teed off a perfect shot. The ball faded into the backdrop of Mount Fuji. Turning back with a gleaming smile, she said, "Then, I return home refreshed from my business trip, not worn out." The image now dissolved into a large jet floating over a perfect layer of clouds. "TrekNet, now available with first class through AirAtlantic," said a new voice. "Don't just fly somewhere: have an adventure."

Riley found herself strangely fascinated with the three-dimensional ads that sprung up all about the airport, noting that they seemed to change based on whoever was nearest to them at any given time. She looked about with the eyes of a child. *It's not like I haven't seen any of this before,* she thought. *Yet, it is.* The experience felt particularly new somehow. Arisu touched her shoulder.

"Come on, we need to keep moving," Arisu leaned closer and whispered.

As they walked, they passed more ads and stores. From some, loud music poured out while others were quiet and had only a few people standing about looking at shirts or framed pictures of Boston. Passing a booth that sold salted pretzels and hotdogs, Riley stopped. The aroma beckoned her. She, at least, noticed the empty ache of her stomach.

"I'll make you food as soon as we get to where we're going," said Arisu. "But we can't stop now."

Riley nodded, but still didn't move. She stared at the picture of a pretzel, its salted surface impeccably captured forever within the picture. She wished she could reach out and take it. As she lusted over food, however, something else drew her ear. Someone spoke to anyone who would listen. She turned, looking for the speaker. A few yards away, a man sat in a crumpled heap on the ground. A black cylinder about a foot in width sat before him. From it, an image projected into thin air. At first, the image appeared as nothing more than a convoluted mess of scribbles.

"This is for you," the man said, as he scribbled on a flat screen in his lap. As he did so, each scribble appeared in the projection. "This is for all of you," he repeated.

Riley walked toward him. Arisu reached for her, but Dante stopped her. He shook his head, "Let her." Arisu looked sharply at Dante and shook her arm free from his hand. Riley, ignorant to all of this, stood before the drawing man. For the first time, she realized the man's entire upper body twisted oddly to his left, one shoulder higher than another.

"This was done so that you could be who you are, so that you may live," the main announced, never lifting his eyes from his screen.

Riley gazed at the crude and monochromatic projection, which was clearly several generations behind the holographic ads populating throughout the airport. As she stared, it took shape for the first time in her eyes. Black scribbled lines merged to form a nearly abstract shape, yet clearly visible to someone like Riley: a crucifix.

The man stopped scribbling and looked up directly at Riley. Riley stared back.

"This," the man pointed. "He did this for you. So you could be who you were meant to be."

Riley looked again at the three-dimensional crucifix, then back to the man. "No. He didn't do it for me."

The man locked eyes with her. "He sees you," he insisted. "He sees your heart. He knows who you really are and he loves you. He knows every one of his children."

Riley took a few steps back, shaking her head. "You don't understand. I don't think He— not me."

A tear slipped down the man's cheek and he returned to his drawing. Arisu stepped up to Riley, taking her hand.

"Come on," she whispered in Riley's ear. "The sooner we go, the sooner this will be over."

Riley looked into her eyes then over her shoulder at the world around them. People rushed by her with the hustle and bustle of a busy freeway, while she stood, frozen in place, enveloped in this familiar, yet alien and unrelentingly lonely world. At last, Riley shrugged and looked back at Arisu.

"You're the boss," she murmured.

"Wake up," Rikard nudged Thomas. "We're here."

Thomas jerked up straight and looked about. People stood and gathered their baggage from the overhead bins in the cabin of the jet. He rubbed his eyes and yawned. Rikard sat coolly next to him, waiting for people to clear out before he began fetching his bag and exiting. They'd landed first in Orlando where some passengers got off the jet, a few more got on, and the jet was refueled before taking flight to Boston. This particular airline specialized in high-profile business and political figures that were willing to pay for smaller, faster, and more private travel accommodations.

"We have to report in, you know," Rikard said.

Thomas nodded slowly. "Yeah, sure."

"But you'd rather not?" Rikard looked over at him.

"Oh, no, whatever. It's all good with me," Thomas lied. "I was going to report in as soon I got back. I just needed more time to gather information on Violet and Arisu."

Rikard laughed, closing his eyes and shaking his head. He leaned down so he could speak more softly. "You don't have to play this game with me, Thomas. I can see right through your bullshit. So how about we both play it straight?"

Thomas swallowed, but maintained eye contact.

Rikard sighed. "I should kill you. I really should. What you have done has jeopardized this whole project in ways you can't even begin to comprehend. You haven't the slightest clue how closely you came to completely derailing this delicate work and pissing off a lot of people. Important people. Powerful people. So you're right to not want to talk to Jones. But you're going to and I'm going to be sure you do. What I need you to do, in the meantime, is play it cool. In other words, try to run and you *will* get hurt. I'll do it in broad daylight. It makes no difference to me, but I think it might to you. You seem like the type of vermin that really values his insignificant little life. Are we on the same page now?"

Thomas swallowed again, harder this time, "Yeah."

Rikard smiled. "Ah, good. Let's keep it that way." He looked around, seeing that most of the people were now gone. "Time to hustle."

THE DOOR SWUNG OPEN with the slightest of creaks. Dante stepped in first, checking the place over. Arisu stood with Riley in the dimly lit hallway. A florescent light at the end of the hall flickered and buzzed slightly. The sound of a loud television set bled into the hall. The worn green carpet on the floor smelled musty. Riley looked up and down the hall as a cat skittered past them. She looked back to Arisu, who kept her eyes on Riley.

"Still waiting for something magical to happen?" Riley asked.

"What do you mean?"

"You keep looking at me as if you expect, any second now, that Violet will just pop out of me. I wonder which would make you more excited, that she might show up or that I might finally be gone, out of your way."

Arisu looked down, "Look, I realize you and I don't know each other all that well. That's making this all a lot harder than any of us thought it would be, but I wish you wouldn't talk like that. I have nothing against you, Riley." She looked back up at her. "I've told you before how all of this works."

"But it's not working, is it? By the time we landed, Violet was supposed to be here. Instead, we're both still stuck with me. So... what does that mean?"

Arisu pressed her lips together, her eyes focusing on something down the hallway. Riley didn't move. She stared, waiting for an answer. Arisu looked again to Riley. This time Arisu's eyes seemed to glisten slightly with a hint of new moisture.

"Full assimilation will most likely take place," she said.

"What does that mean exactly, full assimilation?"

"It's, uh," Arisu pressed her lips together again.

Just then, Dante stepped out of the apartment. "All clear," he said. "Just as we left it."

"Good," Arisu snapped out of her daze. "Let's get inside. I believe I promised you some food."

They stepped into the door. Dante remained in the hallway.

"I'll be headed out then," he said.

"Wait, why?" Riley looked back at him.

"It's okay, Riley," said Arisu. Then she turned to Dante. "Go ahead as planned. Make contact with the insider. I'll wait to hear from you."

Dante nodded, looking one last time at Riley before he headed down the hallway. Arisu closed the door and turned slowly. Riley didn't need an explanation.

"This isn't quite turning out as planned, huh?" Riley pointed out what was becoming painfully clear.

Arisu shook her head. "Not quite. But that's okay. We'll improvise. It'll come together. Dante just has to contact the informant we have working within the program. In the meantime, we wait here, get some food, and get some rest."

Arisu walked passed her and into the small kitchen. Riley turned and followed. The small apartment smelled stale. Aging IKEA furniture spotted the light brown carpet. Dust covered the kitchen counter, the table in the dining area adjacent to the kitchen, and the coffee table in front of the sofa. The long, white vertical blinds on the window hung shut. Riley walked over to it, and peeked out. The city, eleven floors below, looked pretty much like the Boston that Riley recalled. Yet somehow, it had changed. Lit by a bright sun, the place seemed new and unfamiliar yet wholly part of her. She put her hand on the glass, feeling the coolness against her skin. *It's all new to me,* she thought. *It's all new to me because I'm new to it. I've never been who I am right now. I'm forever changing, it seems.*

She turned, finding Arisu looking at her. Riley smiled, but her smile faded all too quickly. Some part of her wanted to alleviate the anxiety Arisu must be feeling, to have the ability to be the person Arisu needed her to be. But, of course, that would mean embracing an uncertain future, most likely some form of oblivion. But maybe, oblivion was something to be welcomed and not avoided. As a life-long Catholic, facing oblivion felt unfamiliar. Is this what a dying atheist might feel? Then she reminded herself that she was not a life-long Catholic after all.

Arisu sighed. She opened a cupboard above the kitchen bar that faced the compact dining area. There stood a small, round table with four chairs. She removed a few boxes and set them on the bar. She looked at Riley again, who hadn't moved.

"I'm sorry," she said. "You can take a shower if you like. I'm sure that after the flight, you might want to unwind. The bathroom is down the hall, next to the living room. In the bedroom, you'll find a few of Violet's old clothes."

"Okay," Riley nodded. "Yeah, that sounds nice."

Riley opened her mouth to speak more, but realized no words had formed within her mind. Everything just felt so off kilter, so out of place. She wanted to say something; to somehow make things better for Arisu, but the truth was that she was the one who was terrified. She was the one who faced the most uncertain future of all. Or, perhaps, the more accurate way of thinking about it was that she was the only one faced the possibility of no future at all. She closed her mouth, turned, and headed down the hallway.

RILEY FOUND SEVERAL DRESS shirts, black and grey pants, jeans, and a few folded t-shirts inside a box at the bottom of the small closet in the bedroom. She slipped into the clean clothes, feeling slightly more awake and refreshed after the shower. The formal clothing seemed too foreign to her, so she dug through the box of t-shirts. All the while, she pictured herself dressed up and standing in a sterile white lab. She pictured microscopes and computers, but was that accurate? That couldn't possibly be right. In the box, she found a light grey t-shirt with the Red Sox logo on it. She looked through the jeans and settled on a faded pair that were not quite her style but seemed like they would fit more comfortably. Right now, comfort felt like the most valuable criteria.

The shower hadn't been a long one, but a good one none-the-less. All things considered, she was starting to feel better. Her body was revitalized at least, but she still felt like she was in a mental fog. She was also increasingly hungry, but it felt positively wonderful to be alone for a moment. With the hunger came the reflex to pray. Having made fasting a regular part of her life, Riley had come to associate the two things. She stared at the water painting of a lighthouse that hung on the room's wall, her mind drawing a blank. Right then, she did not feel it was possible to pray. Did God listen to the prayers of an artificial personality? She wanted desperately to affirm that God must be wise enough to see through such circumstances, but something stopped her. *Maybe it's wishful thinking,* she wondered. *Or worse, maybe it's programmed thinking. How can I trust any of my past experiences? How can they be the basis for my faith?*

She looked the bedroom over. A twin bed with sheets sat in the corner, a small, brown dresser in the other. She had a hard time imagining that this would have been a regular living space for someone. But could it have been Violet's apartment? *No,* she immediately answered himself. *Violet's is much bigger.* She stood in silence, analyzing her last thought. Somehow, she knew Violet's apartment to be much larger than this one. Yet, she could not summon a mental image of what her apartment might look like. She did see, however, a portrait of an old man wearing glasses and smoking a pipe. Riley tried to stare at it with her mind's eye, but the picture faded.

"Riley," Arisu called out.

Riley walked down the short hallway to the living room and kitchen. She found Arisu stirring something on the stove; her back turned. Riley felt an overwhelming urge to walk up to her. She stopped, however.

"Riley," Arisu called again.

"Yes," she answered.

"Oh," she said, turning. "I didn't realize you were right there. How was the shower?"

"Good. I needed that."

Arisu smiled, setting down the wooden spoon she had been using to stir the rice. "Well, this has a little time to go yet. I think I'm going to take a quick shower myself. You mind keeping an eye on the stove for me? You don't have to do anything. Just keep the rice from burning."

"Sure," Riley shrugged.

Arisu disappeared into the bathroom, leaving Riley alone in the living room. She glanced over at the stove, feeling no desire to get any closer to the kitchen at the moment. Figuring the food would be fine for the time being, she turned and sat on the sofa. She looked up at the corners of the wall in front of her. Sure enough, small projection units hung there by the ceiling. Now, how did she turn it on?

"Television on," she tried. Nothing happened. She frowned, thinking of what else to try. "TV on." But still, nothing. It was possible that Arisu had a voice-specific system in and it didn't recognize Riley's voice.

Looking before her, she spotted a remote control on the rickety coffee table. She chuckled at her assumption that this apartment had been equipped with a voice activated three-dimensional television. Arisu didn't seem to be living large. Now she questioned if the thing would even work. As she snagged the remote from the coffee table, she heard the water begin to flow from the shower.

A peculiar thought crept into her mind. She wondered if Arisu trusted her enough to leave the door unlocked. Not that she intended to do anything. Nevertheless, as she saw it, one would only go off to take a shower and leave the bathroom door unlocked if the other person in their home was someone to be trusted. Had Arisu locked the door? Even though Riley remained, did she display that kind of trust?

She smiled and shook her head. *Hang on a second,* she thought. Riley wracked her brain, trying to recall if she had actually locked it or not when taking her shower. Even as she tried to convince herself that she had locked it, she felt a growing certainty that, in fact, she had left it unlocked without thinking. If so, why had she not locked the door? *Do I really trust Arisu?*

Riley sat there, dusty remote in hand, speculating if she might be able to quietly turn the knob and feel if the bathroom door might open. Was it just the desire to gain this insight into Arisu's trust of her? But then what? She wouldn't dare go in, would she? Then again, after seeing how Arisu had defended herself in the airport in Brazil, Riley figured she might leave the door unlocked anyway. Even naked and wet, she would still present a serious threat to any intruder. Her mind lingered too long on that last thought. Glimpses from the memory of Arisu's reflection in the mirror when Riley had bandaged the cuts on her bare back had now joined the tempting chaos. Riley blushed, knowing that it was increasingly difficult for her to deny that there was something there, beneath the surface. What had Violet and Arisu meant to each other? Was Arisu even a lesbian?

Riley had not allowed herself time to think about her own sexuality in such a long time that to suddenly speculate about someone else's orientation now felt utterly incongruent with any reality she knew. *But you're not living any reality you've known,* she reminded herself. She thought she'd left all of that behind when she'd taken her vows and entered the ministry. She was far from being the only nun or priest that had walked away from a life and identity that wasn't 'straight' and discovered a new identity, even comfort, that was based in chastity and ministry. But now, everything was upside down and she suddenly felt dizzy again. It was simply too much to contemplate at the moment. Her whole world was changing far too rapidly.

Holding the remote out, she hit the power button. The projectors whirred into action. Before her, a large image of a mountain landscape formed.

"Welcome," said the built-in voice of the OS.

The words "Violet's Mobile Drive" appeared over the mountain tops." Riley looked down at the remote. She hit the TV/CPU Mode button. The image changed to a baseball game—the Red Sox up six over the Cardinals in the top of the seventh. She grinned then hit the button again. The mountains and words returned. *Well, that's how that works,* she thought. *Now to see what sweet little miss Violet left us on this hard drive.* She paused, feeling odd about referring to Violet in such a way. She was Violet, after all… wasn't she? But to say, '*What did I leave for myself?*' didn't ring true either. *Who am I supposed to be, after all?* She accessed the hard drive. A list of files and folders appeared on the screen. She stared, lost as to where she might begin to look. What would be helpful? What could she digest quickly before Arisu came out from her shower?

Pictures!

Using the remote, she scrolled through the list. A good way down, she came across a folder labeled "Pictures." She opened it. Several thumbnails popped up. She clicked the first one. Bay waters led to the Boston skyline in the upper third of the picture. Riley advanced to the next one. She saw now a picture of the same skyline, only tighter and showing less water. Next, she saw a woman standing on a peer. She faced away from the camera, but immediately Riley felt sure it was Arisu. She advanced again. Sure enough. Arisu leaned against the railing of the peer and smiled at the camera. Next up, a closer picture; Arisu's hair had been tossed by the breeze coming off the harbor. Riley stared into her frozen eyes. Though it frightened her, she had to admit how attractive Arisu was frozen there in the breeze, the light of the setting sun falling over her skin and dark hair. Riley advanced.

On the screen, she saw Arisu with a woman who had an arm around her waist. It took Riley a long moment to realize that she looked at herself. Well, it wasn't herself… really. The hair was flowing and too elegantly styled; the dress she wore too low cut; the necklace simple but charming; the makeup on her eyes and lips elegant and not overstated— but still out of character for a woman who had little use for makeup. This was Violet.

Violet smiled naturally to the camera and Arisu stood close to her with an easy familiarity, smiling with more warmth than Riley had ever

170

seen on her face. Riley's mouth dropped open. Was this a friendly hug? *Come on,* she told herself, *you know it's more.* In the bathroom, the shower turned off. Riley glanced down the hallway, then back at the screen. She advanced the pictures, stopping only long enough to catch a glimpse of each.

Violet and Arisu held each other closely, looking into each other's eyes. Violet and Arisu walked, hand-in-hand, down the peer. Arisu sat at a table, leaning her chin on her hand, looking off at no particular thing. Violet sat at a desk, papers flung about; Violet and Arisu on a beach; Arisu in a bathing suit, standing in ankle deep water; Violet, in a slightly more modest swim suit with her arms around Arisu; Violet's darker skin contrasted beautifully with Arisu's lighter complexion as the two woman's lips met in a playful and carefree kiss—

Riley stopped. *I knew this, didn't I? I knew it all along.* She stared at the picture. It was Violet, alright. Riley's eyes washed over the image of Arisu, the smooth skin of her legs and shoulders exposed. A sensation came over her, like her hands could recall the feeling of the small of Arisu's back and her hair tickling her face. *Late August in Chatham,* she found herself thinking. While she knew Chatham was on Cape Cod, when was the last time she'd actually been to the cape? And yet, she could almost smell the salty breeze.

I've known this all along, haven't I? Or maybe I only feel like I've known this now that I'm certain—fully certain. She'd had her suspicions early. It certainly explained why she felt so drawn to Arisu in the first place; why she would have even trusted her at all. Had instinct and attraction been the reasons she had chosen to trust Arisu? Was this why she had been willing to come along on such a dangerous journey, what had, at first, appeared to be such a ludicrous notion? Could it be that buried deep within her remained some vestige of the attraction Violet had toward Arisu? Riley felt distinctly woozy now, but this dizziness felt new, as if the world was turning while she remained still. *Now I know,* she thought. *Now I know for sure!*

Or do I? Do I know anything, she couldn't help but question. Everything about her world was changing too fast. She found herself thinking again.

Movement in the corner of her eye caught her attention. She snapped her head up—which she had not realized until now had slumped down to her chest while she was lost in thought. Arisu stood in the doorway from the hall. She wore a white robe. Her wet hair tangled down her shoulders. She looked at Riley, eyes expectant, but said nothing. Riley looked into her eyes. Neither spoke for what felt like a very long time. Somewhere inside, caught deep in her gaze, Riley knew she felt something for Arisu. Had she loved her? Rather, had Violet loved her? And even if Violet had loved her, could she—or should she—love her now? At last...

"Violet?" Arisu asked; her voice was soft and tentative.

Riley felt herself smile faintly and her body rise to her feet without her consciously willing it to do so. She looked on as Arisu stepped slowly closer with her hand reached out, touching Riley's face. Riley felt the warmth of Arisu's soft hand, still damp from the shower. All the while, Arisu barely blinked, holding her gaze, as if it were her only means of survival. She drew closer.

The dizziness took over Riley's senses. Arisu noticed the change, her eyes tightening, darting between Riley's eyes in search of something. Riley fumbled back to the sofa, Arisu helping her down slowly.

"What's happening?" Riley pleaded. "What's happening to me?"

Arisu didn't answer; the light in her eyes had been suddenly extinguished.

HER ARMS REACHED OUT, not finding Arisu there anymore. Riley sat up, looking around the silent apartment.

"Arisu," she called. "You still here?"

She looked back at the screen. The picture of Arisu and Violet kissing, which had at first resembled the original picture, now faded into shapes and colors losing their distinct pattern and structure. After a few seconds, even the colors faded away.

"Arisu?" she yelled.

"She's right there next to you."

Riley turned her head, finding Sofia leaning casually against the wall. Riley looked about, confused by Sophia's appearance.

"What are you talking about?" she said, standing.

"She's right there next to you," Sofia smiled. "While you once again slip into this world—this inner place—she awaits patiently, just as she always has; right along the border to the outer world."

Riley looked down at herself then around the apartment trying to make sense of what was happening. "I'm inside my head again? But this looks exactly the same as the apartment. I didn't feel any loss of consciousness. Did I pass out?"

Sofia stepped away from the wall, walking to the window. "As you draw closer and closer to assimilation, the barrier between this inner world and that world out there becomes less and less obvious, perhaps, even less important."

Sofia pulled the vertical blind apart just enough to peek out. The light that came from the slit seemed brighter than before.

"How can that be?" Riley demanded. "How can it not be important? I swear I'm losing my mind."

Sophia turned abruptly, letting the blinds flap shut. They clapped together, moving in waves.

"You're becoming someone else," she said. "Of course it will feel like insanity. None of us has the ability to step into another person's mind, to truly become someone else. That has remained an indissoluble metaphysical barrier for every person. As connected as we might be, an individual is still an isolated being in so many crucial ways. But you have been granted this transcendent gift."

"Well, if it's a gift, I'd like to give it back now, if it's all the same to you," Riley shot back.

"Riley, stop fighting it," Sophia said, shaking her head. "Otherwise, we end up just running in circles. We've been through this before."

Riley shook, tears brimming in her eyes. "I know. I know. I *know*. Why can't this all end? Just end. Sofia, make it end."

She looked at Sophia, feeling the tears run down her cheeks. Sofia returned a sad, knowing smile and stepped closer. Reaching out gently, Sophia took Riley into her arms. She leaned in close, her lips right by Riley's left ear.

"It will in time," she whispered. "It won't be long, now. You can feel it. You're changing. You are no longer the Riley you once were. Everything is changing, my dear."

The walls around them flew out to infinity, vanishing completely. Riley gasped, looking about. The city around them seemed lit by a bright moon, its blue light casting long shadows. The sky, however, appeared to her as a dull and starless blue. The floor they stood on began to fall. Riley gripped Sofia tightly, feeling the cold rush in her stomach from the sudden drop. Building tops rushed passed them, the rushing wind deafening in her ears. Riley closed her eyes, losing all sense of direction. When she opened them again, they stood in the street. She let go of Sophia cautiously and looked around, down at the ground, and up at the building tops.

"How did we get here?" she said.

Sofia said nothing.

"Why do I feel like everything's falling apart?" she asked.

"Everything must fall apart before it can be put back together," Sophia answered. "Isn't that how the universe works? You should know, Violet. You're the scientist here."

Riley, still staring up at the buildings, turned in a circle as a new thought pushed its way to the surface of her mind. "Deconstruction is the first phase of construction." She stopped and looked at Sofia. "You have to take it apart in order to make a new totality from the individual pieces. The whole system's design is based on the usage of data already present. We never created completely new personalities, did we? Holy shit!"

Sofia smiled as a brick fell from above. It crashed into the pavement. Riley walked up to it, stooped down, and picked up a piece of the shattered red brick. She stood, looking up to see if more bricks might be on their way. She felt no concern that one might strike her.

"It's not so much a death," Riley mused. "More like a metamorphosis."

Sophia didn't respond, but when Riley glanced at her, she smiled gently and nodded, indicating that she was finally on the right track.

"But I'm not really Violet yet," she continued. "Why did she try to kill me?"

"Deconstruction. She, Violet, is nothing more than a mental entity you created to deal with the deconstruction. She reacted merely as you thought she might react or ought to react under the circumstances. Survival is such a primal instinct, it's hard to bypass even within this state."

"But now I don't really have a need for her," Riley marveled, "because I'm becoming her." She stood still, staring at the ground. "I am becoming more and more like her with each passing moment. I'm no longer afraid. Riley has to fade. Riley was never real. Not in any true sense, at least. She was based on a composite reality of several people."

She rubbed her face with her hands, taking a deep breath.

"No, no, no," Riley groaned. "I am still Riley. I'm still here. I don't want to die. I don't want to face oblivion. There's nothing past this moment for me. I can feel it creeping up inside me. Nothing. It's reaching out for me. I don't want this… and yet, I do."

Surprised by her own boldness, she reached out and caressed Sofia's gentle face. "This is it, isn't it? The moment everything changes."

Sophia's hair whipped about as a strong breeze picked up. She nodded, a single tear slipping down her cheek, "If you want it to be."

17   TARKOVSKY AND WARHOL

At this moment in history, we may have more in common with our Stone Age ancestors than with our near-future descendants.

- David Eagleman

DANTE SAT ALONE. PEOPLE passed him, never once even glancing at him. He held his smartphone, reading through the day's news. At this time of the day, the large bookstore seemed to be a good place for a casual meeting. He kept his eyes mostly attached to the phone while only occasionally looking up. His eyes would wander slightly, looking around the conveniently furnished reading area of the bookstore—if it could still be called that since more and more of the store had become increasingly consumed by other merchandise. At the opposite side of the room, a large window looked out over a small park that was home to the Irish Famine Memorial, two stories down from where Dante sat. Across the narrow street sat The Old South Meeting House, its red brick walls were dwarfed by the plethora of glass and metal structures that, together, comprised modern Boston. Yet, the Old South Meeting House had been preserved and was still celebrated for its historical significance as the site where the Boston Tea Party gathered prior to their notorious act of defiance against the British crown. Dante felt it fitting to be sitting across from such a place. He felt a new confidence that their plan, while having wandered from the charted path, had now begun to navigate itself back to the original course of action. He just had to wait a little longer, be patient, and to carefully massage each detail into its proper place.

The news consisted mostly of the usual political brouhaha and several profoundly unfortunate events happening across the globe. One article, however, caught Dante's attention. "NeuroCorp About to Launch Judiciary Campaign," declared the title. Dante skimmed the article, finding only vague information about a project designed to bring about a central rehabilitation of the minds in violent criminals. That was, after all, the only non-classified information available to the public. It was also merely the tip of a heavily contaminated iceberg. What did have him worried, however, was the article's indication that the timeframe for a congressional hearing had been pushed forward due to recent protests and demonstrations from human rights organizations and religious groups. The exact time, however, did not appear in the article. There was an increasing pressure and concern over the project. Dante couldn't imagine that Jones approved of having the congressional hearing sooner. Two possibilities occurred to him: either there was genuine concern in Washington over the project or there was a power play to shut down non-classified projects and move them all into DARPA's hands. While Jones was working alongside scientists from the Defense Advanced Research Projects Agency, he was also a financial analyst desperately trying to prove their R&D expenditures had yielded a high enough Return on Research Capital (RORC) to justify their continued investment in the project.

Dante set his smartphone down on the table and stared off. Jones knew all too well that Arisu was at the brink of retrieving Violet, and, in doing so, could possibly collapse the whole project. Perhaps there was a third possibility. Maybe Jones was pushing ahead as quickly as possible in order to gain the necessary approval that would allow him to launch the criminal justice program sooner than expected. By spinning an argument from an emotional or social appeal, instead of from productivity or profitability, the financial metrics may become far less important. In three—maybe even two—years, Project Sleepwalker could be in full swing. Criminals, plucked out of crowded jails, penitentiaries, and death row, unwillingly given a whole new existence and placed back into society—more likely, placed into shitty jobs and lives that no one in their right mind would opt for—the social benefits could be argued as more profitable than the sunk financial costs, *habeas corpus* be damned. Terrorists would also be captured then neutralized at the foundation of their ideology. After all, this was the only logical conclusion of the "war on terror", which had been started decades earlier. How else does one wage a war on a worldview other than by completely rewiring someone's brain?

Could Jones perfect the system in time? Could he fix the flaws? It seemed unlikely. But did that matter? One thing Jones did have on his side was persistence. He would press on, working all of the Sleepwalker scientists long and hard until they had achieved the desired results. But, did he have what it would take for a congressional hearing? Dante doubted this. Yet, knowing Jones, Dante also knew that the man probably had some secret that he and Arisu had not yet guessed. Maybe Jones just hoped to demonstrate the potential so that it could possibly buy him more time.

For Dante, hope remained in retrieving Violet. She had mattered to the project, to Jones. She still mattered. Otherwise, why wouldn't Jones simply have had her killed? Done correctly, it would have been a much neater solution than trying to tuck her away in Brazil. But, then again, maybe Jones really was the bleeding heart liberal that he presented himself to be and he couldn't work up the never to kill. Either way, Jones was rushing, which usually led to mistakes, and they had Violet—or would soon. Dante felt as if he might know what Jones' next moved would be.

Pulling himself out of this stream of thought, his eyes locked on to a blond woman looking through greeting cards by the entrance. She wore faded jeans and a light blue dress shirt. Slipping his phone into his jacket pocket, he stood and quietly left the bookstore. Passing the stands of cards, he stopped and picked one up from the "Get Well Soon" section.

"We all have sick friends," Dante said, not looking up from his card. "Mine's just a little confused, you know?"

"We should get out of here. I'm not so sure about this place."

"Ladies first," he said, setting the card back on the shelf.

She walked away, going down the escalator from the second floor, then heading for the exit. He waited a moment longer, seeming to scan for another card. Once she had stepped through the door, he made his way slowly down to the exit. Stepping out into the clear and humid day, Dante relished the familiarity of Boston, after having been in Brazil for almost four weeks helping Arisu with the final stages of tracking Riley. People walked the sidewalks. A bus rolled by. Cars stopped at the intersection's light. Others buzzed through the green light. The city moved, while by the front door of The Old South Meeting House, the blond woman stood, waiting for Dante. He stopped next to her.

"Good to see you, Tess," he said.

"How was the trip?" she asked.

"I've had better," he shrugged. "I've also had much worse."

She looked at him for the first time. "Shall we walk?"

He nodded and they headed down the sidewalk. Neither spoke as they moved away from the historic building, past the entrance for the subway—or 'The T', as it was known locally—and moved through the wafting smells of fresh coffee and baked goods emitting from a nearby coffee shop. They took a right on Spring Lane, a cobble stone alley meant strictly for pedestrians. The buildings towered on either side of it. Alleys like this always made Dante feel he had suddenly stepped through a portal into another century. The illusion was broken only by a short man walking out of a tiny electronics shop wearing customized smart glasses. They walked on, stopping at another intersection and waiting for their turn to cross. Once they reached the other side, they turned to their left, and waited for the crossing light to turn green.

"I hope you have good news," Dante said.

Tess shook her head. "Have you been following the news at all?"

"I noticed a certain article in today's *Boston Globe*."

"They're serious about all of this, Dante. They're pushing up the timeframe. Every string is being pulled, every effort made to speed up the legal process. That means our timeframe just got a lot shorter. After the airport fiasco in São Paulo, things have gotten rather tense around the office."

"Oh. So you've heard."

She scoffed and shook her head. "Word gets around. It's not supposed to, but come on… this is Violet we're talking about. Too many people are worked up."

Either because she was uneasy or simply functioning as any native Bostonian might, Tess looked at the gap in traffic and ignored the Do Not Cross signal. Dante followed her.

"Please tell me you have Violet," she said.

Dante said nothing. She looked at him.

"You don't have her?" she asked.

"Oh, we have Riley, or Violet, or whatever you wish to call her. We have the body. We don't have the mind. Sounds a little like a bad philosophy joke, really."

"Why don't we have the mind?"

"Something's wrong. I'm not sure what's happening. Arisu still holds out hope that Violet will emerge. However, I'm afraid it has become too much of a mess."

"You mean, assimilation?"

"I'm afraid so."

"Of course; we're fucked," Tess shook her head. "What do we have to go on? There's no guarantee of what will come out after assimilation is completed. We don't even know exactly what Violet was planning. I knew this was all a pipe dream—"

"No, it's not!" Dante put out a hand, stopping her. "This is not a pipe dream. It's not over yet. We didn't come this far to drop this."

She shook her head and walked on. Dante followed, catching up.

"Besides," he continued. "It's too late to drop it. You know as well as I do that we're in too deep now. We could all try to walk away, but what then? They'd find us. You know they would. We will always be a threat to the project, to Jones, even after the project gains approval. And, you also know that all it would take to gain overwhelming public support is simply one catastrophic event. Something even one-tenth of the scale of 9-11 would convince nearly everyone in D.C. to fast track this thing and start capturing and reprogramming alleged terrorists within days.

And, naturally, at least half of those caught would be innocent except for their being in the wrong place at the wrong time."

"Do you think the public will let that happen?" Tess countered.

"Years of vocal public pressure and a two-term president who actively wanted to close Guantanamo didn't change that situation, did it?"

Tess frowned, "You might have a point. For all the sweet talk Jones spouts about saving lives, word is that he's surrounded by right-wing nationalists with all kinds of dreams for this technology. Rumor has it they've already proposed a program for illegal immigrants."

"Now that's a conspiracy theory even I'm not sure I can buy," Dante retorted. "But yes, Project Sleepwalker is a comforting thought to a frightened nation—a frightened world—that can't manage to wake up from the violent nightmare of clashing ideologies and cultures. Naturally, speculations on how it could be used are sure to abound."

Tess sighed. "So, what, we stay the course?"

"What other option do we have? They are on the verge of something. And so are we."

"But if we don't have Violet…" Tess said softly.

"We can't lose hope yet," Dante replied. "But one thing is still bothering me. What was Thomas doing in Brazil? Why was he after Violet?"

"Oh that," Tess rolled her eyes. "I haven't gotten a straight answer, but it's obviously not any official business for Jones or the project. Thomas is nobody; Jones wouldn't even send him to pick up his dry cleaning."

Dante nodded, "Ah, I see. Then it is as Arisu suspects."

"Tech espionage."

"More than just technology," Dante said. "The nation with a tool like this has a serious power advantage. Control minds and who cares about the people's hearts. Who else wants Violet?"

"The Chinese, the Russians, North Korea—your guess is as good as mine. Israel?" Tess shrugged.

They stopped at another intersection. Exchanging a quick and nearly silent good bye, she crossed the street. Dante waited to cross the adjacent street. In no time, Tess disappeared into the current of people walking the sidewalks. Moving quickly between cars, Dante crossed his street, heading back in the direction of the bookstore. He come to another intersection and had to wait for traffic.

Standing there with his mind full of pressing questions, something caught Dante's eye. A man, about 30 years old, was looking right at him from across the street. The man wore a grey suit. He averted his eyes when Dante looked at him. A sudden sinking feeling crept over Dante. He recognized the man. He was one of Arisu's subject retrieval team members back when she had still worked for the project. Since then, he had gone rogue. Dante turned and started down the sidewalk in the opposite direction.

RILEY OPENED HER EYES. Arisu sat on the floor by the sofa. She stared at the projection, currently displaying a picture of her and Violet at a restaurant. By the looks of it, probably a small Italian place in the North End. Riley looked at the picture for a while. Those two people in the projected image seemed happy, younger, and much freer than she felt now. Had she ever felt that free? Violet appeared genuinely happy. Arisu's eyes sparkled in a mesmerizing manner, the distinctly Japanese features of her lean face all the more beautiful when combined with her obvious state of ease in the photo. Recognition washed over Riley as she stared at the picture.

"So, I guess we might as well be honest with each other," she said.

Arisu looked up at her. Riley now could see that her eyes were red. Riley stared at her, overtaken by awe. She'd never seen her so hurt and vulnerable before. And yet, even in this state, she appeared to Riley wholly beautiful. But a moment later, frustration crept back into Riley's mind and heart.

"What is it that you want?" she asked. "Do you need Violet so you can destroy this project; to do what is right? Or, do you just need

Violet… for yourself?"

Arisu looked down, pressing her lips together. A fresh tear slipped down her cheek. "Would it be wrong of me to say that I need both?"

Riley sat up. "Wrong? Not sure I know what's right and wrong anymore." Turning, she positioned himself on the sofa so that Arisu might sit next to her. Riley gestured for her to do so. Arisu moved up onto the sofa.

"I need you to tell me the truth," Riley said. "I'm falling apart. Everything I know is about to come to an end. *I'm* about to end. At least that's how it feels. And right now, everything I know, or I thought I knew—none of that seem to matter much. I'm lost, Arisu. I have no idea who I am. So, all I'm asking for—begging for—is some honesty."

She nodded, not looking at Riley.

"We—Violet and you—were in a relationship?" she asked.

"Yes," she said quietly.

Riley smiled. "I'm beginning to know Violet now, Arisu. She's inside me… somewhere. I can feel her there. The memories are coming back, more and more, memories that aren't mine. I can't place them all, but the feelings, the pain, the joy; it's all in there, somewhere. I just have to sort it out. Why didn't you tell me before?"

Arisu said nothing for a long moment. "I—" she began then sighed. "I was worried about how you'd react. I mean, fuck! They made you a nun. I didn't know what they'd managed to do to you."

Riley nodded, starting to understand. She looked at Arisu, trying to imagine what she might have been feeling throughout this process.

"Maybe you could have hinted at it," Riley said softly. "Maybe mentioned it at some point, that you're a lesbian."

"Well," Arisu grinned a little, "it didn't exactly come up. Besides, I'm not a lesbian. I'm bi."

Riley smiled a little at this, noting that somehow this news also felt familiar, now that she had heard it. "Okay, now we're getting somewhere. I just wish things would have gone differently."

"We had so little time," Arise said. "We need Violet."

Riley frowned, annoyance rising within her at this familiar refrain.

"It seems to me, what you people keep forgetting is that, even if I am an artificial personality installed over your beloved Violet, I still hold the keys. I still call the shots," she pointed at her head. "If we're going to make this work, I need you to be straight with me."

Arisu cocked one eyebrow up and the corners of her lips rose slightly. "Now that's definitely something Violet never asked me to do before."

Riley blushed and smiled. Images, whether they were constructed or actual memories of her and Arisu together, quickly flashed through her mind. "I mean, I need you to trust me with the truth, all of it. Can you do that?"

Arisu, smile fading, slowly nodded. *She truly is beautiful*, thought Riley. *I can see why Violet fell for her.* It was more than physical beauty. It was the way Arisu looked at her in such moments, the way she had smiled a moment ago.

"In the meantime," Riley smiled. "I seem to recall that you were making us some dinner."

STEAM BILLOWED FORTH FROM the rice as it sat in the bowl in front of Riley. She dished out some long, thin noodles and placed them on her rice. Chunks of chicken and broccoli followed. Then she topped it with just a bit of Soy sauce. It didn't seem like much, but Riley was quite ready to inhale the whole bowl and refill it for a second devouring. Still, she hesitated. Arisu noticed this. She smiled, waiting for her to take a bite. Maybe it was just the fact that everything was changing so quickly, but Riley felt the need for something familiar and comforting. She bowed her head slightly and breathed a silent prayer, the words spilling out of her mind with little effort. Despite this, she wondered just how much she really believed the words that she produced so easily.

She raised her head, her hand instinctively rising so that she might cross herself. She stopped mid-motion, staring at it as if she no longer recognized her own hand. She took her fork and thrust it into the bowl of food. Savoring the first bite, she smiled at Arisu. "It's good," she said. "Very good."

"You're just starving," Arisu shook her head. "It's just a throw together meal. There's really not much here that's any good. I had to get a little creative with this. I hope the chicken and broccoli are okay. It's just the generic frozen stuff."

"It's fine. Creative is good. Creative is keeping us alive."

"In more ways than one," she murmured under a slight grin.

For the next several minutes they ate in silence. Riley's eyes wandered about the room, noticing the rather uninspired decorating. Only a few bland pictures hung on the walls. She figured them to be the kind of thing one picked up at a store for a few bucks and placed randomly about a room that was desperately in need of some character. Of course, the end result would always be a room with only an initial appearance of character. Anyone with mildly developed aesthetic sensibilities would quickly pick up on the cheapness of these "works of art" and would pass the whole issue off as just another example of some people's inability to appreciate beauty in art. She stopped chewing. For the first time, at least that she knew of, she had to evaluate where such reasoning came from. Was this something emerging from Violet, or was this Riley? She stared blankly at the wall for a good while. Violet had been a scientist. But did she like art? Did she listen to classical music? Rock? Rap? Did she care for movies? What kind of movies? Novels? Who was her favorite author? Images flooded Riley's mind; pages of books, scenes from films, paintings from von Gogh to Andy Warhol, an orchestra, a lone cello playing a haunting melody, a jazz band playing on a corner stage in a dimly lit joint late at night. The world before Riley faded. She felt herself fall into the music and the images. All of them clearly stood out as parts of her. Until now, they were undiscovered consciousness. None of them seemed out of place. They had always belonged there, as part of her. Even still, she could not distinguish to whom such experiences had first belonged.

She blinked, returning her awareness to the room. Arisu now chewed her food quietly as she observed Riley. She bore no smile and her eyes seemed heavy with exhaustion. She swallowed and looked down at her bowl.

"I'm seeing so much more," Riley said. "I can see and feel and know so much more than before. It's hard to explain. But I still can't place it all. I can place certain feelings and memories into the right context now that I know a little more about Violet. But, there are some things that I can't place anywhere."

"Like what?" Arisu asked.

"Well, first of all," Riley looked around. "Whose place is this? Even as more things start to feel familiar, as you start to feel more familiar…"

She glanced at Arisu in time to see her eyes narrow a little and the corner of her mouth twitch slightly. Riley felt warmth in her face even as she felt a familiar sense of comfort in that look from Arisu.

"This is my place," Arisu sighed. "Well, my new place. Things have been rough since I left the project. I spent most of what I had in savings traveling and tracking down leads until I found out where you were."

Riley looked around with new understanding. The sparse and rundown apartment confronted her now as a testament to Arisu's commitment to finding Violet. She looked at Arisu, but she was staring down at her food.

"And then," Arisu continued without looking up, "I had to stay in Brazil for some time while Dante and I devised a plan for extracting you. I wanted to do it right, to find the right time. But Thomas showed up and…"

"Thank you," Riley whispered. The words ushered forth from her lips with surprising sincerity.

Arisu looked up, and Riley could see the threat of tears in her eyes. Unsure that she was quite ready for this, ready to be the emotional comfort that Arisu likely hoped for, Riley grasped for a shift in topic.

"So this is your place. What about Violet? Did she like art? I can tell that I have a particular appreciation of art. But part of that may be just a lingering thing from Riley… or me. I mean, as a nun, I'm surrounded by art, such as icons. Well, I was, at least. But my appreciation of it seems different now."

"Violet did like her painters," offered Arisu.

"Painters," Riley nodded. "Yes, painters. Warhol. She…" Riley looked at her and smiled with delight. "I like Andy Warhol. Well, maybe like isn't quite the right word. Maybe I'm… amused. Yeah, that's it. I find Warhol's work amusing and not just his painting." It came to her as a pure realization, an emotional statement with a beautiful period at its end.

"What else do you recall?" Arisu probed.

"Violet liked classic films. She… she was fond of Andrei Tarkovsky. But what Violet didn't truly value was Tark's use of profound Catholic imagery in his films, especially in *Andrey Rublyov*, a film about a priest and artist. This meant little to Violet, but it takes on a whole new significance to me now; a different sort of appreciation."

Riley burst into laughter. Arisu observed, almost shocked.

"It's truly amazing, Arisu. I can see things in a completely new light. Step by step, things become clearer. You can't expect to get the big picture by staring at the whole thing. You have to focus in on small parts. You have to get close enough to see the details of just a fraction of the big picture and then, bring only that bit into focus." Riley sat back in her chair, forgetting about food. "Somehow, I suspect that this whole process just doesn't work without a certain amount of priming along the way. Amazing, it's almost invigorating."

Arisu smiled, her eyes lit with joy. "You know, now you're starting to sound like Violet."

"It's because it's all here," she tapped the side of her head with her finger. "We just have to start sorting it out." She grew quiet and sighed. "The catch seems to be that Riley somehow is still here too. It's not quite like Violet is returning and Riley is gone. It's a merging of the two."

"Assimilation," Arisu nodded.

"Which means, in the end we will arrive at an entirely new entity," Riley said, her voice soft.

She stared at Arisu for a long moment, afraid to say anymore, but bubbling with excitement. Finally, she burst.

"We're creating a new person, Arisu. I'm not sure this is what the project or you, for that matter, had in mind for me, but here we are."

They returned to the food momentarily. Riley dished out more for herself. Arisu concentrated on the bowl before her. This lasted for only a few minutes. Riley finished only half of her second bowl and pushed it aside.

On the bright side, Riley no longer felt the gloom of having to face some sort of annihilation. What had been laid before her now seemed like a personality overhaul.

"I'm still becoming something else," she said. "I know this isn't what you were hoping for. But, can you tell me more?"

"More about what?"

"More about us? Or Violet and you, to be precise. I have memories, more like fragments, really. But, then again, no real context emerges yet. So, it's hard to place things together; to draw any significance from it. It's hard to differentiate between a memory and my imagination."

"Imagination, eh? What exactly do you see in there?" Arisu probed with a playful grin.

Riley laughed and then stared off, lost in thought.

"When you think of me," Arisu said, more softly now, "what comes to mind?"

"We worked together."

"But you already knew that."

"We went to a concert? Classical music, I think."

"We went to a few of those, actually."

"We drank imported wine on your birthday, an Italian *Pinot Grigio*. It was at a restaurant. Then, you talked me into trying sake. I had never had it before. It was strong. We went to a concert hall for... I can't recall the particular symphony. Afterwards, we went to my place." She looked into Arisu's eyes. "We made love. I held you there next to me for an hour, talking in whispers. Then, we made love again."

A slender tear slipped down Arisu's cheek. Blood rushed to Riley's face. She looked away.

"I'm sorry," she said. "It's just that... I still feel so much like... Riley. And yet, I now can recall every curve of your body and the way you look when you're asleep next to me."

"Violet," Arisu said, locking eyes with her.

And for a brief moment, Arisu did indeed lock eyes with Violet, for Riley felt whatever part of her was still holding on to Riley fade into her mind's recesses. She watched another tear drift down Arisu's cheek. She watched as Arisu wiped it away, her lips pressed together as she sat still.

"Violet," she said again, but the word was no more than a cracked whisper. "What do we do now?"

"You know as well as I do what we have to do next, Sparkle."

Arisu gasped.

Riley shook herself out of the trance. She looked at Arisu now with pleading eyes, longing for some explanation. Arisu sighed heavily and stood. Covering her mouth with her hand, she excused herself. Riley sat alone and in silence at the small, wooden table. She heard the door to the bedroom close. Moments later, she heard the unmistakable sounds of the sorrow Arisu could hold back no longer. Or was it fear? Maybe some unfortunate mixture of the two now manifested itself in her. Riley rose from her seat and walked to the bedroom door. Her hand reached out to knock, but she stopped an inch short of the wooden surface. Her fingers relaxed. Her hand opened. She pressed her palm against the door, taking in a deep breath.

"Arisu," she said softly. "Arisu."

Riley opened the door, finding Arisu collapsed on the bed. She moved slowly, sitting next to her crumpled body. Riley's hand touched her arm and Arisu looked up, her face a display of agony and longing. She helped Arisu sit up and took her into her arms. Arisu rested her head on Riley's chest.

"I've never known anyone quite like you," Riley said. "You've been so very strong so far. Don't leave me now. I need your help. We can make it. I can't guarantee what the outcome will be, but we can get through the clouds in my mind. We have to stop the project, right?"

Arisu looked up at her. "I need Violet to do that."

"I know."

"Riley, I wish you didn't have to go through this. I'm so sorry. I think you are…"

That moment, Arisu's phone emitted a series of musical notes, clear and pleasing. She pushed away from Riley and stood. Heading to the living room, she answered the incoming call. Riley followed.

"Where are you?" she said into the phone, still wiping away the remains of tears. Her face grew pale. She looked at Riley with wide eyes. "I understand," she said and then hung up.

"We have to leave!" Arisu said to Riley.

18 BATTERY WHARF

[I]n not too many years, human brains and computing machines will be coupled… [and] the resulting partnership will think as no human brain has ever thought before.

- J. C. R. Licklider
(Creator of ARPANET, the precursor to today's internet)

LOCATED IN THE OLD Coast Guard Base right on Boston Harbor, a rather uninspired rectangular building housed the central computers and research labs for the project. When the Coast Guard had moved to a new facility, NeuroCorp was able to lease the building as part of the development deal they had made with the U.S. Department of Defense. The only stipulation was that the project attract as little attention towards itself as possible. This initially presented no problem to Jones. After all, the last thing he, or anyone on the project, had any desire to do would be to call attention to what they were doing. But then the possibility of profiting in the commercial sector presented itself with side projects connected to the R&D from NeuroCorp. The grey building bore no marks or emblems aside from an old Coast Guard base signage, which was now mostly rusted and faded. Parking could be found on the east side of the building. From there, one could see the bay.

Often, Jones had stepped outside in the wee hours of the morning to gaze out over the bay. Ships came and went while planes circled Logan Airport. On clear nights, the light of the stars and moon reflected off the bay's surface. Despite major development, Boston still managed to maintain a certain level of peacefulness. Of course, it didn't hurt that directly next to the base was a luxury hotel and condos. Sitting at the tip of the North End neighborhood, Battery Wharf had become a place for the wealthy and connected to congregate. It certainly made things easy for hosting politicians and other influencers when they needed to pay NeuroCorp a visit. As such, the location on the harbor afforded a level of serenity. For Jones, at any rate, Los Angeles seemed too crazy; New York too self-absorbed; Washington DC— well, it was both crazy and self-absorbed; a magical shit storm. Sure, it had its sort of American "royalty" to it, but he didn't much care for the political "super stars." But, political star power did open doors. They demanded he be close. He longed to be far from them. Let them peek in when utterly necessary, he had always figured, but no more than that. He needed them to keep their distance so that progress could be achieved. So far, Boston had worked well enough. After all, Boston and neighboring Cambridge had long been one of the hubs for budding tech companies. He had lived in San Francisco for a while developing one of his first tech ventures, but when that folded, he found employment through a tech company in Cambridge. Awhile after that, Jones launched NeuroCorp.

Jones, leaning against the side of the building, chuckled lightly. As he stood there, looking out over the bay lit by bright sunlight, he heard two sets of footsteps approaching him. He pushed off the building and stood up straight. His pudgy belly pushed out past the suit jacket he wore. He turned the corner and put out his hands.

"Well, well," he said, "Looks like you boys finally decided to join us back here. How nice of you."

Rikard and Thomas stopped. Rikard grinned with a certain dark delight. Thomas just stood there, probably waiting for what might come next. Jones wanted the little bastard to squirm.

"How was the flight?" Jones carried on in mock friendliness.

"It was a flight," Rikard answered.

"Get some rest?" Jones asked.

Rikard glanced at Thomas, "As much as can be expected."

"Wonderful," Jones smiled, "Shall we head inside?"

Jones opened the small metallic door by punching in a code for the security system. The three men stepped inside. Immediately inside the door stood a small room where a guard sat with a magazine, a mug of coffee, and a small radio playing pop music. The young guard stood up, setting the magazine aside. Jones glanced at it.

"Is that the new *Filmmaker Quarterly*?" Jones asked.

"Sure is," said the guard.

"Anything in there about the new fellow from Egypt?"

"There's an article on him. Haven't finished it yet, but good so far. It's pretty wild what he's been doing," the guard beamed with enthusiasm.

"Drop it by my desk when you're done, if you don't mind. I'll have to read that," Jones said. "But there's no hurry. I'm kind of in the middle of a few things right now, anyway."

The guard nodded, shifting his attention to the two men accompanying Jones into the building. Thomas nodded and forced a smile. Rikard made the slightest of motions with his head in acknowledgement, but otherwise remained straight-faced. The guard removed a small tablet with an attached scanner from his belt. He pointed it at each man, a beep emitting from it each time. Detecting the needed access beacon that each man wore inside a piece of clothing or in their wallet, the tablet connected to the network, searched the facial recognition database, and approved the men for entry.

"I'll just need your cellphones," said the young man.

Jones pulled his out and handed it over, as did Rikard. Thomas reluctantly handed his over as well. The guard pecked a few more commands into his tablet and the door at the right corner of the room opened.

"Have a good day, gentlemen," the guard gestured towards the door.

Jones, Rikard, and Thomas left the room. The guard took his seat again, returning to the magazine. The door slid shut behind them. It latched with a loud metallic clank that echoed in the concrete and metal hallway. Rikard glanced back at the door then to Jones.

"What is it that you find so great about having a young punk like that as a guard when you could just have the whole system automated?" Rikard asked.

"Ah, yes, automation," Jones grinned. "We once believed automation would save the world. Automation is a dream of the past, Rikard. Sure, we have a wonderful security system. But systems can be hacked. Even the best systems can malfunction or be broken. Each new development generates new hackers with new skills, new tricks. They're as bad as bacteria. What doesn't kill you does indeed make you stronger. And smarter. What I have are young minds and strong bodies that give me something more than a series of ones and zeros to work with. They give me loyalty."

"I assume that's why you insisted on making that little scene in there?" said Rikard.

"Oh, come on," Jones laughed, "You and I both know that what's-his-name, ah, Ghinarro, is a fantastic up-and-coming independent filmmaker. I honestly like what I've seen of his work so far. Not that I've seen much. But you see; caring keeps such people loyal to me. I'm more than his boss. I have an interest in him and what he likes."

Rikard shook his head, "Do you pull that shit with me?"

Jones rolled his eyes, "Ha! By no means, Rikard. I wouldn't patronize you like that. After all, I pay you more than enough to not give the tiniest shit about your favorite color or song—if you're even capable of appreciating such things."

"Ah, the perfect boss," Rikard sighed with a smile. He looked at Thomas. "You haven't said much."

Thomas snapped his attention suddenly to the other two men. "Oh, I'm still feeling jet lagged. I'll be fine."

The three walked into the large, open main floor with several computer works stations. Men and women worked at their desks, staring at screens intently. The three took the stairs at the back right corner up to the balcony that ran along the edge of the building and overlooked the main floor. Doors leading to labs, computer rooms, and more research facilities lined the rest of the warehouse. They passed several. Here and there, a scientist popped out of a door, walked down the hall with tablets in hand, and punched in a code to another door and disappeared. Jones led the way, finally stopping at a door to his right. Several more doors stretched on past this one, along both sides of the hall. He punched the code in. This door, however, did not immediately unlock. Instead, a small panel slid open on the wall next to the door. A chin rest projected out of the opening. Jones placed his chin on it and looked into the light that came from the opening. "Approved," said the automated voice once the retinal scan had been completed.

"Sorry, boys," Jones turned to them. "But you're going to have to do the same thing before this door opens. New protocol."

Rikard turned to Thomas, "Ladies first."

Begrudgingly, Thomas complied. Rikard followed. The door finally unlatched and Jones led them in. Inside, wall to wall, the room teemed with computers and technicians. Clear screens displayed data, charts, pictures, and live footage of people moving about their lives. Dimly lit, the room felt like the world's quietest rave. Lights blinked and changed colors as computers processed over five zettabytes of data per second, which is roughly 5 million petabytes per second. Technicians touched screens, talked to the computers, and some even used keyboards. The array of technology spanned a vast gap of three, maybe four, solid generations of industrial and scientific development in computers.

"Oh wow," Thomas breathed.

"That's right, Thomas," Jones grinned. "All this time, and this is the first I have let you set foot into this room. And here it is, all the glory and all the truth."

Rikard walked away from the other two men, still looking mostly unimpressed, though his eyes quickly darted about, soaking up the environment. Thomas looked around the room more slowly, not paying much attention to Jones; even less to Rikard.

"So, I have to ask you this," Jones said. "Why would I bring you here now?"

Thomas snapped his attention fully to Jones. "Ah, you… you feel it's time I learned more about the project."

Jones grinned, "Well, yes, actually. And why would I want you to learn more?"

"Because… knowledge is power," Thomas tried.

"Ha!" Jones shook his head. "You know, we really latched on to that for some time, knowledge. But, you know what? The denial of knowledge may provide us with more power than we ever expected. Science has always advanced most when someone develops an unfair advantage. That's why history celebrates Galileo's telescopes. In the 1600s, when Anton van Leeuwhoek developed a secret method for creating, at the time, the most powerful microscopes in the world, he discovered single celled organisms. A tradesman turned scientist wielded amazing power because he possessed tools that no one else did. That's what Sleepwalker is about, our unfair advantage in the world. It's not just knowledge that is power, but the knowledge to control knowledge. The lie holds the power, Thomas. That's something we must come to grips with. The lie has always held the power. Why do you think, for as long as humanity has been present on this planet, that we have told fabricated stories to each other? People go to movies, stream television shows; fiction means so much more to us than fact. People hardly read the news today. Television news digressed to a flashy set of half-truths with great visuals or sound bites. In fact, an entire goddamned election was guided by fake news, some of which was propagated by another country. Even the infatuation with 'reality television' quickly degenerated into a well-controlled cheap fabrication of reality."

Rikard frowned at Jones, "That's quite a nice lecture, professor. But this isn't sociology class."

"On the contrary," Jones shook his head and walked over to a large clear screen that displayed several views of people walking the streets of Boston. "This is the beautiful marriage of sociology and psychology. And these two have their own dark little affairs with philosophy. This is the greatest lie, fiction, and story that humanity has ever told. And we… we are the dream weavers *and* the dream catchers. We stand at the brink of something magnificently new. This makes everything we do here incredibly delicate."

Jones leaned over and whispered to a technician sitting at the computer. The woman touched the screen, opened a series of files, and arranged them on the screen. Jones thanked her and turned to his two pupils.

"But you see," he continued, "Even as I work with lies to generate a better existence for people who otherwise would be obliterated from this planet by a system built on killing our nightmares—our sociological mistakes, as it were—I prefer to have some awareness of the truth."

"So you really are all about saving live?" Thomas said. "Keeping death row inmates from dying?"

"I won't lie to you on this, Thomas. I'm no fan of our penal system. It may be true that, in some cases, we should just kill off some sick bastard who hasn't an ounce of dignity and respect for life. That's just how life works sometimes. But, I have to start somewhere. What I ultimately want to provide is the opportunity for people to start over. Why should we spend all our money on caging our social misfits? Why not make them fit; the fittest? And why should people live in misery over the mistakes of the past? Haven't you ever wanted to start over? Forget that nightmare from childhood. No one should have to live with the burden of an abusive father, or of being molested, or watching your classmates die in a mass shooting, or mourning a breakup or the loss of a loved one. In one, maybe two generations we could program out of people the need to resort to violence as promulgation or proselytization of an ideology or religious view. It would be the end of terrorism as we've known it."

Rikard stood slack-jawed, for the first time letting his surprise show through. Thomas now kept his eyes fixed on Jones. Both men obviously felt uncomfortable with Jones's chatty new mood. Jones looked from one to the other and smiled.

"Come on, you two," he said, "You look a little worried."

Thomas cleared his throat, "Well, this is just a bit new to me. I've been working for you for—"

"—Four years," Jones interrupted, "And now, I'm telling you more in a few minutes than you have learned in four years. Maybe I've been a bad teacher or maybe you've been a lousy student. At any rate, I keep my eyes open. I always protect my interests against any possible threats. This is too important, you see."

At this, Thomas stiffened. He glanced at Rikard, whose lips curled in a cruel smile. Jones nodded with satisfaction. He had Thomas right where he wanted him. The poor man had no idea, not the slightest inkling, just how badly he'd managed to mess up any prospects for his future in the field, or his future, period.

Jones spoke again, "I think you know what's going on here, Thomas. So, I recommend that you come out with all you know, all you planned."

Thomas stood, frozen. Jones observed the man as tension visibly mounted inside of him. Thomas cleared his throat again. He looked from Rikard to Jones and back again.

"What do you mean?" Thomas attempted.

"Oh, come on, Thomas," Jones raised his voice. "Give me the benefit here. You know I know. So let's be honest. You struck a deal with the Brits. You struck a huge deal. But, the problem is, you have no clue what you have gotten yourself into. You were going to hand over Dr. Murphy to them. And the hope was that she would be able to divulge to them valuable information for their program that is quite similar to this one. Am I missing anything, or did I at least capture the spirit of your conspiracy?"

Sweat beads rolled down Thomas' face. His breathing had become quicker and shallower as Jones spoke. Jones stared at the trapped and scared, little rat.

"So what do I do with you?" Jones asked. "Tell me what to do with you?"

Thomas didn't move, unable to do more than stare blankly off into nothingness.

"Deer in the headlights," Rikard chuckled. "The sad thing is, I think he honestly thought he might get away with it."

Jones turned to Rikard. "That he *believed* he could, I have no doubt. But, that leaves us here with an annoying problem on our hands, a liability of sorts. I need to know how much he communicated to our British friends." Jones looked at Thomas again, "You see, Thomas, they were going to pay me good money to share information with them; very good money. We would have been funded for a full three years, enough time to get this thing rolling at full steam. But you got in the way, they offered you a fraction of what they offered the program, and they knew that they could get exclusive information that I would not sell to them for any price. Information I could not sell to them because of our contracts with the Department of Defense, the National Security Agency, and the Central Intelligence Agency."

Thomas' eyes widened at this, "So, it's true. You are developing projects for DARPA."

"Oh, are we starting to appreciate the magnitude of the shit storm you created?" Jones taunted. "And to think that you believed you knew enough to actually pull this off. So now... now, now, now. Now that I have you here, I guess I can do as I please."

"Hold on," Thomas raised his hands. "I didn't really share that much with them. My deal was pretty much to deliver Violet. That's it, really. You kept me on the edges of the project anyway. I really have no idea what actually takes place here. Not the inner workings. I was just developing software applications for the installation process."

"Ooo," Rikard shook his head, "Playing the ignorance card. A little late for that, isn't it? You did work directly under Violet."

"Now wait," Thomas said, "I haven't delivered her..."

"Only because it proved to be more difficult than you thought it would be," Jones growled. "What is it that you want from me, some kind of mercy? Well, you're in luck. I'm going to extend mercy your way. I'm going to let you go. I'm going to let you deal with the people who hired you. After all, I do believe they'll want the three quarters of a million back that they'vw already paid you."

Thomas' eyes grew wide. Jones laughed.

"Oh yeah," Jones said, the satisfaction gleaming in his eyes. "We knew as much. Plus there's... oh, I don't know... the US government will be interested in trying you for treason. I can make one phone call and you'd be shipped off to an undisclosed holding facility for the CIA where they'd likely have a lot of questions for you."

Thomas looked around the room again. "That's why you brought me in here. That's why you gave me top level security clearance all of sudden. You set me up, you piece of shit."

Jones laughed hard at this. "You set yourself up. And in the end, turning you over to the CIA is a good backup plan. But I think I might be able to come up with a far neater solution."

Thomas shook his head as he stared with incredulity at Jones.

"Take a good look around," Jones said softly, "enjoy it while you can. Because, when you wake up, you will feel... like a new man."

Thomas visibly shook. "Wait a second. I can go away. I can disappear. I'm telling you. I can do that. I haven't really damaged anything."

"Damaged anything?!" Jones screamed. "Violet is out of our hands. Arisu *has her*. And your British friends are close by, I'm sure. That's actually the worst thing you could have done, you dumb fuck!" Jones turned away, letting his anger subside. He looked at Rikard and clicked his teeth together. "Get him out of here," he snarled.

A FEW CLOUDS MOVED through the sky over Boston. Along the busy streets surrounding Faneuil Hall, new cars sat in the early evening traffic. At the stoplights, projected images provided entertaining advertising to those waiting to go through the red light. People walked quickly down the sidewalks. Blending into these people, Dante kept his head down. He had not wanted to go this direction, but what choice did he have? He had lost sight of the project agent, but was sure the man hadn't lost him. He pushed his way past a crowd that was gathered to observe a street performer balancing plates by the statue of Sam Adams. Dante crossed the street and cut through the Holocaust Memorial Park and continued until he reached the entrance to North Station where he slipped inside and took the stairs that lead down to the subway platform. A crowd of people waited for the next train on the Orange Line. He could also take the Green Line. Neither option really helped him get back to Arisu's apartment, but he had to shake off his tail.

He looked about for a place to wait inconspicuously. A spot on a bench was open several yards from him, but no one stood near it. Right next to it, an advertising panel flickered. This drew too much attention to that spot. Though his legs ached and longed for a rest, he chose to slowly wade his way deeper into the still crowd.

He looked at the entrance. A few more people walked down: a businesswoman, a student with a backpack, two older men, and a young couple hand-in-hand. It disturbed him to no end that project agents would be after him already. He couldn't let down his guard. He felt sure that the moment he did, they would pounce upon him. On the other hand, he wondered if, now, he might be running into a trap. Fleeing so quickly, he might run without looking forward and fall right into their web. And these brown recluses would be sure to attack with no mercy. Still, he couldn't sense them near at all. His link-up provided him with a certain amount of traffic and subway information, when he was able to tap into open internet and cellphone signals. Nothing seemed out of the ordinary, thus far.

He looked the place over again. Just then, a young man dressed in a dark grey suit walked down the steps. Instinctually, Dante felt their presence again. The man stopped half way down the steps and looked the place over. Dante tried to keep his head down and still observe the man from the corner of his eye. The man's lips moved and Dante felt sure he now talked to someone else through the hidden network of microphones, which all project agents wore on their clothing. Dante felt the man's eyes lock upon him. Instead of hiding, Dante looked up and locked eyes with the man. Judging from the small bulge under his suit coat, Dante could tell that this one carried a handgun. But in such a public place, that gun would not be coming out so soon.

The next train arrived. On the opposite side of the tracks, people exited the cars. The doors slid open on his side. People funneled in. Dante wedged into one of those human funnels.

The man trailing him walked quickly down the rest of the steps and managed to make it into the train right as the doors closed. Already out of the train and on the other side of the tracks, Dante walked briskly towards the steps. The man was still searching for any sign of him inside the train. Only as the train began to move along its magnetic field did he see Dante standing on the steps, looking back at him.

19 INSTALLATION

Emotions do more than add richness to our lives—they're also the secret behind how we navigate what to do next at every moment.

- David Eagleman

THEIR FOOTSTEPS ECHOED DOWN the hall despite the thin layer of green carpet. Arisu stopped at the stairwell and listened. Nothing. Riley stood next to her, a small black bag in her hands. They proceeded down the stairs. Reaching the bottom floor, Riley stopped. Arisu, however, kept moving. She looked back at Riley with concern.

"Come on," she said. "There's a garage below."

Reluctantly, Riley followed. They reached the large metal door. It stuck on her first attempt, so Arisu put more force against the cold metal. It crashed open. The sound echoed off the concrete walls in the damp and dimly lit garage. Several cars sat near the door, most of them older models that looked a little worse for wear. Arisu walked down the row of vehicles and stopped next to a silver Jeep. She turned to Riley, pointed to her own eyes, then waved her finger in a half circle. Riley nodded, gathering that Arisu meant for her to keep a look out. She glanced slowly around the parking garage. Arisu walked to the driver's side of the Jeep and lowered herself to the dirty concrete ground. Lying on her back, she pulled out her smartphone and turned on the camera's flash. Using it as a flashlight, she searched the underbelly of the vehicle for anything unusual. It seemed to take a long time, though Riley assured herself it couldn't have been more than a minute or two. Satisfied, Arisu stood up. Riley, still keeping the lookout, glanced at her. Arisu nodded and pointed to the Jeep and Riley walked to the passenger side as Arisu hit the automatic unlock on her keychain. As quietly as they could, they climbed aboard.

Once they had pulled out of the garage and on the street, Riley tossed the bag behind her seat. She looked out at the vaguely familiar Boston streets. She'd been too distracted when arriving at the apartment building to give the neighborhood much thought, but now she wondered if it might be Boston at all. Maybe it was Lynn, North of the city. It made sense to her, but she still didn't feel connected to the place. When in Brazil, Boston and its many neighborhoods and surrounding communities had been a memory, an awareness that she had come from there. Now that she found himself here, she couldn't actually bring herself to remember clear specifics—at least not with the same inherent sense of familiarity one might have expected. Street names only bore a distant connection to things in her mind, if at all. The place felt the same and different all at once. But then again, with every passing moment, Riley felt different. It was hard to explain. Just… constantly different.

"So, this is the car you left?" she turned to Arisu.

"It's Dante's, actually," she said.

The light turned green. Before oncoming traffic had the chance to react, Arisu cut in front of them with a quick turn to the left—banging a left, as it was known locally.

"What were you checking for? A bomb?"

"No. A bomb would be too big. Too much attention would be drawn to it. I just needed to make sure it hadn't been tampered with, like it wouldn't start or worse, wouldn't stop. I didn't find any of the usual signs of someone planting a tracking device. Although, I suppose they could have covered it up well. It's a chance we're going to have to take for right now."

"Where's Dante?"

"Try to relax for now. He's good. He'll be there."

Riley frowned and looked back out the window. "We seem to find ourselves in this situation a lot, at least since we met in Brazil."

Arisu smiled, "Sorry, I'm still being vague."

"Yeah. A little. And here we are in a car, driving to who-knows-where." She turned to Arisu. "I know more now. I'm learning, no, recovering more with every passing minute. But it doesn't feel like enough yet. We need to go somewhere."

"Okay," Arisu kept her eyes on the road. "What did you have in mind?"

"Violet's apartment."

She looked at Riley, eyes wide. "No. We can't go there."

"Why not?"

"Too risky."

Riley grinned. "Thank you," she said, looking out her window again.

"What? What do you mean?" Arisu demanded.

"Oh, nothing," Riley shrugged.

"No," Arisu said, anger creeping into her voice. "It is something. What is it? You have to tell me."

"Not so fun being in that position, is it?" she turned to Arisu again. "I can recall where Violet lived. I think I might be able to get there. And, judging by your reaction, it's still there. Otherwise, it wouldn't be risky. It would be pointless."

Arisu sighed, "Damn it."

"Please, Arisu," Riley said. "I'm learning to trust you. Try to trust me. I'm here. I'm in this, for better or for worse. There's no exit for me now. I want all of this to be over with. But, until I can really reconnect with Violet, I have very little to work with."

"You have me," Arisu said softly.

She glanced over at Riley, and in that fleeting second Riley could see pain, anxiety, and longing in Arisu's eyes.

"What if that's not enough?" Riley said as gently as she could.

"We can't go there, Violet," Arisu said; her voice soft but determined.

"But it's there. It's intact. I know it. They left it intact exactly for this sort of situation. When bringing Violet back, they needed to be able to place her right back into a very familiar environment, *her* environment."

"And that's why it's too dangerous," Arisu raised her voice. "It's theirs, Riley. They keep it well guarded."

Riley looked back out her window at the world outside. The setting sun cast long shadows. More clouds gathered in the sky. Most of the streetlights were now on. Arisu took an entrance ramp to the highway. They drove for several minutes in silence.

"Get the bag," Arisu said, at length.

Riley complied without a word. Reaching behind her seat, she pulled the bag around and set it on her lap. She looked at Arisu, awaiting further instructions.

"Inside, you will find a Z-57 and several cartridges," she explained. "The cartridges are in the side pouch."

Riley frowned at her, unable to hide her incredulity. When Arisu said nothing else, Riley opened the bag. Sure enough, just on top of the things Arisu had packed into the bag sat a silver and black handgun. Riley looked up and blinked, then turned to her.

"What am I going to do with that?"

"Stay alive," she said.

"Do I even know how to shoot?"

"Well, judging from the way you handled yourself at the roadside stop and the airport, you seem quite capable of defending yourself." She glanced at Riley, "Though I'm not quite sure how you came by those abilities."

"Really? I was hoping you could help me with that part. So far, I find nothing about Violet that would account for that."

"It's noise," Arisu said. "It must be. That's the only thing I could think it would be."

"Noise? That would be, ah…" she rubbed her forehead. "It's there, I can't quite recall it. But it's… ugh, I can almost remember."

"It's spectral interference. This interference, this noise, it is a phenomenon that the project encountered with some subjects implanted with new personalities. It's a result of residual data that doesn't fit into a particular category. Therefore, it can't be placed within a proper programming pattern for the subject's brain. The mind has to interpret this as something, so it often ends up as an odd memory or, in some extreme cases, a bit of strange behavior, like a phantom skill. Usually, it's nothing drastic. Some subjects had nightmares; others had an out-of-character desire to play a certain sport or musical instrument, though they had no reason to do those things. A couple of times, a subject just left the country due to some sudden desire to go see the pyramids in Egypt or Big Ben in London. But I have never seen anything quite like what you have. Although, spectral interference might be an explanation, at least in part, for why you sleepwalk."

Riley sighed. "I kind of miss the days when my sleepwalking problem ws my biggest concern. But, I'm not sure I can buy that noise has made me an expert in self-defense."

"Violet could have planted something. She might have prepared for this exact situation," Arisu granted. "Maybe she managed to prepare her own special type of 'noise', in case she was ever supplanted. Maybe it was her way of giving you a fighting chance, so to speak."

"But she didn't tell you?" Riley asked.

"No," Arisu shook her head. "And I'm just speculating, but if Violet did anything like that, she might have decided that it was best to keep it a secret, even from me. You know… just in case."

Riley stared down at the gun for a long minute. Unsure if it was the thought of carrying a gun that had affected her or carsickness had set in, she felt her stomach turn. She looked out the window again. The world around her had gotten much darker in mere minutes. Heavy clouds hung over the towering Boston skyline straight ahead. The darkness of oncoming night seeped into her heart as their Jeep crossed the Zakim Bridge and into the tunnel.

Riley zipped the bag shut without taking the gun.

THOMAS STOOD HIS GROUND, watching, as all around him technicians prepared his Installation Bed. It looked like nothing more than the usual hospital bed, except it did not move or tilt up. A subject would be out cold for quite some time while the installation process took place. Once this initial phase was complete, he would be taken to the Phase

Two bay where he would lie dormant for nearly a month. Nanites would swarm his brain and scientists would hover over his body, keeping him alive. Thomas shuttered. He still wore his clothing, despite having been instructed several times to remove them and put on the pasty white body suit. Once more, a short, stern woman stepped up to him. This time, she took hold of his elbow.

"Come on Mr. Coleman," she barked. "No use in delaying."

With lightning speed, he shook his arm free from her grip, brought it around her, took hold of her arm with his left hand, and twisted her arm hard behind her back. Everything stopped. Technicians and scientists stared. Security sprang into action. Thomas used the woman's body as a shield, making his way to the door. The guards drew their Tasers, the only weapon they could carry inside the compound. The first shock struck the woman's ribs. She went limp. Thomas thrust her forward towards the approaching guard. He ducked the next shot, barely. He came up with a hard uppercut to the guard's stomach. His left hand pried the Tazer from the guard's right hand. In an instant, he had the guard turned, facing away from him, and the weapon aimed at his heart. The man coughed and gasped for air.

"I can get three rounds off before you bring me down," he announced. "They'll go right into his heart."

The three remaining guards halted their advance. Thomas moved slowly for the door. The guards crept along with him, still maintaining the same distance.

"Open the door!" Thomas yelled. "Open it!"

The guard closest to the door hit the access button and the door slid open. Four agents poured in. Caught off guard, Thomas stared at them in surprise. The guard he held hostage delivered a hard elbow to his stomach. Thomas gasped. The agents pounced. Unable to make sense of what took place next, Thomas hit the ground. The world spun in a frenzy of kicks delivered to his torso. He couldn't breathe, and his lungs burned. Pain took over. After a moment, the frenzy stopped. He gasped then spat blood on to the floor.

"Give it up, Coleman," one of the agents said.

Thomas felt a sharp pain in his left arm. He discovered a technician bent over him, emptying a syringe. The room blurred into a blue and green mess. The laughter of the agents echoed painfully in his head. Then, darkness came and with it, a bizarre peace.

"WELL, HE DECIDED TO give us a bit of a show after all," Jones said, leaning against the back of a chair in the control room.

Rikard still stared at one of the security monitors. "What do you gain by reprogramming him?"

Jones stood straight. "Still haven't caught on to my methods? I'm not reprogramming him! I'm just sedating the sonofabitch. He'll basically wake up with a hangover; a hangover and the ever present knowledge of how badly he fucked up and how close he came to just vanishing."

Rikard turned to him. "So that's it? You're tossing him out?"

"It would seem that way, wouldn't it?" Jones winked. "At any rate, you and I have to move on. Our problems haven't gotten any smaller."

"The agents lost Dante," Rikard groaned.

"More or less," Jones raised his hand. He pointed to another monitor. "Randy, bring up Tess's file."

A row of several pictures and a video feed of a woman working at one of the computer stations in the complex were displayed. Rikard stepped closer, glancing at Jones.

Jones gladly continued, "This is Teresa Eleanor Gomez. She's, a defector. She's on their side now. But we still have the power to influence her. I've called off the agents. Let them regroup. In just a few minutes, Tess will be contacting them. She will arrange for a meeting. And then, my friend, Violet will walk right into our hands. Arisu brought her all the way here. Now she can hand deliver Violet. Very kind of her, don't you think?"

Rikard frowned as he muttered, "I doubt Arisu will hand you shit."

"Oh, come on. Have a little more faith in me," Jones shook his head.

THE JEEP SAT QUIETLY in the dimly lit parking lot of a small municipal park, the old combustion engine still humming. Dante glanced at it as he walked calmly across the park. He passed a couple on a bench. They paid no attention to him, too wrapped up in their conversation. Dante strolled by on the cobblestone path. The scent of freshly cut grass still hung in the air and, judging by the bits of grass shavings on the sidewalk's edge, Dante figured this must have been the day's last stop for a crew of city groundskeepers.

He approached the Jeep. Still several yards away, the doors opened and Arisu stepped out. She stood by and waited. Dante nodded his greeting, not wanting to call any more attention to them than necessary. Once he came within just a few paces from the vehicle, Arisu smiled at him.

"Glad to see you made it alright," she said.

"It was a close one," Dante admitted. He leaned down and peered into the car. "How's she doing?"

Arisu's look said it all. Dante lifted his hand for a slight wave to Riley, who simply nodded in return. Dante shook his head.

"This isn't good, Arisu. What are we going to do if we can't get Violet to emerge?"

The melody that emitted from Arisu's smartphone kept her from answering him. Reaching into the Jeep, she plucked it up from between the seats and answered the incoming call.

"Arisu," came Tess's voice came over the phone's speaker, "Are you in a safe location?"

"For the moment," she said.

"Is Dante there?"

"I'm here," Dante volunteered.

"Good," Tess said. "We need to meet tonight."

Dante looked at Arisu, frowning. Arisu shrugged. "Why?" she said.

"I managed to recover Violet's original phone." Tess explained, her tense voice becoming softer. "I can't hold on to it for long. I have to get it to you right away."

Arisu and Dante stared at each other, eyes wide. "Tess," Dante said, "How did you get a hold of that?"

"I can't explain right now. We just have to meet. They will know very soon that it's gone. I have to get it to you before they get to me first."

"Alright," Arisu said, "Where do we meet you?"

RILEY LOOKED OUT THE windshield as Arisu parked the Jeep. Dante sat next to her, looking out the passenger window. This particular Back Bay street was dark, with seemingly few streetlights. Arisu turned around and looked at Riley, who sat in the back. She held out a handgun for Riley, who looked at it carefully.

Is this where I'm headed? God, is this who I am now? Riley shook her head.

"Riley, come on," Arisu said. "I don't know where you learned to fight the way you do, but we have to play it safe."

Riley shrugged, "I'm not sure why I know how to defend myself so well. Was Violet really into self-defense classes? Was she a scientist by day and NRA member on weekends? I'm missing something here."

Arisu frowned, glancing over at Dante.

"We all seem to be missing something," Dante muttered.

Arisu shook her head, "Don't think we have time to work that all out right now."

She thrust out the gun to Riley who looked at it again. Her hand nearly rose to it, but she stopped. *Where are you? Where am I in this? I can't pretend I know anymore what is true or not, but this feels...*

Even in the privacy of her mind, Riley couldn't quite form the words. But she felt certain that she could not—would not—carry the gun. Everything was changing so rapidly that she needed to hold on to some sense of normality. Riley Bekker did not carry guns.

"I'm not walking into a public place with a gun," she said, at last.

At this, Arisu and Dante exchanged surprised glances.

"You're not going anywhere," Arisu said.

Riley raised her eyebrows. Even as she did, she could see Arisu's jaw tighten. Vague feelings of long lost arguments washed over her as she stared at what felt like a familiar expression on her girlfriend's face. *Violet's girlfriend*, Riley corrected herself.

"If we take you," Arisu said, "we run the risk of walking you right into a trap."

"Or, we can run the risk of me waiting right here for them to spring a trap on me," Riley pressed back. "Either way, this doesn't strike me as an ideal situation."

Arisu looked at her now with the same stern eyes. Riley stood her ground, amazed at how calm she felt. Arisu blinked and turned to Dante.

"This could be a trap," she said. "But if we bail out now, I guarantee that we will never get our hands on Violet's phone. And not just that, but Tess will be exposed. She can't go back now."

"Why does the phone matter?" Riley jumped in.

"You kept encrypted notes," Dante offered up. "And since you always had your phone on you or locked up, it was a relatively safe place for such notes."

"Notes on what?" Riley muttered. But even as she did so, she saw a brief flash in her mind's eye of the phone. A feeling of dread washed over her.

"They were notes on the ethical failures of the project and illegal engagements," Arisu answered. "Of course, Violet knows all of that by heart."

An unbidden sense of guilt washed over Riley. "Right," she nodded, "but without Violet here…"

Arisu looked away.

"Besides," Dante jumped in, "we can't leave Tess hanging. They may already know the phone is missing and be coming for her."

"That means we're wasting time," Riley opened her door.

"You're not going in there," Arisu grabbed her arm.

Riley locked onto her eyes, jaw clenched. "To waiver now would be a terrible mistake, Arisu. Risks will have to be taken. Sooner or later this whole thing is going to hit the fan. And when it does, you won't be able to protect me."

Something changed in Arisu's eyes. Her grip loosened and her hand slid to a rest on Riley forearm. Her touch was warm and gentle. Arisu turned to Dante.

"We'll go in," she almost whispered. "Just Riley and I. You stay here. If it is a trap, we have to get out of here fast. Keep it running and be ready to drive up and get us out of there. Do your thing and, you know…"

She nodded her head toward Riley.

"I'll do my very best to keep an eye on things from here," Dante said flatly. "Are you sure about this?"

Arisu looked back at Riley, who did her best to repress her own growing fears. Arisu nodded.

"Okay," Dante nodded once.

The three of them climbed out of the vehicle and stood on the sidewalk. Arisu walked to the back of the Jeep, opening it. She rummaged through a bag that had been left in the Jeep before her trip to Brazil. Riley leaned close to Dante.

"What just happened?" she whispered.

Dante smiled. "I don't know. You tell me, Violet," he winked.

Dante walked to the driver's side and climbed in. Riley watched him, but all the while she replayed his words in her mind. *What did he mean by that?* Arisu closed the hatch and stood by the Jeep in the dim streetlight. Lifting her shirt slightly, she slipped a handgun into the waistband of her pants, near the small of her back. Into her back pockets she slipped two extra clips. Riley couldn't help but notice Arisu's lean abdomen when she had lifted her shirt. In a rush, Riley's mind retrieved long lost memories of touching Arisu's bare skin. The smell of her hair suddenly surrounded her. For a moment, she felt embarrassed by the familiarity of these thoughts. However, something inside her also found great comfort in those memories. For an instant, Violet gazed at the woman she had loved. Indeed, she truly was beautiful—more than

Riley had let herself recognize. Arisu now stood straight and had pulled her shirt down. In spite of the heat, she retrieved a jacket from the bag in the back of the Jeep. She slipped it on, allowing it to cover the handgun.

Turning to Riley, Arisu looked her in the eyes. "You're sure about this?" she asked, her voice low.

"These days, I'm sure of very little," Riley grinned weakly. "But I am sure that I can't sit by anymore. I can't let the two of you always put your lives on the line for me. If I understand this correctly, Violet picked this fight. Maybe it's time she started fighting it again, however that might work out."

The corner of Arisu's mouth curled up slightly. She nodded. "Then let's do it." She turned and walked across the street.

20 EASTERN STANDARD

[A]t the turn of the twenty-first century, a new field called nanobiology, or nanobio-technology, came into being. Once relegated to the pages of science fiction, this burgeoning new discipline allows scientists to 'couple' biological systems with machines. In 1999 DARPA awarded grants for biohybrid programs. The stated goal was to create cyborgs--part living creatures, part machines.

- Annie Jacobsen

LOCATED ON COMMONWEALTH AVENUE, just a short walk over Big Pappy Bridge from Fenway Park, Eastern Standard was a lasting establishment in Boston. Riley and Arisu walked down the sidewalk together. Arisu's eyes scanned every person they shared the sidewalk with. Riley tried to swallow back the rising butterflies in her stomach. As they reached the front entrance, with its red canvas covering that extended onto the wide sidewalk, Riley and Arisu both instinctually reached for the door, their hands brushing lightly for a moment. Arisu allowed the hint of a smile to escape her lips before she lifted her hand, allowing Riley to pull the door open.

Inside, Riley looked over the place and spotted Tess, whom she managed to now recall vividly. Tess was sitting at the bar with her back to the door. Riley slowly began to move in her direction.

Arisu hung back by the door for a moment and looked around. When asked by the lanky host if she'd like a table, she feigned having just spotted who she was looking for and also headed for the bar.

Riley took a seat next to Tess, who had a martini glass before her. "Hi Tess," Riley said, just above the din of people and the music.

Tess glanced over. "Violet?"

"Not quite," Arisu answered as she approached.

She wore a broad smile and reached out to Tess. Following the queue, Tess stood and acted as if meeting an old friend. They hugged and, for the brief moment they were close, Tess whispered, "I might have been followed."

The three of them settled back at the bar. Riley didn't like having her back turned to the room, but at least large mirrors lined the wall in front of her. The mirror was partially obscured by liquor bottle that stood on the shelves before it. It made the place feel bigger, but Riley's heart raced inside her chest as she felt confined, trapped.

"I saw my chance," Tess said in casual tone, "and I figured this was as good of a time as any, since you're in town."

"Your boss didn't mind?" Arisu asked.

"He's been a little distracted since Thomas and Rikard got back," Tess answered before sipping her martini.

The bartender approached and asked what Arisu and Riley might like. Arisu ordered a seven and seven, Riley asked for gin and tonic. Riley watched Arisu's reflection as she scanned the room in the mirror. Briefly, their eyes met. The bartender returned with their drinks.

"So, the phone?" Arisu asked.

Tess reached into her small purse and retrieved a slender smartphone. Riley recognized it instantly. A quick rush of dizziness hit her as she recalled how she had encrypted the notes on the phone. She had used an app that appeared to be a collection of old video games.

"It hasn't been wiped?" Riley whispered.

"Not that I know," Tess said, sliding the phone over. "But, I made sure it was off. I guarantee the moment you power that thing up, they'll be tracking its location. You might want to build yourself a Faraday cage before you turn it on."

Riley nodded and reached out for the phone. Tess surprised her by reaching out her left hand and grasping Riley's hand. She squeezed firmly with her sweaty palm. Riley looked into Tess's wide eyes.

"I'm sorry, Violet," Tess said. "They took my brother."

Riley felt a sharp prick in her hand and she pulled it away. She stared with unmasked horror at Tess.

"What did you do?" Arisu muttered.

A tear slipped down Tess's cheek. "It's just a sedative."

Riley felt a prickling numbness expanding out from her hand. She had to fight it, she had to stay alert.

"Goddamnit, Tess," Arisu whispered.

Tess turned to Arisu, "I'm sorry. I was—"

Suddenly, Tess's whole body stiffened and her muscles began to spasm. She arched her back and fell. Riley caught her. Arisu looked around the room but saw no one.

"Is she okay?" the bartender said, approaching.

"Call 911," Riley shot back.

Tess foamed at the mouth now, her body convulsing. Riley recognized what was happening.

"They're killing her," she said to Arisu. "They must have injected her with nanites of some kind, one of the weaponized projects. It's attacking her nervous system."

"We have to go," Arisu ordered.

"We have to help her!"

"She sold you out."

Riley felt her arms shake as she held Tess. The convulsing woman felt heavier by the second as the numbness moved up Riley's right arm. She could already feel the world around her slowing down. Involuntarily, Riley let Tess slip to the floor. But as her body crumpled, Tess reached out her right hand and grabbed Riley's arm. Another sharp pain shot through Riley's skin.

She looked down at Tess's fear-filled eyes and hit the floor. *Sonofabitch, did she just give me a second dose?* But this time the skin on her arm burned. Even as her mind fought to stay alert, Riley realized what had happened. Tess had anticipated that Jones wouldn't hold up his end of the deal. She had armed herself with a stimulant to combat the tranquilizer.

"We have to go," Arisu said, grabbing Riley's arm and pulling her along.

"Hey," the bartender called after her. "The ambulance is coming! Where you going?"

"We can't leave her," Riley protested, her speech slightly slurred.

"We can't stay," Arisu fired back.

Arisu didn't look back as she rushed to the door. Riley felt herself pulled along, her mind swirling with the effects of the sedative, which had a definite head start over the stimulant. They pushed their way out the door. Riley's blurred vision registered a man standing on the sidewalk. Was that…

"Arisu," Rikard called out.

"Run," Arisu ordered.

She pulled Riley to the right, bumping into a waiter before jumping over the velvet rope that marked off the outdoor dining area. They rushed past a vendor selling Red Sox t-shirts. They were just a few paces from the subway entrance which descended below the street. Riley turned her head back in time to see a smeared shape that she was certain had to be Rikard, in hot pursuit.

"We can't leave her," Riley muttered as she collided with someone's shoulder.

"Any time now, Dante," Arisu blurted out.

She led Riley down the steps that descended into the Kenmore T stop. Riley stumbled on the steps and Arisu had to pull her up. *Why are we going down here? Dante can't pick us up down here.* Arisu pulled her along, through the tunnel that led to the subway access gates, to the other side of Commonwealth Avenue, which allowed people to enter from either side of the wide and busy street. Up ahead, two tall men in suits locked eyes with Arisu.

"Shit," Arisu hissed, "we're going in."

"Arisu," one of the men called out to her. "Stop right there."

A wave of nausea washed over Riley and she blinked. Inside her chest, her heart fluttered and began to race. The stimulant was kicking in. A new level of awareness seemed to grab a hold of her mind. She felt Arisu's hand on her arm, holding on tightly. Her hearing picked up not only the sound of the crowd walking and talking, but on the subtlety of Arisu's breathing. They were short, anxious breaths. *She's scared that she's about to lose me again.*

The two men approached. Riley watched them with increased clarity. The dizziness was pervasive, but she could see more clearly now, her adrenaline was pumping. The world around her felt as if it was slowly tipping over on to its side but, at the same time, she felt ready to fight. *Should I have grabbed a gun after all? No! Too many people; way too many people,* she argued with herself.

Arisu made a move to the entrance gates but was stopped by Rikard's voice.

"Don't do it," he called out from behind them.

Both Riley and Arisu looked back. He was approaching from the direction they had come. People brushed past him on their way to experience some night life in Back Bay. As Riley brought her head around to face forward again, she caught the eyes of three young men passing by who seemed to have noticed that something out of the ordinary was happening here. The tallest of the three tapped one of the others on the arm and they stopped. They were muscular with short hair and carried themselves in a way that unmistakably told Riley they had fought overseas. *Tall one's a Navy Seal, maybe all three of them.*

"Is she okay?" the tall one asked Arisu.

"She's not feeling well," Arisu said automatically.

"Roofied," Riley managed. She pointed back at Rikard then to the other two agents. "That asshole and his buddies over there slipped something into my drink."

"Yo," the tall man called out to Rikard, "you slip this girl something?"

"That's none of your concern," Rikard shot back. "Now move along."

"Oh, but I think it just became my concern," the tall one stepped closer to Rikard.

One of the other two approached Arisu and Riley. "What do these guys want?"

Riley jumped in before Arisu could say anything. "They're just a little upset I'm not interested in them. Not my type." She leaned her head on Arisu's shoulder and planted a playful kiss on her cheek.

The man talking to them looked back at the two men who stood a few yards away. "Motherfucker," he shouted back in a distinct Boston accent. "What year is this? Are you fucking serious, dude? And it takes three of you assholes to chase down these two?"

"These women are wanted criminals," Rikard growled.

"Like hell they are. Show me a fucking badge, bro," the tall one stepped closer to him.

Rikard smiled, "I don't think you want to deal with the trouble you're about to get yourselves into. So I sincerely recommend you move along."

"I sincerely recommend you show me a badge, bro."

"Okay," Rikard shrugged. He reached into his suit jacket.

Riley knew what Rikard was going for. Would he really pull a gun in a crowded tunnel in Boston? She watched him over her shoulder, feeling as if everything were now moving in slow motion and beat him to the punch.

"Gun!" she screamed before Rikard could produce one. "He's got a gun!"

The tall Good Samaritan tackled Rikard, throwing him to the ground. The two agents rushed forward, but the other two good Samaritans blocked their way. People screamed and rushed about, trying to get out of the tunnel. Riley watched as people pushed past the two agents. Suddenly, one and then the other crumpled to the ground. Dante stood just behind them, Taser in hand.

Behind Riley and Arisu, the tall man landed a hard blow to Rikard's face with his right hand, as he held Rikard's right wrist with his left hand. "Drop it," he yelled at Rikard.

"Gentlemen, we thank you for your help," Arisu said to the two men closet to them, "but our ride is here and we gotta go."

"Don't you want to call the cops on these three?"

"Next time," Arisu said, walking off.

"Sorry, things to do," Riley said, giving them a quick wink.

Reaching Dante, they rushed out. Behind them they heard more yelling as the tall man and Rikard still fought. Then, they heard a new yell: "he's getting away."

Rushing up the stairs that led to the entrance on the other side of Commonwealth Ave, they burst out onto the street. Riley still struggled with being able to travel in a straight line. As they reached the sidewalk, a hand grabbed her arm and pulled hard. She spun around and found another agent in a grey suit.

She gave it no thought. She delivered a hard blow with her knuckles right to the agent's throat. He gasped and dropped. But as he fell, another man in a suit just behind him produced a gun with a silencer. Riley had only enough time to drop hard to the sidewalk and kick at his leg. She only got a glancing blow in on his shin, and he stepped back. His gun pointed down at Riley.

"You don't want to do that," Riley said. "I'm too valuable."

"Actually," the agent smirked.

Riley watched as his finger moved over the trigger. She felt a horrible bolt of electric dread shoot through her as she realized he was going to execute her right there. Then his right shoulder jerked back with a loud crack and a red mist of blood filled the air. His gun dropped as he fell back, crying out in pain.

Looking back, Riley found that Arisu had her gun out. She rushed forward and pulled Riley to her feet.

"Let's go!" she barked, pulling Riley along.

There was pandemonium on the street now and people ran away from the scene, screaming. Dante had double parked the Jeep just across the street. They dove in and he threw it into gear. He made a u-turn and peeled down Commonwealth Ave, away from Back Bay.

AT FIRST, HE BECAME aware only of the dull, yet powerful ache in his head. Something wet and cold touched his face. He moved his hands, but they felt heavy and weak. Slowly pushing himself up to a sitting position, Thomas became aware that he rested on a sidewalk. Lying on his side, water splashed from a gutter and onto his face. His head throbbed now that he was vertical. He groaned. *What happened?* The memory of the struggle came to him. Why could he remember that? Why hadn't they reprogrammed him? How long had it been?

"Oh, damn it, Jones," he muttered, "You piece of shit."

Just had to mess with me, he thought. *I'm not important enough to be reprogrammed.* That would have been a waste of millions of dollars of resources and expensive nanobots. A dose of sedatives, however...

A man walked passed him, giving him no thought. Thomas figured he must look like a drunk who had passed out along the street. He stood slowly, his head still hurting. His sense of balance seemed intact; though maybe a little slow to adjust. *What exactly did they inject me with?* He put out his hand, stumbling forward, and braced himself against the building's brick siding. *What day is it?* He looked about. *Or rather, what night is it?* Another person walked passed him in the opposite direction of the last.

"Excuse me," he said, his voice coming out more like a cough. "Excuse me, please, what day is it?"

They ignored him. He knew he had to at least get himself straightened up before he could figure anything out. *But where am I?* He looked about. The building he leaned against appeared to be an old apartment complex. He spotted a liquor store not too far down the street from him. Beyond that, he saw a large parking lot stretching out before a grocery store. It didn't feel familiar. He felt sure he was still in Boston, but he could not place this neighborhood. At least, not while in this state of mind. Automatically, he reached for his phone in his pocket. *Oh, right. Jones made me turn that in to the security guard.*

Thomas gathered his strength and stumbled forward. *I'm going to kill you, Jones. I'm going to give you some of your own shit. Then, let's see who's smarter.* As he walked along, his left arm still using the wall to brace himself, the thought occurred to him that his British employers might like to hear from him. This latest development wouldn't go over well. It was at that moment that Thomas realized Jones's plan. *The son of bitch is going to let them do the dirty work. He doesn't want to deal with the body right now. He'll let them do it.* He stopped walking. He had to come up with some plan. The money he had so far might be able to get him out of the country. *But they'll track me.* He started walking again. *Then I'll just finish the job. I'll stick it to Jones once and for all.* He laughed lightly to himself. First, he needed to go back to his place.

Checking his other pockets, he discovered his wallet. Nothing had been removed from it. He stood by the street corner and looked about. A block away, he spotted the entrance to the orange line on the T. Maybe he was in Jamaica Plain? He walked towards it, feeling the pain in his head with every step. At the station, he found the doors locked. Seeing a digital clock inside, he realized how late it was. It was nearly 1 AM; the trains had stopped at least a half hour ago. He didn't have his phone to request a taxi or rider service. Walking a few blocks, he found a bar. There, he managed to use a phone and request a cab. Ten minutes later, he climbed into the taxi. The sudden acceleration made his head swirl with renewed pain. Nausea stirred up in his stomach. He covered his face with his hands and rubbed his forehead.

At home, he could rest a bit. He had to recover. Then, he would have to devise a plan. Right now, however, sleep tugged on his mind and body. He wasn't able to concentrate. He lay down in the taxi seat—it was extremely uncomfortable—and slept.

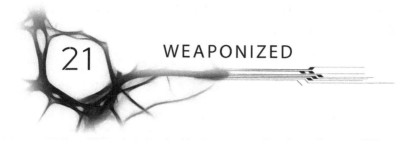

21 WEAPONIZED

In 2007, in a solicitation for new programs, DARPA stated, "Human brain activity must be integrated with technology."

- Annie Jacobsen

ARISU WHIPPED THE CURTAINS shut. Dante stood by the door. They looked at each other without moving for nearly a minute. They listened carefully to the news report on the TV; the news anchor concluded his report as if there were no cause to question the official report.

"Authorities say the shooting may have been gang related," the news reporter on the TV said. "No one has been arrested, but witnesses are talking to the BPD."

"No one arrested?" Arisu said stared at the television incredulously.

"They're cleaning it up fast," Dante mused. "I didn't realize Jones had such deep connections."

"What are they doing? That agent was going to shoot Violet."

"Maybe we have to consider the possibility that, in their minds, it's simply safer to have her dead than run the risk of losing her to the wrong people."

Arisu looked away, not responding.

The motel room smelled musty and damp. The lamps cast a yellow light over the brownish walls. Two full size beds sat side by side, a nightstand between them. Only one alarm clock sat on the stand. From behind the closed door of the bathroom, they heard Riley heave. The disgusting splatter of vomit into the porcelain toilet was barely dampened by the closed door. Arisu looked off, taking a deep breath. Dante moved away from the door and took a seat on the bed closest to

Arisu. Moments later, Riley stepped out of the bathroom. Water ran down her face. She quietly sat on the other bed, closest to the bathroom door. She looked down at the floor for what seemed to her like eternity, not speaking.

"Feel alright?" Dante asked.

Riley moaned.

Dante looked at Arisu, who turned from the window. She took a seat in a poorly padded chair in the corner. Dante sighed and turned back to Riley.

"How much longer are we going to do this?" Riley asked.

Arisu did not respond. Instead, she leaned forward and placed her face in her hands. She took in deep, steadying breaths.

"Who was Violet, really? I knew those three men in the tunnel were Navy Seals. I just knew. And I defended myself again… until that last part."

Arisu looked at Riley and shook her head. Riley looked up at them for the first time. Arisu looked off. Dante made eye contact, steady and yet worried.

"I endangered the lives of people who have nothing to do with this," Riley said. "But I feel like I'm not any closer to knowing the truth. And now, Tess is dead, but for what? What are we really playing at here?"

When no answer came, Riley stood and paced the small room. Dante stood as well, but just watched her.

"They killed Tess. Those assholes killed Tess!" Riley sighed.

In a flash, Riley punched the wall. The boom echoed. Riley leaned against the wall, tears streaming from her eyes. Arisu now stood, shaken. Dante stepped closer.

"Easy now," Dante tried to reach out for her.

Riley retracted, moving away from his hand.

"Dante," said Arisu. "Maybe you could go get us all something to drink."

Dante turned to her, frowning.

"I need to talk to Riley," she explained. "Give us some time alone. Please."

He softened and nodded. Taking one of the room keys, he headed out. As the door closed and latched, Arisu stepped closer to Riley.

"Riley," she said softly. "I'm sorry. I'm sorry that this happened. We took a risk. They're obviously much more aware of our plan than we expected."

She laid a hand on Riley's shoulder. Riley turned, and to Arisu's surprise, took her into her arms. It was a moment before Arisu could compose herself, before she could remember that, despite how this felt, this still was not Violet holding her. *So what?* The thought startled her, but she remained still, wrapping her arms around Riley. After a minute, Riley loosened her hold and let go slowly. Arisu took her by the hand and led her to the bed. They sat side by side.

"Riley," she spoke softly, "Look at me."

She did, her face stern, tears drying under her eyes.

"At least remember this," she continued. "I'm here because you got us out of there. You did some fast thinking in that tunnel. I hate to admit it, but I was in over my head. You got us out of there alive. And I'm sorry about Tess. I know you two... Violet and Tess worked together a lot."

"She was a good person," Riley said, "A damn good scientist. She helped me compile the list of violations and doctored test results. She... used to tease me about liking you. She shouldn't have put herself on the line for us, Arisu. She should have run away."

"Riley, she was used. That whole thing was well planned out. When she gave away that it was a trap, she knew what would come next. The fact that she dosed you with that stimulant saved your life."

Riley hung her head. "She shouldn't have ever helped Violet. No one should have. You should have never helped her."

"Of course I helped you," Arisu shot back.

"But they're too powerful. What can we do? What did I think you could do? We can't take them down."

"Don't say that," she grew stern. "We have to stop the project."

"Why?"

Arisu looked at her in shock. "Why? Because Jones is going to unleash a whole world of problems on this country that not even he is prepared to deal with. The system is far from perfect. Violet knew this. There will be consequences. But, even if it's perfected, that's worse than the project's flaws. We would all be in danger. This goes beyond terrorists and violent criminals, Riley. This is about every last person on the planet, from now to eternity. Our government will be able to reprogram people, important people. Government officials will become nothing but puppets. Celebrities, artists, rock stars, religions, political parties, entire ethnicities, you name it. All of them will be in the project's sights sooner or later. Once Jones hands this thing over to the people who originally funded it, it'll all go to hell. A society based on the ability to think freely will become extinct. Merely the illusion of free thought will be all that remains. We will all believe every thought that goes through our minds will be our own original thoughts. But will they be? Maybe, maybe not, but we will never be for sure."

Riley sighed, staring off.

"You said something back there," Arisu continued. "You said something about weaponized nanites."

Riley looked back at her frowning. "Yeah."

"Are they weaponizing nanites?"

Riley stared off, lost in thought. "I… I can feel something there. It's…"

"They probably hid those memories well," Arisu sighed. "So it's true. Jones is working with DARPA. It sure would explain a lot."

Riley looked back at Arisu, eyes wide. "I wish I could remember."

"You will," Arisu smiled. "This is what we're fighting, Riley. And, if Jones really is selling some of this tech to DARPA or doing research for them in exchange for other resources, then this is only the tip of the iceberg. We're basically the Titanic and, if it's all the same to you, I'd rather survive the impending collision."

"I think I want to throw up again," Riley managed a weak smile.

"No pressure, huh?" Arisu laughed.

Riley shook her head and sighed.

"More importantly," Arisu said, her voice now barely more than a whisper, "the woman I love asked for my help. So, of course I'm helping her. That's why."

Riley looked up at Arisu, whose eyes glistened with the threat of tears. Arisu never quite figured out if it was Riley or Violet acting in that moment, but Riley leaned forward, reaching up to Arisu's face, and kissed her lips. Arisu melted into the kiss, relenting to the touch which she had missed so much.

But, a moment later, Arisu pulled back.

"I'm sorry," Arisu said. "I miss Violet."

Riley nodded. "I think she misses you too."

In silence, Arisu looked at her for a long moment. Was there any chance that it was Violet who sat next to her? Had it been Violet who kissed her? Was it even possible at this point that Violet could ever return?

"If even half of what you're saying is true," Riley said, "then we do have to stop the project, no matter what!"

Arisu perceived a new fire behind those eyes. She wanted to believe that, even if she could not recover Violet, this fire now blazing in Riley's eyes could carry them to the end. She also conceded to herself that all they really needed was the knowledge Violet held. Whether or not Violet ever returned seemed to be inconsequential next to the ultimate goal of stopping the project. They were going to have to give their lives. Arisu saw no other way.

"That was a nice speech, by the way," Riley grinned.

"Thanks," she smiled, her mood becoming lighter. "But I can't take credit for it, really. It's basically what Violet said to me—what convinced me to join the fight."

"You sure there wasn't anything else?" Riley smirked, knowingly.

"Well yeah," Arisu nodded.

"You really loved her," Riley said, softly.

Arisu paused, her smile fading. "Love her. I still love her. That hasn't changed. At least, love as we understood it. Maybe nuns see love differently."

Riley shook her head. "'No greater love is there than this: to lay down one's life for another.' Isn't that what you've been doing this whole time?"

Arisu nodded just slightly. "It's beautiful. Who said it? A saint? A philosopher?"

Riley smiled, looking away. "Jesus."

Arisu smiled, "Well, that's embarrassing. I probably should have known that one. Sorry, can't say I've ever been to mass. Church is…"

"You don't have to apologize," Riley interrupted. "The sad truth is that I'm not even sure I understood what that meant till now." Her face grew bright, her eyes wide. "And that's the thing, Arisu. That's the thing that gives me hope. I can't honestly say I really believed, not 'till now. I can't honestly say I knew love 'till now. They can program personalities on top of other personalities. They can give the illusion of life experience, but they can't program faith, or love, or hope… or even joy. All of that has to come from somewhere else, somewhere deeper; somewhere real. It's the raw stuff that makes us human. It's *this* more than anything else that will keep us from forever becoming mere biological hard drives. Don't you see, in a very real sense, we've already won. They are the ones fighting a losing battle. You can program the human mind, but not the spirit. It transcends that ability."

Riley laughed, startling Arisu, who watched as Riley shook her head and laughed again. A few, thin tears streamed down her cheeks.

"What is it?" asked Arisu.

"That's what Violet began to see, I think," Riley said. "At least, in part. None of this, which comes to me now, feels new. It's like I've known it all along. I just haven't put it into words. I haven't been able to find the words." She looked at Arisu, her hands reaching out and taking hers. "What if that's the big flaw? What if that's it? Violet finally came to the realization that humanity at its core transcends such technology. Has there been a perfect personality implant? Wait… You don't even have to answer that. I know there hasn't been one."

Arisu pulled her hands from Riley's and stood. "That can't be it. It's too simple."

"Too simple?" Riley frowned.

Arisu sighed then snapped her finger. "The phone," she said. "We need to check the phone."

Arisu had forgotten about the phone in the aftermath of the escape and Tess's murder. Apparently, Riley had too. Riley pulled out the phone and looked at it.

"We can't power it up here," she said. "We're going to need a Faraday cage, like Tess said, or some other means to be completely off grid."

"Faraday cage?" Arisu asked.

"It's a structure often built out of thin wire mesh that blocks out radio waves of any kind. It would make it so Jones can't spot the phone's location the moment it powers up. The phone doesn't need to be on any networks. We just want to access local files."

"Right. Which brings up another issue," Arisu sighed again. "What are the chances that there's even anything on that phone?"

"Only one way to find out," Riley said, standing up. "We'll just have to make a Faraday cage. There has to be a hardware store around here."

Arisu smiled, "You know, you are starting to sound a lot like Violet."

Riley smiled weakly.

THE DOOR LATCH CLICKED so loud it made Thomas' head hurt. He stood against the door in his darkened apartment. Normally, he would have felt relieved to be home. He had been out of the country for nearly two weeks. *How did I expect to get away with this?* He moved forward, his hands sliding along the cold wall. His fingers ran across the touch-switch. The light came on. The sight of his living room finally brought a feeling of relief: the bookshelf filled with novels, the old UHD television unit facing the sofa. He stood a few feet away from the sofa, it's back facing him. The light cream colors of the walls, the brown of the carpet, all things he knew so well. He breathed a sigh of joy.

"How was the trip?" a feminine voice said softly.

Rising from the sofa, where he could not have yet seen her, a woman stood. Her blond hair brushed her shoulder. He recognized the eyes, the high cheekbones, and the usual business slacks, white shirt, and slender suit jacket.

"Oh, Janet," Thomas shook his head. "You scared the shit out of me. What the hell are you doing here?"

"You know," she continued in her crisp British accent, her voice becoming more of its usual growl. "I think I should be asking you that. You were supposed to return from Brazil with this Violet lass."

"Things didn't go as planned."

"You don't say," she cocked her head to the right. "We managed to gather as much. So maybe you could start by filling us in, you know, with details. We would love to know them."

Thomas moved into his kitchen, nothing more than a small area open to the living room where the carpet gave way to tile floor. He grabbed a glass from the cabinet above the sink and filled it with tap water. Grabbing a bottle of Advil from the top of the microwave, he popped a couple of pills and washed them down with the water.

"Jones is too smart," he said. "I should have known."

Janet walked to the edge of the carpet, "You assured us that you'd be able to give us Violet. We know about Jones's little helper, ah, what's-his-name…"

"Rikard," Thomas spat the word out with obvious disgust. "But he wasn't the whole problem. I didn't count on Arisu."

"Arisu?" Janet repeated, as if it were some new term she had yet to learn in a science class. "Is this the traitor girl?"

"That's the one. She and Dante surprised me. They managed to convince Riley that…"

"Riley?" she raised her eyebrows.

"Yeah, Riley. That's the personality that was installed over Violet. They managed to convince her to trust them instead of me."

He leaned against his counter. She crossed her arms. Thomas looked down at this glass of water. Janet cleared her throat. He looked up. She stared at him with cold eyes. He marveled that anyone could manage to pull such a sexy look and demeanor, and yet be so completely cold and repulsive. As far as Thomas was concerned, Janet was the definition of "bitch"; not that she didn't treat him well enough, most of the time. Yet, he always felt suspicious of her, figuring she would eventually betray him. He always felt on edge around her, like she was a wild animal ready to strike at any moment. He looked apathetically back into the chill emanating from her cool, blue eyes.

"What are we waiting for?" she said.

"You want me to go fetch her for you… now?"

"Violet is here, isn't she? This Arisu brought her back to Boston. What is it that they plan to do? Why bring her back?"

Thomas shook his head, "They want to blow it all to hell. They want to destroy the project. Basically, they want Violet for the same reasons you want Violet. She knows it all. She was quite valuable, I guess, not that I honestly understand it."

"What do you mean?"

He pushed off the counter. "It's just that Violet is a young, agile woman. She's attractive and she seems able to fight. But she's supposed to be a scientist who made some big breakthroughs in neuroscience. She worked on the project from the beginning, I guess. There's got to be more to her than we've been told. She fights like a soldier. She holds key information to the program. And right now, everything revolves around this one woman. How often do things really revolve around one person? The more I think about it, something seems way out of whack."

"Well," she turned and walked to the sofa. "Whack it back into place. And do it quickly."

She plucked up a small, black purse from the sofa and headed for the door. She opened it and stopped. Thomas walked into the hall.

"How does twenty-four hours sound?" she said without looking back.

"Uh, to get Violet?"

"No, to go to the sodding mall," she spat back. "Yes, get Violet, you bloody nitwit."

"I'll do my best."

"Fuck your best," she snapped. "You have twelve hours."

"Wait," he protested, "You said twenty-four."

But she was out, slamming the door behind her. His headache, which he had begun to forget, throbbed. He stepped forward and leaned against the door. Looking down at his watch, he saw the time: 2:34 A.M. *Might as well make some coffee. Sleep's out of the question.* He walked back into the living room. For the first time, he spotted a slender, dark green tablet that sat on the sofa. It rested upon a piece of paper. Scribbled in Janet's handwriting were the words, "Use this to keep track of Jones's communications with his agents. Get to Violet first."

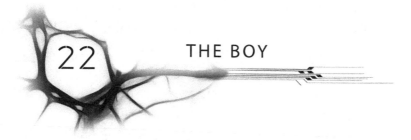

22   THE BOY

The concept of AugCog [Augmented Cognition] sits at the scientific frontier of human-machine interface, or what the Pentagon calls Human-Robot Interaction (HRI).

- Annie Jacobsen

"THIS IS GETTING TOO messy," Jones muttered. "How does she keep slipping past us?"

Rikard rubbed his eyes and yawned. Noticing this, Jones moved for the door. Rikard followed him out of the control room, down the hallway, and into a small—all too clean—kitchen. Rikard felt blinded by the LED lights shinning off the white walls, cupboards, and counter tops. Jones pointed to the coffee maker.

"Better fill your tank," he said.

"Something is wrong with all of this," Rikard said, reaching for the pot. "Riley, or Violet, or whoever the hell she is now; she's too clever for us. Combine that with Arisu and some luck, and we just can't seem to get the upper hand."

He poured himself a mug of coffee. Jones did the same. They both leaned up against the counter sipping and grimacing at the hot, bitter swamp water. But the jolt of caffeine was definitely welcome.

"Some of that luck is Dante," Jones nodded. "But you seem to have your own luck. What happened out there on Commonwealth Avenue? That was a fast clean up job."

"I run a tight ship," Rikard smirked.

Jones stared at him for several seconds. "That you do," he said at last. "Sometimes I just wonder who's actually at the helm of that ship."

"Just be thankful we've got your back," Rikard said then sipped his coffee. "You have a chronic defection problem. Violet, Arisu, Thomas, and now Tess, you're lucky you are still standing where you are."

Jones glared at him. "I am Project Sleepwalker. I am NeuroCorp. There would be nothing without me."

"And pretty soon there might be nothing, because of you."

"How dare you?"

Rikard laughed and sipped his coffee. "Drop the pretense, Jones. You're a fuck up and you know it."

"Fuck up? I anticipated the possibility of more defectors. Tess isn't a real threat."

"You're right," Rikard nodded. "She isn't… now."

Jones' mouth dropped open ever so slightly. "You…"

"We made creative use of your yet to be patented technology," Rikard smirked.

"You killed her," Jones stared off, his voice low. "You had no right."

"You are the one who has no right to pretend that the ground is not crumbling right beneath your feet. Tess and Thomas were a surprise to everyone," Rikard said, his eyes on his coffee. "I let you handle Thomas your way, but I wonder if I'll regret that choice."

Jones stared at the white wall for a good while. Rikard continued to sip his coffee. Tipping his mug up to his mouth, Jones drank the rest of his coffee quickly, still looking straight ahead.

"I have to discover who else may be a traitor among us," Jones said, setting the cup down on the counter. "Thomas has really thrown us for a loop. In the meantime, you need to track them. We need to figure out their next move."

"Easy. They'll eventually need to infiltrate this very complex."

"I'd like to avoid that," said Jones, setting his now empty mug down next to him on the counter.

"How do you propose we avoid that?" Rikard probed.

"Well, they need Violet back, right?" Jones waved his hand in annoyance. "They'll do whatever it takes to get her back."

"To stop the project?" Rikard smirked.

234

Jones looked now at Rikard. "It's not about the project. It's about Arisu. In the meantime, we just need to wait for them to try to infiltrate Violet's old phone."

Jones walked out with a huff of annoyance. Rickard watched him through tired and skeptical eyes.

DANTE BREATHED PEACEFULLY. He rested on his side, facing the window and door. He had agreed to sleep first and allow Riley and Arisu to sleep later, while he stayed awake. For a good while, Arisu and Riley sat on the other bed and spoke in hushed tones. Finally, convinced by Arisu that she ought to relax, Riley took a shower.

When Riley had finished, she found Arisu lying on the bed with her eyes closed. Riley still wore the same clothes that she had on before, but now, she felt refreshed. Her eyes, however, felt heavy. She walked between the beds and knelt next to Arisu. Riley opened her mouth to speak to her, to wake her. She stopped herself however. Instead, she reached out and pulled a strand of hair that had fallen on her face. Arisu's eyes opened slightly and she smiled.

"I'm done," Riley said softly.

Arisu sat up and stretched. "I didn't mean to fall asleep. I haven't been out for long, have I?"

"Not too long," Riley sat on the bed. "I didn't take too long in there. But I am tired. Doubt I can stay awake much longer."

"I'll try to make it quick," Arisu said as she rose and walked into the bathroom.

Hearing the shower start behind the closed door, Riley thought back to earlier in the day when they were at the apartment. It felt like ages ago. Perhaps that was why a shower felt so desperately needed. Perhaps it was the sweat and dirt from the run-in with the agents. Perhaps it was the uncertainty of what might happen next. At any rate, the hot shower felt revitalizing and soothing to Riley's aching body. Having been sedated and then the adrenaline, the hard fall on the street… she was quite sore. An inspection in the mirror revealed a nasty bruise on her lower back.

Riley intended to climb under the covers but, as she sat there thinking, sleep took hold of her. She slumped down on the bed, lying on her back. Sleep came with no warning. It came quietly and swept over her completely.

Burn it down, now
Tell them all that it will end
somehow
It comes to this
the love and bliss
the pain that drove you here
must finally disappear

Riley felt her lips move. The sound of her voice echoed. Her eyes shot open. Green light filtered in through stained glass windows. She sat surrounded by a sea of empty pews. She rose from her seat and walked to the wide aisle in the middle. Long pillars lined the sides of the cathedral. They stretched up to a ceiling that seemed to go on for just as long as it was high. She stared up, but her eyes could not focus. Somewhere, from within this vast place, she heard running water. She looked to the front of the church. Instead of an icon or crucifix, as she had expected, she saw merely a fountain. She walked to it, each step reverberating throughout the cavernous church.

As she walked down the long aisle, a young boy darted across it. He hid between pews. But when Riley reached the pew he should have been, she found it empty. She moved on without consternation, only stopping when she reached the fountain. Shaped like a tower of rock, it jutted up from the ground. It stood nearly seven feet tall. Water trickled down from various openings along its surface. Grass, moss, and flowers grew aside its base. Riley knelt before it and cupping her hands, she filled them with water. She brought her hands to her mouth and drank. It ran down her throat, dribbling down her face, cold as ice. She stood, still looking down at the fountain's base. But now, she found herself in a garden. And, as she looked about, she saw before her, tall trees and lush plants, all in bloom. Something about this place moved her. A feeling of profound peace unexpectedly washed over her. She took in a deep breath and a tear slipped down her face.

"Why have you come back?" she asked Riley.

Riley turned and faced Sophia. She stood among the plants with flowing, white clothes wrapped about her. She did not smile. Neither did Riley.

"I've got to piece this together," she said. "You haven't told me everything."

"The mere fact that you have come to this realization is an indication of your abilities, of your progress."

"You're avoiding straight answers."

"How can I give you straight answers? I am merely a construct of your mind, a creation here only to facilitate."

"Then, maybe, you could start by doing some actual facilitating. Start, by telling me where you come from?" Riley demanded. "Why are you here, in my head? Why would I create you? If Violet was in love with Arisu, than who are you?"

"It seems sad to me that we have come this far only to return to this very early question," she sighed. "Is there not yet a more fundamental question you still need to answer?"

Riley frowned, stepping closer to Sophia. She did not move, her eyes watching Riley closely.

"Who am I?" Riley whispered.

"Answer that," she nodded. "And all of this will fall into place."

"I'm Violet."

Sophia smiled at her now. "Are you, now?"

"Well, maybe not yet. But I'm becoming her. I can feel it. It's... It's ah..."

"Assimilation," Sophia finished the thought for her. "But the process is not yet complete, and you should not assume so much upon yourself so early."

"So early? How long will this take?"

But Sophia turned, stepped back into the bushes, and vanished. Riley called to her, running to where she had stood. There was no sign of her anywhere. Still, she called, her throat feeling dry and hoarse. She dove through the bushes, closing her eyes. Her body struck a hard surface.

Opening her eyes, Riley found that she now lay on a cold, hard floor of a dimly lit room. Desks set up in rows trailed off in every direction. She picked herself up from the ground and looked in all directions. As she turned about, she spotted two people speaking. They faced each other. A woman stood with her back to Riley and spoke to Arisu.

"Why do this?" the woman was panicked. "Because we didn't know what we had gotten ourselves into; we have to do this. They lied to us, Arisu. They told us this was about safety, about the betterment of society. It's really only for the betterment of our world in the eyes of a very select group of people. If we keep going now, we will be doing the devil's work."

"Violet, no," Arisu protested, "We can't get out."

"I'm not talking about getting out now. It's too late for that."

"What then?"

"We're going to fight this. We have to bring this down from the inside."

"That's impossible."

Riley stepped closer, but they seemed oblivious to her presence.

"Maybe it is impossible," Violet shook her head. "But I can't be party to this anymore. They're going to wield a power that they don't even understand or appreciate. They don't really want to fight terrorism. A better criminal justice system is a convenient front. It's always been a façade. It's the easiest way to get test subjects. Soon, this will spread to every level of politics. Freedom of speech and the ability for free thought will be nothing more than a convenient illusion. We will believe our minds are our own just as we have always had. But it will be a lie. We will be a lie."

Riley smiled. Arisu wasn't lying when she said that Violet had given her that speech.

"You helped create this," Arisu yelled.

Riley stopped just behind Violet. She reached out and grasped her shoulder. Turning Violet, Riley looked into black eyes. No skin could be seen on the face, just a mass of contorted raw flesh. Riley screamed, pushing the woman; that thing, away. The body collapsed next to Arisu, who screamed as well. Riley covered her ears and ducked. From above, a bright light flooded the place. Riley cowered on the floor. Arisu stopped her screaming. She looked at her now, as if for the first time. Riley looked up from the ground at her.

"When will it begin?" Arisu asked.

"When will it end?" Riley shot back.

"The two shall become one," Sophia's voice resounded. She walked between desks, her eyes intent on Riley. "This concept should not be new to you, Riley."

Arisu looked at Sophia and smiled, "The beginning and the end; alpha and omega."

Riley shook her head, still crouched to the ground. "You're all crazy."

"Maybe," they said in perfect unison, "But what does that say about you?"

Riley wished she could cry; wished she could lie there on the cold floor and weep until whatever vestige that still remained of her own self could vanish peacefully into nothingness. *God, let it end. Let it be oblivion. It has to be better than this.* To her, nothingness became a mistress of great desire. *There is no paradise for* me, she thought. *Mine is a truly lost soul; an artificial soul, made up of nothing but goddamned ones and zeros triggering synapses inside a brain. What kind of God allows this to happen? Or is God just part of my programming?*

She pressed her hand against the cold floor. Only oblivion could offer her a sweet kiss of lasting relief from the vicissitudes of this hell, this simulated purgatory where she must pay for someone else's sins. Arisu and Sophia crouched next to her. Riley curled into a fetal position and shook. She shivered. She cursed.

"Where is she?" Sophia asked. "Why has she not emerged by now?"

"There are greater problems here," Arisu answered. "There are much greater problems here. I don't know if they were prepared for this."

"They created a monster," Sophia lamented. "Infused with faith, they created a monster that cannot let go of her perceived reality."

"Maybe this is the fittest for survival?"

"Time will tell."

The women stood. Riley watched them as they walked away. Their hands joined and they traveled down an aisle between desks. Riley screamed, calling after them. The light from above vanished. The floor grew colder. She no longer saw them, for she could hardly see at all.

For what felt like a long time, she lay on the floor. She breathed slowly and deeply. Her body relaxed. At last, she stood. To her amusement now, for nothing surprised her anymore, all the desks were gone. Riley stood in some unidentifiable empty space. Some dim sense of light cast itself about her, though it did not come from any particular source. This light allowed for about six or eight feet of visibility in any given direction. She walked forward and the light moved with her. It slowly came to her realization that somehow, she was the source of this soft glow. Maybe she was the light. Maybe she was only light. She walked for a long way, with little ambition for the time being. At last, she reached a wall. She reached out and touched it. Again, to her amusement, she found it to be soft, though it looked like metal. She ran her hand over it. Then she ran both hands over the silky surface. Gripping the wall with both hands, she tore the material open. Yellow light poured into the darkness. She continued to tear at the wall until she had made an opening large enough to step through to the other side. Once through the wall, she found herself in a kitchen. Sophia stood by the stove, stirring something. She wore jeans and a t-shirt, not her usual angelic gown. Over the clothing, she had wrapped an apron.

Her hair did not flow freely, but rather hung in a tight ponytail squarely at the back of her head. She looked up at Riley.

"Where have you been?" she said, but her voice carried a harsh edge Riley had never heard before.

"I should ask you that," Riley shrugged.

Pulling out a chair from the small kitchen table, Riley took a seat. She was unsure of what compelled her to move. It was as if she were watching a movie from within the eyes of one of its actors. Sophia returned to her stirring with a disgusted click of her tongue. Riley watched her, not yet sure what to make of this new development. The skin beneath Sophia's eyes seemed darker. She seemed tired, stressed, and annoyed. For the first time, it occurred to Riley that Sophia seemed human. An actual breathing, living, loving, frustrated, hungry, and thirsty human being stood before her.

"Stop looking at me like that?" Sophia said without looking at her.

"What?" Riley came out of her daze. "What do you mean?"

"I mean, stop staring at me like you're hungry or horny, or both. You know I'm mad at you."

"I'm a little confused right now," Riley said.

"I don't see why," she spat back.

Riley pushed her chair back and stood. She stepped closer to Sophia. Her movements, however, still seemed to be happening without her conscious choice. Her right hand reached out, lightly sliding around Sophia's hip. Riley turned Sophia so they faced each other. Sophia stared at her, anger written on her face. Riley now had both hands on either hip, holding her gently.

"Please tell me what's happening?" she whispered. "I need to know."

Sophia sighed, her arms reaching around Riley. Riley's hands traveled up her back and she pulled her into a tight embrace. Sophia rested her head on Riley's shoulder and cried. Not knowing what else to do, Riley held her quietly, rubbing her back lightly. At length, Sophia lifted her head and looked at her. Her eyes, still red from tears, no longer seemed angry, just hurt.

"Why are you doing this?" she said. "Why do you *have* to do this?"

"Do what?"

She pushed away from Riley and left the room. Riley followed, turning the corner for the hallway. What she saw before her, however, appeared as a long, pale corridor with no doors or windows. No sign of Sophia, either. Riley looked back in the direction from which she had been. The corridor stretched on to infinity with no sign of the kitchen and no doors along the walls of the hallway. She looked in both directions trying to get her bearings, but the hall stretched infinitely in both directions. Well, it looked that way. Not wanting to waste any more time, she took off in a full sprint down the direction she had originally faced. While the walls and floor rushed by, no visible change took place in the distance. The point where the ceiling, walls, and floor met into the distance remained the same. No light appeared at the end of the tunnel. In fact, no real source of light illuminated the corridor. All the same, an evenly diffused light cast itself along the entire length, at least the visible length, of the corridor.

Riley slowed her pace. After a few more strides, she stopped altogether. She did not gasp for breath. Her heart did not beat any harder than usual. It was not fatigue that stopped her, but hopelessness. The thought crept into her mind that hopelessness was really spiritual fatigue, the inability to believe any good will come of the situation, of life, of taking another breath. She stared down the hall and sighed. Clenching her fists, she screamed. The sound bounced off the walls with an almost electronic clang. As she stood there, the thought entered her mind that she ought to try the wall again. Why did she have such a short memory? She reached out to the wall next to her. This one didn't feel soft. It felt very much like the drywall, but drywall could be broken.

Then she saw it in her mind: a memory. Just out of college, she had worked with a couple guy friends of hers on a retirement community maintenance crew. They had worked on some old houses, remodeling. Her friend, Jeremy, had leaned up against some of the old drywall and nearly fell through it. It became the joke of the summer, much to Jeremy's chagrin.

Riley stared at the wall. Where had that come from? *I'm becoming who I always was to begin with.* She delivered a hard blow to the drywall, her fist closed. She had broken through. She pulled her fist out of the wall, leaving a hole behind. She noticed blood on her hand. But when she checked it closely, she found that her hand was not injured. Riley looked up at the hole again, watching as blood dripped from it. *The wall's bleeding,* she smirked.

She kicked several times, breaking the drywall, giving only a slight thought to the notion of striking a stud. In a few moments, a hole gaped open before her. Riley was now covered in blood. A slight glow emanated from the other side, but she could see nothing clearly. Crouching, she stepped through. When she emerged, she found herself in a small bathroom. The hole filled in behind her, leaving only the bathroom's dull, yellowish walls in view. A little boy, fully clothed, sat in the tub. He cried, his knees drawn up to his face, arms wrapped about his legs. Riley crouched next to him

"Don't worry about it," she said, though she had no real awareness of what she meant. "We all go through it. She's a nice girl. But the first crush you have, usually never turns into anything."

The boy looked up at Riley, tears still flowing down his face. Riley looked into the boy's face and felt a twisted sense of recognition. She gazed upon her own young face and yet, not a young Riley, but someone else. The boy shook his head and buried it in his arms.

"You'll end up killing us all," the boy whimpered; his words muffled. He held out a black box with a metal bar that protruded from the top, bare wires coiled about the bar. Riley blinked and was on the verge of asking him what the box was for when the boy shrieked, as if he were being ripped to shreds.

THE SLIGHTEST BIT OF blue light crept in through the curtain's edge. Dawn now quickly took over the Boston cityscape with its abundance of sleek, new skyscrapers. Planes cut the sky, arriving and departing from Logan. The city was coming to life.

Inside the little hotel room, this was not the case. Things were still dark and quiet. This included Riley's mind as she lay there, staring at the ceiling. How long had she lain there now? How much longer would she lie there, helpless? She had never pulled the covers back. She had simply slept where she slumped in exhaustion the night before. Arisu breathed easy next to her. Curled up under the sheets and lying on her side, her back to Riley, she seemed at rest. For Riley, rest seemed beyond reach anymore. She sat up. Arisu stirred a bit in her sleep. She briefly watched her then got up. Arisu opened her eyes and blinked at Riley.

"What is it?" Arisu said, through a yawn.

"I have to go," Riley whispered.

"What? Where?" Arisu sat up now, her hair falling over her face in a dark, tangled mess.

"I have to go to Violet's apartment," Riley tried to keep her voice soft and calm.

"Why do you need to go there?" Dante said, his voice clear and loud in the silence of the room.

Riley turned quickly. "I thought you were asleep."

"I did sleep," Dante grinned from his spot in the chair by the window. "But someone needed to keep watch after you two went to sleep."

"Right, I forgot," Riley admitted.

"But why go to Violet's old place?" Dante insisted.

"I have to prime the pump," Riley explained. "I have to do something. I can't just sit here. We have no clear direction. What's the plan? Wait for them to find us, catch us? I can see it now. You don't have to keep it from me. Both of you took your chances. You got to me in hopes of getting Violet back. If you had Violet, you had a plan. But without her, there's nothing."

"And what do you think you'll get from going to her place?" Arisu moaned in exasperation.

"Things are coming to me," Riley turned to her. "I can recall what her place is like. I can see it. I kept... she kept at least one project computer there. Did much of her work right there, at home. If I can access that, I know she left us something there."

"What?" Arisu said, "What exactly did she leave?"

Riley shook her head. "I don't know that yet. If I did, maybe we wouldn't even have to go there. But I can't remember."

Dear God, why can't I just remember?

"Then how do you know it's there?" asked Dante.

"Because I *do*. I can feel it. I know it," Riley insisted, becoming more agitated. "It's like it's on the tip of my tongue, it's right there in my head, and I can't reach for it. I can't pull it out. Like the title to some really good book you read one summer, years ago. You kinda know the plot, but most of the story, the characters, the places… are gone. You can't pull it up."

"Kind of like a dream," said Arisu with a steady and knowing gaze locked on Riley.

"Yeah. Exactly like a dream," she sighed.

Like a dream I can't remember even while I can't wake up from it, she thought. Riley slumped back onto the bed, her head hanging low. Arisu looked at Dante. Neither spoke in the growing light that seeped through the curtain. Arisu shook her head. Dante sighed.

"What about the phone?" Dante suggested.

"What about it?" Riley shrugged.

"We should at least try it," Arisu offered. "We just need to be in a place with no signal or build one of those ferret cages."

Riley actually chuckled at this. She looked up at Arisu. "Faraday cage. But let's be realistic here. Jones let us get the phone. What are the chances that, even in a Faraday cage, it is safe to turn on?"

Arisu's eyes wandered. She swallowed then looked at Dante.

"She's got us, Arisu," he said.

"We'll work something out," Arisu mumbled.

"Work what out?" Dante raised his eyebrows. "We are stuck. She said it herself. We have no direction. Our plan has come to a complete halt. Until we have Violet, we are going nowhere. All we're doing now is giving them a chance to track us, eventually find us, and take us in."

"But we can't go there," Arisu protested.

"I recognize it's a risk. However, I think it's time we trust Riley. I think she's catching on," Dante continued. "At some point, we are going to have to put this all on the line. We won't be able to hide. We won't be able to run. At some point, we're going to have to dash headlong into the lion's den, guns blazing, figuratively or… maybe, literally. Either way, it's going to be ugly. I know you want to protect Violet at all costs, but this is bigger than any of us. Sacrifices will have to be made."

Arisu stared down at the floor for a good minute. Riley looked at her then at Dante. He flashed Riley a warm, reassuring smile and a slight nod. Arisu stirred, rising from the bed. She looked at Dante for a moment then locked her eyes on Riley.

"Are you sure you're ready for this?" she asked. "Once we set foot in there, there's a good chance we won't get away, hardly any chance at all."

Riley held her gaze. God, help us. If you're actually there.

23 THE APARTMENT

Despite the feeling that we're directly experiencing the world out there, our reality is ultimately built in the dark, in a foreign language of electrochemical signals. The activity churning across vast neural networks gets turned into your story of this, your private experience of the world...

- David Eagleman

BRIGHT SUNLIGHT BOUNCED OFF the pale side of the tall building. Balconies jutted out from the structure, potted plants swayed in the morning breeze. For such an East Coast city, the building itself was quite out of place. The rough stucco material that ran the entire length of it resembled the type of building one would expect to find in southwestern states near Mexico. The apartment complex, however, emanated its own attempt at personality. Riley stood by the Jeep, staring up at it.

"This is it, alright," she said.

"What now?" Arisu questioned her, obviously not seeking direction as much as quizzing her to see if she had thought this far ahead. Riley smirked, recognizing Arisu's sometimes annoying habit. More was coming back to her.

"The two of you follow me," Riley said, eyes still firmly fixed on the building. "We walk right in and I head to my apartment on the sixteenth floor, 1601. My balcony faces east so we can't see it from here. We used to eat out there and look out over the bay. One night we did a little more than eat out there."

Arisu's jaw dropped slightly. Riley smiled at her.

"Well," she managed, "I guess if this place has that kind of effect on you, we should have brought you here a long time ago."

"Obvious risks aside," Dante looked up and down the street. "We should hurry up. We do not wish to call attention to ourselves."

"Okay," Arisu replied, "We'll do the same drill as before. Riley and I will go in. You stay here. Text if anything—"

"—If *anyone* shows up," Dante corrected.

"Yeah," she pressed her lips together. Her narrow eyes became mere slits as she squinted up at the building. "Any ideas as to how the hell we'll actually get into the apartment?"

"I ask for the key," Riley said with a smirk.

Arisu frowned at her.

Riley laughed quietly. "Trust me. Just trust me."

"I guess we're out of options," Arisu sighed.

"Hey, it's only fair. What goes around comes around. Both of you knew it would come down to this at some point."

"Well," Arisu ran her hands over her face and through her hair, "We expected to have…"

Riley just nodded and suppressed a slight laugh. "Such is life, but Dante is right. We better get going."

Arisu's expression changed and she looked at Riley with a strange mixture of surprise and confusion. Riley turned and crossed the street. Arisu followed. Dante crawled back into the Jeep. Riley and Arisu stepped up to the large, tinted glass doors. Riley stopped and turned to Arisu.

"When we go in there," she said, "hold my hand."

Arisu blinked then nodded.

"I have distinct images in my mind of walking into this building with you; you holding my hand. If any of the front desk people are the same…" she trailed off.

They faced the door. Riley reached out and Arisu slipped her hand into hers. But, they held hands as one might hold the hand of a friend or a parent with their child, palm to palm. Riley reached up for the handle but stopped. She moved her right hand, which held Arisu's left, and interlaced their fingers. Arisu looked up at her with the same look she had given her a few moments before, on the other side of the street. Riley smiled softly and pulled the door open.

The front lobby looked much the same as she recalled it. The place was mostly sleek gray and silver with white accents and LED light panels that ran across the ceiling and upper third of the walls. To the right, she spotted the black sofas and coffee tables where business associates and friends of those living in the building would wait and pass the time with a selection of magazines, newspapers, and three-dimensional projection ePapers and television. Large windows next to the sofas looked out upon a lush lawn and garden that belonged to the complex. No one sat there at the moment.

The main counter stood to their left. A young woman, dark and tall, sat on a stool looking down at her computer display hidden by the dark marble counter top. The woman at the counter looked up at them and, in an instant, recognition flooded her face. She smiled warmly, displaying exceptionally white teeth.

"Dr. Murphy," she said, "What a surprise. Welcome back."

"Thank you," Riley returned the smile and stepped closer to the counter.

Arisu said nothing. She seemed to merely look the place over. Riley knew, however, that she was taking careful note of each exit and searching for surveillance, attempting to find any hint of danger or any possible advantage, should they land themselves in a bind.

"Haven't seen you in some time. Where have you been?" the woman asked, her tone still pleasant.

"On sabbatical," Riley maintained a cheerful exterior, while glancing at her nametag. "But I need your help, Leslie."

"Sure. What can I do?"

"I need the extra keys for my apartment," Riley explained, feeling Arisu's gaze turn to her. "Airline lost my luggage and the key was in my bag."

"Certainly," Leslie nodded her head. "Where did your sabbatical take you?"

"Somewhere unexpected," Riley grinned.

Leslie's eyes fell on the small gold crucifix that still hung around Riley's neck. "I guess so," she said. "I'll need you to do a retinal scan to access your drop box. You did leave your spare keys in the drop box, right?"

"Yes," Riley nodded.

Leslie directed her to the end of the counter, where she had Riley lean over the retinal scanning device, which was no more than a small dome on the counter. Riley glanced at Arisu. She shook her head ever so slightly and Riley knew Arisu's concern was that, as soon as Riley scanned her eye, the system would alert Jones of her return to the apartment complex. Likely true, but what other options did they have? Riley gave her a reassuring squeeze of the hand and bent over the dome. The computer beeped. Leslie looked down at the display behind the counter.

"Alright," she said, "Let's get that box."

She disappeared through a door on her side of the counter. A few moments later, she returned with a small, metallic box in her hands. She slid it across the marble. The entire surface of the silver box gleamed in the light. Only a faint line could be seen where the main body of the box segued to the lid. A sudden memory flashed into Riley's mind.

"This is our standard drop box," the apartment manager, Gilbert, had explained. He had held up an open box. "It's air tight when sealed, so I don't recommend using this as storage for your hamster while you're gone." The man chuckled at his own joke. He always did, it seemed. Riley had said nothing. "Anyway," Gilbert continued, "it's fingerprint activated. So, only you can—"

"—Open it," Arisu whispered. "Please. Let's keep moving."

Riley pressed her pointer down on a small, black oval on the lid's center. The box hissed then the lid lifted about an inch off the box. Riley removed it and peered in. A single key, which looked more like two keys crisscrossed lengthwise, sat in the middle of the black, foam padding. In the upper right corner was a small piece of folded paper. Riley reached in, grabbed both, and pocketed them.

"Thank you, Leslie," she said, slipping a few dollars on to the counter next to the box.

"You're welcome." the receptionist smiled politely. "It's nice to have you back."

"That's kind of you. Have a good day."

Riley turned and walked to the elevator. She waved her hand over the sensor and called the elevator down. Arisu stood next to her, their hands still interlocked. Riley felt the warmth of the two sweating palms. They both kept their eyes straight ahead, waiting for the door to slide open. When it did, they stepped in. Riley spoke the command for the elevator to head for the sixteenth floor.

"You know," she said, as they rode the elevator up. "I used to wonder why they couldn't just let me do a retinal or finger print scan for my own apartment instead of having to have a key *and* the retinal *and* the voice recognition."

"And then you realized," said Arisu, "That thieves were killing the people whose apartments they targeted in order to take an eye or a finger. Thus, they could gain the ability to access the apartments."

Riley looked at her, eyebrows up.

"We had this conversation before," she explained.

"Ah," she turned back to the door.

"Not that I mind," she said, "But do we still need to hold hands?"

Riley looked down at their hands, realizing their fingers were, in fact, still interlaced. "No. We don't have to, but maybe I find it comforting."

Arisu smiled slightly and Riley let go slowly. Their hands slid apart, dropping to their sides. Riley stared straight ahead at her reflection in the polished metal. She looked long into the eyes of a stranger. Suddenly, she recalled the piece of paper in her pocket. She reached for it. Arisu watched her. Riley unfolded the paper, which turned out to be no more than a white post-it note. Black ink smudged the paper. Written in flowing cursive were the words, "Congratulations on making it this far. Now, to discover who you really are. Sonic Shadow."

"What is that?" Arisu asked.

"I take it this is a little something I left for myself since I knew no one else would be able to open that box."

They felt the sudden lightness as the elevator slowed and then stopped. The door slid open. She folded the paper and stuffed it back into her pocket. They stepped out, not into a hallway, but rather a small room with one door. A couple of abstract works of art hung on the walls, which were painted in earthy colors. A small, white statue of a nude woman holding a vase stood in the corner. The only door led to Riley's apartment, which occupied the whole level, as did all apartments in the complex.

Riley stepped up to the small display screen to the right of the door. The motion sensor kicked in and the computer greeted her, "Good day, ma'am, and ma'am," said a synthetic female voice, a slight sexy edge to it.

"I was always jealous of that voice," Arisu grinned.

"Yeah," Riley glanced at her. "That's why I never changed it."

She scoffed. "Are you for real?"

Riley shrugged and turned back to the screen, bringing her eye close to the small dome that protruded from the wall adjacent to the display screen. The computer beeped with the completion of the retinal scan. Riley took a step back.

"Please state your name," the computer said.

"Violet Murphy," Riley said, in a flat tone.

"Proceed with key," the computer instructed her.

A metal plate, where the doorknob should have been, slid open and revealed a keyhole hidden within it. Riley slid the key into place and turned it. The door unlocked with a loud click and she pushed it open with ease. She stood just outside the door, staring into the apartment. Her eyes were soaking in the wooden floor, glass table, lush sofa, and the mini bar still lined with bottles of imported liquor. A large rug lay in front of the sofa. All the blinds were drawn, yet sunlight glowed through. Riley wished she could rush in and throw herself on the sofa and simply escape the stress of the last several days. *It's a lie*, she told herself. And yet, she wanted to crack open a bottle of wine and sip it slowly. She wanted to stand out on the balcony, wine glass in hand.

Another urge occurred to her. She'd like to stand on that balcony and smoke a pipe while looking out at the Boston skyline.

"Did I ever smoke a pipe?" she whispered.

Arisu frowned and shrugged. "Not that I know."

Riley smiled, and took the first step into the apartment. Arisu followed her in, closing the door behind them. Riley looked around, soaking in the place with increased familiarity. The front door—if it could be called that—stood at the center of the apartment. The whole place encircled it. Riley walked by the sofa, running her hand over it. She peeked out of the blinds, sighing at the sight of Boston below.

"Riley," Arisu said.

She turned to her.

"We have to keep moving," Arisu said softly.

"You're right," she muttered and moved away from the window. "Let's try my computer."

Arisu followed Riley into the study. On an elegant, hard oak desk sat a computer, sporting three displays side by side. Bookshelves lined the walls. Riley walked over and instinctively turned the computer on. It loaded quickly and stopped at the dialogue box for the operating system's password. Riley took a seat and stared at the screen. Arisu stood behind her.

"Any ideas?" she asked.

"Yeah," Riley brought her hands to the keyboard. "SonicShadow."

"What?"

Riley smiled, "Shadow the Hedgehog was an artificially constructed character in *Sonic Adventure 2*, which was the final game in the franchise for the Dreamcast before Sega discontinued the console. He's kind of like an alternate 'Sonic.'"

"So, the note—" Arisu pointed out.

"Yeah. So, did it mean anything else?"

"Oh, I don't know. Something you dealt with in research, I think. I'd heard you talk about it before. It had something to do with—"

"—regulating undeveloped neurons," Riley interrupted. "We were reproducing neurons so that we could create new paths, new mental connections. We had to develop a specific breed of nanites that could function in this manner, carrying the proper proteins to the developing neurons that relied on this sonic hedgehog factor, which was named after the video game character. Those particular neural pathways make neurogenesis possible, an essential step for implanting new personalities."

"Right," Arisu nodded. "How about we keep moving along?"

Riley tapped in the password. Arisu watched with wide eyes.

"Please state your name," said the computer, this time in a much more generic male voice which lacked the more human features of the "feminine" apartment program.

"Violet Murphy," Riley stated and the computer continued. "I think Violet knew it would come to this. Those words, they used to run through my head all the time."

Well then," Arisu smiled with relief, "not sure I followed all of that, but something seems to be coming back to you. How do you feel?"

"I feel fine," Riley shrugged. "It's amazing. It's all there. It just needs a primer of some kind; something to inspire the thought in the first place. I have to reestablish old thought patterns."

"Well, let's prime it quickly. Keep going."

Next to the keyboard, a pad nearly the size of the screen glowed. Riley touched it and the exact images that appeared on the screen appeared on the pad. She used this to navigate. She opened folders and files, searching for any information on the project. Most files were reports on experiments, proposals for new experiments, theories related to the development of the project. As she scanned the large amount of files, something occurred to her.

"This sure seems like a whole lot of work," Riley said, still looking through folders. "I must have had a lot of time on my hands."

Arisu just frowned, but said nothing. Bent down, she kept her eyes on the computer.

Riley stopped and pulled up a search window. "Okay, let's try this route. I need to search for something."

"Actually," Arisu stood straight and reached for something strapped to her belt. "Let's link the computer to my phone, download what we can, and get out of here."

"What if we don't get what we need?" Riley asked.

"You have as long as it takes me to get this ready."

"Arisu, come on. This isn't that simple."

"I know that. But we can't just dink around here. Someone's bound to show up eventually."

Riley tapped her fingers against the pad. Clenching her jaw, she let out a slow hissing breath. *What do I search for?* Her eyes wondered. A bulletin board hung on the wall behind the computer. Several charts and papers clung to it by pins. *Sonic Shadow*, for whatever reason, the words ran through her head again. *I did that already. It's the password.* Her mind raced, attempting to understand what other significance it might have. She tapped the pad, bringing the search window up again. *Do a hard drive search for something, or maybe even someone*, the voice inside her urged.

So she did.

A barrage of files appeared before her. But near the top a particular file caught her eye and Riley felt a deep sense of recognition. The title of the file: "Sonic Shadow – Who Are You.pdf."

"You ready for this?" Arisu asked, placing her smartphone on the desk.

"I am."

She activated the wireless link and the computer searched for devices near it that were prepared for the uplink. Riley sent first only the top file revealed by her search. Then, selecting a large array of files relating to experiments, plans, and charts of test subjects, she downloaded what she could.

"That's it," Arisu said. "We have to get out of here."

"What if there's more? What if we didn't get the right files?" Riley protested, sudden panic gripping her.

Arisu sighed, turning her head away. She looked back at Riley, "We can't spend much more time—"

The smartphone chirped. They both stared down at it, sitting there on the desk. A text message appeared on the screen. Their blood went cold, their breathing stopped. It read, "They're here."

"Shit!" Arisu grabbed the phone. "We have to go."

Riley stood, looking around the room, as if she might find something to defend herself with. Arisu clipped the phone to her belt again and leveled her eyes with Riley's. The upload would continue until they got out of range, most likely once they left the apartment.

"Is there any other way down, aside from the main elevator?" she asked.

"Jumping?" Riley shrugged.

Arisu pursed her lips and raised her eyebrows.

"Kidding. There is an emergency stairway and a freight elevator," Riley said. "It's right out from the kitchen. Let's go."

It was Arisu's turn not to move.

"Come on, you said it, we have to go," Riley said.

Arisu's eyes wondered down to the floor.

"Arisu," Riley's voice grew hoarse with tension. "What are you waiting for?"

"They'll have covered all the exits," she sighed.

Riley looked at her, jaw locked, eyes narrow. "Then we go up; go to the top of the building. That will buy us some time. We can set off the fire alarms, but we can't stay here. Let's take the freight elevator to the top."

Riley reached out and took her hand. Arisu looked up at her.

"Don't give up on me now," Riley whispered.

They darted through the apartment, passing through the kitchen and into the small laundry room in the back. A single white door sat at the end. Riley ripped it open. Beyond it, the stairs wound upward and downward. The freight elevator doors stood closed. A sickly, greenish light glowed from florescent tubes that lined the stairs. Riley reached out to call the elevator, but Arisu stopped her. She pointed to the stairs instead. They climbed as quickly as possible, their muscles aching. Their breathing gave way to gasping, inspired more by desperation and fear than physical exertion. Nine floors later, Arisu's phone chirped, alerting her of the loss of connection to Violet's computer. That was it. Whatever they had managed to grab, it would have to be enough for Riley. The last set of stairs lead to the clubhouse at the top of the building. They climbed it, stopping at the door. Riley took hold of the handle and shoved the door open.

Bright sunlight rendered them blind for a brief moment. A salty wind from the bay blew over them. Riley raised her hand to shield her eyes from the sun. She glanced at Arisu, who squinted and looked around.

"We're going to get ourselves cornered up here," Arisu said. "What's your plan?"

"We could sun bathe, maybe get something to drink from the bar," Riley grinned. But the humor was lost on Arisu.

They walked as calmly as they could to the bar area, passing the roof-top pool and hot tub. They fought for control over their breathing but still, it came shallow and quick as their hearts thundered in their chests. The clubhouse stood on one side of the roof, nothing more than a simple bar area and grills that residents could use. Only two people sat in the roof deck structure. Riley and Arisu walked passed the two women who chatted over cups of coffee. Riley directed her down a narrow hall. They reached the restrooms and changing rooms. She pulled Arisu into the women's changing room. They found it empty, as she had hoped.

"They'll come looking for us," Arisu said.

"Yeah. I'm counting on that," Riley answered evenly, though she found herself wondering where this sudden composure was coming from.

"What?"

"I need to see what's on that file," Riley put out her hand. "I have to see it. It may be the one thing Violet left for us. Once I've seen it, they can take us."

"You're just going give up?" Arisu raised her voice.

"No," Riley raised his hands to calm her. "Not give up. Give in. Just for the moment. At some point, it comes down to facing them."

"Not like this," Arisu headed for the door.

Riley grabbed her arm and pulled her back. "Arisu, don't."

She glared at Riley. "You're just going to wait to be caught? Who are you?!"

"That's exactly what I'm trying to figure out. Now give me the phone!"

Arisu stared at her. A tear broke free from her right eye. Riley watched it slip down her face then over her jaw line and down her neck. Arisu breathed through her nose, her whole upper body moving with each breath. Without taking her eyes from Riley, Arisu unclipped the phone and thrust it out at her.

Taking it, Riley opened the list of files they had downloaded before they got out of range. She found the one, the first one she had uploaded, and opened it. A news article appeared. Her eyes fell first on the picture of on old man, graying hair, smoking a pipe. Riley looked at him with a strange sense of misplaced recognition, like she knew the face. And yet, it somehow didn't belong there. She scrolled down. A caption below the picture appeared. "Dr. Victor Murphy, scientist, theorist, and government consultant, laid to rest today in St. Thomas Cemetery."

Confused, Riley skimmed the article and then scrolled down further. She found another article. "Jane Doe Rescued in Human Trafficking Bust Dies After A Four Month Coma."

Riley skimmed the article about the woman who had been found in the bust. She had freed several young women and girls from a ring of sex and labor trafficking linked to Central America. Then, she reached the picture of the unconscious Jane Doe in the hospital. Riley's knees nearly gave out. The hair was shorter, her face malnourished and much younger. But, there was no mistaking it. That was Riley lying in a hospital bed. That was Riley being declared dead by an article in the Boston Globe.

She gasped.

Arisu watched her. Riley stepped back, feeling the revulsion course through her body, her muscles began to ache and her stomach started to churn. Her back hit the wall behind her and she steadied herself.

"What is it?" Arisu asked.

Riley said nothing, trying just to keep the floor from coming up and hitting her. What the hell did this mean? Riley forced herself to look at the phone again. She returned to the first article and looked it over again. Victor Murphy had been a leading scientific consultant for several DARPA projects of the past three decades. The article was from five years ago. The second article was from three days before the first. She looked up at Arisu, shaking her head. Arisu stepped closer. *I can't show it to her,* Riley thought. She scrolled down further. The article ended. A simple chart followed, the words, "Sleepwalker Agent Profile" at its top. It bore the picture of a young man and his information.

The chart read:

Name: David Brown.

Age: 27

Marital Status: Married

Spouse: Sophia Angelica Brown

Children: Tiffany (2), and Diane (3)

Riley stopped there, her eyes closing. She slid to the floor, weeping. Arisu rushed to her. She knelt next to Riley.

"What is it?" she asked, "Riley, come on. What is it?"

"You have to go," she sobbed. "You have to go. Get out of here! You have to get out of here now."

"I'm not leaving without you!"

"No, you have to go!"

Riley dropped the phone. It clattered on the floor, echoing off the tile. Arisu looked down at the screen. Her jaw dropped. Picking it up, she scrolled back to the top, finding the articles. She stared for a long minute, scrolling slowly at first, then, with increased franticness, she too gasped.

"No," she said. "It can't be. It's a lie."

Riley shook her head, looking up at her through the blur of tears. "It's not. It's all right there. Worst of all, it has all been in here," she pointed to her head. "The whole time. The whole fucking time!"

"What do you mean?"

Riley just shook her head and stared off into nothingness. Finally, her lips parted and she cried softly, "Sophia."

24   NO WAY OUT

[A]t DARPA, [Michael] Goldblatt became a pioneer in military-based transhumanism—the notion that man can and will alter the human condition fundamentally by augmenting humans with machines and other means. … When questioned about unintended consequences, like controlling humans for nefarious ends, Goldblatt insists, 'There are unintended consequences for everything.'

- Annie Jacobsen

THE BUSHES SCRATCHED HIS face, but Dante paid no attention to that. He watched quietly as project agents looked the Jeep over. Six of them headed into the building. Dante crouched and waited. No message from Arisu had come through on his phone. *Why weren't they responding? I may be forced to stage some kind of distraction*, he figured. But, he had to be certain of the timing. Too soon, and all he would accomplish would be to get himself caught. Too late, and the women may already have been apprehended. He looked down at his phone. *Why don't you respond?*

Closing his eyes, he willed the network of nanites in his brain to try and access any open local network so that he could try to reach Riley. He could not find anything other than what felt like a brick wall. Giving up, for the moment, he returned to watching the agents. They must have been using something to block signals. The agents on the street turned suddenly and headed towards the building. Two dropped back and stood guard by the front door. These agents seemed to have little interest in keeping their presence from being noticed. Rikard led the first group in, guns in hand and dressed in black. Dante counted twelve agents in all. Undoubtedly, another group of six had stationed itself around the block. That meant, most likely, the three of them were up against eighteen well-armed agents. Dante looked down at his phone.

Still nothing.

If communication signals were being blocked, Arisu might be trying to reach him with no success. His phone indicated they had received his message. But that was before the agents had likely activated their signal blocking. He wondered if they were monitoring as well. He hoped they had been too busy getting out of the apartment to respond. He hoped!

They have them already, don't they? This was a mistake. He shook off the thought. The agents could not have reached the apartment already. On his phone, he risked tapping in another message and hit send.

"COME ON!" ARISU YELLED, "We have to get out of here."

She pulled Riley up, who struggled to steady herself. Arisu grabbed her face forcing her to look her in the eyes.

"It's a lie," she said firmly. "You are Violet Murphy."

"No," Riley said. "I'm not Violet; I'm not even a nun. I'm a Jane Doe. Can't you see it?"

"No," Arisu shook her head. "No. No way. There's an explanation for all of this."

"Victor Murphy," Riley shook her head, "is the scientist behind the project."

"You can't just believe this file," Arisu protested. "Why is the profile of a dead project agent in there? I knew David. I was there the night David died. You were there the night David died. It was the night that changed everything for me. That was the breaking point. I couldn't be part of the project anymore, not after what you showed me that night."

Riley's mind flashed with visions of the pursuit of a subject who had escaped. Darren. His name had been Darren. Riley could recall being part of the retrieval team. No, wait! She had shown up to try to save Darren. But she also could clearly recall the pursuit, the black uniform, the gun…

In her mind, she could look down and see the gun in his hands. David's hands! She could recall the event from her vantage point and his. They had been linked somehow. Was it some mind trick like the one Dante pulled in Brazil? The rush of awareness brought on a headache, as old neural connections were forced into place.

"Violet Murphy never existed," she said.

It must have been something in her voice or the iciness in her eyes, but Arisu pulled away. Her hands slid from Riley's face and Arisu stepped back slowly. "What do you mean?"

"David and I are connected," Riley said. "I'm David. David is me. I can't quite explain it yet. But… yes… we're one."

Arisu shook her head, "You're in shock."

"Don't you see? That explains my ability to fight, to shoot, to feel their every move," Riley said, her eyes growing dark and distant. "They'll be on the roof shortly."

"Violet, this doesn't make any sense," Arisu protested, her voice shaking.

"Don't call me Violet," she growled.

Arisu shook her head. "Look, we don't even know if that file was real. What if Jones planted it? Right now, we have to get out of here then we can figure this out. Don't give up on me now!"

In spite of herself, Riley smiled slightly. "Wasn't I saying that to you just a moment ago?"

Arisu smiled, "Yeah. Now stick with me, girl. We have to focus. How do we get out of here?"

Riley took a deep breath and nodded. She wiped away tears and swallowed hard. After a few more deep breaths, she put out a hand. Arisu looked at her quizzically.

"Think I'll take that gun now after all," Riley said.

Arisu nodded and handed one over.

They peeked out of the door quietly. Riley walked down the hall first, gun in hand at her side. The voices of the two women talking in the bar area echoed down the hall. Riley stopped at the end of the hall and glanced at the stairway entrance then the main elevator entrance. Seeing nothing, she popped around the corner, keeping her gun low and out of sight. Arisu followed her. The talking women paid no attention to them.

"You check north and east," Riley said, "I'll check south and west."

They split, heading to the edges of the roof, which was guarded by a tall chain link fence to prevent drunken, careless tenants from falling over the edge. Riley checked the west side first, then the south. On the south side, where they had come in to the building, Riley noticed two agents down by the street, keeping watch over the Jeep. She saw no sign of Dante.

Her heart raced. Her mouth felt dry. She pushed every thought from her mind that did not relate to getting out of this building undiscovered. She knew that being captured was a real possibility. She had even made peace with the fact that it was the most likely outcome of returning to the apartment, but that was before learning her complete lack of identity.

What had they done to her? Who was she really?

No time to figure that out now. She fought off the questions and the inherent anxiety they induced. Everything had just changed for Riley yet again, but this was neither the time nor place to deal with any of it. *Get out of here now, work the rest out later. Arisu's still right about that.*

Arisu returned, crouching next to her by the roof's edge. "There are two agents on guard by the north entrance."

"Same on the south," Riley said.

"So, I guess we'd better assume a total number of sixteen to eighteen, then, could be more. Where's Dante?"

"Can't see him," Riley shook her head.

Arisu looked back at the bar, the main elevator entrance, and then the stairway entrance. "They'll come up. They're in the apartment by now. They may have figured out that we headed up. We're stuck here. Even if we try something like pulling the fire alarm, they'll still come up."

Riley looked the roof over again, "Then we draw them up here. Trap them."

Arisu frowned, but her frown slowly faded as she thought about it. "There's only two ways down from here."

"Elevators or stairs," Riley said through nervous breaths.

"So if we draw as many of them as possible, activate the fire alarm, the elevators are out of the question."

"We have to go down the stairs fast. We'll need to make some kind of barrier," Riley looked over at the grills near the bar. "A firewall," she grinned.

Arisu glanced over, "What are you thinking?"

"Half of those grills run on gas," Riley explained. "We unhook one of the tanks, let it leek just inside the stairway exit, and set up something to spark."

Arisu grinned. "Alright," she shook her head, "how you going to do that?"

"I'll figure that out while I'm getting the tank."

Riley stood and ran across the roof, between the pool and hot tub. The woman who sat and chatted now looked at her with bewilderment on their faces. She slowed her pace as she walked by them.

"Excuse me, ladies," Riley said. "But I would recommend that you return to your apartments right away."

"Oh really?" the one scoffed. "And why is that?"

Riley stopped, realizing she didn't have time to deal with this. Still, she desperately wanted to get them out of harm's way. In one swift move, her gun came out.

"Because the crazy woman with a gun is politely asking you to do so," she maintained the same courteous tone.

The women stared at her with wide eyes. Riley rolled her eyes.

"Go! Now!" She yelled, "Get out of here!"

The women bolted upright and ran for the elevator. Riley headed to the grills. All of the grills were built into a long marble counter. She stopped by the first of the gas grills and opened the small cabinet door beneath it. She looked in. Her stomach turned inside of her as she realized that she could not count on her own mind to develop such plans.

In her haste, she had recalled that some of the grills were gas. As such, she figured that each gas grill would be fed by individual gas tanks. She was wrong. There were no individual gas tanks. A single pipeline split off and fed all six of the gas grills.

Riley looked up at the bar area. Her hands shook, her heart beat even faster, and her head began to pound. She felt as if her eyes couldn't focus. She reached up and pressed the side of her head, as if expecting something to happen. The memory of a helmet came to her, a TMS helmet. Just as quickly, something else came to mind.

Riley ran to the bar and jumped over it. Landing on the other side, she looked around. Sure enough, there was a gas grill for use within the bar. A black hose ran down to the grill's dedicated and, most importantly, portable gas tank. She knelt next to it and tapped the little round tank. It made a hollow clanking sound. *Right, genius,* she chided herself, *like you know what a full or empty tank of propane sounds like.*

She made quick work of unhooking it. Regardless of how full it was, it would have to do. Given how well-maintained the facility was, she put her faith in the likelihood that the tank would be regularly replaced. Next, she searched for a lighter in any of the drawers. She recalled that there was usually a long-stemmed lighter in one of the drawers, used as a backup just in case the built-in lighting system failed. Finding it, but not bothering to test it since all she needed was the spark, she grabbed the small tank from the floor. As she brought it up, the elevator door slid open.

She looked over at the elevator. The two women still stood in front. Riley glimpsed the black suits of the agents within and sprang over the bar; knocking over the coffee mugs the women had left behind. The women at the elevator, in too much of a hurry to wait, charged into the elevator the instant the door opened. The moment of confusion among the women and the agents provided just enough time for Riley to make it across the roof.

Just as she reached Arisu, a shot blew apart chunks of cement from the stairwell wall by the entrance. Riley hit the ground, the gas tank bouncing out in front of her. She watched it roll, hoping a bullet wouldn't strike it. Arisu took cover just inside the doorway of the stairs. She returned fire.

"Don't hit those women," Riley shouted.

She pulled out her own gun, rolling to her back, and fired two high shots as the agents scattered and the terrified women dove into the elevator. She stood quickly, and fired two more high shots. Snatching up the tank, she made it into the doorway just as a bullet blew a fist-sized hole in the open door. Arisu fired three more quick rounds and headed after her. The door slammed behind her. Riley stopped just inside the door and set the tank on the floor. Pointing the valve toward the door, she cranked it open and sparked the lighter in front of it. A bright flame whooshed out at the door.

"Let's go!" She yelled.

They ran down the next set of steps, turned right, and kept going. Quickly, they worked their way down the winding stairs. Above them, they heard the door burst open. Shocked yells echoed through the stairwell from where the agents encountered the flame. Chaos ensued and Riley thought she heard someone yelling for the other to stop, but the door was kicked open again and shots fired.

An explosion shook the building and rang their ears. Dust rained down the stairwell. Riley felt a horrible chill of guilt. One of the agents must have tried to fire a round at the tank to disable it or simply knock it over. Instead, they probably ruptured the tank. With more propane freely accessible to the flame, the remaining gas in the tank had ignited. Had any of them been killed? The explosion certainly felt big enough.

She hit the wall; they were only a few levels down from the roof, her ears ringing. *What have I done?* Smoke filled the place. She coughed, fighting for air. Arisu pulled her up and they headed down the stairs. The fire alarm sounded. It was a shrill, oppressive sound. LED strobe lights blinked at each landing. Sprinklers sprang to life, showering the stairwell with cold water. If not for the safety grip tape on each step, the descent would have been a painfully slippery one. They dashed down the steps as quickly as they could manage without losing their balance.

"What do we do when we reach the bottom?" Arisu yelled, between gasps.

"Call Dante," she answered, "Tell him to get ready."

Riley stopped between floors. Arisu stopped next to her and pulled out the phone. She shook her head.

"I tried earlier. I can't get anything through to him. I bet they're jamming the signal."

"Then we keep going," Riley shouted over the alarm.

Arisu nodded.

DANTE STARED UP AT the top of the building. Smoke billowed into the air. He had heard the shots, which gave him the assurance that Riley and Arisu were still unharmed and free. The explosion, however, surprised him. None of the agents should have been carrying anything explosive. He sucked in a slow breath, held it, and then let it out slowly. Movement at the front of the building drew his attention. The two agents that stayed back for door duty now sprinted into the building. At last, Dante had his chance to start the car and clear the area for Arisu and Riley. He'd still have to be careful, but this would be his best opportunity to act.

He peeked out of the bushes and looked at the door. He took another step forward and turned to the street. The barrel of a gun greeted his face. He froze, not even breathing.

Rikard held out his weapon right at eye level.

DOWN THE STAIRWELL THEY plunged. The descent became dizzying and soon, they could no longer tell what floor they were on or how much farther they may yet have to travel. Water still sprayed from the sprinklers. At last, Arisu and Riley reached the main floor, soaked, sore, and exhausted. Riley didn't stop, however.

Arisu called after her, "Where are we going?"

"The garage."

She stopped before the large door. Arisu followed her down, stopping next to her. A florescent light in the corner flickered. Arisu locked eyes with Riley.

"What is it?" she asked, catching her breath.

The door on the main floor opened. Riley felt her whole body tingle with the sinking sensation of falling into a trap. Still, she ripped open the door and stepped out into the parking garage. Arisu followed. Lights flooded their eyes from all directions. Agents, with their guns raised and flashlights on, waited in a half circle blocking their escape through the garage. Riley and Arisu stood, still panting from their race down several flights of stairs. They raised their hands.

From the door behind them, an agent stepped through and placed the barrel of his gun against Arisu's neck. Riley looked at the man, clad in black, a mask over his face. *I was one of you*, she found herself thinking. David Brown had been a project agent—a hired goon, really. He'd been ex-military, washed up, and in need of some cash. Basically, that's who all these young men and women were. Then again, she wondered if they hadn't also fallen prey to a much larger scheme. It struck her that this mission had never been about preventing the misuse of power. The power was already being misused.

"Nice work, ladies and gentlemen," Rikard stepped out from behind the half-circle of agents.

Another agent, a woman all in black, had followed him. She brought Dante forward at gunpoint. Dante looked at Arisu and then Riley, an apology in his eyes. Agents closed in around Riley and Arisu, one standing behind each of them.

"I think we can peacefully conclude all of this now, can't we?" Rikard continued. "So, drop your weapons, and we all go home."

Riley glanced at Arisu. She shook her head.

"Don't," Rikard stepped closer. "Dante will pay for it if you try anything."

"I'm not what you think I am," Riley answered.

"Uh-huh, sure," Rikard grinned.

From the corner of her eye, Riley saw something quickly dart between the cars behind the agents. She couldn't be sure of who it had been, but someone had just joined the party—albeit, unofficially. Riley kept her eyes on Rikard.

"The guns, now! Come on!" Rikard raised his voice. "I don't really want to be here when the fire truck shows up to clean the mess you made upstairs."

Riley slowly pulled out her gun and lowered it to the ground. Arisu did likewise. She, however, locked eyes with Dante. As she bent over, to place the gun on the damp, cement ground, she kicked her foot back, knocking the gun from the hand of the agent who stood behind her. She then delivered a hard blow to his gut. Dante ducked and rolled over. Arisu fired two rounds squarely at the agent over him. Rikard hit the floor to avoid the bullets. Driven into action by pure instinct, Riley sprang in the opposite direction, snatching up her gun. Arisu ducked behind a car near the door.

As Dante sought cover, a bullet ripped into his left shoulder blade. He screamed and crashed to the cold ground. But then, the unexpected happened. Another shooter opened fired on the agents. From the cars behind the agents, a series of shots rang out. The agents scattered like cockroaches, a new sense of disorder and fear taking over. Riley ran, keeping low. She crouched behind a car and tried to spot the shooter. Popping out from behind a large SUV, Thomas unloaded a whole clip. He succeeded in hitting only cars and walls.

Arisu ran out to Dante. A pool of blood formed where he lay on his stomach. The wound on his back pumped out blood with each heartbeat. She crouched next to him.

"Get—" he moaned. "Get out of here."

"Not without you," she said.

She reached out to help him, but how could she even move him? What could she do? She knew it had been a mistake to—

An arm wrapped itself around her neck. A gun clicked next to her right ear and the barrel pressed hard into her cheekbone.

"Leave him be, Arisu," Rikard whispered into her ear. "Help will be on the way soon enough. As for us, we need to get going."

"You son of a bitch," she spat. "You have no idea what's going on here. You're just a pawn."

"Oh, honey, I'm afraid you're the one who has no idea what's going on here," he sneered, "You don't even know who your girlfriend really is."

He stood, pulling her to her feet. With his handgun raised, he moved down the row of cars. Agents covered him. A large, black electric van whirred around the corner of the garage and stopped near Rikard. The side doors slid open and some of the agents entered.

"Thomas," Rikard called out. "You have some balls, buddy. Just showing up here like this; you just don't know when to give up, do you?"

Thomas fired a shot, which skipped off the van's bulletproof windshield. Rikard ducked. Straightening, he shook his head.

"You're not our real problem anyway," Rikard yelled. "Now come on, Violet, you don't want anything to happen to Arisu, do you?"

Riley, still crouched behind a car nearly sixty yards away, peeked out around it. She spotted the van, Rikard, and Arisu. Rikard held her tight, gun pointed out in Riley's direction. Riley ducked back and looked for Thomas.

"Riley, get out of here!" Arisu called out, her yell cut off by Rikard's arm jerk that choked her.

Riley spotted Thomas moving closer to her, but still in the next row of cars. Just as Thomas crept around the edge of a blue sports car, Riley locked eyes with him. They stared each other down for a second. Then, Riley smiled. She nodded towards the exit to her right. Thomas raised his eyebrows and nodded once. Riley peeked out again to see Rikard.

"Come on, Violet," Rikard howled. "We don't have all day. What do you plan on doing?"

"Riley," Arisu yelled, her voice cracking with the strain, "Just go."

Rikard jerked his arm around her neck again. She coughed. Riley ducked back and took in a deep breath. *They won't hurt her*, she found herself thinking. *They won't do anything to her. Not yet, at least. She's their bargaining power with me now.* Riley looked over at Thomas and brought her gun up, barrel in the air. Thomas did the same. Just then, something changed in the air. Sirens bellowed in the distance. Riley grinned with satisfaction.

Rikard swore and called off his men. He shoved Arisu into the van and turned one last time in Riley's direction. "You've got six hours, you peace of shit. You hear me? She dies in six, unless you turn yourself in; pretty sure you know where to find us."

The door to the van slid shut. It lurched forward and sped right past Riley and out the exit. Riley stood and watched the van go up the ramp and turn onto the street. Thomas stepped out, gun raised. Riley looked at him.

"What now?" she said.

"You're coming with me," Thomas said.

Riley rolled her eyes. "I'm getting really tired of being the center of everyone's attention." She raised her gun and leveled it on Thomas. "You won't shoot me. I'm too valuable, remember?"

"Yeah, well you won't shoot me—"

With a quick jerk down Riley pulled the trigger, delivering a shot to Thomas' leg. The man howled and dropped his gun. He collapsed to the ground. Riley watched, letting out a sad sigh. She stepped closer and kicked his fallen gun away. Thomas grabbed his leg and moaned. Riley looked down at him.

"Thanks for the help, Thomas," she said, "I do sincerely appreciate your timing, but I can't get caught by Jones or you. The sad thing is that I'm not even the person who everyone thinks I am. Keep pressure on that, they'll have you in surgery in no time. I tried not to hit anything vital."

Thomas groaned with pain. "You shot me, you bitch."

"Yeah, well, you drugged me, you creep," Riley shrugged.

With that, Riley jogged down to Dante, snatching up Thomas' gun along the way. Reaching Dante, she stooped down. Dante breathed, but he'd lost consciousness. Riley wanted desperately to stay and help him. The sirens grew closer, however. She couldn't stay. She took Dante's smartphone. Riley stood and looked the garage over. There wasn't any time to hack a car here. For now, she would have to go on foot, but what then? What would she do after that? One thought consumed her mind, *I'm not Violet. I'm not the woman everyone seems to think I am.* She put the guns away and ran hard.

25 REDUNDANCY

The riddle of whether free will exists also revolves around the ambiguity in defining *free will*.

- Dean Buonomano

She stared at Rikard, her eyes narrow and dark. Her wet hair clung to her face. Rikard grinned at Arisu, shrugging slightly. The van swayed while travelling down the road. Arisu breathed hard, still feeling her body ache from the chase and confrontation. Her wet clothing felt heavy, cold, and constricting. She said nothing knowing that, soon enough, she would be at the project's main facility and Jones would have plenty of questions to ask. She would have to speak, whether or not she agreed. She wouldn't even put it past Jones to implant her with some new system of nanites that might facilitate her willingness to share information or, at least, loosen her tongue a good bit. Did they have such a thing? But, then again, she didn't put it past Jones to use old-fashioned physical force and intimidation.

He should know her better than that by now. Some punches and kicks wouldn't quite do the trick. Cutting fingers off might do the trick though. Was Jones even capable of that? She shook the thought away; her imagination was running wild now. Surely, that was all. This was a government sponsored project and torture would be looked on rather negatively … maybe. Or maybe, if no one found out … she had dealt with enough politicians during her days on the project, retrieving rogue subjects, to know that they wanted the appearance of innocence, but no more than the appearance. Then again, if anything became traceable evidence, they could be in serious trouble. Most likely, Jones would resort to simple words and threats. Then, maybe he'd implement some of the project's technology or so she hoped.

"How you feeling?" Rikard asked.

Arisu frowned, not answering. *What does he care?*

"Arisu," he insisted, his tone of voice changing as if he were putting aside some act and now actually showing that he cared. "How are you feeling?"

"Oh, just peachy," she muttered.

A broad grin stretched over his face. Rikard shook his head. "You really are one of a kind, Arisu. Sorry things are turning out like this. It shouldn't have been like this, at all."

"What the hell do you care?" she spat.

His grin faded and she thought that, for an instant, she detected some sadness in his eyes. Something drifted over him for an instant. His eyes wandered then returned to her. He grinned again, but this time it was forced and not as self-assured.

"We just need Violet returned to us safely," he said.

"You have a funny way of going about that," she grinned through her rage. "In case you failed to notice, your dip-shit goons were firing lethal rounds back there."

"Yeah, well, your girlfriend blew up three of my men."

"What choice did we have?"

"There's always a choice, sweetie," Rikard sighed. "I've always had a certain respect for you. I'd hate to see you wasted when this is all said and done."

Arisu frowned but didn't respond. Was he threatening her?

"This thing," Rikard said slowly. "It's bigger than us. And if there's one thing you have made abundantly clear, there are some snags that are going to have to be stitched up."

"*Snags?* Is that what you call Violet?" She shot back.

Rikard sat back and smirked. "She's more like the proverbial canary in a coal mine; a valuable canary we need back, incidentally."

"Good luck with that," she sighed.

"Oh, I don't need luck. I've got you. She'll come for you."

Arisu looked down feeling as if her body were suddenly three times as heavy, "I wouldn't be so sure of that."

WALKING ALONG THE COLD, busy street, she muddled into a world of incertitude coalescing with her present surroundings. Streetlights glowed in the growing darkness. Headlights moved past her. Violet, Riley, whomever she would turn out to be, walked on. Her blank eyes stared ahead. She took in each breath as if it might be her last. *And who would care?* Her whole existence now culminated into a mesh of lies. If only she could really believe—believe it deep within herself, with that sort of self-recognition that constantly reminds a person of who they are, that she really was Violet Murphy. But there had never really been a Violet Murphy, had there? And who was David Brown? Why did she have these memories that seemed to belong to David? What had they done to her? To him?

The system works, she figured. It really works. Look at me. She shook her head. But what if it's a lie? How can I believe anything anymore? One thing, however, countered that thought quickly. Sophia. What about Sophia? How did Sophia fit in to all of this? Was she merely a product of Riley's confused and reprogrammed mind? Something about Sophia felt so… tangible.

People walked by Riley down Boston sidewalks, but it might as well have been anywhere else in the whole damn world. Who were these people? How did they interact with her? How did their existence intersect with hers? None of them made eye contact with her and she made no effort on her part to establish any. With shoulders slouched, she simply walked on and wrestled with the thoughts in her mind. *They have Arisu, Dante is in a hospital, somewhere, and I'm not Violet because there never was a Violet.*

What the fuck do I do now?

Her body straightened with a sudden realization. They did this to me. They know I'm not really Violet. I'm nothing but a human hard drive and they still want me. What they need is access. All I have to do is turn myself in. They can have me. As long as she lives, they can have me. I'm nothing anymore. I'm a fucking biological memory card.

She stopped walking and stared up at the sky. Something deep inside her longed to call out in prayer, just as she had before, when she believed herself to be a nun. *I'm not a nun*, she shook her head. *I can't pray, I can't ask for the help of something I was just programmed to believe in.* She stared at the growing blackness that stretched out above her, above the building tops and streetlights. *Why not?* The question slipped into her mind quietly. *Why can't you?*

So she did. Letting down her guard, she implored for some unseen help. She prayed in much the same manner as she had as a nun in Brazil, though it felt as if she'd never done it before; as if this were the first real prayer she had ever sighed. All at once, it felt familiar and new, like listening to an old song but truly hearing the words for the first time; like soaking in the melody and finally understanding the emotion behind it. Stillness encompassed her. Taking her eyes off the dark sky, she walked again.

A LONG PIER STRETCHED out over the water. Light poles were intermittently lined up along both sides. She needed to think, to give up on the place where her soul had been ripped from her body. She had lost track of time, her feet hitting the pavement in a steady rhythm. At some point, her clothing dried in the summer night air. She hadn't known that she was coming here, but yet, here she was. A few people walked by; some were talking, some laughing. No one paid attention to Riley. She stared out at the water's surface, which reflected back the light from the poles above. She had to turn herself in. She knew it. Yet, something held her there. She couldn't will herself to the project center. *Where is the project center?* She looked out at the cityscape; the buildings freckled with light against a dark sky that glistened off the surface of Boston Harbor.

Her eyes locked on to it and she knew it with every atom of her being. That's why she was standing here in this park, this pier. Just across the bay was Battery Wharf. And there, stood the old coast guard building, right on the waterfront. *There you are.*

Once again, Sophia came to mind. She had to be connected to either Victor Murphy or David Brown. She focused hard on the memory of Sophia in the kitchen. Whose memory was it?

It washed over her suddenly: Sophia was David Brown's wife. Yes, it made sense. The memories rushed forward with new rapidity. Riley shook her head, marveling at the certainty of the notion. *I am David,* she thought. But how?

Redundancy.

The word entered her mind with such force that she felt the world around her threaten to melt itself down into a puddle of dizzying colors. She gripped the hand rail before her.

"It was all about redundancy," said Violet.

Shaken, Riley looked to her right. There stood a woman who looked very much like herself. But her hair was tied neatly in a bun and she wore a silky blue dress shirt and slacks.

I'm losing my mind, Riley thought.

"You can't really lose something you've never truly had," Violet smirked.

"How are you here," Riley whispered.

"Visual reproduction of a person can be manipulated at a neural level," Violet shrugged and leaned on the rail. "It's quite basic. After all, what you see is just your brain's very selective interpretation of the outside world filtered through your eyes and then transmitted to your visual cortex as electrical signals. Did you know that colors as we think of them are a construct of the brain? The objective world outside of your brain is not exactly colorful."

"Blah, blah, blah, am I right?" David said, stepping up to the rail on the other side of her. "But that's not what you're really asking. You want to know how this got so complicated."

Riley looked at him, unable to speak.

"Redundancy," David went on. "They'd never tried it before. But Victor Murphy was too important."

"So they stored everything they could in two places," Violet nodded.

"It didn't take so well with me," David grinned.

"Then you died," Violet said softly, the weight of guilt clinging to those words.

Riley glanced at the two figures she was standing between. Well, two figures that she imagined herself to be standing between. "So, I was the other backup for Victor?"

"For good measure, they tried connecting our minds as well," David explained. "But mostly, you just got... me. Thrilling, I'm sure."

Riley shook her head. "Then why was Sophia my guide?"

"How each mind responds to the process is a mystery," Violet said.

"I need my guide," Riley found herself saying. "I need Sophia."

"I have done all I am capable of doing," Sophia said.

Riley turned to find Sophia in her white flowing gown, walking toward her, eyes bright.

"Hi sweetie," David said softly. "I'm so sorry... about everything."

Sophia flashed a slight sad smile to David and then returned her focus to Riley.

"How is any of this happening?" Riley said. "If this is a dream, I want to wake up."

"It's best if you think of it as a dream within a dream," Sophia answered.

"What do you mean? None of this is real?"

"That would make this a lot simpler, wouldn't it? But, in its own right, this is real; it's just as real as anything you've ever experienced. You have been through quite a bit. Few could endure such a high level of programming and withstand it the way you have."

"Geez," David chuckled, "I'm standing right here."

Riley reached back and held the rail for support.

"It's time," Violet said softly. "You need to search within yourself. You know the answers. It's all there."

"You're ready for this," Sophia smiled.

Riley straightened up and looked into Sophia's eyes. "Do you know the answer?"

Sophia nodded, "But only because you know the answer. Remember, I am merely an assistance program that adapted itself to already present mental constructs."

"AAP," Riley grinned. "That's right, Assimilation Assistance Program. I helped write that particular... no... I guess Victor did."

"But you hold all that Victor held."

"Not all," she raised a hand in protest. "Due to the amount of overwriting and reprogramming, not all the information transferred from Victor has remained intact. It's sort of a generation loss. When it comes right down to it, the brain is an analog storage device. There's a generation loss involved with the transfer of information.'"

Riley stopped. What am I saying? I know this? She nodded, smiling. I do know this.

"What do I do now?" she asked.

As Sophia spoke, the words came also from Riley's mouth. "Assimilate. Complete the process. Become what you have been destined to become. Do not fight the inevitable. Rather, embrace what you can become."

Riley gazed at Sophia one last time. A breeze blew through the trees and her guide drifted away into nothingness. She would never see her again. She was sure of it. Next to her, David sighed. The world became dim and narrow and Riley spoke no longer. Glancing about, she found that David and Violet were gone as well. Riley felt herself let go from within, like a silent explosion of energy inside her chest. Riley faded as well, though not completely.

Silence washed over her and she felt herself lying on her back. Time lost any significance to her once more. The beautiful oblivion settled over her. As it did, she knew quite well what took place. Her mind flowed with notions, thoughts, and memories, all of which she knew belonged there but, until this moment, they could not have been accessed.

She felt Victor's childhood in a small town, his parents' divorce, his failed relationships, his marriage to Joletta Holland, his divorce twelve years later, long hours working on theories.

She felt David's tortured school life, his failure to make it on the basketball team, his first kiss, his first night with his wife, his memories of Sophia pregnant, and his memories of Jones barking orders. Every mental barricade broke, and emotion and memory rushed forward like a powerful river that silently carried the inner life of each person. The three rivers met, an unholy trinity manufactured by the hands of humanity and imposed upon a silent victim who still remained out of reach. Maybe she was afraid to remember that life, that past, that reality? Maybe it was best forgotten?

What is this place?
   What is this thing we call the soul?
      It eludes every notion and every attempt to pin it down.
   We claim it's here or there.
      But is it anywhere?
  Is it really within or maybe, it was beyond us all long?
      Ever the joy of humanity has been broken by the soulless.
  What makes a person who they are and not someone else?
      What keeps one from connecting, truly connecting?
  What exactly does it mean to be unique?
      And what is eternity, if not working out these very questions?
  But every step uncovers a new mystery.

Three rivers became one and alone, she accomplished that which she'd feared for so long.

SHE OPENED HER EYES and stared into the light. It hurt initially, the dull ache traveling through the back of her eyes and deep into her skull. She took several deep breaths, hoping the pain would ease. She brought herself to a sitting position and sat on the peer. Smiling, but wishing she could cry. Tears seemed out of the question, like attempting to draw water from a long, dry well.

Who am I now? No response came to her. I am three and yet, I am none of these. The real me seems long gone, just a lost soul that I never really knew. Instead, I'm here now, some mixture of these three persons that I have never really been before. This is the real nature of assimilation. This is the beast which they have released from the Abyss. I am something new. Something unpredictable. Something even they could not have planned for.

She looked out at the city across the bay and took in a deep breath of the salty air. The vacuum that had demanded some form of self-identity pained her within, pleading for something apparently unattainable. *I am Riley*, she thought. *Not the same as I was, but new.* An odd and amusing thought occurred to her. She recalled the New Testament story of Saul's encounter with Christ on the road to Damascus that blinded him temporarily before transforming him from a persecutor of Jesus' early followers into the Apostle Paul, the author of most of the New Testament.

I have traveled down a backwards road to Damascus, an epistemic road, a metaphysical journey. She grinned, mulling over this information that sprung forth from the religious knowledge placed within her. She was seeing it from a whole new perspective. She'd been blind all this time, stumbling about while hoping for some sense of direction in the darkness. But now, she could see.

In that moment, she felt more sure about who she was than she had in a very long time. She also felt a profound and devastating sense of loneliness that weakened her entire body.

"Sophia," she whispered.

Nothing.

Finally, the tears came.

What did they do to me?

Her eyes locked on the old coast guard building and a new thought flooded her with such force, she shook where she stood.

What are they doing to Arisu?

In that moment, everything else vanished. Her mind saw only Arisu.

Riley saw her with a clarity she had lacked before. She understood that in spite of all the obstacles, Arisu had loved her and she had loved Arisu. No, 'had' was the wrong word. She loved Arisu *now*.

A chill breeze blew in from the harbor. Longing for some last bit of direction, she opened her mouth to call Sophia. But, she knew that Sophia was gone now, gone for good. *Once assimilation takes place, the AAP is dissolved. It no longer has a purpose*, the thought rang distinctly in Violet's voice.

She stood and walked to the metal railing that ran along the edge of the pier. She leaned against it and looked out over the dark water. Her eyes leveled with the distant shore. She smiled. Again, she breathed a prayer to whoever might be listening.

Where do I go now? She looked about. Come on, please. Tell me where to go now.

Come to me, came a thought that seemed outside her mind.

She stopped breathing for a second. Where had that come from?

Come find me and together, we can get Arisu back.

A grin formed on Riley's lips. Hello, Dante. It's good to hear from you, old friend.

RILEY AMBLED DOWN THE long corridor, the white walls reflecting light back into her squinting eyes. A feeling of familiarity washed over her as she progressed down the halls of Mass General Hospital. It felt eerily like the journey through the endless recesses of her mind, except, in this hallway, medical personnel swept deftly about. Strewn throughout its entire length were empty stretchers, hospital beds, and patients waiting with family. Riley kept her eyes aimed at the floor. She felt her time slipping away; she had to find Dante.

Gliding up to the receptionist desk for the fourth floor of the hospital, she found no one present. That seemed just as well. She knew the hospital room number anyway. She slid past the desk and down a much narrower hall. A nurse stepped out of a room and walked by her.

Riley kept her eyes low and the nurse never said anything. However, she did feel the man's gaze upon her as they passed each other. Still, she behaved as one who was well aware of her actions and had no need for fear. Fear? It felt so distant to Riley now. It wasn't that she was confident, she simply did not experience fear the same way she had before. *Maybe I have nothing left to lose at this point. So, what's left to fear?*

Turning a corner, she strolled a few more paces. She glanced up at the room numbers as she passed each door— 809, 811, and, across the hall, 810. She needed to be farther down the hall. She moved on with a steady demeanor.

She watched the numbers out of the corner of her eye. Reaching 827, she stopped by the door and listened. She could hear a baseball game, likely coming from the television inside. *Nice! The Red Sox are up 5-1, bottom of the 8th!*

Startled, she turned her attention back to the hallway. A doctor, her stethoscope was dangling from her neck while her eyes focused intently on an electronic chart that she was holding in her hands, was moving quickly in Riley's direction. Driven by some instinct to gather information at every step of the way, Riley noticed the doctor's name tag that glowed, "Rachel Olsen, MD." Riley ducked into the room before Dr. Olsen looked up from her work. Riley hoped she hadn't been planning to look in on Dante.

To her surprise, Riley stared down at a short woman wearing a hospital security guard uniform. She sat on a chair and stared at the projection of the game in the corner. The guard looked up, surprise in her eyes. Riley smiled. The guard frowned, brushing aside her dark hair.

"You need something?" she asked.

"Yes," Riley nodded. "I'm here to check in on the patient."

"What? You a doctor? What's your name?"

"Dr. Murphy," she said the first thing that popped into her mind.

The guard squinted at her, nodded, and finally smiled. "Dr. Violet Murphy, huh? Nice to finally meet you." She stuck out her hand. Reluctantly, Riley shook it.

"And you are?"

The woman reached into her jacket and produced a badge. "Special Agent Monica Ray. Sorry for the deceiving outfit."

Riley stared at the badge before her. Sure enough, there it was: FBI. Riley took a step back.

"She won't bite," Dante groaned.

Riley looked over at the man lying in the hospital bed.

"Have a seat," Agent Ray offered, pulling up a chair next to Dante.

Riley complied, still looking from Dante to Agent Ray, quite perplexed.

"Hey there," Dante whispered.

"How you feeling?" Riley asked.

"Slightly shot," Dante smirked.

Riley smiled.

"Glad I can finally introduce you to my partner," Dante said.

"Partner?" Riley glanced at Agent Ray then back to Dante.

"Sorry, I've never told you the whole story," Dante said. "My name is Agent Fernando Gomez. Arisu and I worked together in the FBI several years ago. She left, started working for the project, and I, eventually, went undercover. I became a volunteer test subject for medical research with NeuroCorp, I met you, and you can figure out the rest from there."

"So, the cancer..."

"Oh, that's real. Part of why I was perfect for some undercover work."

Riley stared off. Accessing the newly recovered memories, she let them begin to wash over her. Yes, it was all there. She worked to piece it all together; bits of hurried and hushed conversations from the early days of her conspiracy as a whistle blower. She could recall the night she learned of Arisu's past at the FBI. She, however, was not undercover. She had been fired after refusing to drop an investigation in to a foreign diplomat with deep ties to companies within the telecom, energy, pharmaceutical, and arms manufacturing industries—that last one particularly benefitting certain dictators that he had befriended. Arisu had been forced into a tough position, watching helplessly as her name was dragged through the mud inside the various law enforcement networks. That is how she ended up taking the job as a highly skilled mercenary for NeuroCorp.

A lump formed in Riley's throat at apprehending all of this new, yet old, information. It also deepened her resolve to rescue Arisu, the woman who had already been dealt an unfair blow in life and yet, still set out on an impossible quest to find Violet. What was Arisu feeling, now that they both knew the truth concerning Violet? *No!* There was no time to speculate. It was time to act!

Riley turned back to Agent Ray, "So, why the rent-a-cop outfit?"

"FBI badge draws more attention," Dante's words slurred. "I'm supposed to be a two-bit crook, you know—just till I heal up."

"You called me here. What do we do now?"

Dante shook his head, his eyes closing. "I can't stay awake for long." Dante coughed. "Something's wrong. I can't tell for sure, but something feels wrong with the nanites."

"Like what? Are they not healing you?" Riley said, unable to hide her concern.

"He's bleeding internally," Agent Ray offered. "So far, it seems the nanites aren't doing anything to stop it."

"How do we get them to stop the bleeding?" Riley asked then stopped. She stared down at the floor as the information flooded her conscious mind. "A significant trauma or injury can overwhelm the system. They're designed to battle his cancer, and even that is a balancing act. Damn it, Dante! I'm sorry."

"Don't be," he formed a weak smile. "You have to go get Arisu."

"But," Riley said. "What do I do?

"I can link up with you. I can stream everything you know, everything you are experiencing, right to FBI headquarters."

"Did I plan this?"

"No," he shook his head. "It's more of a fail-safe. Not even Arisu… she doesn't…"

His eyes closed, and he breathed slowly. Riley watched him then turned to Agent Ray.

"What are you doing now?" Ray asked.

"I need to get Arisu back." Riley stood. "I'm going to turn myself in."

"But, then you're in their hands," Ray said.

"But Arisu will be free. Assimilation has already happened. I'm evidence of both the power and weakness of the project."

"Exactly," Ray nodded. "That's why we can't let you turn yourself over to them. Despite all the trouble they went through to keep Victor Murphy's memories intact, don't underestimate their desperation when you show up and try to blow the cover on the whole thing. They will kill you."

Riley considered this. She nodded. "And they might just kill Arisu too. She's just a means to draw me to them."

"So we go in with a team—"

"No. They will kill her. I have to go in alone. I have to go in myself and get her out of there. It's the only way." She looked into the FBI agent's eyes, who watched Riley quietly for a moment. "I need a phone. I need to be able to call you. If I call you, can you wake Dante up? Can you make sure he links to the FBI headquarters?"

"We should get more agents," she said, shaking her head.

"If we do and Jones finds out, everything will be shot to hell. And, if that's the case, Jones would kill Arisu himself just to pay me back."

"Jones isn't dumb," Agent Ray pressed. "He knows he's being watched. Killing Arisu might be too risky. He may have powerful allies, but no one wants blood on their hands—at least, not traceable blood. Honestly, I'm more concerned about Jones' allies. And, I think *you* should be more concerned about what happens to Arisu's brain."

Riley locked eyes with Ray, absorbing those last words. Ray had a point. It was one thing to consider losing Arisu to death, but it was somehow even more horrifying to contemplate losing her to the erasing and reprogramming of her entire being. She looked out of the hospital window at the glowing city lights, contemplating her next move. "Okay. Have a team on standby. Have them close, but not too close. Jones can't suspect anything. I have to show up first. I have to make sure they won't do that to her."

"So you really love her, then?"

Riley looked back at Dante then Agent Ray. She nodded. "Yeah. I do."

Agent Ray pulled out a cellphone and handed it to her. "Call Dante's number. It's the last number dialed. I'll try to wake him and you make sure to get out of there alive. This thing is much bigger than us. We're not even supposed to be on this case. There are powerful people at work here. If you and Arisu get killed or erased, they can just sweep this whole thing under the rug and move on with a new plan."

"Then why keep me alive in the first place?" Riley shook her head.

"You'll have to take that up with Jones," Ray shrugged.

Riley looked down at the phone. It was getting late. She had to go now. She had to get Arisu out of there. Looking back up, she sighed, "Thank you. Thank Dante for me, for everything, for protecting Arisu."

"Hey you," Dante murmured.

Riley looked over at the bed, finding that Dante had cracked his eyes open, fighting to stay conscious.

"You're talking like you're going to die or something," Dante said.

Riley approached him. She smiled in spite of herself. Then, she reached down the collar of her shirt, grasped the crucifix around her neck, and undid the clasp. Riley looked at it in her hand for a moment before setting it on Dante's chest. "Hold on to this for me."

"Why? Are you coming back for it?" Dante smiled, bleary eyed.

"Yeah, I am. I don't think I'm done with that yet."

Riley turned and walked past Agent Ray before she or Dante could say anything else and headed out. She dashed quickly for the elevators. She had to get back to the North End, back to where she had hidden her guns. Then, she would go right to Jones, straight to his front door.

26   VIOLET

The Bible said that God made man in his own image. The German philosopher Ludwig Feuerbach said that man made God in his own image. The transhumanists say that humanity will make itself into God. [T]ranshumanism is the inevitable and logical extension of enlightenment thought, which exalted the power of human reason.

- Sebastian Seung

SALTY WIND BLEW IN from the harbor. The lights shone brightly along the walkway. Riley stood still, letting the wind encircle her. She was feeling rather petulant, pissed off, ready for a fight—any fight. In the distance, a boat's lights reflected off the dark water's undulating surface. Clouds had rolled in, a storm silently brewing in the darkness. Out over the top of the city skyline, lightning flashed. The storm was still too far for the sound of thunder to reach her ears, but it would only be a matter of time before the thunder arrived in earnest. She looked out over the water then back at the building. She could feel the weight of the guns where they were pressed against the small of her back. They had created the wrong woman to fuck with. It was time to bring in a storm all her own. *Can I do this any other way?*

Her hands reached up to her neck, her fingers running over the place where the crucifix used to hang. *Am I a killer? Can I kill again to end this? To save her?* Her mind vibrated with the rush of information about the project center, as well as David's military training and the project's operative skills. It all stretched out before her mind's eye, an epistemic blueprint of destruction. A shiver ran down her tense spine and she fought off tears.

"Is there any other way?" she whispered. "Is there any other way to get her back?"

Arisu had come for her; she searched, risked, found, and fought for her in Brazil. Specifically, what now had Riley woke was the part of her that had fallen in love with Arisu. It had been there all along, just under the surface, but she had pushed it away. She had been a nun. How could she allow herself to love a woman? Her devotion was supposed to be entirely in Christ, her Savior. Was Christ still her Savior now? How could an artificial personality, let alone a blending of personalities, find salvation? Certainly the Kingdom of God was not meant for the freakish product of multiple assimilated personalities. Though she was no longer a nun—had she ever been a real one?—she breathed out her prayer again: *Is there any other way? Does it even matter?*

She walked quietly along the harbor side walkway that stretched for miles around Boston Harbor connecting various wharfs and piers. She passed a young couple, their dress shoes clicking on the sidewalk, as they made their way back to the luxurious hotel not far from the old coast guard building. The man and woman paid no attention to her and she carried on with relief.

Rounding the corner, she looked up at the building that housed the project's main facilities, bluish LED light from a street lamp splashed across the metallic door. It looked so inane, so simple. Inside, however, something grand and terrible awaited her. She recalled the last time she had been there. Well, not really her; Violet had been here. At that time, she had the box, the one from her dreams; the one with the coiled wire around the metal bar. Riley sighed then swallowed hard in spite of the tightness in her throat. *They must know I'm here. What are they waiting for?* She stood there, unable to move but anticipating something.

Nothing happened.

Her eyes stared intently at the small door. No one came. *Is this the right place*, someone inside her asked. *Yes, yes it is. I know it. I know this place. I've been here. This is it!*

"This is it," she said as the stepped forward. She raised her voice, "I'm here! Jones! I'm here now. We can end this."

Her voice bounced off the building's side and skipped across the water. A dog barked in the distance. Waves lapped up against the rocks and the wooden poles supporting the piers. The tide was receding; even the ocean knew it shouldn't be around here tonight. The wind picked up and slowly died down again. She reached into her pocket, grabbing the phone Special Agent Monica Ray had given her. She made the call and brought it to her ear. She waited for Ray to pick up.

"Violet," she said.

"Close enough," Riley answered. "Are you ready? It's time to wake up Dante. Keep him awake for a long as you can."

"Okay."

"Thank you," she said then hung up without waiting any longer.

The door creaked open. Out came a young guard followed by two agents. Riley looked each in the eye—the young man, the woman, and the balding brute. She kept her breathing steady. They stepped closer to her. She took a step forward. They slowed their pace. Riley felt her stomach tighten. Her head began to spin. She clenched her fists, fighting for composure. She wanted to collapse, to weep, to turn herself in, to give up. *Why can't I? Why can't I give up? No. You can't do that. They win. You can't let them win. No one else should have to endure this!*

With her eyes still on the three approaching figures, she reached to the small of her back and pulled out the two handguns she carried. They stood their ground, staring her down, guns raised at her.

Dante, are you there?

Headlights rounded the building and a black, electric SUV whined to a stop, its lights blinding her. More agents poured out of it. Riley squinted, trying to get a count of how many were there. Did it really matter?

Dante, are you there?

The sound of guns being cocked and readied, feet shuffling over asphalt and the wood of the pier, filled the night air. Somewhere overhead, Riley could hear a jet coming in for a landing at Logan across the harbor. She smiled and held the guns out limply, posing no threat to anyone.

"Drop your weapon," Rikard yelled, though Riley couldn't quite spot him in the glare of the headlights.

A dream she used to have several times returned to her now. Darren, she had tried to save Darren. No, wait, she had tried to capture Darren. *It's all true,* she thought. *It's a composite of several unique experiences— the same story told from different perspectives.* She was an agent, she was Violet trying to stop Arisu and her team; she was Victor with his insights that lead to breakthroughs in nano-engineering. Suddenly, the flavor and smell of Victor's favorite pipe tobacco came to her. She saw the lab, recalled long conversations with Jones down white corridors. With this memory came another, a darker memory. A truth she had learned, but had been forced to forget. It shook her. But it also gave her hope.

Dante, are you there?

Yes. I'm here.

Riley smiled.

"Drop your weapons, Violet," Rikard yelled.

"Where's Arisu?" Riley replied.

"Inside. Now, drop your weapons or you'll never make it in to see her."

Riley dropped the gun in her left hand. Her right hand brought that gun up to her temple. "Why kill me now?" she yelled. "You've kept me alive this long, why would you kill me now? What if I do it myself?"

"You won't do that," Rikard called back from beyond the headlights.

Are you getting this?

Loud and clear!

"Why am I so important?" Riley cried out.

"Because," came Jones' voice now. He stepped out from the door into the building. The heavy metal door clanged behind him as it shut. "You are how we've kept one of the most brilliant minds alive and creating. Victor Murphy has been dead for years. We needed you to keep him alive. We had two of you. David volunteered, but it didn't work out so well for him. You, on the other hand, have been a brilliant success."

He's right. David Brown had volunteered. Riley could see it in her mind. Sophia had left him. After three tours in Afghanistan, David had changed. Their communication broke down. She had gone to Seattle where she had family and the opportunity to create a new life, to teach literature at a university. David, left with little, began to work for the project. While on covert mission, he learned of the plans to implant Victor's memories into a test subject. David had been on the team that extracted the Jane Doe from a Central American trafficking ring, which brought in sex workers for various, major public events. A police bust led to their capture, but the Jane Doe had suffered serious injuries including a broken arm and serious head trauma that landed her in a coma.

Riley saw it all in her mind with startling clarity. She glanced at the scar on her arm. Had she ever been to Alaska? She had memories. Were they real? Maybe someone had been to Alaska, but it was unlikely that the Jane Doe had ever been there.

Then, the memory of the destruction of the stored data—a whole array of massive hard drives—that represented Victor Murphy's collected memories. Violet had done this before she had been reprogrammed. *I'm the last copy. And they didn't know how to pry out what they needed, so they hid me and hoped they could figure it out at some point.*

"Now we need you to complete Victor's work," Jones went on. "Why you ever got it in your head to destroy the project is beyond me."

"Because it doesn't work," Riley said, lowering the gun from her temple. "Because it's wrong; what Victor Murphy failed to see was that the essence of an individual is more than electrical impulses in the brain. This thing you want to do, it should never happen."

"We are building a better world," Jones stepped forward. "There may be flaws in the project now, but we can perfect it. That's why you are still alive, Violet. Now tell me, have you finished assimilation?"

"Where is Arisu?" Riley demanded. "You can have me, but you have to let her go."

Jones stepped closer now, a smile creeping across his face. "So, you still love her. How remarkable."

"Jones," Riley said. "Take me and let her go. You have what you need." She dropped the second gun. "I'm right here."

Agents moved in fast, grabbing her arms and pulling them behind her. Riley did nothing to fight them. She stared at Jones.

Are you getting this?

Yes.

"The thing is, Arisu knows too much," Jones said, walking up to Riley. "How could we possibly let her go? Maybe we can do some adjustments first, you know?"

"Don't you touch her," Riley spat back. "She's no threat to you. How can she prove anything? Your project is so buried in red tape, you have deniability. How could she prove this to anyone? You have me."

"You might be right, but it's best to clean up certain messes quite thoroughly," Jones said.

"Like you cleaned up messes before?" Riley cried out. "You had all those rogue test subjects captured and brought back here. Then, when the programming didn't take, you had to destroy the evidence, so you just kill them off. It was easy enough. They were death row inmates, so who cares, right? After all your talk publicly condemning the death penalty as—what was the word you used—barbaric, was it? That was just rhetoric though. So, how about we talk about the subjects killed in the field, the ones we couldn't retrieve safely. What about them?"

"Progress has always come at a high cost," Jones said.

"Really, that's progress?"

Dante, are you still with me?

"Is the cost ever too high?" Riley pressed on.

"You have become a liability," Jones nodded. "Take her in!"

The agents shoved her forward.

Dante! You still with me?

She stared at the building. A sinking sensation turned her stomach as she realized that Jones might have thought of the possibility of Dante and her linking up. He was likely jamming their ability to communicate or, maybe, Dante was no longer conscious or, worse yet, alive.

As she was pushed through the door, the horrible realization that she was alone threatened to completely undo her.

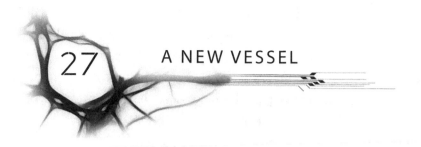

27   A NEW VESSEL

Our lives now are only partly biological, with no clear split between the organic and the technological, the carbon and the silicon. We may not know yet where we're going, but we've already left where we've been.

- D. T. Max

HER BODY MUDDLED ON, as if she were suffocating. Every step down the familiar hall clutched at her soul, wresting her life away from her. She was ushered into a large room lined with computers. The florescent lights and white walls stung her eyes. *This is the programming room next to the servers,* she found herself thinking. *They've rearranged a little, but I recognize it.* Jones stopped in the middle of the room and Riley was forced to stand before him.

"Do you know where we are?" Jones said, staring at her with something akin to anticipation.

Riley nodded.

"Good," Jones smiled. "That means our dearly departed Dr. Victor Murphy is still in there, the parts I care about anyway."

"Where's Arisu?" Riley said.

"No point worrying about her," Jones waved her off. "You should be more concerned about yourself."

Riley looked around the room, thinking. "You're going to prep me for extraction," she said.

"Yes," Jones nodded. "I'm glad to see you're tracking right along with me here. Technicians are getting the extraction room ready, so I thought I could show you how we've improved our system in your temporary absence."

He turned and waved at the computers, "All of this is new. We have made significant advances in our neural-network. Victor was a brilliant man and he helped us advance not just the nanotechnology that makes our work possible, but he also developed the AI system that monitors and guides our entire process. I wish I could show it to Victor. He was right. Once we broke past the nano-scale barriers for computing, Moore's Law held up. That means that the nanobots we install today are even better than the ones already inside you. And, with the continued development of five-dimensional glass discs capable of storing several thousand petabytes of data, each, our new server system is smaller and much more robust."

Riley smiled. "Show it to me," she shrugged.

"Ah, if only it were really you, old boy," he wagged his finger at her.

"So you do recognize that a true personality overwrite is not possible," she said.

Jones raised his eyebrows in an exaggerated expression of incredulity. "Oh, it isn't?" He stepped closer to her, looking her up and down. "Do you remember who this body you inhabit belonged to?"

Riley searched her mind. Who was the Jane Doe in that article?

"You're probably wondering who you *really* are," Jones smiled. "There is no *real* any more. You are what we made you. We succeeded in our first overwrite. When Victor was diagnosed with cancer, we knew we had to act. Unfortunately, it was much too severe for treatment, even with medical advancements in nanobots. Computational power and storage wasn't quite up to speed to simply upload his entire connectome—you do recall the term, I hope.

"Yes, a connectome is a map of all neural networks that make a person who they are," Riley said with ease. "It's the wiring diagram for your personality."

"Wonderful," Jones smiled. "I'm glad to see the assimilation process has worked so well. I was worried there for a while. I mean, you do have a lot going on in there."

"More than you'll ever know," Riley said, flatly.

"Where was I?" Jones looked off. "Oh yes. We couldn't just upload

Murphy's connectome to a computer system like the transhuminists have been proposing for decades. We could store the data, but the processing power to replicate the functioning of consciousness isn't quite there, yet. So, we went to work extracting his connectome. He thought it would be interesting to have his mind implanted in two subjects. He wanted to try a male and a female. David was easy enough but, for you, we needed to provide appropriate alterations. We didn't want to run the risk of errors due to unexpected dissonance between personality and body."

"So you created Violet Murphy," Riley muttered.

"Yes."

"But then..." Riley searched her mind for more. "Something happened. I... can't place it."

"Ah, yes. We made sure to leave some gaps. David proved to be a problem. Too much of the original David remained. In the end, it was safest to just let David be David and focus on Violet. Meanwhile, you had gaps in your connectome implant. So we decided to clean house and begin again. But then, you figured it out and staged a little accident for the servers that housed Victor's backup."

Riley blinked, trying to recall. Her nightmare rushed back to her: the box with the coiled wires, entering the server room after hours, and then running through the halls to get away from the powerful magnetic burst.

"The investors weren't happy about that one," Jones continued. "That server system cost several million dollars. The new neural-server costs even more. But fortunately, no EMP could possibly wipe the data from the glass disks and they'll be around for 14 billion years or so. Just think, once we advance computational power, we can dispense with these bodies and upload our connectomes to a synthetic system."

"Oh, so you're only after immortality, that old chestnut. And here I thought it was going to be something big," Riley rolled her eyes and shook her head.

"I'm just helping humanity evolve."

"But, in the process, you lost Victor's backup," Riley said. "So that's why you merged David's mind back into mine."

"Lost? You destroyed it, you little shit," Jones spat back. "And yes, we tried filling in all the gaps of Victor's connectome by merging our work on David with what we had in your brain. It was sloppy, I have to admit," Jones shrugged. "But, we needed to fill gaps as best we could. It was a risk we were willing to take in order to preserve Victor. His brilliance was astounding. He could have taken this project to whole new levels. But alas, at some point we all have to let go of what could have been and embrace what must be."

Riley stared at him, a chill running down her spine. "How Zen of you. You don't care if you get Victor back anymore."

"Oh, I want desperately to archive all you have to offer us. Victor's insights are still quite valuable, but I'm afraid we are done with this—" He looked her up and down. With an air of disgust and a wave of his hand, Jones droned, "—particular vessel. You've shown us what happens with multiple installations. The assimilation of various connectomes becomes too convoluted, too much noise and chatter. We needed to keep you safe while we brought our new neural-net server online. We've had to move the schedule up slightly due to some unforeseen interference, but we're ready now."

So this was it.

"Have you already killed Arisu?" Riley whimpered softly.

Jones cocked his head to the side. "You still care for her? You know what I never have figured out. Were you gay before the installation or is there some level of sexual re-orientation due to the fact that you have both David and Victor crawling around inside that brain of yours?"

Riley stared at Jones, a tear escaping her right eye and traveling down her cheek. "Does it matter?" she asked.

"The information would be invaluable in terms of our scientific knowledge," Jones said. "But, in practical terms, no. It doesn't matter. It's all over now."

Riley stared at the man with such hatred that she felt as if she might miraculously will herself to compress all of the dark energy growing inside of her. And then, explode, killing herself, Jones, and the whole fucking project. But then, a thought struck her upside the head.

"The server isn't ready," she blurted out suddenly.

Jones' eyes flickered. "It's ready."

Jones was bluffing. She could see it in his eyes.

"You son of a bitch," Riley screamed. "You're going to extract Victor from me as best you can and use Arisu as a new temporary vessel."

Jones looked up at the ceiling. "Like I said, Victor was brilliant. I should've known you'd figure it out."

"Fuck you," Riley spat back. "I figured that out all on my own."

"Such language for a nun," he smirked at her.

"You're so blind. You're just going to make the same mistake again."

"Oh no," Jones shook his head. "We've made improvements. We'll be mapping and extracting only the relevant information. It's actually quite fortunate that you're here now. This is our next level of development and testing. It's so nice of you and Arisu to volunteer for the job."

Riley looked around at the men and women gathered nearby. She looked at Rikard. "Are they all your test subjects?"

"Oh, come on now," Jones raised a hand to his chest as if insulted. "I'm not a barbarian. We only test on criminals."

"I wasn't a criminal."

"You were nobody. And once Victor is no longer inside you, you'll be nobody again, nothing but a liability."

Another tear slipped down Riley's face, this time from her left eye. The door behind her opened and Jones looked beyond her to whoever had entered.

"Ah, good," he said. "It's ready."

HER HEART BEAT AGAINST her ribs like a thrashing caged animal in its final throes of fight or flight. They walked her down the long, white hall. The agents dispersed, leaving Rikard to escort her. Riley stared off into her impending oblivion. She could recall the process clearly. First, they would shave her head. Then, they would place a flexible helmet of electrodes that would communicate with and manipulate the nanobots inside her brain and spinal cord. If they really had significantly improved their nanotechnology over the last couple of years, then they were sure to also inject her with a whole new colony of nanites.

Where are you now? What do I do?

They arrived at the installation room. Three technicians awaited her. There were two beds. Arisu lay in one. She was dressed in a hospital gown, her arms and legs strapped down. Her mouth was taped shut. Tears leaked from her eyes as she watched Riley enter the room.

Riley stared into her eyes—those trapped and terrified eyes—and felt something inside of her break. A desperate hopelessness struck her like a spear to the chest and she gasped for air. Suddenly, an image—an angry face rushed to the surface of her mind. Who was it? She felt a rage rising inside of her. No, it wasn't just rage for her current circumstance or what they were doing to Arisu. This was the memory of an older rage, of a deep desperation, the last violent lash of a cornered animal. She saw the face again: a man with dark eyes and a mustache. He had brought her here. He had promised her safe passage to America. But what he had really done was enslave her and she hated him for it. She hated him more than anything she had ever hated in her life. She remembered that swiftness with which he attacked when she was distracted by loud knocks on the door of the basement apartment. He shoved her hard. She could see the floor and the edge of the coffee table coming up to meet her.

She blinked as a hand touched her. It was one of the technicians. "Come on," the tech was saying, "you need to disrobe."

Riley clenched her fists. *Okay, David.*

She grabbed the tech's wrist and spun him around, slamming him into Rikard. They both hit the wall. She dived over the bed and crashed into the equipment on the other side. Pulling at the cables, she ripped every connection she could find, from computers, medical gear, and directly from the wall sockets. Several alarms sounded.

"Stop her!" Jones shouted.

Rikard arose and whipped out his handgun. As he brought it up,

Riley grabbed a metal stand for the saline solution and swung it around, striking Rikard on the head. He collapsed. Another technician looked at her with utter terror. The third reached out and tried to seize her. Riley grabbed his hand and twisted the fingers with such swiftness that she barely registered the popping as his bones broke. The tech stumbled back, screaming in pain.

"Stay right there," Riley barked at Jones, metal stand still in one hand.

With her free hand, she loosened one of the restraints on Arisu's wrist. The moment the buckle was undone, Arisu's free hand began working on her other arm.

Rikard moaned and got to his knees, holding a hand up against his bleeding head. The uninjured techs and Jones stared at Riley, eyes wide and mouths open.

"There's nowhere to go," Jones said, clearly making an effort to seem calm.

"You got that right," Riley said, panting.

"You can't leave here," Jones continued. "There's no point in fighting."

"I'm not letting you do this to Arisu," Riley said. "You have no idea the hell you put her through."

"Shut up!" Jones screamed. "I'm done with you. I'm done with this mess. You have stood in the way of the greatest achievement in human technological evolution for long enough. I am done with you!"

"Yeah," Rikard said, staggering to his feet. "You're done alright."

His gun came up. The burst and muzzle flash filled the room. Blood splattered on the sterile white walls. Jones stared at Rikard with a look of utter bewilderment and then, anger. Riley gasped.

Jones looked down at the hole in his chest then back up to Rikard.

"You," Jones gasped as he stumbled back to the wall.

"That's right," Rikard muttered. "I'm here to clean up your mess. As it turns out, the greatest liability hindering this project's success was you."

"You can't," Jones struggled, "You won't... you're done."

Rikard shook his bleeding head. "No, you're done. My real bosses over at the DOD gave me a clear directive this morning: clean house. And it's to be a very thorough cleaning."

Jones slid down to the floor as Rikard raised the gun. Without any forethought, Riley drove forward, striking the gun with the metal stand. Rikard yelled in pain and the gun clattered on the tile floor. Riley dropped the stand and dove at Rikard, shoving him into the wall. He gasped, but fought back, trying to reach down for the gun. In desperation, she kicked the gun across the room.

Rikard delivered a hard blow to her ribs. The air rushed from her lungs, which burned sharply. She collapsed on the floor, all her energy vanishing to focus on the ability to breathe again. Rikard, face covered in blood, looked down at her.

"You stupid bitch," he said.

"Who you calling a bitch?" Arisu growled.

Rikard looked up just in time to see the muzzle flash of his own gun. The bullet struck his right eye and exploded out the back of his head, covering the wall and door behind him with blood and gray matter. He stood there for what seemed like a very long moment. Finally, his knees gave way and his lifeless body collapsed.

Arisu looked around the room at the terrified and cowering techs. "You can get out of here now," she said, "unless you want to wind up like him."

They rose slowly and stepped over Rikard's body, making their confused and hasty exit. Riley gasped for air, feeling the sharp pain in her ribs, which were likely broken. She looked over at Jones who clutched his wounded chest and fought to keep breathing.

"We overestimated a few things, old boy," she said to him, feeling the words come out of her mouth almost on their own. "There just might be more to us than the mere firing of neurons."

Jones locked eyes with her, his eyes wide with the primal fear of facing death.

Arisu knelt next to Riley, asking her how she felt. Slowly, she helped Riley to her feet. Riley screamed out in pain as she pulled her up. But, as Riley stood, she looked into Arisu's eyes, which had been devoid of hope mere minutes ago and, in spite of her pain, wrapped her arms around Arisu and brought their trembling lips together. Arisu gripped her tightly, putting all of her seemingly abandoned hope into that painful and liberating kiss. They parted and Riley gasped in agony and relief. She sobbed into Arisu's shoulder, a torrent of inexpressible emotion pushing its way out of her.

Through the tears, exhaustion, and aching, Riley was barely aware of traveling down the halls. Arisu carried her, as best she could, with one arm while with her other arm, she was unafraid to fire at anything that moved, though she had little hope of hitting much. Lacking direction from either Jones or Rikard, the other agents seemed to scatter with little concern for stopping them. Likely, they were preoccupied with getting out of there before the situation got worse.

Too late.

When they reached the exit, Arisu kicked open the door. A blinding light, wind, and the whir of a helicopter confronted them. They stopped; Arisu lowered her gun and sighed.

"FBI, drop your weapon and come out with your hands up," boomed a voice over a bullhorn.

Arisu smiled at Riley, letting the gun fall from her hand.

"Stand down!" came another voice. "Stand down! That's our informant! They're with us."

Riley recognized Agent Ray's voice even in all the chaos. Riley looked up into Arisu's eye, her body becoming limp. Try as she may, her grip slipped. Arisu, shaking with shock and exhaustion, could no longer hold her. The ground rose to meet Riley. She barely registered pain form the impact. Her head spun. She saw the mustached man, Sophia, Victor Murphy, Violet, and Arisu together. Memories and associated emotions washed over her with wave after wave of simultaneous discovery and familiarity.

Her eyes saw the world on its side as feet approached her, but her mind was a million miles away. She let go and let it all come rushing into her.

"Riley," Arisu said, falling to her knees next to her. "Come on, babe.

Stay with me, we gotta get out of here. Come on, Violet."

It took far more effort than it should have for Riley to move her hand and reach out to Arisu, who desperately grasped Riley's hand and held it tight. Lights flashed and feet rushed past her, but Riley found Arisu's eyes, which were filled with new tears.

"It's okay," Riley said.

The world around her spun and faded to black.

As it did, Riley heard Arisu lean in close and whisper into her ear, "You hold on, Riley Bekker. You hear me? I love you."

EPILOGUE:

Ana

A hundred thousand Parkinson's disease sufferers worldwide have implants—so-called brain pacemakers—to control symptoms of their malady. Artificial retinas for some types of blindness and cochlear implants for hearing loss are common. Defense Department money, through the military's research arm, the Defense Advanced Research Projects Agency (DARPA), funds much of this development. Using such funding, a lab at the University of Southern California's Center for Neural Engineering is testing chip implants in the brain to recover lost memories.

- D. T. Max, "How Humans Are Shaping Our Own Evolution"
(April 2017 issue of *National Geographic*)

You have to remember DARPA's job isn't to help people. It's to create 'vast weapon systems of the future.'

- Annie Jacobsen, author of *The Pentagon's Brain*

THE SUN CUT THROUGH the increasingly bare trees. A brisk breeze sent orange and yellow leaves fluttering over the grass. A few of them became trapped on the headstones before being coaxed onward by a fresh breeze. Arisu stood in a black dress among a sea of black clad men and women. The casket bore an American flag. Next to it stood a large picture of a handsome dark skinned man in a suit and tie, smiling.

Dante had faded slowly as his cancer became too aggressive for the nanites to fight off. In the end, he had opted for a total system shutdown. The nanites were merely prolonging an inevitable and painful process. He had set his remaining affairs in order and said his goodbyes.

Several high-ranking members of the FBI, NSA, and CIA were

present at the funeral, as well as several others, whose exact jobs were a mystery to most. Because of the risk it posed, Riley remained in one of the black SUVs parked in the cemetery—though even this was known to only a few key people. With her were two well-armed FBI agents. Riley looked out the window, wishing she could be out there with Arisu. Absentmindedly, she ran a finger over the crucifix around her neck.

As the quiet and dignified graveside service was concluded, the crowds slowly dissipated. Agent Ray and Arisu returned to the SUV and climbed in. Agent Ray sat in the middle row with one of the two agents. Arisu climbed into the back seat next to Riley, who smiled sadly at her. Arisu returned the smile and sat down quietly. As they pulled out of the cemetery, Agent Ray looked back at them.

"You two all set?" she asked.

Riley and Arisu exchanged a glance and then both nodded to Ray.

"I've arranged for you to be taken to Logan in the morning," Ray continued. "The agent taking you will be the only other person who knows where you're headed."

"Thank you," Riley said.

"You two stay safe out there," Ray smiled. "It was a risk brining you back."

Riley looked over at Arisu. "We couldn't stay away. Not for this."

Ray nodded.

"Any updates?" Arisu probed.

"We're still trying to find any ties Rikard had to the Department of Defense and who might have had a vested interest in the project," Ray explained. "So far, nothing, but the one thing we have determined is that the investment structure for the project, both in terms of government funding and private funding, was not exactly by the book. We've uncovered at least four shell corporations that Jones had set up in order to funnel the money into the project."

"Speaking of Jones," Arisu smirked, "how is that asshole holding up?"

Ray smirked. "It's been a slow recovery. The angle at which he was shot did a lot of damage to his intestines and liver. But, he'll live... as long as we protect him. He's convinced that there are plenty of people who will want him dead before he can ever testify before a grand jury."

Riley nodded, knowing this was quite true.

"The names you gave us so far have been good leads," Ray said to Riley. "Tricky to pin them all directly to the project, but good leads nonetheless. Got anything more for me?"

Riley closed her eyes, slipping away from the moment, searching through the other halls of her mind. She blinked and returned her focus to Agent Ray.

"If the Department of Defense really had a vested interest in the project, it can only mean they were looking to militarize the project in some capacity. Victor Murphy had thought of this possibility. Within the project servers will be encrypted files with proposals for possible combat applications. I know for a fact that you'll find the plans to use an Intelligent Nanite Hive System, similar to the one inside me, for the extraction of information from enemy combatants. There are also theories on activating rage and suppressing empathy in soldiers, at will."

Ray raised her eyebrows. "Impressive. Not to play devil's advocate here, but might that not be a good thing?"

Riley chuckled. "It's too much power. The moment we're in there—inside someone's mind—we can get to everything. We can blackmail them, torture them with living nightmares, rewire them; we can rip from them the very core of who they are. Soldiers become robots unable to question unjust orders. The human rights violations will rack up quicker than anyone will be able to track them. And, we will create a whole new type of enemy in the process."

"You think others will copy the technology?"

"Only a matter of time," Riley sighed. "That's how it almost always goes, especially when it comes to military advantage. You think the world had a problem when we were involved in a nuclear armaments race with the USSR, just wait until China and Russia catch wind of what we've been up to."

Ray nodded. "Well, shit. Not to just go and prove your point, but we did get your boy, Thomas. He's being held in a secret location for the time being. We don't want whoever he was working for to find him either. It gets a little fishy there since he claims they were a British tech company, something called SciRebral, Inc., and that he was just doing your basic industrial espionage. But we checked. There is no SciRebral Inc."

"Could be British Intelligence," Riley suggested.

Ray grimaced at this. "Thomas said that too. It gets pretty hairy accusing one of our closest allies of trying to steal highly secretive experimental technology from us."

Riley nodded.

"But, we'll keep digging," Ray said. "Meanwhile, you two keep your heads down, stay alive, and get ready for when we need your testimony. This isn't going to be an easy case. Shit, it's going to be a challenge just to convince some people this is even possible. Then, we have to try to get our aging Supreme Court justices to understand this when they're already having trouble understanding rudimentary 3D projection patent lawsuits. Meanwhile, there's information leaking to the press and plenty of reactions."

"So I've seen," Riley replied. "In the current political climate, there's already groups bent on demonizing entire scientific disciplines. This won't help much. Whatever we do, I don't want to hurt legitimate and ethical work in the fields of neuroscience and nanorobotics."

Agent Ray raised dubious eyebrows, "Doubt I can help with that. I have to investigate this case and make sure we have enough to prosecute everyone involved."

"I know," Riley nodded. "But there is real good that can be done, if this technology is in the hands of far more ethical scientists, free of political or power-based motives."

Ray smiled. "I have to admit, I expected you to be just a little more bitter. Look at what they've done to you."

"Oh, I've got my fair share of bitterness," Riley said. "I also intimately understand what this technology is capable of, for ill or for good. The one thing Dr. Victor Murphy never counted on was that his knowledge might be preserved in someone with a fundamentally different view of the world, a different ethos of morality than him. I see what he saw, but I also see what he never saw: the true power to heal and make whole, not to merely subvert and repress."

Ray looked at Arisu and said, "She's not one for relaxing, is she?"

"Never has been," Arisu smiled at Riley.

"Must be a hit at parties," Ray chuckled, "I guess that explains the request you put into the bureau for a top of the line pro-tablet with all the latest encryption," Ray said to Riley. "The work continues."

"No," Riley shook her head. "A new work begins. We can turn this towards better purposes. The advancements Project Sleepwalker brought about can still be…" she searched for the right word.

"Redeemed?" Ray offered.

"Sure. We can give all of this a happy ending, a eucatastrophe of sorts."

"Sister Riley, the scientist and philosopher," Arisu grinned.

"I won't pretend to understand what you just said, but you'll get that tablet," Ray said warmly, but then leaned in closer, "I caution you though; don't expect the bureau to not come poking around with questions about your work. People are really spooked."

Nodding, Riley sighed and looked away. She felt Arisu squeeze her hand as she heard Agent Ray say, "But I do know what Dante would have done. And I trusted him through an awful lot."

"Thank you," Riley beamed, looking back at Arisu.

"How are you two holding up?" Ray asked, more softly.

"We're good," Arisu said. "Great, actually."

"We got married," Riley said, looking at Arisu. "Well, technically, we eloped."

"One day, it would be nice to be back and throw a proper reception," Arisu smiled.

"Yeah," Ray nodded. "That's great. Congratulations. Who proposed?"

"She did," Arisu said. "I was… shocked."

Riley laughed. "You're the one constant in my world and you're shocked that I want to spend the rest of my life with you?"

Arisu blushed slightly, something that Riley rarely saw happen, and looked away.

"Anyway," Riley continued, "the way I see it, I'm finally in a position to decide for myself who I want to be. So I choose to be Mrs. Riley Ana."

"You're taking Arisu's name?" Ray marveled.

"I don't need any further connections to Dr. Murphy and I'm sure that the name Bekker has no basis in reality for me."

"Can't argue with you there," Ray replied. "But I see you're still wearing the crucifix."

Riley glanced down at it. "Yeah," she said softly. "Still figuring all of that out as well."

Ray smiled politely and faced forward.

Riley stared out the window as they drove on. There was still much to be worked out, so much to be uncovered, as far as the project was concerned. There was also plenty that Riley wished she could discover about Jane Doe. It was down there, buried under layers of memories from several people. Part of her felt sure about the need to find herself, but another part of her recognized, given everything she had been through, everything that had been imposed upon her mind, that she would never be that lost person, no matter who she had been. Some part of her knew that the only direction was forward. She and Arisu would have plenty of time to talk in Iceland, plenty of time to process and speculate. They would only be there for six weeks. Then, it was off to Tokyo. They would keep moving around the globe for awhile. Yes, they would have plenty of time to talk. More importantly, they would have all the time in the world to begin building a happier future together.

Looking back into Arisu's eyes, Riley returned the squeeze to her hand and smiled. She leaned over and laid her head on Arisu's shoulder. The future was uncertain, but she wasn't alone. She had the women she loved. And for the first time in her life, she could finally decide who she wanted to become.

Acknowledgements

It took me 15 years to complete this novel. This story started its existence as a short film I made with my college friends, Andrew Gilbert (who co-wrote that script with me) and Scott Peercy, as well as my then girlfriend (now wife), Danae. I developed the idea further into a novel, which I began writing my senior year of college during a novel writing course taught by Kim Peterson. Following graduation, I completed the manuscript and took a shot at finding a publisher. Finding no bites and becoming quite busy with my pursuit of a career as a filmmaker, I set it aside. As the years passed, I toyed with the manuscript on occasion, revising then changing the ending, which I struggled to find satisfactory. Then, I moved to the greater Boston area, the original setting for the novel after a previous visit. Since Boston became my home, the desire to revisit this story only grew with time.

In recent years, I've rediscovered my love for novel writing. I also rediscovered this story under a new light. In particular, I found that, while the bones of the plot were good, I wanted an even more compelling lead character. A major re-write and expansion ensued, which resulted in both the change of the lead character (Riley, instead of Paul), and a brand new ending. I also built upon some ideas which I was too young to deal with at the time, with any real insight, even though I was attempting to write something complex and sub-textually personal.

In writing this novel, I have relied greatly on the help of several people for whom I am extremely grateful. I would like to thank my wife Danae, Andrew Gilbert, Scott Peercy, Ben Bowers, Andrew Shaw, Michael and Michelle Breniser, Heber and Lori Hernandez, Jeremiah Hawn, Brenan Campbell, Dominic Kaiser, and my parents Jim and Pat.

In addition to these people, there have been those who have greatly affected this work through their intellectual stimulation during that first draft, which I wrote while I was still in college: my spiritual mentor Dr. Chad Meister, my writing mentor Kim Peterson, Dr. James Stump, Bob Staples, Jon Sabo, Tim Erdel, Beth McLaughlin, and Robby Prinkert.

In this recent, in depth version of the story, I have greatly benefitted from conversations with Trevor Duke and the writer's group we co-founded: Writer's Block. My many thanks to Penny Crosby, your enthusiasm for my writing is a major source of encouragement. Deion Moore, a neuroscience student himself at the time (now graduate), thank you for several helpful and stimulating conversations. Specifically, Deion suggested that I read *Connectome: How the Brain's Wiring Makes Us Who We Are* by Sebastian Seung, a book which was instrumental for the final moments of the story.

In the rewriting process, I have also drawn significantly from the astute and inspiring work, *The Brain: The Story of You* by David Eagleman. I also got to pull double duty in the final stages of research, both as a sci-fi author and parent by reading *Welcome to Your Child's Brain* by Sandra Aamodt & Sam Wang. Annie Jacobsen's *The Pentagon's Brain: An Uncensored History of DARPA, America's Top Secret Military Research Agency* provided me with fascinating and disturbing insights into what has gone on and what is likely going on right now within the military-industrial complex, in terms of scientific research aimed at a weaponized, transhumanist future.

Ultimately, this book would not be nearly as sharp, clear, and legible if it were not for Eric Bumpus, my editor and long-time friend. His suggestions have ranged from correcting my atrocious spelling to economic terms, additional research, and really nerdy references we geeked out over. His tireless work on this manuscript took it from its rough state and elevated my writing skills, all in the service of making the story and characters more compelling and engaging. Thank you, my friend!

To all of you, thank you. The journey has been long, but a lot of fun and indubitably fulfilling.

Other Works by Mikel J. Wisler

Novels:

Unidentified

Non-Fiction:

Short Films 2.0: Getting Noticed in the YouTube Age

Short Stories:

Suspicious Behavior

Amnesiac

Empathy O.D.

Learn more about Mikel J. Wisler's writing and filmmaking by visiting

www.mikelwisler.com

Communicating Belief and Intellect

Doxa (v): Doxa (from ancient Greek "glory", "praise", "to appear", "to seem", "to think" and "to accept") is a Greek word meaning common belief or popular opinion.

-- A Greek-English Lexicon

Noûs (n): (in Greek philosophy) mind; intellect.

-- Random House Kernerman Webster's College Dictionary

Media (n):
A substance that makes possible the transfer of energy from one location to another, especially through waves.

-- The American Heritage Science Dictionary

DoxaNoûs Media is a publishing company focusing on fiction and nonfiction within the areas of science, entertainment, business, politics, theology, and civil discourse.

www.Facebook.com/DoxaNousMedia

Twitter: @DoxaNousMedia

CPSIA information can be obtained
at www.ICGtesting.com
Printed in the USA
LVHW081702260919
632367LV00009B/147/P